PR...

INDIA BLACK

Berkley Prime Crime titles by Carol K. Carr

INDIA BLACK
INDIA BLACK AND THE WIDOW OF WINDSOR

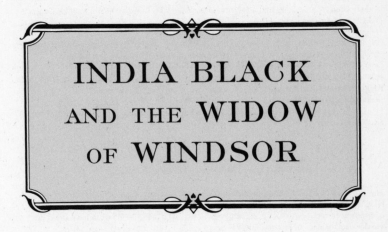

INDIA BLACK
AND THE WIDOW
OF WINDSOR

Carol K. Carr

BERKLEY PRIME CRIME, NEW YORK

THE BERKLEY PUBLISHING GROUP
Published by the Penguin Group
Penguin Group (USA) Inc.
375 Hudson Street, New York, New York 10014, USA

Penguin Group (Canada), 90 Eglinton Avenue East, Suite 700, Toronto, Ontario M4P 2Y3, Canada
(a division of Pearson Penguin Canada Inc.)
Penguin Books Ltd., 80 Strand, London WC2R 0RL, England
Penguin Group Ireland, 25 St. Stephen's Green, Dublin 2, Ireland (a division of Penguin Books Ltd.)
Penguin Group (Australia), 250 Camberwell Road, Camberwell, Victoria 3124, Australia
(a division of Pearson Australia Group Pty. Ltd.)
Penguin Books India Pvt. Ltd., 11 Community Centre, Panchsheel Park, New Delhi—110 017, India
Penguin Group (NZ), 67 Apollo Drive, Rosedale, Auckland 0632, New Zealand
(a division of Pearson New Zealand Ltd.)
Penguin Books (South Africa) (Pty.) Ltd., 24 Sturdee Avenue, Rosebank, Johannesburg 2196,
South Africa

Penguin Books Ltd., Registered Offices: 80 Strand, London WC2R 0RL, England

This book is an original publication of The Berkley Publishing Group.

Copyright © 2011 by Carol K. Carr.
Cover illustration by Alan Ayers.
Cover design by Rita Frangie.
Interior text design by Tiffany Estreicher.

FIRST EDITION: October 2011

Library of Congress Cataloging-in-Publication Data

Carr, Carol K.
    India Black and the Widow of Windsor / Carol K. Carr. — 1st ed.
        p. cm. — (A madam of espionage mystery)
    ISBN 978-0-425-24319-0
    1. Victoria, Queen of Great Britain, 1819–1901—Assassination attempts—Fiction. 2. Nationalists—Scotland—Fiction. 3. Spies—Great Britain—Fiction. I. Title.
    PS3603.A7726I55 2011
    813'.6—dc22
                        2011000273
PRINTED IN THE UNITED STATES OF AMERICA

10 9 8 7 6 5 4 3 2 1

ACKNOWLEDGMENTS

My thanks to Maestro Nick Evangelista of the Missouri State University Fencing Society for answering an endless list of questions about the art, science, and history of fencing. I am also grateful to Debra Kendrick-Murdoch and to Nick for demonstrating the finer points of the sport and graciously "doing it one more time" so the author could experience the sights and sounds of an actual bout. Any errors made or liberties taken with regard to the fencing scenes in this book are attributable solely to the author.

INDIA BLACK
AND THE WIDOW
OF WINDSOR

PROLOGUE

"Alafair, you stupid girl. It's *First* Samuel. *First* Samuel, for goodness' sake." Mrs. Evangeline LeBlanc rustled to the table in her black silk gown, taking up the heavy Bible from the table and flipping rapidly through its pages until she'd found the correct chapter and verse. "First Samuel, chapter 28. You had the pages turned to *Second* Samuel, chapter 24."

Her daughter shrugged. "Really, Mama, do you think any of these people will notice whether it's First Samuel or Second Samuel or a page from Mrs. Gaskell? It's so dark in here you can't see your hand in front of your face."

"Exactly as we like it, my dear. And, yes, details always matter. We don't need some old biddy wandering over to refresh her memory about the encounter between Saul and the spirit of Samuel, and instead reading about some avenging angel flattening Jerusalem at the Lord's command. It just wouldn't do."

Evangeline LeBlanc (born Elsie Gooch in Catahoula Parish, Louisiana, and whose most recent residence had been the women's ward of the New Orleans municipal jail) cast an experienced eye over the room. The parlor of the little rented house was suitably respectable for a medium of Mrs. LeBlanc's reputation (which was still wholly intact in Great Britain, if a bit tarnished in the States). True, the rooms were the tiniest bit shabby, but in an odd way that added to the verisimilitude of the experience; the people who came to see her were less interested in the quality of the lace antimacassars on the sofa and more concerned with her ability to contact the recently departed. The state of the room indicated a woman preoccupied with spiritual matters rather than earthly affairs. She couldn't afford to be flashy, as that drew unnecessary attention to the fees she charged and the status of her bank account.

There was nothing flashy about the room now. It contained only the required articles for the séance. The round oak table was covered with a white lace cloth, and in the center stood a crystal ball. Two white candles in gleaming brass candlesticks stood north and south of the ball. The Bible, now open to the correct page, was situated on the western side of the crystal ball, and a piece of perfect white quartz acted as a paperweight. To the east of the ball, Alafair LeBlanc had positioned a bud vase containing a single white lily, its fragrance reputed to attract spirits. In the event any mischievous, or downright evil, spirits appeared, Alafair had laid out their defenses on a sideboard: a wicked-looking knife of Sheffield steel, a delicate silver bell and a salt cellar filled to the brim with coarse rock salt. Mrs. LeBlanc had never had the occasion to test these defenses against any ill-mannered apparitions, but then Mrs. LeBlanc had never actually been successful in contacting any spirits of any sort. The accoutrements of her trade were there for the comfort of her clients.

"The room looks perfect," Mrs. LeBlanc said. She cocked her head critically at her daughter. "Should we go over things again?"

Alafair wheezed in exasperation. "No, Mama. We've done this dozens of times."

"Another round of practice wouldn't hurt. If we'd only covered that bit of string in New Orleans, I wouldn't have spent seven months in the pokey, listening to whores scream for morphine or a drop of rum." Mrs. LeBlanc sniffed. "Jail is no place for a woman of my sensibilities. It nearly shattered me."

Alafair dropped a comforting arm around her mother. "That was the past, Mama. We've done really well here in London. Your name is known all over town. Everyone who is anyone wants you to conduct a séance."

Her mother dropped her eyes modestly. It was true. Londoners were coming out of the woodwork for a chance to have Evangeline LeBlanc contact dear Uncle Piers (he was fine in the morning, but cholera acts so swiftly) or sweet little Mary (who knew there was an abandoned well there?).

"Of course," Alafair went on, "we got terribly lucky when Lady Bancroft was run down by that hansom cab, just after you warned her to expect bad news by horse. Probably wasn't expecting it to be quite such bad news, though."

"I was only trying to scare the woman," Mrs. LeBlanc said indignantly. "I didn't take to her at all. What a snob. Acted like we weren't fit to wipe her feet. I just wanted to put the wind up her."

"Her death was regrettable," said Alafair, without the slightest hint of regret. "But it's been good for business. The swells are lining up to see you. Just look at the size of the fish we've landed tonight."

There had been more involved in landing this particular fish than Mrs. LeBlanc had shared with Alafair, but then the girl need not know everything, especially since Mrs. LeBlanc found herself a bit uneasy about this specific detail. Still, bills must be paid, and if she did her job well, quite a lot of bills would be settled out of tonight's work. She looked at the clock and clapped her hands. "Mercy! She'll be here any minute. Look sharp, Alafair, and mind you don't snag your ring on that wire again or there will be hell to pay."

Alafair rolled her eyes. By now she was used to her mother growing anxious as the time arrived for the séance. Mrs. LeBlanc would turn snappish, like she had about First Samuel, and then pace the room in circles, muttering under her breath and wringing her hands. Alafair had mentioned it once, only to endure a diatribe about the similarities of séances to theatrical productions and the strenuous preparations her mother had to undergo in order to present a realistic performance. Like most artists, though, Mrs. LeBlanc would be ready when the curtain rose.

They heard the jangle of harnesses and the ring of iron shoes on the cobbled lane outside the house. The driver of the coach shouted hoarsely, slowing his charges to a standstill, wheels crunching to a halt in the rime of frost on the stones.

"She's here," said Mrs. LeBlanc, who made a dash for the mirror, tucked her fading grey ringlets into her cap and ran a finger over her eyebrows.

"How do I look?" she enquired of her daughter.

"Very correct," said Alafair. "And quite trustworthy."

Mrs. Leblanc spared her a quick smile, flung herself into a chair with her hand on her chest and breathed deeply to calm her nerves. "Go to the door, dear, and welcome our guests. And don't forget to curtsey," she shouted after Alafair as she smoothed her dress and checked one last time for escaping curls.

Alafair opened the door and found herself staring at the chest of a tall, slim footman wearing a cloak and hat against the winter chill. He removed the hat and inclined his powdered wig at her.

"Mrs. Evangeline LeBlanc?"

"I am her daughter, Miss Alafair LeBlanc."

The footman pirouetted and bowed prettily, his arm sweeping gracefully backward to indicate the stout, dark form that had appeared at his elbow.

"Her Majesty, the Queen," he said, then stepped aside as the little figure marched resolutely into the hall, brushing past Alafair with barely a glance. Alafair bent a knee and wobbled dangerously, rising just in time to snare the first of many garments the Queen was beginning to shed with the help of a lady-in-waiting who had accompanied her. Alafair collected shawls, scarves, cashmere gloves and a severe bonnet in varying hues of black from the Queen, then held out her arms as the men and women who were participating in the séance with Her Majesty discarded their heavy coats and cloaks, bonnets, top hats, mittens and gloves. Alafair staggered under the weight, wished they had hired a maid for the evening and pondered the task of escorting the Queen into her mother while carrying the contents of a clothing shop.

Her mother had anticipated her, though, and now appeared in the parlor doorway, looking serene and somewhat otherworldly, as a good medium should. Alafair had no idea how she managed the transformation from nervous wreck to confident guide to the world beyond the grave, but Mrs. LeBlanc was not to be underestimated.

She dropped an elegant curtsey. "Your Majesty. Welcome to our humble dwelling."

Alafair opened the door to the dining room and dumped her load of coats and gloves on the table. It would be hell to sort out later, but at the end of the evening everyone would be so excited by what they had witnessed, so eager to talk about it among themselves, that they wouldn't notice the wait while Alafair frantically matched gloves and untangled scarves.

The Queen dipped her chin at Mrs. LeBlanc's greeting and examined her new spirit medium. Mrs. LeBlanc smiled encouragingly, in a cordial, American sort of way, but did not speak. The Queen, though a devoted believer in communication with the spirits of the departed, was known to be skittish and unpredictable when dealing with even her closest advisors, and Mrs. LeBlanc was grateful for the suggestion she'd received to permit the Queen to make this slow perusal of her face and figure. She was confident she could pass inspection: her grey hair was sensibly covered by a lace cap, her clothes sober and her expression combined both a quality of aloofness from the sordid affairs of this world and a quiet assurance that you'd soon be speaking with your loved one from the next. Having practiced this expression in her mirror hundreds of times, Mrs. LeBlanc could now slip it on and off like a mask.

While she waited quietly for the Queen to finish her examination, Mrs. LeBlanc studied the Queen. Nearly sixty now, plump, with heavy jowls that accentuated her receding chin, a strong nose, pale blue eyes and the expression of a dedicated eater who has just been informed that dinner will be late. Her late husband, Prince Francis Albert Augustus Charles Emmanuel of Saxe-Coburg and Gotha, had been dead sixteen years, but Victoria still wore widow's weeds. Local rags had taken to calling her the

"Widow of Windsor" due to her extended mourning period. To-night, her black gown was of the finest Henrietta cloth, trimmed in crepe and sporting the nine-inch long lawn cuffs known as "weepers." A cambric handkerchief was tucked into one, ready to be whipped out and put to use if dear departed Albert made an appearance. In the slightest of concessions to those who thought the Queen had worn her mourning clothes too long, she had adorned herself with a jet broach and rings.

The Queen and Mrs. LeBlanc held each other's gaze for a few moments, then the Queen nodded slightly to her retinue, and there was a great whoosh of expelled air as the ladies and gentlemen realized the Queen was satisfied.

What a job, thought Mrs. LeBlanc, following this old pussy around, catering to her every whim and cringing when she was displeased. Made faking conversations with dead people seem positively pedestrian by comparison.

"Won't you come into the parlor, ma'am? Everything is prepared." Mrs. LeBlanc stood aside and let the Queen enter. She took in the room quickly, noting with approval the arrangement of the candles, the Bible and the lily in its vase. She seated herself at the table, and the three women and two men who accompanied her settled into chairs. The Queen peremptorily rapped the seat beside her, and Mrs. LeBlanc sat down.

"It is a rarity that I seek solace from anyone other than Mr. Lees." The Queen wasted no time in getting down to business.

"I understand perfectly," said Mrs. LeBlanc. As a thirteen-year-old schoolboy, Robert James Lees had gone into a trance just after Albert's death and conveyed messages from him to Victoria. Rumour had it that during the past several years, Lees had lived at Buckingham Palace for long stretches of time, so that Vicky could converse with her husband whenever the mood struck her.

Mrs. LeBlanc smiled gently. "I have the greatest regard for Mr. Lees. I have not yet had the good fortune to meet him, but I hope to do so soon. He is highly respected in America."

"He is a most empathetic man and most gifted. He has a rare affinity for the spirits of those who have gone before us. My dear Albert finds him a most congenial medium through which to speak to me. While he lived, the prince and I were inseparable, and I depended on him for so many things. Now that he has passed on, it is such a comfort to be able to consult with him as needs dictate."

"I sympathize, ma'am. I too have lost a husband." Well, not so much lost him as never quite found him. Given Alafair's colouring and temperament, her father was likely Charlie McClelland, the cardsharp who haunted the Mississippi riverboats, relieving commercial travelers of their hard-earned profits. Or the culprit could have been Frank Summers, the itinerant preacher who was always skating out of town after pocketing the contents of the collection plate.

"Then you will understand how important my dear Albert was to me and how much I long to speak with him whenever I can."

"Of course I do. And if he is ready to speak to you tonight, you shall have the chance to say all that you would wish to him."

"Dear Albert always comes to me," said the Queen. "I am a spiritually receptive person."

I'm counting on it, thought Mrs. LeBlanc. Victoria Regina she might be, Queen of Great Britain and Ireland and Empress of India, but she was desperate to contact her dead husband, and in that frame of mind, she would ignore all evidence to the contrary and believe Mrs. LeBlanc had the power to summon spirits.

"Shall we begin?" Mrs. LeBlanc placed her hands on the table and extended her fingers until her pinkies touched that of the

Queen on one side and the bewhiskered old gentleman on the other. The rest of the group likewise stretched out their hands until their little fingers rested against those of their neighbors.

Alafair glided discreetly behind a small desk tucked into the corner, out of the line of sight of everyone except her mother, and surreptitiously fingered the elaborate arrangement of wires and twine located beneath the desk.

Mrs. LeBlanc closed her eyes and inhaled deeply. The group around the table muttered and rustled until finally the noise subsided to an expectant silence. The Queen sat like a statue, staring into the flame of the candle on the table before her. Minutes passed, and the room was quiet. Alafair studied the circle of participants and smiled. The bewhiskered gentleman looked bored out of his skull. Probably wished he were tucked up at his club with a brandy and soda, and a lively game of whist to occupy his time. None of the others looked very excited at the prospect of hearing from Albert again, either. After twenty years, the gossip from the spirit world must be getting pretty stale.

Mrs. LeBlanc spoke softly. "I am seeking Albert. Come, Albert, and commune with us."

Silence. The air stirred, and the candle flame guttered. The Queen sighed. Alafair carefully replaced the tiny fan of peacock feathers.

"Come, Albert," said Mrs. LeBlanc. "Your friends are here. Your wife is here. They want to speak to you. Leave the realm of living souls and move among us."

The only sounds in the room were the ticking of the clock on the mantle and the crackle of the fire in the grate. There was a muted popping sound, like a cork being pulled from a bottle, and a blue flame erupted among the coals. Alafair let the thin wire slip from her fingers, as the group at the table started in their seats and shifted nervously in anticipation.

"I feel your presence, Albert," said Mrs. LeBlanc. "Will you speak with us tonight?"

The scent of lilies filled the room, and the Queen drew in a long, quavering breath. "He is here," she whispered. "I feel his presence."

Alafair snorted silently and replaced the atomizer behind one leg of the desk. She was as bored as the whiskery gent. She'd done this so often, she could have done it in her sleep.

"Are you there, Albert?" asked Mrs. LeBlanc. "We seek your companionship and counsel tonight. Please, do not fail to appear to us."

The table tipped to one side and rocked gently.

"Albert," cried the Queen. "Oh, Albert, my dear."

Mrs. LeBlanc removed her foot from the lever beneath the table and pressed another. A tapping sound, like fingers rapping gently on the old oak table, resonated through the room.

"Drina?" The sound had emanated from Mrs. LeBlanc, but the voice belonged to someone else. It was deep, guttural, and overlaid with a thick German accent. The Queen's hand quivered against Mrs. LeBlanc's.

"It must be him," whispered one of the ladies-in-waiting. "Only her family calls her that."

"Albert, are you there?" asked the Queen in a tremulous voice.

Mrs. LeBlanc shivered. Her eyes closed and her head lolled to one side. Alafair stifled a yawn.

"I am with you, my darling Drina," said Mrs. LeBlanc in the harsh tone of a Teutonic aristocrat.

"Are you well, my dear?" asked the Queen tenderly.

Alafair bit back a guffaw. He was dead, for Christ's sake. How well could he be in those circumstances?

Mrs. LeBlanc forged on. "I am quite well. And you? Are you also well?"

"Well enough, dear. Just the slightest indisposition. Nothing for you to worry about. I fear I have had some difficulty sleeping, and my appetite has decreased recently." The Queen paused for breath, and the German voice spoke hastily.

"I'm sure you'll feel better soon. And the children? How do they fare?"

Victoria inhaled sharply, and the group around the table stirred uneasily.

"The girls are doing wonderfully, Albert. And Arthur, Leopold and Alfred are such fine gentleman. But Bertie—" The Queen's voice rose in indignation as she contemplated the ribald exploits of her son Albert Edward, Prince of Wales and heir to the British throne.

There was a strangled moan from the participants in the sé-ance, and Mrs. LeBlanc, realizing she had started down a path leading to disaster, interjected swiftly in the heavily accented voice: "My dear, do not trouble yourself about Bertie. All will come right in the end. Trust me."

"I do wish that I could, Albert, but he is such a trial. There's not a serious bone in his body. All he wants to do is drink and carouse and chase women. I don't understand why you could not have had greater influence on him while you were with us."

Mrs. LeBlanc was quickly developing sympathy for poor Al-bert. Generally, those left behind were looking for reassurance from the departed, not an opportunity to complain about their health or harangue the poor dead relatives about their lack of parenting skills. The Queen was still cataloguing Bertie's deficiencies for her departed husband. At this rate, the séance would drag on for hours, as Bertie's deficiencies were both manifold and extensive. Mrs. LeBlanc seized the bull by the horns.

"My dear wife, I know how you struggle to rein in Bertie and to see that he is provided with the training appropriate for your successor. I do not like to see you so exercised by these trials. I beg you not to concern yourself with this matter and to take care that you do not injure your health by worrying excessively about our son. My time with you is brief, and soon I must return to the others. I have come to you tonight with a request, Drina."

The Queen straightened in her chair, her face avid with curiosity, and Bertie's shortcomings forgotten for the moment. "Anything, anything at all for you, my dear."

"I miss you terribly, and the children as well."

Tears seeped down the Queen's heavily powdered jowls. "And we miss you."

"I remember all the happy times we shared at Osborne and at Windsor. But most especially I long to relive those halcyon days at Balmoral."

The Queen sniffed and nodded lugubriously. "They were happy times indeed."

"If I could return to you, I would ask only that we might spend the rest of our lives there together."

"What, even in the winter?" Her Majesty looked dubious.

"Yes. I would go this instant, if I were there with you. My one regret is that we never took the opportunity to spend the holiest of days there together with our family. I would so dearly love to spend the Christmas holiday there, with friends and family, and hold a ghillies' ball for the servants, and dance to a reel together just as we used to do."

The Queen's lip trembled. "Ah, yes. What wonderful times we had at those balls."

"Will you go now, this instant, to Balmoral? Will you give me the satisfaction of spending Christmas at our Scottish home, where I may visit you in spirit and observe the close bonds of our family once again?"

"Well," said the Queen, "you know I always spend Christmas at Osborne."

"Please go, my darling. How I long to be with you there in the Highlands. It would mean so much to me if you would accede to my wishes, just this once, and spend the holiday at Balmoral. It is my heart's desire. Please, do not disappoint me."

"Er, no, of course not," said the Queen. "I should never dream of disappointing my dear husband. I shall inform the master of the household at once that I will be spending Christmas at Balmoral."

While Alafair distributed coats and mufflers, Mrs. LeBlanc accepted the compliments of the Queen's party on a successful communication with the spirit of Prince Albert. She curtseyed to the Queen, now swaddled in furs and scarves, who gave her a grave nod.

"I should like to see you again, Mrs. LeBlanc. I have spoken to dear Albert on several occasions, but he has never been quite so, er, explicit about his wishes. You must be exceptionally talented as a channel for spirits."

"Thank you for your kind words, ma'am. I am glad that I could provide such a direct communication to you. I should be pleased to wait upon you at any time."

The Queen shuffled to the door, and the footman swept it open for her and her entourage.

The bewhiskered gentleman dropped a coin into Mrs. Le-Blanc's hand. "With Her Majesty's compliments," he said as he tipped his hat.

The last of the party to leave sidled furtively to Mrs. LeBlanc's side. "Most convincing, madam. You remembered every detail. Well done." The voice was a soft Scottish burr. A handful of coins cascaded into Mrs. LeBlanc's outstretched hand. "Remember, not a word to anyone, or you may find yourself back on a ship to Louisiana, Miss Gooch."

ONE

"India," French hissed, "at last I have you where I want you."

His face was inches from mine. I could feel his breath through the mask, hot with lust, and his eyes were aflame with it. There was a sharp pain in my left breast, I was sweating buckets, and my knees felt as though they could give way at any time. I had never seen French like this, and it worried me.

But only for a moment. I've found myself in a bad patch or two, and if I do say so myself (and if I won't, who will?), I'm at my best when the chips are down. The options in this situation were the usual ones available to a woman physically threatened by a man: attack (my preferred method but not always the wisest), submission (only if every other option had turned tail and fled over the hill) and deceit. Now there's a world of possibilities in the latter, and so I turned my mind to how best to practice that glib and oily art (as old Willie Shakespeare put it). It didn't take long for me to decide on an approach. French is as predictable as a vicar's afternoon appointment with the sherry bottle.

I gave him a look of maidenly meekness. "Ow," I said. "You're hurting me."

French sprang away as though I'd produced a viper from my pocket. "Oh, I say. I didn't mean to injure you."

You can always count on the English gentleman in French, at least until he sniffs out that you've been relying on his good manners to take advantage of him. Then, he can be a right brute. The moment when French discovered that I had been pulling his leg was looming on the horizon like a Malay pirate ship, so I dropped my act and went in for the kill.

His foil hung at his side. I gathered my strength and lunged toward him in a perfectly executed *flèche*, my arm thrusting forward and the button that covered the point of my foil slamming into French's fencing jacket at the breastbone. The blade of the foil bent wildly and skittered off French's chest as my momentum carried me along the fencing strip, but as I passed him, I let out a great whoop of victory. A touch for India!

"That's a touch," I cried when I'd halted my headlong rush and turned back to face him. I ripped off my mask and pushed my hair from my face.

"Oof." French was recumbent on the strip, cradling his sternum and breathing raggedly. "That wasn't a touch; that was a bloody ambush." He pushed himself to a sitting position and regarded me reproachfully. "That was underhanded, even for you, India. You misled me, and when I dropped my guard, you attacked."

"You're the one who said that fencing was in part the art of deception."

French probed his chest for an entry wound. "Within accepted conventions, it is."

"That's ridiculous. How can you deceive someone if you have to follow rules about how to deceive him?"

French ignored my question, as he no doubt knew there was no adequate response to it.

"That maneuver of yours would be frowned upon at L'Ecole d'Escrime Français. In fact, you'd be tossed out of every *salle d'armes* in France."

"Well, I learned the art of self-defense at L'Ecole d'Boulevards d'London. 'Needs must' is the school motto. And if you don't know how to wallop a gent in the bollocks, you can't graduate." I tossed my mask to one side and wiped the sweat from my face. "Really, French, I do appreciate your interest in my personal safety, but I've done alright on my own up to now. To be honest"— and surprisingly, in this case, I was—"I'm not sure fencing is for me. A well-aimed kick in the testicles is more my style. And if the situation requires it, I'm a fine shot with my revolver."

I carried my .442 Webley British Bulldog with me whenever I traveled at night or into any of the more questionable districts of London. I'd used it on several occasions, including a few weeks ago when I had cut down a sabre-wielding Terek Cossack guard from the Russian Embassy who had been about to filet me while French had been occupied wrestling with Major Ivanov, the tsar's agent in Britain. I opened my mouth to point out how very effective my Bulldog had proved against the Cossack's great killing sword, the *shashka*, but French was glaring at me as he got stiffly to his feet.

"Do not," he said, in a warning tone, "blather on about how effective your Bulldog was against the Cossack. If I hear one more word from you about that, I'm going to be ill. I am well aware that in most cases, it is more advantageous to hold a gun in your hand than a sword. However, there may be times when you don't have your Bulldog on your person, and you find yourself threatened by an assailant with a knife or a club or even a sword. The object of teaching you how to fence is to provide you with an additional means of self-defense if, at some time in the future, you should find yourself wishing you hadn't left your revolver on the fireplace mantle. I should think you would be glad to learn a few new tricks to protect yourself, given your, ah . . . profession."

Dear French. Always so solicitous of my feelings, except when he isn't. My profession, as he so delicately referred to it, is in fact prostitution. I am the abbess of Lotus House in St. Alban's Street, an elegant and luxurious establishment catering to the upper echelons of the civil service, minor aristocracy and our brave military lads (officers only, of course). The whores I employ are attractive, clean and generally devoid of any ambition other than getting their hands on the next bottle of gin. I feed them well and keep a doctor on retainer to ensure the girls don't provide anything to the customers that they shouldn't. I run a tight ship and am justifiably proud of my services and my reputation, which has improved by leaps and bounds over the past few years. I'm not in the first rank of brothels just yet, but give me a year or two and the old abbesses will have to step aside or get shoved out of the way.

No doubt you are wondering how the madam of a brothel came to be learning the art of fencing from a handsome British blue blood with blue-black hair and arrogant grey eyes. Surprisingly, our relationship was not of a business nature, unless you could call French's attempt at blackmailing me not long ago (enterprising as it was) "business." It's like this, you see. One of my regular customers, a spaniel-faced cove named Archibald Latham, expired on the premises of Lotus House not long ago. Naturally, I had to dispose of the body before any of the other madams got wind of the situation, or they would have made my life a living hell, spreading the word that the bints at Lotus House were a bloodthirsty lot and Latham had been killed for the contents of his pocket. As it turned out, Latham had passed over the River Jordan due to natural causes, probably as a result of the stress and strain of his work at the War Office. On the day he died at Lotus House, he was carrying a memo containing vital information about the state of the British military.

Russia and Britain had been rattling sabres at each other over Russia's threat to attack the Ottoman Empire, ostensibly to assist their Serbian cousins who were being put to the sword by the Sublime Porte's rascally military irregulars, but in truth because Tsar Alexander II was a bit sulky over not possessing a warm water port for the Russian navy. Naturally, the British government didn't want the Russian bear anywhere in the vicinity of the Mediterranean, where it might come roaring out of its den and cut off British access to the Suez Canal and the route to India. In consequence, the British government had been trying to intimidate the Russians with talk of the number of British Tommies champing at the bit to have a go at the Russians again, just a few decades after the debacle of the Crimean War. I know, hard to credit, but you know how these diplomats are: they fancy themselves as master strategists, just because they've gone to public school and read a little Cicero.

Normally, I'd have shoved Latham's papers in the fireplace and put a match to them, just to get rid of any evidence that the old goat had been in my establishment, but in this case I didn't have the chance. Russian agents had been shadowing Latham and took the opportunity his death presented to spirit away the case containing the War Office memo, a memo, which, you've no doubt realized by now, contained an accurate depiction of the strength of the British Army, which was just about large enough to repel an attack on Penzance by the combined forces of Norway and Sweden.

Apparently, the Russians weren't the only ones interested in my spaniel-faced friend. French (in his role as agent for the British prime minister) had also turned up, demanding the case, just as I and my assistant Vincent were preparing to deposit Latham's body somewhere along the Thames. When I couldn't produce the cursed case, French (setting aside his usual courtly instincts) had coerced me into helping him recover the memo, informing me just how easy it would be to remove Lotus House from my ownership if I did not.

It turned out to be quite a ride. Along the way, I met that dear old queen (Disraeli, not Victoria), swanked away the evening at a ball at the Russian Embassy and found myself in the middle of an extended pursuit of the Russian agents and the stolen memo through the snowy English countryside, culminating in a crossing of the English Channel that still leaves me nauseous when I think about it. (It was during this adventure that I had dispatched the Cossack guard with my beloved Bulldog.) Well, there's much more to the story of course, but I don't see why I should tell it to you here. I've written it all down as the first volume of my memoirs, to be published just as soon as French stops trying to teach me to fence and I can find a publisher willing to suspend disbelief at the prospect of a prostitute riding to the rescue of Her Majesty's government. If you want to know how things turned out, you'll just have to fork over a few bob at your local bookseller's.

"I'm always glad to learn a new trick," I said (not pointing out that I'd also turned a few in my time), "but I don't see the point of learning *this* trick. I mean, it's all very well for a bunch of poncy poofs to prance up and down a painted rectangle on the floor, flicking each other with this poor excuse for a sword, but when I'm in trouble, I'm usually in need of more than a French vocabulary and a keen sense of fair play."

French sighed, vexed at my stupidity. "It is not a 'painted rectangle'; it is a piste. And fencing is not just 'prancing about,' as you so ignorantly portray it. The object of fencing is to thrust your sword into your opponent without allowing him to touch you. This requires an exquisite and exacting combination of strength, timing, precision, quickness of mind, and resolution. It requires subterfuge, cunning and sleight of hand."

"I believe I possess all of those characteristics in abundance. Don't forget, I've had to live by my wits all these years, and I've managed to do so without any knowledge whatsoever of a *dessus*." I pushed a hank of wet hair from my eyes and contemplated myself in the mirror along the wall. My raven black hair lay in sodden streamers around my face, and my creamy English complexion (kept so at no little expense by creams and unguents, and the denial of any indulgence in opium) was flushed with heat and shining with perspiration.

"Besides," I said, "I'm sweating like a whore at Evensong, and these clothes are hideous." The long, quilted jacket was made for a man, and consequently strained to bursting over my ample bosom and fit entirely too tightly around my hips. I looked as though I were about to be carted off to Bethlem Royal Hospital for a fortnight's cure.

"Never mind how you look, India. Why do women always worry about how they look? We're fencing, for God's sake, not having tea with the Queen. Now put your mask back on and let's begin again. And this time, please try to control the point of your foil. The object is not to slash with the foil but to use your hand to manipulate the point to touch your opponent in the target area."

"Why can't I just lop off his arm and be done with it?"

"Damnation, India. The reason beginners learn to fence with the foil is so that they will grasp the importance of controlling the point of the blade. Control of the point is everything. And if you don't mind my saying so, you could benefit a great deal by learning a modicum of self-control."

"Oh, don't get sniffy, squire," I said, but I put on my mask.

There was no arguing with French when he was in this mood, and I had found that our fencing practice had at least one unexpected and delightful side effect: my figure (despite my buxom appearance) was growing lithe and strong. I was so strong now, in fact, that I could slice my cook Mrs. Drinkwater's Dundee cake with one hand and a dull knife. This was a considerable accomplishment, since Mrs. Drinkwater, when she wasn't swilling the cooking sherry or passed out on the deal table in the kitchen, was capable of producing baked goods that a prison gang couldn't break with pickaxes.

French pushed his mask on securely and raised the point of his foil at me. "Now, please assume the correct stance."

Resignedly, I placed my feet at right angles to one another, bent my knees slightly, lifted my own foil in my right hand and put out the left arm to balance my sword arm.

"Excellent," said French.

"Well, this part's not so bloody difficult, is it? It's all that other twaddle that's confusing. And why can't we speak English? I mean, why can't you just say 'put your feet together,' instead of 'rassemblement'?"

"Your accent is atrocious."

"It's odd, but I can't recall having had the advantage of an education at Eton and Oxford."

"Never mind," French said soothingly. "Once you can execute a *redoublement* with speed and accuracy, I shall attempt to teach you how to pronounce the word correctly."

That did it. Nothing gets my back up like condescension, especially from the likes of French, whose chestnuts I had pulled from the fire once or twice on our previous escapade.

"En garde," I cried, with no attempt to roll my "r's." I surged forward, waving my foil, aiming at the smug smile I could sense behind French's mask.

He met my blade easily with his own, flicking mine to one side as though it had been a circling gnat. In the next instant, the button of his foil came to rest against my jacket. I looked down in some dismay, for I really detest being beaten so easily, and especially by French. Perhaps I should have been less impetuous in my assault.

Naturally, like all men, he could not leave well enough alone.

"You see, India. I was correct. You lack control. You allowed your anger to carry you along on an ill-planned and poorly executed attack, which I parried with no difficulty."

I shoved the blade of his foil from my chest and took up my position again. "Come on then, you pompous git."

For the next hour, we danced and capered up and down the length of the piste, our blades ringing as they clashed together. French moved with suppleness and grace, now parrying my thrust with a minimum of effort, now executing a perfect *balestra*, jumping forward slightly (which caused me to take a short step backward), then lunging after me with his sword arm thrust forward. I caught the blade of his foil with my own, turning my wrist sharply to push the tip away from my target area, then rotated the

wrist back and surged forward in a counter attack, my eyes focused on the seam in French's fencing jacket. He evaded my
thrust, tilting his hips and swiveling his torso, and then came at
me again. He feinted once and nearly drew me in, but I detected
the hesitation in his blade and drew back before he had time to
straighten his arm and touch me in the target area.

While French executed his moves with the elegance of a Russian ballerina, taunting me with his superior technique, touching
me at will, I hopped about like a chimpanzee just let out of its
cage, attempting to block his advances and launch a counterattack. French kept shouting instructions to me in his impeccable French accent (well, I assumed it was impeccable, dashed if I
know, really, since I don't speak the language). One thing I was
sure of, however, was that any number of incomprehensible com-
mandments would not improve my fencing. I was staying in the
bout through sheer willpower and cussedness. The muscles in my
thighs burned like fire and my lungs felt seared, but I'd be damned
if I'd give up until I'd acquainted French with the feel of my foil
planted firmly in his chest. I renewed my offensive with vigor.
Once the tip of my foil was an inch from the cloth of his jacket,
but he deftly raised his blade and deflected my own, then spun
effortlessly away. Twice more I came within range of touching
him, lowering my head and charging like a mad bull, hoping to
catch him off guard with the quickness of my movements, but
again he pirouetted out of reach of my blade, shaking his head in
disgust.

"Less enthusiasm, please," he said, "and more finesse."

I'd had several customers in my time that could have benefitted from those instructions. Alas, enthusiasm was all I had at this
point (and it was waning fast). Any finesse I might have possessed
had vanished like an oasis in a sandstorm. Well, that left guile.

Hadn't French told me that the premier fencers used various means (within the conventions of the sport, of course) to distract, confuse or startle their opponents? I'd do the same, and to hell with the conventions.

French was waggling the point of his foil at me, looking for an opening. He began to advance slowly.

"Mungo?"

"What?" French checked his progress.

"Your name, is it Mungo?"

French has never disclosed his Christian name to me, and I've amused myself often since I've known him by guessing just what moniker his parents had bestowed on him.

"Of course not. That's a ridiculous name."

"Sholto?"

French put down his sword in disgust. "It is not Mungo. It is not Sholto. Nor is it Ivo. Are you ready to fence now?"

"Agmondesham?"

"Bloody hell. No one is named Agmondesham. At least not in this country."

"I beg to differ, sir. Agmondesham Vesey, the Irish MP."

"Irish. Proves my point exactly."

"Hereward?"

French advanced on me like lightning. I raised my blade to fend him off and retreated. Rapidly. He looked very annoyed. Good.

"Wilberforce?"

"No," said French. He was almost within range. Just a few steps more and my trap would snap shut.

"Eglantyne?"

"Wherever do you find these na . . . ?"

I slithered to one side, and his point went flying past my left sleeve. I stepped into his oncoming body, my foil outstretched. Got you now, you bastard, I thought, just as he whipped his foil back into position and slid the blade down mine until our sword guards met with a resounding clang. He pushed me back, rather casually, and buried the button of his foil against my breast.

"Damn and blast!" I was cross. Usually, the name game drove French to bouts of inarticulate exasperation. Who knew he could fence under such conditions?

I discarded my mask and collapsed in a heap on the floor. "It's no good, French. You've exhausted me. I'll never learn this bloody sport, and frankly, I don't give a tinker's damn if I do."

French removed his mask and wiped his sleeve over his brow. "It isn't just sport, India. It's a killing art."

"Well, I shall just have to hope I don't encounter any pedigreed Germans with dueling scars and a murderous disposition. If I do, I shall run away as fast as a rat up a drainpipe."

French tucked his legs beneath him and sank down beside me. "It's the French and Italians you should worry about. They fight with skill; displaying a dueling scar on your cheek would be tantamount to admitting you were a poor fencer. Germans are brutes, charging and slashing like barbarians. Come to think of it, you fight a bit like them."

"I'm not overly fond of the Krauts. They always smell of stale beer and sausage, and they're too frugal for my taste. However, I would point out that their ancestors toppled Rome, thereby proving that civilized fighting is an oxymoron. I'll put my money on the inhuman savage any day."

A husky cough cut short French's reply. We turned simultaneously to behold the fellow who had interrupted our conversation.

"I do hope I'm not intruding." He was as squat and pale as spring's first mushroom, with a lumpen nose and sharp eyes.

"Harry." French rose to his feet. "Don't worry, you're not inter-fering with our lesson. We were finished." He turned to me and offered me his hand, pulling me to my feet. "May I present Miss India Black? India, this is Harry Parkman. He works for the prime minister."

"Miss Black," said Harry, with a secret little smile that I didn't much like. "I've heard of you."

"Oh, yes? From whom?"

"Why, the prime minister, of course. Lord Beaconsfield him-self. He holds you in great esteem." He gave me the once-over. "And I can certainly see why."

I don't mind being scrutinized by men; it's been my stock-in-trade for many years, so why should I complain now? Besides, I don't think I flatter myself when I say that even sweaty and di-sheveled as I was at that moment, I was still a damned handsome woman, capable of turning any man's head.

"How is the old reprobate?" I asked.

Harry laughed and French scowled.

"I mean that only in the political sense, of course," I hastened to add. French had a soft spot for Benjamin Disraeli, first Earl of Beaconsfield, the present prime minister of Great Britain and French's employer. Well, I must admit I was rather fond of the old boy myself. Any Jew (yes, I know, his father had converted to the Church of England, but Dizzy would've joined the Ancient Order of Druids if it would have improved his chances of becoming PM) who could climb the greasy pole to the summit of British politics deserved some respect, in my book. I always root for the under-dog and the outsider, and Dizzy, with his Jewish ethnicity, his outlandish clothes, his dyed black ringlets and his hooked nose, was the epitome of a social pariah. Not unlike, I might add, a prostitute.

"The prime minister sends his regards, and requests that you and Mr. French consult with him tonight at ten o'clock at his lodgings in the Langham Hotel." The request sounded oddly formal coming from this little toadstool.

"You can tell him we'll be there," said French.

Just like the man, I thought. Never bothers to consult me; just feels free to commit me to any sort of undertaking without so much as a by-your-leave. And I'd have certainly enquired why Dizzy wanted to meet with us. But I suppose French was merely complying with convention by not deigning to ask the messenger any questions. He'd reserve those for Dizzy himself. Still, I had to admit my curiosity was aroused. What could the prime minister want with me? French worked for the man, so if Harry had said Dizzy wanted French to make tracks for Hong Kong, there'd be French on a ship headed east. But if the great man himself was summoning me, then he must have need of my special talents. I'd rather enjoyed myself chasing that damned War Office memo all over Kent and across the English Channel, shooting Cossacks and matching wits with the tsar's agents. Truth to tell, the excitement of running my own establishment had begun to pall; riding herd on a group of bints was no easy task. I mean, there are only so many times one can tell a girl "no discounts for your favorites," or put off the local wine merchant until the next ship arrives from India and disgorges a group of sex-starved cavalry officers on Lotus House. I was growing weary of the necessity of providing constant attention to the niggling details of operating a business (and God, there are a lot of them). I needed a new challenge to stimulate my interest, and perhaps the prime minister had something in mind. My spirits rose at the prospect.

* * *

At the appointed hour that evening, French and I presented ourselves at the door of Dizzy's hotel room. Since the death of his
wife a few years before, the prime minister had given up his London residence and rented rooms at the Langham Hotel, a discreet
and elegant establishment. I thought French might prefer to enter through a side door, so as not to put my womanly charms on
display to all the venerable Tory duffers having their after-dinner
port in the lobby, but we marched straight through the reception
area and up the stairs, while the old coots waggled their eyebrows
and looked enviously (but erroneously) at French.

Dizzy himself opened the door to us, grasping French's hand
in a manly grip and bending over mine like the gallant he was. I
admit to some shock at his appearance. It had been a few weeks
since I had seen him, but he seemed to have aged several years.
He'd always had the appearance of an aging Levantine roué, with
his tinted, thinning curls and sensuous lips. Now he looked positively ancient, his face heavily creased with lines and white as
paper.

"Welcome," he cried, flinging open the door and ushering us
into a large sitting room, where a fire, ferociously hot, burned
brightly in the grate. I removed my hat and gloves and took in the
room. Not to my taste certainly, but decorated in the style of the
day: dark green wallpaper with a scrolled overlay of vines and
leaves in a rich cream colour, matching fabric on the chairs, an
excess of Queen Anne furniture in mahogany and rosewood, and
an assortment of busts, pictures, mosaics and ferns adorning every available space. The drapes were velvet, in the same dark green
as the wallpaper, with a heavy gilded valance. Against this somber
(and in my view, oppressive) background, Dizzy stood out like a
macaw in a mortuary. He wore a silk dressing gown of crimson,
soft slippers of scarlet leather tooled with his crest and a scarlet

fez with a black silk tassel dangling over his ear. A single black ringlet corkscrewed out of the fez over his forehead. Lord. If the man didn't have style, at least he had courage.

He petted and cosseted us, pushing us into chairs nearest the fire and summoning a prim youngster to serve us drinks (brandy and soda for French, and a neat whisky for me), all the while prattling on about the events of the day, the state of the Conservative Party, the damned Russians (and here he looked a bit like the fiery old Disraeli, for he hates the Russians as only a former Jew can hate a regime that purges its Jewish population in periodic orgies of violence). When we'd received our drinks and the young man had delivered a cup of warm milk (warm milk!) to the prime minister, his torrent of speech finally subsided and he sank into a chair beside us. For a moment we sat in silence (quite uncharacteristic when Dizzy was in the room), sipping our drinks, with French and I waiting politely for Dizzy to get around to the reason for our visit and him staring gloomily at the fire. Finally, he stirred and spoke.

"You'll be wondering why I've summoned you here." Politicians are great creatures for the obvious.

Dizzy sighed morosely. Good Gad, I wondered, what could have happened? A revolt in Firozabad? Those demented Afrikaners stirring up the Zulu again? The Suez silted closed?

"The Queen," intoned Dizzy in funereal tones, "is spending the Christmas holiday at Balmoral."

Well. Bit of a letdown, really. What did I care where the old bag ate her plum pudding on the day of our Lord's birth? I glanced at French to see if he found this news as disturbing as Dizzy and was relieved to see that he looked as puzzled as I felt. Dizzy was staring at us expectantly, obviously awaiting our response to this doleful news.

I tried to think of something to say; deuced difficult though it was. "Er . . . I take it that that is not her customary practice." Not bad under the circumstances. Sometimes I surprise myself.

"Indeed not!" Dizzy expostulated. "She has never done so in the past. She always spends the holiday at Osborne, her home on the Isle of Wight."

"Well," said French carefully, "if she wants to make a change, is that not a good thing? She has been rather restricted in her habits since the prince died. Perhaps an alteration of her usual schedule would benefit Her Majesty's health."

Dizzy looked aghast. "Mr. French, I do not object to her changing her holiday plans. If she wanted to spend Christmas in Kathmandu, I should not mind. No, sir, I should not mind in the least. The problem, however, is that she requires that I also go to Balmoral, as minister in attendance, and I am not well. Not well at all, at the moment."

He settled back in his chair with a "there, how do you like that?" air.

"I see," said French.

I did not. How to approach this? Stupidity always works. "Minister in attendance?"

"Yes," said Dizzy. "The Queen must always be accompanied by a senior member of the government, to deal with correspondence and any issues of importance that might arise when she is away from Windsor."

"You said, 'a senior member of the government.' Does that not mean that someone else could go instead of you?"

"Of course," Dizzy groaned. "But the Queen insists that *I* accompany her to Balmoral. God, what a disaster."

Spending the Christmas holiday confined in a draughty stone house in the middle of the Cairngorm Mountains with Vicky and her retinue did indeed sound like a dreadful proposition, but I figured Dizzy had no one to blame but himself. He'd gone out of his way to woo the Queen since he'd become prime minister, flattering her egregiously, calling her the "Faery" (difficult to believe, I know, since she's built like a brick lavvy, but there you are), sending her flowers and valentines, collaborating in her deification of her dead husband, Albert, and basically fawning over the woman until the rest of her ministers and attendees had to leave the room because they were feeling nauseous. Can't say I blamed Dizzy, though. As a result of his loving attention to this plump, homely woman, he had more influence over her than any previous prime minister. He had unparalleled access to her, and now, it seemed, he also had an invitation to Balmoral.

"I abhor that pile of stone," Dizzy sniffed. "Her Majesty, as you know, always insists on the windows being left open to let in the fresh air, and since she can't abide coal fires, it's like living among the Esquimaux. I swear there were icicles on the wall of my bedroom the last time I was there. A man can't even console himself with a bit of tobacco. If you want to smoke, you have to go outside and stand in the cold. It's uncivilized, I tell you. Uncivilized."

Quite a predicament for the old chap, but it didn't really sound like a problem requiring the abilities of India Black. Or French, for that matter.

He must have been as perplexed as I was, for he drained the last of his brandy and soda and asked, "Why does the Queen want to go to Balmoral at this time of year?"

"Because," Dizzy said bitterly, "Albert told her to go."

"Sent a telegram, did he? 'Dear Vicky, go to Scotland. Al.' Is that it?"

French looked daggers at me and I shut my mouth, but Dizzy seemed undisturbed by my appalling lack of etiquette.

"He communicated with her through a spirit medium." Dizzy rose and staggered to the sideboard, where he replaced his glass of milk with one of brandy. He took a large gulp. "You've no doubt heard the rumours: the Queen believes that Albert speaks to her from beyond the grave. She consults mediums quite frequently. Apparently, Her Majesty has just seen an American woman, Mrs. LeBlanc, who is all the rage among the aristocracy at the moment. People claiming to see their dead rat terriers and that sort of rot." He seemed to realize that he was skirting near the edge of the cliff labeled "casting aspersions on the Queen's sanity," and made a beeline for safety.

"Oh, what does it matter if the Queen believes that she speaks to her dead husband? If she derives some solace from these séances, then there can't be any harm, can there?"

I supposed not, as long as Albert was only comforting his widow and not instructing her to declare war on the State of Vermont, for example.

"She's never recovered from his death," said Dizzy, coughing. "Do you know, she's kept his rooms just as they were on the day he died, with a clean nightshirt on the bed and hot water brought in every morning for his shave?"

Sounded like certifiable behavior to me, but I suppose one of the privileges of the monarchy is going mad while everyone goes on bowing and scraping, pretending you're merely the tiniest bit eccentric.

"Is there something we can do for you, sir?" asked French.

Dizzy's courtesy reasserted itself as he noticed our empty tumblers. "Oh, good Lord, I've let your glasses run dry. You must have another, by all means. I'll call Ralph."

"You needn't bother. I'll manage for us all." I was grateful for the chance to do something other than listen to the old man (fond as I am of him) whinge about our sovereign, even if it meant serving drinks, a decidedly servile role I usually despised. I replenished French's drink and mine, looked helplessly around for the jug of warm milk and decided that what Dizzy needed was another stiff brandy.

"Thank you, my dear," he said when I placed the glass in his hand. It trembled slightly. That wasn't like Dizzy. He must indeed be ill, for he set great store in presenting an air of imperturbable insouciance.

"Perhaps you could explain to the Queen that you're not feeling up to the journey and that a stay at Balmoral might have deleterious effects on your health," I suggested.

Dizzy smiled weakly. "It's true I'm not up to my usual standard of robust vitality, but I fear the Queen has little sympathy for her ministers when she wants them by her side. They are expected to be there." He looked glum. "Besides, if she thought the trip to Balmoral might kill me, she'd likely jump at the chance to ask me to carry a message to Albert. No, I shall have to go, regardless of my health. Why, I'll even have to procure a note from my physician, advising the Queen that I will require a warm fire in my room and extra blankets. I've had to do so before, you know."

"Is there something else that's troubling you, sir?" asked French.

"Ah." Dizzy rubbed his nose. "Very perceptive of you, Mr. French. Indeed, there is another matter that causes me concern. Enough concern, I might add, that I felt it necessary to invite you and Miss Black here tonight to discuss it with me."

Now we were getting down to brass tacks, which suited me perfectly. I never was one for sitting around sickrooms and soothing fevered brows with a cool hand. I empathized with Dizzy, but I'd been growing increasingly impatient (and bored) as the minutes ticked by without a hint as to why French and I had been summoned.

"Russians again?" I asked.

"Worse," said Dizzy. "The Scots."

"Have they crossed the border and attacked York?"

Dizzy laughed mirthlessly. "That might be a less difficult issue to resolve. No, the clans have not risen and there's no revolution in sight. There are, however, a few men and women who refuse to acknowledge the legitimacy of the British monarchy in Scotland. Have you heard of the Sons of Arbroath?"

French rose from his chair and raked the coals vigorously. "The Scottish nationalists? The group that is agitating for an independent Scotland?"

"The very same. Not that the idea of an independent Scotland has ever truly died out among the Scots. Quite a few of them still loathe the Act of Union of 1707, convinced that the Scottish parliament signed away Scottish freedom in exchange for trading privileges with the English colonies. You know that old saying of the Jacobites? 'We are bought and sold for English gold.' Many Scots continue to hold that view."

French nodded. "They do have a legitimate grievance. The act was shabbily handled by both members of the Scottish aristocracy and the English government, being pushed through the Scottish parliament by men who were rewarded with gifts of money, monopolies on trade, and grants of peerages. It's difficult to argue that the majority of the Scots agreed with the decision to join England, especially as Scotland relinquished the right to govern itself."

"It's been nearly a hundred and seventy years since the act was signed. Surely feelings have died down by now," I said.

"Certainly not among the Sons of Arbroath. They are fanatics.

They will do anything to achieve their aims, including murdering the Queen."

French resumed his chair and directed a question to the prime minister. "What do you know?"

"India, my dear, would you mind fetching that shawl across the bed and bringing it to me? There's a draught in here."

I certainly couldn't feel a draught as French had just stoked the fire and the room was infernally hot. But I fetched the shawl anyway and draped it gently around the old man's shoulders, tucking it in and giving him a friendly pat on the shoulder as I did so. He smiled up at me in his charming way, and I felt a lump rise in my throat. Good God, this wasn't like me at all. I hurried back to my seat and gulped down some whisky to steady myself. The last time I'd felt something akin to sympathy was . . . well, it had been so long ago I couldn't remember. Sympathy was bad for business, and I'd vowed never to make a decision based on that most unreliable of emotions. Still, I couldn't help feeling a wee bit of compassion for the old gallant.

"As you're aware, Division A of Scotland Yard is responsible for the Queen's personal safety. Superintendent Robshaw, the head of A, is a reliable chap, not given to seeing threats where none exist. His informants have heard rumours that the Sons of Arbroath intend to assassinate Her Majesty."

"Is the intelligence accurate? The sources trustworthy?" asked French.

"Robshaw thinks so, and if he does, I must. There is more, however. It seems the Sons of Arbroath have learned of the Queen's impending visit to Balmoral and are planning to execute her there, on Scottish soil, in a daring act of defiance."

"How would they manage to do that?" I asked. "Surely security there will be as tight as a corset on a fat woman." The penny dropped. "Ah, I see. There's a fox among the chickens."

Dizzy nodded, the black curl on his forehead bouncing. "It would seem so. First, the Sons of Arbroath have learned of her plans to go to Balmoral, which are not widely known at this point. That would imply that someone has leaked the information to them."

"Could they have picked up gossip on the street?" French was contemplating the flames in the fireplace.

"It's possible, of course. But I only learned of her plans myself the day before yesterday. What is more worrying, however, is the rumour that the assassination will occur at Balmoral. The Queen will take a few attendants and servants with her, and some of the local Scottish nobility will be invited to join her for a few days to celebrate the season. The Scottish servants who customarily wait upon the Queen when she is at the castle will of course be there. Robshaw is inclined to believe that the killer or killers may have infiltrated one or more of these groups of people. You are correct, India. Balmoral will be well defended from any assaults that originate from outside the castle. But the Queen is vulnerable if the would-be assassin is among those who are *within* the castle."

Dizzy hugged the shawl tightly around his shoulders. "I want you both to go to Balmoral. Mr. French, you will accompany me as my private secretary, but your real purpose will be to observe the Queen's guests and ensure that none of them pose any harm to Her Majesty." He paused. "Will it be difficult for you to leave your fa—"

"Father," interjected French, quickly.

"Er, quite. Will it be difficult for you to leave your father during this time of year?"

"He understands the demands of my work, sir. Thank you for inquiring."

My ears had pricked up at this exchange. I had a difficult time imagining French as a dutiful son, attending church with the pater on Christmas morning and sharing roast goose with the aged geezer at luncheon. Certainly, I knew he had parents, somewhere, at some point in his life, or he wouldn't be gracing this earth with his presence. But he'd never mentioned any details regarding his hearth and home since I'd known him. And I could have sworn that Dizzy had been preparing to say something other than "father." Well, I'd winkle the information out of French later. I scorched him with a glare, and he looked away. Guiltily, I thought.

Dizzy turned a bright eye upon me. "And Miss Black, dear Miss Black. You exhibited such ingenuity and bravery in that affair of the War Office memo."

Brace yourself, I thought. When Dizzy turns on the charisma, India Black is liable to end up in the soup.

"It would be extremely helpful if we were to have a sp . . . er, a source among the servants. We need someone trustworthy to ascertain if a traitor lurks among them. Where, I thought, can I find someone who has the intelligence, the courage and, may I say it, the *brass* to play such a role?" Dizzy looked appealingly at me, like an ancient and adoring hound. I had the urge to scratch his ears.

"The prime minister is right, you know," said French. "You have the nerve to carry it off, and that will be half the battle. Servants' quarters are usually closed to outsiders, but if anyone can find a way to wriggle in, you can, India."

Now, I know what you're thinking. They were flattering me shamelessly, courting me like lovers. Don't fall for it, you're thinking. A lesser woman might, of course, but then India Black is no lesser woman. Their compliments might sound like so much flaming balderdash, but the truth is they were right: it would take guile, confidence and a set of bollocks the size of cannonballs (alright, I didn't have *those*, but I was only speaking in the figurative sense) to infiltrate the closed circle of the Queen's servants, and luckily, I possessed all those attributes in spades.

French and Dizzy were gazing at me expectantly.

"I shall consider your proposition carefully," I said. Well, you just can't do what men want without making them wait a bit; tends to make them more appreciative when you finally say yes, don't you know?

French rose briskly. "It's settled, then."

Damn that man. "It is not settled, French. I shall have to think it over."

French put on his hat. "While you're cogitating, I'll visit Superintendent Robshaw tomorrow, discuss the details of security around the castle perimeter and inform him of our plans."

"Excellent." Dizzy beamed at me.

"I shall be at Lotus House tomorrow at one o'clock, India. Why don't you provide luncheon for us, and we'll formulate a plan of action."

"But, French, I haven't said that I'm going."

He hefted his malacca walking stick. "Oh, but we both know that you will, India."

Damn *and blast* that man.

TWO

When I had told French that I had to give some thought to disguising myself as a dowdy lady's maid (or God forbid, as the peon who had to empty the chamber pots), I'd meant it. You may think me unpatriotic for not throwing myself in front of the horses to save Victoria Regina, but I had mixed emotions about the whole thing. I mean, Vicky was not what you'd call the cream of the crop when it came to monarchs. There was that unhealthy obsession with her dead husband, for one thing. Long after anyone else would have pulled themselves up by their bootstraps and soldiered on, the Queen was still mooching about Windsor Palace and bemoaning the loss of Albert. In fact, she hadn't shown her face in public for years, *years*, after the old boy kicked the bucket and departed for That Better Place. She carried with her a miniature of the late prince, and when she came upon an especially scenic view, she whipped it out for Albert to share. Not for her the state of digamy.

She was also a bit of crank. There was her list of prohibited activities: speaking in loud voices in her presence, saying hello to her on one of her afternoon walks, building a coal fire in her rooms or bringing a bishop to luncheon. She adored planning funerals and memorials. Her servants were not allowed to leave her residence before she did, no matter the time of day. Then there was her propensity for exotic servants: those Indian fellows, decked out in flamboyant costumes like circus entertainers, who occupied their time cooking curries in the courtyard, trying to teach the old bat to speak Hindi or standing stiffly behind her while she ate her meals. She was so attached to the kilt-wearing farmer's son John Brown from Balmoral that she'd brought him to London with her and given him a room down the hall at Windsor. The two were so inseparable that the newspapers had spread rumours of a secret marriage and called the Queen "Mrs. Brown." Garden-variety stuff, really, you say. Just like my potty old aunt Dorothy. Completely harmless. Just humour the old gel when she goes off on one of her tirades about the bloody bishops.

But your aunt Dorothy isn't the Queen of the United Kingdom of Great Britain and Ireland and Empress of India. In any other family, Her Majesty's eccentricities would have meant a locked room in the attic and a lifetime of meals on trays. In short, our present monarch is hardly the epitome of regal rule, and there's no denying that the Empire could do better. That brings us to the other side of the coin. If the Sons of Arbroath (and I must remember to ask French about that; I've a fair bit of history, but arcane Scottish lore isn't one of my interests) succeeded in slaughtering the Queen like a pheasant during the hunting season, the heir to the throne was Albert Edward, the present Prince of Wales, universally known as Bertie. Now if Bertie had shown up at Lotus House, I'd have been glad to see him, for he was a wastrel of the first order, with a propensity for drink, cards, race-horses and fast women. Just the type of customer you can count on to spend his sovereigns not wisely but well at your establishment. I suppose it must be hard on the chap, being portly and middle-aged now, and who likely had expected to be occupying the throne already but for the longevity of his stout little mother, who, despite possessing a hypochondriac's assurance that every time she sneezed she was about to join dear departed Albert in the netherworld, was as healthy as a plow horse. Bertie hadn't done much to assure Mama that he was fit for the throne, however, running as he did with a fast set, impregnating women right and left (he even kept a doctor on call for those willing to have abortions), leaving a trail of bastard children throughout England and losing a packet at the gaming tables. In short, while Bertie would always be welcome at Lotus House, it was quite another thing to consider him opening Parliament and making state visits to Paris (all those whores and all that champagne!).

Given the choice between a dissolute rake on the throne or a neurotic, overweight widow, I'd plump for Vicky, which is why I was seriously debating a jaunt to Balmoral with Dizzy and French. Do not think, however, that I would do anything foolish such as jumping into the path of a speeding bullet to save the woman's life. If I could deflect an assault with minimal damage to myself, I would probably expend the effort, but the jury was still out on what I was willing to do to save Britain from Bertie.

There were other, indeed more important, factors contributing to my decision. The first was that the holiday season was notoriously slow around the brothels of London. All the customers were tucked up with their families, pretending a degree of amity that didn't really exist, watching their children open presents and listening to their wife prattle on about the neighbors. Things would pick up after Epiphany, when hordes of relieved customers would appear at the door of Lotus House, clamoring for their favorite bints and a bit of sex that didn't involve their partners closing their eyes in dismay. My friend Rowena Adderly, proprietress of the Silver Thistle and an experienced abbess, could easily look after things while I was gone, provided the price was right and I didn't mind returning to find my best-looking whore trailing back to the Silver Thistle for a few nights of bliss with Rowena.

And as I have already indicated, I was fed up with the tedious task of running Lotus House, especially when the girls had all the time in the world to sit around and bicker while the revenue dried up. My prior escapade with French had sparked a current of excitement that needed a bigger outlet than umpiring spats over hair combs. I was, in short, as bored as a priest on Monday. I needed a change of scene. All things considered, I would have preferred the Greek Islands at this time of year, but if that wasn't in the offing, then the Scottish Highlands would have to do.

But I must confess to another reason for considering Dizzy's request. It amused me to cavort among the most powerful men in the land, men who wouldn't dare acknowledge me if they met me on the street but who weren't too proud to rely on a whore to help them out of a jam now and then. I enjoyed grabbing a pew near the seat of power, patting a government minister on the shoulder and handing him a drink, offering my services (so to speak) and getting the poor devil off the hook. You may say it smacks of arrogance and that it's unseemly for a lady to gloat, but as I'm not a lady, I don't care ha'pence for your opinion.

* * *

"India!" Rowena squealed. "Come here, you delightful slut. Where have you been keeping yourself?"

I endured a crushing embrace and a less than surreptitious squeeze of my womanly assets. Rowena, as even the dullest of readers will have gathered by now, is a tom, albeit the prettiest one in London. She's an island girl: dark, voluptuous and seething with eroticism. She's developed a nice business at the Silver Thistle, specializing in providing dusky maidens like herself to soldiers, sailors and civil administrators just home from the colonies and longing for the pleasures they enjoyed under the Southern Cross.

I extricated myself from her grasp (which was a bit like trying to peel off an enormous leech) and regarded her warmly. Despite her carnal interest in me, I consider her a friend and someone I can rely on when the chips are down. She'd played a peripheral role in the War Office memo affair, accompanying me to the Russian embassy and sharing a brief period of captivity there, so she was not surprised to hear that I was about to become embroiled in another mission with French.

Indeed, when I mentioned his name, she pursed her lips and gave me a shrewd look. "The dashing Mr. French, eh? Not my type, of course, but he is attractive. If you like men, which damn it all, you apparently do, India."

"Some men," I corrected her. "Well, a few men. And despite what you think, I don't find French attractive at all. If you'd spent several days in his company, you wouldn't find him alluring either."

She harrumphed and looked at me knowingly, but she didn't say anything else, probably because she didn't want to lose her chance at some additional profits over the holidays. Friends we may be, but business is business.

So we shared a cup of tea and some lovely scones (no use providing the recipe to Mrs. Drinkwater; the effort would be wasted) and haggled in a good-natured way over how to split the proceeds from Lotus House while I was away in Scotland. There were a number of details to work out, like who gets which dress on which night, and what to do if a girl faints or expires when she's with a customer (I usually apologize, tell the customer I mistakenly thought he had expressed an interest in necrophilia, and offer him a 10-percent discount on his next visit).

We settled on a list of rules, with Rowena making a little moue of disappointment when I told her the girls were off-limits.

"You'll ruin them for the customers," I said. I knew it was a waste of time, as Rowena would be bedded down with the prettiest strumpet in the house before I had reached King's Cross, but one does have to make the effort to stamp one's moral authority on a situation.

I was lounging in my study late that morning, with my feet up and a preprandial whisky in my hand, enjoying the fire and waiting for French to grace Lotus House with his presence, when Mrs. Drinkwater staggered into the room, narrowly missing the pretty little French table I'd taken in payment from the impoverished third son of a peer. She was gasping like an out-of-condition prizefighter in the tenth round. Tendrils of hair had escaped the bun at the nape of her neck, and her face was pink with the effort of producing a suitable repast for me and my guest. Lord knows what we'd be eating today, but I felt sure we wouldn't enjoy it. I should have made French spring for luncheon at a nice restaurant. Why he wanted to dine here was a mystery beyond the comprehension of mortal man.

"What is it, Mrs. Drinkwater?"

The cook placed her hand on her bosom and inhaled noisily. "I tried, miss; I really did."

Burned the joint, I thought with satisfaction. Now French will have to take me out for a decent meal.

"It's that blasted boy." Mrs. Drinkwater rung her hands and burped loudly. Obviously, she'd been in the cooking sherry. Again.

"Boy? You mean . . ."

"'Allo, India."

I should have guessed. A stench had quietly pervaded the room, heralding the arrival of Vincent, last name unknown, a street arab who occasionally (and for an exorbitant price) assisted me in dealing with some of the problems encountered in running a first class brothel: vetting the girls who came round looking for work, performing the odd bit of blackmail for me when necessary and, in one instance, helping me dispose of Sir Archibald Latham's body. Vincent had subsequently proved himself to be a loyal foot soldier in that business, extricating French and me from a rather sticky situation. Frog-faced, crack-voiced and wily as a hen-killing weasel, he was a good lad to have on your side, the only disadvantage being that he smelled like a troop of infantry-men who'd made a forced march from Karachi to Calcutta with-out soap and water while subsisting on rancid monkey.

"Hello, Vincent," I said, gliding casually across the room to crack the window and then steering him away from the uphol-stered furniture to a suitable hard-backed chair. If the boy ever sat on one of my cushions, I'd have to burn it.

I settled into my own chair, glanced at the clock and smoth-ered my dismay. French would be here any moment, and if Vin-cent learned that his hero's arrival was imminent, there'd be no dislodging him with dynamite. French and Vincent had struck up an unlikely friendship (well, I suppose it wasn't any more unlikely than my relationship with French, though I had the advantage over Vincent in looks, hygiene and literacy), with French admiring the boy's pluck and Vincent respectful of French's manly virtues. French had even gone so far as to upgrade the boy's wardrobe, replacing his habitual rags with a set of fine . . .

"Vincent," I cried, "where are your clothes?"

He looked at me, perplexed. "Got 'em on, don't I?"

"I meant the ones French bought for you."

"Oh, those. They fetched a good price from ole Silverstein."

"You *sold* them?"

He shrugged. "They smelled funny. An' they hitched me."

"I hope you have a better explanation than that to give to French."

Vincent's eyes gleamed. "Is 'e comin' 'ere? When?"

I opened my mouth to lie, but just then I heard the rap of a malacca walking stick on the front door, and Mrs. Drinkwater lurched past the study on her way to admit my visitor.

"That's 'im now, ain't it?" said Vincent, jumping to his feet.

Oh, hell. I scurried after him, but it was too late to intercept him; he'd met French at the door and the two were shaking hands manfully and enquiring about each other's health. French's eyebrows had shot skyward when he'd first laid eyes on Vincent, but being the gentleman he was, he didn't enquire about the whereabouts of the clothes he'd bought or the aroma that enveloped Vincent (French had also arranged for Vincent to enjoy a weekly bath, which, in retrospect, had been a deuced optimistic prospect). I suppose all those years at public school with fellows nicknamed "Stinky" and "Grubby" had inured French to malodorous lads.

French handed his coat and hat to Mrs. Drinkwater and strode into the study, making for the fire, with Vincent on his heels like a newly hatched gosling.

"It's a damnably cold day," French said, warming his backside. "And I'm famished. Superintendent Robshaw's entertainment allowance only runs to weak tea and stale biscuits."

"Robshaw. Ain't that the cove from Scotland Yard?" Vincent had made himself comfortable on the sofa. Bugger. "You been to the Yard today? 'Ow come?"

Mrs. Drinkwater plunged into the room, her stained apron flapping and her hair askew. "Luncheon is served, Miss Black." She jerked her head at Vincent. "You can have some bread and dripping in the kitchen."

"Mrs. Drinkwater, set another place at the table, please. Vincent will join us for the meal." French bestowed a charming smile on my cook, which he no doubt used to great effect on the maids at his country home but which left Mrs. Drinkwater unimpressed.

"Suit yourself," she sniffed, and gave Vincent a dark look.

You will notice that the bastard didn't bother to consult me. I was in the bread and dripping camp with Mrs. Drinkwater, but French and Vincent were already on their way to the dining room, nattering away about knives and brass knuckles, from the snatches of conversation I could hear as I followed them.

As I expected, the meat was charred beyond recognition, the potatoes boiled to mush, and the peas had been cooked into a sticky green gruel. French looked momentarily dismayed, but Vincent dove in with all the grace of a suckling pig on the sow, chewing with his mouth open and grunting softly in satisfaction. Vincent was not a critic of a free meal. No doubt French was wondering why I employed a cook as shockingly bad as Mrs. Drinkwater. His cook had probably been trained in Paris and could whip out a *turbot sauce mousseuse* without blinking an eye, but then French's chef didn't work in a brothel. I counted myself lucky that I'd found a cook willing to work with a gaggle of naked women and a score of priapic, inebriated gentlemen parading through the halls on a daily basis. Unfortunately, Mrs. Drinkwater insulated herself from these conditions by drinking copious amounts of gin, sherry, wine, beer and even the odd bottle of vanilla extract. As you can imagine, this did not improve her cooking.

Vincent helped himself to seconds while French pushed his potatoes politely around his plate. "So wot's up at the Yard, guv? Those blokes need us to sort out some trouble for 'em?"

I prayed fervently that French would concoct some story about our involvement with Robshaw and the Yard, for if Vincent got wind of the plot against the Queen, he'd be in Scotland afore us, as the old song goes. But my prayers went unanswered (due, perhaps, to my never darkening the doors of a church); French launched into a summary of our meeting with Dizzy, which Vincent lapped up, hanging on every word and all the while forking food into his mouth as though he'd never eaten before.

"Blimey," he said when French had finished. "Wot do we do now?"

"India and I will go to Scotland tomorrow," said French.

He'd known that I would go, of course. I resigned myself to arguing with him later about his presumptuousness. Not to mention that music hall interchange between he and Dizzy regarding holidays with the French family, or was it the French family patriarch? French had some explaining to do.

"Wot about me?" Vincent cried through a mouthful of peas. I had to look away.

"There's no place for you at Balmoral," I said.

"But I could run errands for ya or deliver messages, or follow some of them hassassins around and report back to ya," he protested. A tiny glob of peas landed on my lace tablecloth.

"You look perfectly at home on the streets of London," I told him. "But in Scotland you would be as out of place as a donkey in the derby. The only people who will be there will be the Queen's guests and her servants."

"I could 'ide in the stables. They got stables there, don't they?" Vincent looked appealingly at French. I could see French was weakening.

"The idea is impractical," I said firmly.

"We'll discuss it later, Vincent," said French. "Now let me tell you what I learned from Superintendent Robshaw today."

On your own head be it, I thought. If French couldn't say no to Vincent, then French would just have to figure out what to do with the boy. Perhaps he could at least be persuaded to take another bath, being that he was going to be consorting with royalty.

French made himself comfortable, with a glass of wine at hand. "As you would expect, Scotland Yard keeps a watchful eye out for any individuals or organizations who pose a threat to the Queen. There's always some disaffected Irishman who's willing to take a shot at Her Majesty over the home-rule issue. And there has always been a small group of Scots who were passionately committed to independence for their country."

French paused for a sip of wine. Now that the history lesson had begun, I could see that Vincent was losing interest rapidly; French would have to conjure up some tales of derring-do and swordplay, or the boy would be asleep with this head on the table before long. No surprise, really, given the amount of food he had ingested.

"Most of the Scottish nationalists have been ineffective organizations, consisting of a few crackpots who failed to attract many followers and ended up fighting amongst themselves. You know how the Scots are: a more cantankerous lot doesn't exist." French obviously hadn't spent much time behind the scenes at his local brothel.

"But in recent months, a new group has appeared, rumoured to have connections to the Scottish aristocracy and headed by a mysterious figure called 'the Marischal.' Where previous groups were content to issue broadsides and hold up the odd mail train, this new organization has not hesitated to use violence. They have claimed responsibility for the murder of two Scottish magistrates and an English judge."

This was more like it; Vincent's nose was quivering.

"My whiskers! And this 'ere marshal is the one who done it? Ain't a marshal got somethin' to do with the law?"

"Marischal," French corrected him gently. "And you're correct, Vincent. 'Marischal' does mean marshal in the Old High German language. The word originally meant 'keeper of the horses,' which was an important role, but over the centuries the position evolved into that of a marshal, someone responsible for keeping the peace. The word is also used to designate the highest rank in the military. It's an interesting word, with a fascinating etymology."

Vincent now looked wide awake, but my eyelids were drooping. French must have noticed, for he emptied his glass, refilled it from the bottle nearby and plunged on.

"The Marischal did not choose his name randomly. In 1320, fifty-one Scottish peers signed a document that became known as the Declaration of Arbroath, in which they asserted their independence from the English king Edward I. You'll remember him, of course, as the 'Hammer of the Scots.' The king even had the phrase carved on his tombstone, in Latin. He is reviled in Scotland for the brutality with which he crushed Scottish attempts at independence. Robert de Keith, then the Marischal of Scotland and one of the most influential men in the country, opposed Edward and put his signature to the declaration."

I stifled a yawn. I admit to sharing Vincent's views on history. Hangings and beheadings and torture are diverting, but my interest wanes when it comes to tales of sitting around a table and putting pen to paper.

"So the Declaration of Arbroath is the inspiration for a collection of fanatics bent on throwing off the English yoke?" I asked. "And they are killing government officials to achieve their objective?"

"Yes," said French. "And now they have targeted the Queen. Robshaw's men have heard that the present Marischal exerts a powerful influence over the Sons of Arbroath. He is charismatic, eloquent and passionately committed to the Queen's death. Robshaw is convinced that the Sons and the Marischal constitute a significant threat to Her Majesty."

"And Dizzy wants us to protect her. So what's the plan?" I asked briskly. I doubted that there was one; French had a preference for improvising, but I had been a participant in some of his hastily devised schemes, and my predilection was for carefully planned enterprises that did not leave one staring down the barrel of a revolver.

"I suppose you'll go as yourself."

"Yes," said French. "As Dizzy suggested, I'll go along as his private secretary."

"And I suppose you've got me seducing various household servants and reporting back to you on their political views?"

French glanced quickly at Vincent, to see if this graphic depiction of my presumed role had reached his tender ears, but Vincent was chewing meditatively on a piece of burned meat and ignoring the conversation. Probably devising a means of hiding himself among French's baggage and joining us in the Highlands.

"I've arranged for you to act as a lady's maid to the Dowager Marchioness of Tullibardine, a distant cousin of the Queen, who has been invited to spend the holidays at Balmoral."

"How on earth did you manage that, on such short notice?"

"Oh"—French waved a hand vaguely—"the marchioness is always in need of a maid."

My antennae quivered. "Am I expected to seduce the marchioness? Because if I am, I may just stay in London and send Rowena along with you."

French snorted, the most inelegant sound I'd heard him make in our brief acquaintance. "Good Lord, no."

"You seem inordinately amused by the idea."

"She's rather old, India. No, you will only be required to act as her personal assistant. In fact, the two of you share a similar personality. I expect you'll get along famously. Here," he said, handing me a packet of papers. "I've prepared letters of recommendation and a summary of your experiences as a lady's maid among various Scottish aristocrats. All of it false, of course, but it will add credibility to your story, India, if you can rattle off the duchesses and baronesses for whom you've worked."

"Presuming none of them are friends or acquaintances of the marchioness."

"Not to worry. None of the ladies listed there have any connection whatsoever with any of the guests invited to Balmoral by the Queen. And should anyone enquire, they are each prepared to swear that you were in their employment on the dates specified and that you were an exemplary servant."

"Should I bring the Webley?"

"I wouldn't. You'll have no privacy in the servants' quarters, and it would look deuced odd for a lady's maid to be carrying a revolver. I will, however, provide you with the necessary uniforms. Jot down your measurements for me, please."

I scribbled down some notes for him, hoping that the British government had a good supply of costumes in my size, and passed it to him. He rose from the table. "I shall see you at the station tomorrow morning at nine o'clock. Wear something dowdy and servant-like. You do have something frumpy in your closet, don't you? It wouldn't do to arrive at the station in that sapphire silk gown you were wearing the other evening."

I assured him I would be sporting suitably cheap and practical clothing. I'd have to raid the bints' wardrobes, but no doubt there would be a few threadbare dresses and shawls tucked away from their days as fishmongers' daughters, milkmaids and flower peddlers. I escorted French to the door, with Vincent dogging his steps and begging to be allowed to tag along to Scotland. Knowing French's resolve, I resigned myself to seeing Vincent somewhere in the vicinity of Balmoral. I trundled upstairs to conduct my scavenger hunt and to acquaint myself with my virtues as domestic help.

A few minutes before nine o'clock the following morning I passed through the entrance to King's Cross for my rendezvous with French. At his instructions, I'd sent my luggage on ahead to be placed on the appropriate train. French was waiting for me on the platform beneath the arched roof, a newspaper tucked under his arm. He nodded approvingly at my drab appearance, noting the shabby brown wool dress and tweed coat I'd liberated from the brothel's occupants. He took my elbow and steered me into a nook in the wall, between the ticket office and a tearoom, where he handed me a parcel wrapped in coarse paper and tied with string.

"Your uniforms," he said.

"I hope they fit, French."

He shrugged impatiently. "You needn't worry. We know how to do these things."

"For your sake, I hope you do."

"Now, look over there," he said, gesturing over his shoulder. "That's the Queen's train. Her coach is in the rear. The coaches in front will be occupied by some of her guests and the servants she is taking along from Windsor."

The Queen's train looked like any other except for the rear coach, which was painted a glossy black and bore the Queen's coat of arms in gilt upon the doors, and the great-coated army of grave-faced coves patrolling the platform around it.

"Robshaw's men?" I asked.

"Yes. In addition to the men you see here, he'll have operatives on the train itself and at each station along the way. Agents from the Yard will inspect every inch of track between here and Balmoral. No one gets on this train without a special pass."

He rummaged in his pocket and produced a document. "Here's yours. You'll be in No. 14, in a private compartment. Normally, you'd be expected to travel with the other servants, but since the marchioness will join the train at Perth, I thought you should enjoy the comforts of a first-class carriage alone while you can, without being subjected to speculation and inquisitiveness from the other servants."

"Thank heaven for that. I'm not sure I'm up to the task of making conversation with the Queen's equerry just yet."

French pointed down the platform. "There's Robshaw. Just as

well that you see him now. Once he's at Balmoral, he'll be occupied with securing the perimeter of the castle. We won't catch a glimpse of him then."

Robshaw was a tall, thin chap with a supercilious nose and a set of luxuriant side whiskers the colour and texture of a seal's pelt. His trousers were sharply creased, his hat was freshly brushed, and the shine on his boots was blinding at twenty paces. He tipped his hat to a passing gentlewoman, displaying a pair of spotless dove grey gloves, glared at a flying smut that had dared to land on his forearm and brushed it disdainfully away. If he cared half as much about Vicky's security as he did about his appearance, the Queen was safe indeed.

"Looks a bit of a fusspot," I said.

"He's got an eye for detail, which is just what one needs in his job. Never leaves anything to chance and always has a trick up his sleeve." French checked the time. "We'll be leaving soon. When the train arrives in Perth, the marchioness will be escorted to the carriage and introduced to you by Sir Horace Wickersham. He's provided a letter of reference for you to the marchioness."

"I confess to having some doubts about this. It's not really my nature to toady to the upper class."

"I have my doubts, as well," said French, fixing me with that cool grey stare of his. "Remember our fencing lessons; control the point. Don't let your emotions get the better of you. And for God's sake, don't tell the marchioness to bugger off no matter what she does."

"Bugger off, French."

He smiled. "One other thing." He removed the newspaper from under his arm and handed it to me. "You'll want to read this. The Marischal has published a letter on behalf of the Sons of Arbroath. They have announced that they intend to kill the

Queen and pursue a campaign of public executions until the government of England capitulates and emancipates Scotland."

"That ups the stakes a bit."

"Considerably."

"And I'll bet Vicky's pantaloons are in a bit of twist."

French's lips twitched. "I'll see you in Scotland."

"Wait. How will we communicate?"

"Not to worry," French called over his shoulder. "I shall be in contact with you."

"You bloody well better be," I muttered, and headed for my carriage, studiously avoiding looking directly at any of Robshaw's men. You never know but what one of these steely-eyed fellows from Division A of Scotland Yard had once been an ambitious youngster walking a beat around Lotus House. Being a woman it was difficult to forget, I thought it best to keep my head down and my gaze averted. Sometimes my profession can be a liability, but as it affords me a great deal of money and the liberty to do what I like with it, I can endure the occasional inconvenience.

I handed my pass to the joker guarding the door to my carriage and waited while he scrutinized it with the avidity of Shylock reviewing his accounts. There was a tremendous commotion around the Queen's train, with crates of wine and parcels of provisions being trundled aboard and red-faced men shouting instructions, and even, I noticed, several Thoroughbreds being loaded into a horse carriage. The steeds were plunging and stamping at the noise and the steam, and a few grim-faced lads were hanging on to their halters. Some swell must be making the trip under the erroneous impression there were no horses in Scotland.

I watched idly for a moment, and then a striking figure caught my eye among the toffs and their stable boys. It was French, but he was no longer the sober gent with whom I'd just conversed. He wore a vermilion frock coat with a black velvet collar, a low-cut brocade waistcoat and slim-fitting trousers the colour of smoke. He strolled languidly around the edge of the crowd, watching the horses and twirling his malacca walking stick in his hand. Somehow he had contrived to alter his appearance: his thick black hair was tousled and his eyes heavy lidded, as though he had just arisen from his bed in the nick of time to catch the train (or, perhaps, never made the acquaintance of the bed at all last night). I watched with interest as he sidled over to a staid gentleman in an elegant black suit and leaned over for a confidential word. The somber fellow looked startled, then vexed and finally positively outraged. He said something blistering to French and stalked off, leaving French with a look of impish delight on his face. What the devil was he up to? French usually conducted himself with tedious rectitude (barring the odd case of blackmail, as I've previously noted). Now he looked like a louche member of the Upper Ten (Thousand, that is, being a reference to the crème de la crème of English society, which, of course, contains its share of rotters and scoundrels, only they're the richest rotters and scoundrels in the land and, therefore, above the law). French yawned and consulted his watch, then shouted instructions to one of the lads, who was holding a fine grey gelding and waiting his turn to lead the horse onto the carriage. I can't say I was surprised to see Vincent, decked out in a new suit of clothes. I wondered what the secondhand clothing market was like in the Balmoral area.

I won't bore you with the details of the trip from London to Perth. I'm a Londoner, born and bred, and I get vertigo if I have to leave the Big Smoke. Green fields and clear blue skies are fine for some folk, but a steady diet of cows, clover and quaint little villages is not to my taste. What do people do out here? I wondered. Besides churn butter, make sausage and polish the brass at the church, of course. If I'd had the misfortune to be born somewhere rustic, I'd have died of ennui by the time I turned thirteen. Consequently, I didn't glue myself to the window and admire the scenery like most travelers would. I browsed through the newspaper French had given me and noted the hysterical threats against the Queen by those infernal Scottish nationalists. I briefly contemplated a perusal of the Bible I'd brought along to impress the old battle-axe to whom I'd soon be apprenticed, but it's never been one of my favorite books: too much fire, brimstone and punishment, and shockingly rude things to say about harlots. In the end, I closed the curtains in my compartment, put up my feet and stretched out for a long snooze. I figured sleep would be a rare commodity once the marchioness got hold of me.

Many hours later, we pulled into the station at Perth. Jolted awake, I rubbed the sleep from my eyes and drew back the curtains. There wasn't much to see, other than a bustling train station that looked much like any other. I noticed a few well-dressed ladies and men on the platform, waiting to board, and concluded that other members of the Queen's party besides the marchioness were boarding here. French had instructed me to wait in the carriage until Sir Horace arrived to introduce me to my employer, so I cooled my heels and hummed a few songs, killing time, until I heard some timorous footsteps in the hallway and a gentle knock upon the door.

"Miss Black?"

I rose to my feet and smoothed my skirts. "Come in."

Sir Horace Wickersham was a ruddy old squire with a cast in

one eye, a halo of fluffy white hair and the confidence of a bullied mouse.

"Hello," he mumbled. "Hello. Very nice to meet you. Very nice indeed." He glanced briefly at me and blushed. His eyes skittered away from mine and toured the compartment. "Did you, um, have a nice journey?"

"Yes, it was fine."

"Good, good." He stared with some fascination at my Bible. "I asked, you see, because the rails are sometimes quite uneven, and the journey can be most uncomfortable."

"It was tolerable," I said.

"Um." He now seemed mesmerized by my hat. At this rate, the train was going to be leaving for Aberdeen before the marchioness boarded.

"I'm looking forward to meeting the marchioness," I said brightly, trying to prod the old codger into action.

"Yes. Quite." Silence, while Sir Horace examined the floorboards of the carriage.

"Does she need some assistance in boarding?"

"No. No. I'll fetch her." He shuffled his feet and spun his hat in his hand like the captain of a ship headed for the rocks. "Look here," he said stiffly, "has anyone told you about Her Ladyship's, um, habits?"

"Habits?" I echoed. Damn that bastard French.

"You know, the—"

"Horace?" It was less a voice than the cawing of a demented rook.

Sir Horace leaped like a show jumper at the last hurdle. "Joshua and Jeremiah! It's the marchioness."

I was preoccupied with planning slow tortures for French, but Sir Horace's reaction snapped me back to attention.

"Where are ye, Horace? Damn and blast, ye must be here some-where. Come out where I can see ye."

Sir Horace darted to the doorway. "In here, m'lady. I was just conversing with Miss Black. Catching up on old times, you know." He laughed nervously.

"Bugger the old times. Come and help me, ye fool. I need an arm to lean on." The raspy voice subsided into a raspy cough.

Sir Horace roused himself to action and disappeared into the corridor to escort the Dowager Marchioness of Tullibardine into the carriage. Oh, French, I thought. The torture will be long and slow. I pasted a smile on my face and prepared to meet my employer.

I had thought that voice had issued from an amazon, but the marchioness was a tiny woman, no bigger than a flea and as wob-bly on her feet as a faulty skittle. She shuffled in on Sir Horace's arm, leaning on a cane, and flopped like a rag doll onto the bench, from which she glared up at me through rheumy eyes. She was accompanied by a musty odor, equal parts camphor, tobacco and lavender. I had been harboring a secret fantasy of a kind, ma-tronly and progressive aristocrat, one who was careful not to overwork the help and who made sure they were paid generously. My fantasy dissolved in smoke when the marchioness looked up at me. God, what a death mask. Her Ladyship's skin was the co-lour and texture of the papyrus on view at the British Museum. Someone (and from the looks of it, it must have been the old girl herself) had applied a thick dusting of powder, which had settled into the cracks of her face. A wide streak of rouge had been smeared under each eye, giving her the appearance of a Coman-che ready for the warpath. Her eyes were clouded with cataracts, and her mouth hung open, displaying a few discoloured teeth and a vast expanse of mottled pink gums. And her hair—good

Lord, what was I going to do with that rat's nest? Still, knowing that a great deal was at stake (i.e., the Queen's life), I hid my dismay and tried to look servile and obsequious, which, if you're as naturally handsome and confident as I, is deuced difficult.

The marchioness poked me in the shin with her cane. "Who's this?"

Sir Horace grimaced apologetically at me. "This is the girl I told you about, m'lady. India Black. Your new maid. You'll recall that I recommended her; she gave excellent service to my late wife."

"Indian? What sort of name is that for a lass?"

"It's India, Your Ladyship," I corrected her gently.

"India." She stared balefully at me. "Damned silly name. Who names a girl after a country? Especially one full of little brown people who don't eat beef. Somethin' wrong with them, I say. Give me a good bit of rare English beef any day. Horace, where's my snuffbox?"

Sir Horace rummaged hastily through the marchioness's baggage until he produced a beautiful little mother-of-pearl box with a painted miniature of a dyspeptic geezer on the lid. He offered it to the marchioness, who dipped a yellow nail into the snuff and shoveled it into her nose, inhaling deeply. She sighed like an addict smoking the evening's first pipe of opium, then her face contorted in agonizing pain. I sprang to my feet, looking wildly at Sir Horace for assistance, but it was only the commencement of a series of violent sneezes from the marchioness, who, I don't mind telling you, could have benefitted from a handkerchief. So could I; I wiped a few droplets from my skirt and shuddered.

My employer swiped her nose with the back of her hand. "Well, Imogen, tell me about yerself."

"It's India, ma'am," I said.

"Damned silly name."

Before she could cover the racial and dietary characteristics of the Hindoos again, I launched into a brief précis of my experience as a lady's maid in various grand Scottish houses. The marchioness listened attentively, closing her eyes and nodding at the mention of the Baroness Haggis and the Duchess of Kneeps. I finished my spiel and glanced at Sir Horace, who was wearing out the brim of his hat again and stealing glances at his watch.

"What are ye doin' still hangin' about, Horace?" the marchioness snapped. "Get off the train or ye'll be going to Balmoral with us, and ye know how the Queen hates uninvited guests."

Sir Horace looked relieved, tipped his hat to me with a sympathetic smile, kissed the marchioness's hand and vanished. I couldn't help but envy him.

"Don't just stand there gawpin', girl. Put away my things and find a rug fer me. It's bloody cold in here."

THREE

And so my life as a lady's maid began. I stored the marchioness's luggage and covered her thin frame with an ancient woolen rug, moth-eaten and smelling of wet dog. I propped her upright in the seat and poured her a cup of tea from the bottle Sir Horace had thoughtfully provided, and I dipped her biscuits into the tea so as not to strain the few remaining teeth in her skull. All the while she peppered me with questions. Where was my mother from? Had she been in service? What about my father? I don't mind telling you that I'm at my best when it comes to total fabrication; it's all that practice I've had in telling gents how handsome and clever they are. I spun a grand tale for her, of a family tradition of decades of humble service to the great (nugget of truth in that, I suppose), until the marchioness tired of the subject and spied the Bible on the seat beside me.

"Ye're a Christian, Ina?"

"It's India, ma'am," I corrected, not for the first or last time that day. Well, that sent her off on another tirade over the foolishness of my mother, who'd seen fit to christen me for a country renowned for heat, dust, cobras, squalor, monsoons and swarthy little nudists who worshipped cattle. The Mussulmen (heathens who wouldn't appreciate a good piece of gammon) and the Sikhs (damned fine soldiers, but they never cut their hair, and they wear those peculiar undergarments) didn't escape her wrath either. When she'd vented her contempt for the jewel in Britain's crown and fortified herself with more snuff (I stood well clear this time and succeeded in avoiding the worst of the deluge), she snorted happily and reverted to her question.

"Ye're a Christian, Irma?"

"Um." I wouldn't say I'm superstitious, but why tempt a bolt of lightning from the Old Chap Upstairs? "As much as any other person, I suppose."

"Ye can read the Bible?"

I hefted it in my hand. "Yes, ma'am, I can. My father was a great one for the Good Book. He taught me to read it at an early age." There was a low rumble of thunder on the horizon, but I figured a white lie in service to the Queen might deflect any lightning bolt from the heavens. "Would you like me to read to you?"

"Proverbs," she said, giving me a sideways glance. I sighed. Hours to Aberdeen and all of it to be spent in moral instruction. Why couldn't she have been a Song of Solomon type, or at least enjoyed the Psalms? I cracked the book and started reading, with the marchioness grumbling and scratching beneath her wool rug and snuffling like a truffle-hunting pig as she inhaled tobacco.

Sometime later, just as we had reached that delightful verse about the dog returning to his own vomit, I detected a stillness in the seat opposite me and looked up to see the marchioness sitting silently, head slumped forward, a tiny line of dark flakes issuing from her nose. I put down the Bible without a sound, grateful that the old trout had succumbed to sleep. If reading aloud from the Bible was the marchioness's chief entertainment, then by the time I'd finished my assignment, I'd be able to take up a second line of a work as a missionary to the godless infidels in Africa.

This thought amused me no end, and I whiled away a good bit of time imagining myself urging the inhabitants of the Dark Continent to turn to the light, until it occurred to me that the marchioness seemed preternaturally quiet. I got up from my seat and peered closely at her. I waved a hand in front of her face, but the movement did not arouse any response. Her withered bosom lay motionless; I could detect no rise and fall indicating that she was still breathing. Bloody hell. What if Her Ladyship had crossed the River Styx (barking orders all the while to Charon, or "Charlie," as she'd no doubt call him)? What would happen to my mission if the marchioness had kicked it? There couldn't be too many doddering old pussies lying around sans maid and with an invitation to Balmoral in their pocket. I was contemplating my options, wondering how I was going to reach French to break the news and staring rather absently into the marchioness's face when her eyes popped open.

"What are ye doin', ye silly goose? Get away from me."

No need for that directive, as I'd nearly fallen over myself springing to the other side of the carriage. I couldn't have been more surprised if she had died and her corpse had reached out and throttled me.

"Sorry, m'lady. I thought you were ill."

"I'm never ill. I merely closed my eyes for a second. Now where were we? Ah, yes. 'As a dog returneth to his vomit, so a fool returneth to his folly.' Carry on, Ivy."

That journey was the longest of my life. First we read the Bible, and then when the old lady had grown tired of the uplifting maxims of Proverbs, she had me rummage through her bags until I found a battered copy of *Bleak House*. Not the most uplifting of Dickens's stories, but at least it was a better read than Proverbs, and I started in heartily enough, until the marchioness demanded I "do the voices." She was quite insistent, and so I delivered, in my opinion, a credible rendition of the different characters. The grasping Richard Carstone and the wicked Tulkinghorn were easy enough for me, having a good deal of acquaintance with such characters, but that Esther Summerson was a hard slog; I'm not at all sweet or long-suffering, and I tend to think that Esther is a bit of a stick. It's confoundedly difficult for a lady of the evening to portray a virtuous ninny. My performance was not improved by the fact that my audience kept nodding off, but every time I stopped reading, the filmy eyes flew open and that rasping voice commanded that I continue. So I persevered until the chimneys of Aberdeen shot into view and we transferred onto the tracks that led to the village of Ballater, where the railway ended and we would complete our journey to Balmoral by horse and carriage.

By then I was so hoarse I could have croaked. I'd have given a half share in Lotus House for a pint of ale and a stiff peg of whisky. I could only hope that the marchioness's time at Balmoral would be occupied with luncheons and teas and reminiscing with the Queen about dear departed Albert. Otherwise, I'd have no time for detecting, not to mention a bad case of laryngitis. It was tempting to blame French for saddling me with this snuff-dipping, narcoleptic bibliophile, but in truth I realized it was my own fault for agreeing to come to Balmoral (the fact of which I did not intend to inform French). The next time I felt the urge for adventure, I'd just have to take up needlework or bicycling or, God forbid, fencing.

Fortunately for my voice and my patience, the marchioness's interest in reading had declined in favor of enjoying the Scottish countryside. I followed her example and gazed out the window, to be greeted by a bleak landscape of rocks, hills, roaring burns, snow-covered firs and larches, and sheep. We passed several wind-blasted hovels of stone and sod, thatched with heather and looking as cold and desolate as the last outpost before the Arctic Circle. To the west, the ice-shrouded peaks of the Cairngorm Mountains gleamed in the sun. Here and there in the twilight, tiny pinpricks of lights shone from isolated cottages. Picturesque, I suppose, if you liked desolation and gloom. It was a bit mournful for my taste, though I could see how it would appeal to the melancholy Widow of Windsor.

At the station at Ballater, a footman appeared to usher the marchioness to the Queen's waiting room in the station. Her Majesty had her own private room, no doubt with a roaring fire and refreshments. I was instructed to wait in the carriage (without so much as a cup of tea) until the horses were harnessed and the carriages were ready to depart. I took a turn in the hallway, stretching my legs, and watched as the nags were hitched to a series of landaus and broughams. All the crates and parcels that had been loaded onto the train in London were now unloaded onto a dozen wagons and carts. The effort to get the old bag to Scotland was considerable, and on behalf of the British taxpayer, I was outraged. All this because the dead prince had wanted his wife to holiday in the Highlands. Surely, there were better uses for the money expended—a nourishing meal for homeless children, a hospital for the poor, a reduction in the property taxes for the owner of Lotus House. Perhaps it would be best if the Marischal and his band of fanatics dispatched the Queen and all her near relatives. I was not sure the country could afford them.

A footman appeared to collect the marchioness's luggage and my own.

"Follow me," he said. "You'll be travelling to the castle with Her Ladyship and Lady Davina Dalfad, Countess of Haldane. And her maid, of course. The countess is one of the Queen's ladies of the bedchamber."

Was she now? Being one of those myself, I thought perhaps the countess and I might find some time to share a few amusing anecdotes of our experiences. Perhaps not.

"How far is it to the castle?" I asked the footman.

"Nine Scotch miles or thereabouts. You'll be there in time for tea. Here's the coach. Watch your step." He handed me into a comfortable vehicle, handsomely swagged out with tufted leather seats and velvet curtains. I took the only seat available to me and surveyed my fellow passengers.

I shared a bench with the countess's maid, who nodded her head in my direction but did not smile when I sat down. She had a prim little mouth and an air of superiority. I decided I did not like her. The marchioness sat across from me, swathed in the same moth-eaten rug she'd used on the train. And next to her, straining not to come into contact with the marchioness's covering, sat Lady Dalfad, the Countess of Haldane.

Handsome in her youth, no doubt, with those high cheekbones and the sculpted mouth, thick honey-coloured hair now changing to ash at the temples, and sea green eyes that flickered briefly in my direction and then dismissed me. Age had softened the flesh of her face, however, and there was a web of thin lines at the corners of her eyes.

"Ida, my snuffbox," the marchioness commanded. I poked about in the old gal's valise until I found the container and handed it over.

The countess stiffened.

"Would ye care for snuff, my dear?" The marchioness extended the delicate little box to the countess.

Her lip curled. "Thank you, no. I don't partake of snuff." She turned away, adding under her breath: "Filthy habit."

"Suit yerself," said the marchioness, loading a fingernail and inhaling noisily. I pulled my handkerchief from my sleeve and bent my face to it, feigning a speck of dust in my eye. The top of my hat absorbed the shower that inevitably followed. The countess's maid mewed with disgust and dabbed at her skirt. The countess cringed. The marchioness returned the snuffbox to me with what I swear was a wink. She sponged her upper lip with her coat sleeve and grinned toothily at the countess (no small feat, with so few teeth in her head).

"Invigoratin' stuff," she said.

The countess nodded coldly.

"I hope they've got tea laid on when we get there. I'm famished. Nothin' to eat all day but some toasted bread and a few biscuits." The marchioness smacked her lips.

The countess looked down her nose. "The Queen always provides generously for her guests."

"I should hope so. Filthy rich, she is."

An expression of pain crossed Lady Dalfad's face. "Really, Your Ladyship, I think that comment extremely rude."

I waited for the marchioness to whack Lady Dalfad across the shins with her cane. I'm no expert on the peerage, but I do know that a marchioness outranks a countess. She might be one of the Queen's ladies of the bedchamber, but the countess was walking on thin ice, speaking to the marchioness like that. I felt a stirring of outrage on behalf of my employer, but I shouldn't have troubled. The marchioness just chuckled and coughed loudly, spitting up flakes of snuff and swabbing them away with her gloved hand.

We rode the rest of the way to the castle in stony silence, the marchioness dropping off to sleep a couple of times and then starting awake whenever we hit a bump or crossed a bridge. The countess's maid sat rigidly in her seat, staring at the floor, and Lady Dalfad occupied her time by peering out the window at the great conifers that lined the road, and the craggy hills beyond. What a delightful house party this was going to be. I could only hope that I wouldn't have to share a room with the countess's maid.

The sun was setting as we pulled into the drive of Balmoral. It was an impressive old pile, if your taste runs to massive granite buildings in the neo-Gothic style, complete with castellated gables, a porte cochere, and towers crowned with turrets and crenellated battlements. There was a bleakness about the building that all the hustle and bustle of the arrival of a trainload of servants and guests could not dispel. The castle was nestled in a valley, surrounded by the Cairngorms. The rocky heights of Lochnagar, that dark and forbidding mountain, towered over the place. It had begun to sleet; tiny pellets were bouncing off the roof of the coach and pinging against the window. I shuddered. Trapped here for three weeks with the likes of the marchioness and Lady Dalfad. I could only hope that the Sons of Arbroath were an efficient lot and would attempt to knock off the Queen sooner rather than later.

The coach was driven to the front of the castle, where the marchioness and the countess were assisted to the ground and escorted through the main entrance into the building. I caught sight of Dizzy's profile through a carriage window (no mistaking that bowsprit). He was bundled in rugs and blankets, shoulders hunched against the bitter cold, and he looked thoroughly miserable. French stood bareheaded in the courtyard, his black hair blowing in the wind, smoking a cheroot and talking animatedly to the cove he'd annoyed at King's Cross. The cove looked even less amused than he had in London. French broke off his monologue to bark orders at his stable boy. Vincent had many gifts; he was a first-rate fingersmith, blackmailer and cracksman, but unfortunately, none of those were useful in leading an ill-tempered gelding across the icy cobbles to the stables. The lad had a tight grip on the halter, but his feet were dangling in the air, and the horse was dancing across the courtyard toward a cart laden with crates of French wines. French strode after the duo, shouting instructions. I was eagerly awaiting the destruction of the Queen's entire stock of champagne (well, it would serve French right for allowing Vincent to tag along), but alas, a hoary figure with bristling eyebrows jumped forward as spryly as a youth and rescued Vincent, snagging the horse's halter and taking him in hand.

Our carriage started forward and I lost sight of the show. We circled the castle and arrived at the servants' entrance. I was delighted to see a welcoming glow in the windows and an open door, spilling warmth and light into the growing darkness. I needed a cup of tea, or something stronger, if it were on offer.

The countess's maid and I alighted from the carriage. The footman collected our luggage and motioned for us to follow him into the house. He dumped our bags unceremoniously in a heap on the flagstone floor.

"Wait here for Miss Boss, the housekeeper," he flung over his shoulder as he disappeared into the bowels of the castle.

We didn't wait long, for the housekeeper arrived within minutes, bearing a notebook and pencil, pink with exertion and looking very cross. Now most people you meet are inconsequential little swine that have as much presence as a wet flannel. Miss Boss was a formidable biddy, with a tiny squashed face and the beady eyes of a watchful bird of prey. She gave me a look that said, "I've seen your type before, girl. Stay out of the pantry, don't make any unnecessary noise, and if I catch you flirting with the male servants, I'll skin you alive." I found myself nodding, though she hadn't said a word.

She consulted her list. "India Black, lady's maid to the Dowager Marchioness of Tullibardine. You'll be sharing with Flora Mackenzie. She's the cook's daughter and a housemaid. She'll be able to help you find anything you will need for the marchioness." She checked her list. "Effie Clark, Lady Dalfad's maid. You'll be in your usual room, with Lady Thorne's maid. You know the way. I'll have your baggage sent up. India, follow me."

We hustled through the kitchen (a cavernous space capable of feeding a smallish army) and into a hallway, where a boatload of servants was milling about, jostling against each other as they scurried to and fro, bearing linens and teapots, scuttles of coal and platters of sandwiches.

Miss Boss bore down on a lone footman. "Robbie, Robbie Munro. This is Miss Black, lady's maid to the Dowager Marchioness of Tullibardine. Miss Black will be sharing with Flora. Fetch her luggage and show her the way, please."

"Yes, Miss Boss." Robbie gave me a diffident smile. Well. Things were looking up. Munro was a comely lad with golden red curls, a dimpled chin and the manly physique of a member of the Household Cavalry. He wore a black waistcoat and jacket, and a kilt in the Royal Stewart tartan. He collected my bags, hefting them casually and tucking them under his arms.

"This way, miss."

It was a mighty long hike to the room I'd be sharing with the housemaid. I've heard there are a hundred thirty rooms in Balmoral, and I do believe we traversed each one of them. We marched along what seemed like miles of corridors, with Munro setting a ground-eating pace the likes of which hadn't been seen since the march to relieve the siege of Lucknow. I scampered after him, trying to match his stride and straining for a glimpse into some of the rooms as we passed them. Not being the recipient of many royal invitations, I was curious as to how the other 1 percent live. We exited the servants' staircase and entered the main corridor. I can't say I cared much for the furnishings here, which consisted of large numbers of stags' heads mounted on walls painted to look like marble, assorted pictures and busts of the dead Prince Albert (draped in black crepe, in case anyone in the English-speaking world was unaware he'd joined the great heavenly choir some years ago), heraldic shields and an astonishing array of Scottish weapons: axe heads of granite, serpentine and greenstone; dirks; basinet helmets; spears; pikes; great two-handed swords that looked as though they should be wielded by giants; broadswords; flintlocks; targes; and dozens of *sgian dubhs*, those nasty little pigstickers the Scots love to carry in their stockings and whip out after a dram or two. An aficionado of edged weapons would have thought he'd died and gone to heaven. If Vincent got word of the abundance of arms within reach, there'd be no telling how many daggers and such he'd cart away in his luggage. I hoped the Queen had insurance.

We passed a few open doors that led into some of the sitting rooms and parlors and such, and I have to admit at being rather shocked. Not from the elegance or the grandiosity, but from the sheer bloody awfulness of the rooms. The Queen and Prince Albert had clearly been besotted with Scotland; the carpets on the floor were the Royal Stewart tartan or the green Hunting Stewart tartan (pretty, I suppose, in a throw rug, but covering what seemed like acres of floor, it was a bit much), the curtains were tartan, the chairs and sofa were upholstered in the same tartan designs, and the wallpaper was covered with thistles. I felt woozy.

Munro grinned at me. "It's something, isn't it? I couldn't believe it myself. I've never seen anything like it."

"Have you been here long?"

"A few days. I'm just learning my way around the place."

As if to prove his point, we turned a corner into a dead end.

"Must have taken a wrong turn back there. Ah, here we are. This way." We set out again, Munro carrying my bags effortlessly.

"What is your job here?" I asked.

"I serve at meals, open and close doors for guests, and if any of the gentlemen guests require a valet, I perform that function as well." He leaned closer to me, and I could smell the pomade on his hair. "I don't mind telling you, I'm a bit nervous."

"So am I. I was just hired by the marchioness today. I've never met her before, and the first thing I have to do is attend to her at the Queen's castle." Might as well play up my inexperience (fact) and my anxiety (also fact); the handsome Munro might take pity on me and show me the ropes. He might also provide some intelligence about the other servants.

"Not to worry. You'll do fine." He opened a thick oak door. "Here we are. This is the marchioness's room. Her baggage has been brought up already, as you can see. I'll take your luggage on to your room. Once you've put away the marchioness's things, come back to the kitchen and have your tea."

The marchioness's room resembled all the others at Balmoral: a plethora of tartan and thistles, with watercolours of the sur-

rounding Cairngorms and Highland lochs on the walls. A wood
fire had been lit in the fireplace, and I stood before it warming my
hands for a bit while my head stopped spinning. Lord, a few
nights in this place and I'd never be able to read a Walter Scott
novel again. Unpacking the old girl's things was the work of a
moment: clothes in the wardrobe; combs and brushes and powder on the dressing table in front of the window; Charlie Dickens,
the Bible and her snuffbox on the table beside her bed. I checked
to see she had a good supply of wood and candles, then hoofed it
back to the kitchen. I was famished.

I should have left a trail of bread crumbs to follow, for it took
me a good long while to find my way there. You'd think you
could follow the smells, for it was teatime with dinner not far
off, but in a castle the size of Balmoral the smell of food cooking
didn't penetrate the granite walls and long corridors. I'd been
busy gaping at the hideous décor and not paying any attention
to the route Munro had followed, so I had to bumble around
the halls, peering into doorways and over balustrades, trying to
figure out where I was going. If not for the directions proffered
by a succession of po-faced servants, I might still be wandering
the halls of the Queen's Highland retreat. I finally staggered
back into the kitchen, having taken the two-shilling tour of the
castle.

Miss Boss pounced on me like a hawk on a field mouse. "You've
arranged Her Ladyship's belongings?"

"Yes, ma'am."

"Then let me introduce you to some of the servants you will
need to know."

We made a hasty circuit of the room, with Miss Boss intro-
ducing me to a dozen bewhiskered gentlemen in kilts (Royal
Stewart, naturally) who acted as under butlers, footmen, equer-

ries and such. I thought the odds were good that I'd remember
their names, as they were all Archie or Jock. Surnames seemed in
short supply in Scotland as well, as they shared just a few: Grant,
MacBeath and Macdonald. As we were introduced, each muttered some greeting in an incomprehensible Scottish accent. I
might as well be in Hungary, I thought. Thank goodness for
Munro and Miss Boss. I could at least understand them when
they spoke.

I met Edith Mackenzie, the cook, a tubby, moon-faced woman
with freckles and untidy red hair under her white cap.

She smiled pleasantly. "Call me 'Cook.' You've far too many
names to remember as it is. There will be bacon and eggs and
spotted dick for your tea, when Miss Boss is finished with you."

That couldn't come soon enough, in my opinion, but Miss
Boss had more introductions to make. She pointed across the
room to a tall, balding chap with a guardsman's mustache.

"That's James Vicker, the deputy to the master of the household. Usually, the master of the household accompanies the
Queen from Windsor to Balmoral, but he's ill, and Mr. Vicker will
be serving as the master in his place. Mr. Vicker is responsible for
sleeping and dining arrangements, and entertainments. You
must do whatever he tells you to do."

I wasn't sure the chap would be up to the task. Vicker was
white with stress, the remaining tufts of his hair standing in soft
peaks around his forehead, which was creased with worry. Bad
enough to take on the diva's role after years of being an under-
study, but to be uprooted from the familiar confines of Windsor
on the Queen's whim was no doubt a considerable strain.

"And *that*," Miss Boss hissed, "is Mr. Brown." The feisty housekeeper looked apprehensive. "You must also follow Mr. Brown's

instructions. He's a sharp tongue on him, but pay no mind to it. Just do as he says."

I'd been dying to see John Brown, farmer's son and former ghillie, now the Queen's close confidant, who called her "wumman" and slept down the hall from her. He was a rustic-looking gent, with a dense brown beard and craggily handsome face. Good-looking, if you like a bit of rough, which apparently Her Royal Majesty did. He'd started service at Balmoral as Prince Albert's ghillie, guiding him on hunts for stag and accompanying him to the lochs for salmon fishing. After the prince's death, Brown had managed to worm his way into the Queen's good graces (no one was quite sure how, as he was reputed to be a drunken lout with the manners of a moor pony), and now he lorded it over Her Majesty's household.

A group of dusky gentlemen trouped past, decked out in sapphire tunics and blousy pants, with white muslin turbans adorned with peacock feathers, and carrying pots, pans and a number of jute bags. One had a chicken tucked under his arm. The scent of cardamom and turmeric wafted after them.

Miss Boss frowned. "Her Majesty's Indian servants. We don't cook for them; they prepare their own meals in the courtyard. They don't do much when they're here, just loiter about all day and shiver. They only work at mealtimes. One of them stands behind the Queen, ready to assist her."

I'd have given a sovereign to see the marchioness's face when one of those little brown buggers appeared in the dining room.

I surveyed the kitchen and felt my spirits sink. It looked like an international convention of domestics. I could imagine the topics they'd discuss: "How to Deflect Sexual Advances from Your Employer," "What to Do When Your Employer Expires on the

Chamber Pot," "Ten Tips for Removing Stains from Egg Cozies," and so on. The English servants were impassive, the Scots dour (you expected something else?) and the Indians odiferous. Finding an assassin in this motley crew would be like unearthing a killer at Sanger's Circus. Where to begin? I didn't think it likely that one of those Indian chappies would be dedicated to the cause of Scottish nationalism, but who knows? He might have befriended a Glaswegian merchant in Bombay and over chai and chapattis discussed their similar desires for an independent nation. And how was I to even communicate with these Hindoo brethren? I could barely understand the Scottish accents I heard around me. Well, a hot meal, a stiff peg of brandy and a good night's sleep, and I'd be ready to tackle the anthropological society meeting in the morning.

"Here's Flora," said Miss Boss. "Flora Mackenzie, Cook's daughter. You'll be sleeping in the spare bed in her room."

Flora was a looker. A strawberry blond curl had escaped from the mass tucked into her cap, and her brown eyes sparkled wickedly. She had a rosebud mouth and a dusting of freckles across a pert nose. Rowena would have taken one look and begun purring. Flora would do well in the Big Smoke, with that mocking smile and devilish gaze. The toffs would eat her up; all I'd need to do was shorten her skirt and lower the bustline of her white blouse, and the money would be rolling in. I debated the ethics of doing a bit of recruiting for Lotus House while performing my patriotic duty of guarding the Queen and decided I shouldn't jeopardize my disguise.

"Och, you're a beauty," said Flora. "The fellows will be all over you. I'll have to put a lock on the door." She giggled good-naturedly, and I was relieved to see that she wasn't going to be the jealous type. Every man within a fifty-mile radius was probably wound tightly around her little finger, and yours truly posed no threat at all. She took my arm and steered me toward a table laden with steaming platters of food and urns of smoking tea. Warm as sunshine, she was.

"Tuck in, dearie. If you came on the train, I'm sure no one thought to feed you all day. Take as much as you want, but don't tarry. You'll have to be upstairs in a thrice to dress the marchioness for dinner."

I hadn't thought of that; I'd been looking forward to putting up my feet and having an early night. Damn. I consoled myself with the thought that French was no doubt doing yeoman's work as well: having a brandy and soda or four, sitting down to a lavish dinner followed by a vintage port, a Cuban cigar and a strenuous game of billiards. My attempt at consolation failed. Morosely, I ate a hearty supper and drank several cups of strong, sweet tea, fortifying myself for the ordeal to come, while Flora pelted me with questions and sparred flirtatiously with the footmen. After the meal I followed Flora up the stairs to the servants' quarters on the top floor, down a draughty hall and into a spartan room containing two single beds, a plain chest of drawers, a bedside table with a candle and a box of matches, and a second table in the corner, where a pottery jug and bowl indicated that I'd be enjoying invigorating sponge baths during my stay. It was as cold as the North Pole in there; even an Inuit would have found it chilly.

"No fires during the day," Flora said cheerfully. No doubt they were used to this temperature in Scotland. "We'll light one tonight, after we've finished our duties." She pulled open a drawer. "You can put your things in here. I'll take your spare uniform down to the laundry each day and bring it back each night. The Queen doesn't like to see anyone without the proper amount of starch in her skirt."

She flopped on the bed. "Ooh, that feels nice. I've been running my legs off since we heard the Queen was coming. Sent everyone into a flutter when we heard she was on her way. Poor Miss Boss almost had a fit."

Flora turned over on her stomach, elbows on the bed and her chin in her hands. "I don't mind a bit of excitement. Usually, it's dead up here this time of year. But now the Queen's come and the ghillies will get their ball, just you wait and see."

"Their ball?"

"Och, you don't know about the ghillies' ball? We always have one in the fall, when the Queen comes. It's ever so much fun. All the servants and the ghillies are invited, and the Queen leads it off with a grand march around the ballroom. Then we dance and drink and drink and dance until dawn."

"Sounds marvelous," I said. "What are the choices for men around here?"

Flora hooted with laughter. "Rough and hairy, and that's how we Scottish lasses like them. But I've got my eye on someone new this year."

"Robbie Munro?"

"How did you know?" Her eyes narrowed. "You haven't got plans for him yourself, have you? I must warn you, I've already picked that flower out of the bouquet."

"Not to worry, Flora. I've got a beau back in . . ." Bloody hell, where had I supposedly worked before the marchioness had employed me?

I needn't have worried about supplying a name. Flora heaved a great sigh of relief at the news and bounced off the bed.

"Have you anything to wear?" She rummaged hastily through my things, which unsurprisingly yielded nothing in the way of a party dress. She fingered the dull woolens with dismay. "Well, now. We'll have to find something for you. None of these will do. But we're about the same size, and I'm sure I've got something that will fit you."

She sprawled on the bed again. "Did you meet Effie, Lady Dalfad's maid?"

"The countess's maid? Oh, yes, we've met."

"Bit of a twit," said Flora. "Gives herself airs."

"So does the countess," I said, remembering her condescension toward the marchioness.

"You'd expect that, wouldn't you? They all do. The nobs, I mean. I say"—she bounced upright—"did you see that good-looking fellow with the black hair waving in the wind? The one with the grey gelding? I've never seen him here before. Do you know him?"

I disclaimed all knowledge of French.

Flora examined her manicure, which, truth to tell (she being a housemaid), was not in the best of condition. "He's a handsome devil. Looks a regular scoundrel." She giggled. "I *love* scoundrels."

Miss Boss opened the door. I suppose the idea of knocking first had yet to make it to the Highlands. Then I remembered that I was a servant and expected to perform such niceties, not personally experience them.

"Flora! I've been looking all over for you. The Princess of Wales's sitting room needs a dust. What have you been doing with yourself? Wasting time gossiping, of course. Now get on your feet and get downstairs. And you"—she glared at me—"the marchioness is ready to dress for dinner. You've thirty minutes."

I bolted out of the room, hastily arranging my cap. Truth to tell, I was the teeniest bit glad to get away from Flora's prattle. My head was still spinning from the journey, not to mention meeting the marchioness and the legion of servants whose names I would never remember.

"Not that way," roared Miss Boss.

I reversed direction and scurried past her. I needed a cartographer in the worst way. I hustled out of sight of the housekeeper and down the stairs, where I lassoed a housemaid carrying a dustpan and broom and extracted directions from her to the marchioness's room. I was haring along like a hunted rabbit down one of the hallways when I turned the corner and ran smack into the most notorious womanizer in Britain: Bertie, Prince of Wales and the heir to the throne. He was a middle-aged swell with a spade beard and the girth of a pregnant Percheron, but elegantly dressed in tweed trousers, soft leather boots and a Norfolk jacket. He looked like an ordinary chap, but the dark circles and sagging pouches under his eyes marked him as the libertine he was.

Poor old Bertie. He liked a bit of fun and wasn't too particular where he found it: actresses, prostitutes, the wives and daughters of his closest friends. He wasn't a discriminating chap, our Bertie, but then he had so little to do with his time except drink, dice and whore. His mama (Her Royal Highness) despised the poor stick, blaming him for his father's death. It's like this, you see. Bertie was away on maneuvers with his army unit in Ireland when some of his fellow officers decided to play a joke on him and invited the actress Nellie Clifton to his tent. A scandal ensued, and a few weeks later, Prince Albert, though ill with the typhoid fever that eventually killed him, traveled all the way to Cambridge to remonstrate with his son about his ethical shortcomings. Two weeks later poor dear Albert shuffled off this mortal coil, leaving Bertie with lashings of guilt and the Queen with an intense dislike of her own son. But I digress.

The prince caught sight of me and assessed me the way most gentleman do, starting at the toes of my shoes, eyeing with approval my trim waist and luscious breasts, and ending his survey with an appreciative smile at the sight of my milky skin and cobalt blue eyes. His wife, Princess Alexandra of Denmark, was following close behind her husband, rattling on about their son Albert Victor's education and daughter Louise's accomplishments at the piano. She couldn't help but notice that Bertie's attention had wandered away from her fascinating conversation and was now focused on me. She glared at me, a look that contained enough cyanide to quell a lesser woman, but I was sanguine. I've never understood why wives direct their poison at other women; it's their wandering husbands they ought to take outside and beat with a horsewhip. I'm a handsome woman, and there's no point in trying to hide my light under a bushel; why should I be blamed for a man's natural reaction to me?

The princess stalked past, head high, looking down her nose at me (which took some time, as it was quite a nose—one of those you see frequently on the faces of the inbred European aristocracy). I felt a bit sorry for the old hay-bag. She wore an expression of impending doom, as though she'd just gotten word that another of the prince's mistresses was pregnant. She was followed by several gloomy, horse-faced children (at least the Prince had done his royal duty in that department), who, from their expressions, had learned of their father's nefarious ways from their mother. They sulked along the passageway, out of sight, and I put on speed for the marchioness's room.

She was sitting at the dressing table, wearing a stained silk bathrobe and a look of bewilderment.

"Good evening, Your Ladyship." I dropped a curtsey.

"Ah. There ye are, Irene. I've been wonderin' where ye'd got to. It's almost time for clobber. They put on a superb feed at dinner here. Well, ye can tell that just by lookin' at the Queen, can't ye?"

I picked up the marchioness's comb and brush and looked dubiously at her hair. "I'll have you ready soon, m'lady." I poked experimentally at the white tangles. "Is there anything in particular you'd like me to do with your hair?"

"Just comb it, ye idiot girl. I'm long past the age of carin' what I look like. Passin' presentable, that's good enough for me." She patted the top of the dressing table irritably. "Where is that snuffbox?"

"Here it is, Your Ladyship," I said, retrieving the container from the bedside table and turning to the marchioness just in time to see her insert her nail into her powder box, draw forth a goodly portion of that cosmetic and cram it up her nose. She inhaled deeply, shuddering, then a strangled note issued from her throat and her body quivered. I looked round frantically for something to staunch the inevitable eruption. Where's a blooming towel when you need one? I considered my options—One of the marchioness's dinner gowns? My skirt? (No)—then settled for the closest thing to hand: a pillow from the bed. I clapped it over the marchioness's face just as she detonated.

I was sure the muffled roar would bring Superintendent Robshaw's men rushing in, looking for bombs, but no one came. I removed the pillow and surveyed my handiwork. Well, there was one piece of the Queen's linen that would never be used again.

The marchioness shook herself vehemently, like a wet Scottish deerhound. "Most unusual. I've never had that reaction to Mitchell's snuff before. Must be an inferior stock. I'll have to put a flea in that man's ear when I get home."

"It was face powder, ma'am," I said gently.

The marchioness swung round, her faded eyes alight with suspicion. "Face powder! 'Strodinary! Why would ye give me face powder instead of snuff? Are ye tryin' to kill me, Irene?"

"No, ma'am, of course not," I said hastily. "I didn't . . ." Oh, what was the point? I took a deep breath. "My apologies, my lady. Very stupid of me. It won't happen again."

The marchioness rubbed her face with her hand, then wiped it on her dressing gown. "Don't just stand there gapin' like a fish. Do up my hair and get me dressed or I'll miss the pâté de foie gras. The Grand Duke of Mecklenburg-Schwerin always sends it to the Queen for Christmas."

So I did my best to tidy the marchioness, wrestling her coarse, frazzled elflocks into some semblance of a coiffure, dabbing the powder on her withered cheeks with a practiced hand, applying the rouge sparingly, and otherwise doing what I could with the material at hand. I have to say, I was rather proud of my work when I finished. The marchioness certainly looked less seedy than when we'd met at Perth. She was, in fact, just this side of respectable. Not that the old dear noticed, of course, having fallen asleep while I brushed and combed. I gave her a kindly poke, and she awoke with a snort, gazing wildly around her.

"Balmoral," I reminded her.

"I know where I am," she snapped. I allowed myself to feel a moment of pity for her dinner partners tonight.

I shoved her into her dress while she tottered about like the Prince of Wales on a bender, helped guide her wavering feet into her kid shoes, tucked a handkerchief into her sleeve (not much chance of that being used, but I owed it to the other guests) and placed her snuffbox into her evening bag. Someone knocked discreetly, and I opened the door to find Robbie Munro on the threshold, looking, I might add, simply stunning in a dark green jacket, snowy white shirt and a kilt that showed a fine pair of legs.

He gave me a dazzling grin, which I returned.

"I'm to escort Her Ladyship to dinner," he said.

The marchioness wobbled past me, like a cork on a wave. "Don't flirt with the footmen, Ilene," she hissed in my ear. I tried to look abashed, but I fear that I failed.

It was getting on for nine o'clock when I finally staggered into the room I shared with Flora. I untied my laces, removed my shoes and stretched out on the lumpy mattress, pulling a blanket over me. Someone had lit a mean little fire in the grate. They were generous with the coal here at Balmoral; there must have been three pieces in the fireplace. I shivered. Cyprus next time, I promised myself. Or Athens. The prime minister must need somebody on the spot in a warm climate from time to time. Hell, I'd even take Cairo at this point. I huddled under my blanket, feeling very sorry for myself.

I must have dozed off, because when I came to Flora had bustled in, humming a tune.

"You look ragged, India."

"It's been a long day. And I still have to tuck my old lady into bed."

"That'll be midnight or later, unless she likes to retire early."

"She retires frequently during the day, and I expect she'll drop off once or twice during dinner."

"Old pussies are like that." Flora removed her cap and pulled the pins from her hair.

I struggled upright, brushing my hair from my face and giving it a good scrubbing with my palms. I wanted nothing more than a few hours repose, but the sooner French and I uncovered the would-be assassin, the sooner I could stop wiping the marchioness's nose and head home to London. While I had a few minutes alone with Flora, I might as well see what I could learn about the Balmoral servants.

"How long have you been in service here at the castle?"

She brushed her hair vigorously. "Donkey's years. Since I was a slip of a girl. Mama is the cook here, and it seems like I've always worked alongside her. When I was ten, I was hired to do the washing up, and then I did laundry, and a few years ago I became housemaid."

"I've met your mother. She's very nice."

"Mama's nice to everyone, even John Brown and those heathen chaps from India. She's a good cook, too. She came to work here when the Queen and Prince Albert built the house, and she's been here ever since. Her Majesty's quite fond of Mama's puddings, and she says no one roasts beef nearly so well."

One glance at the Queen's figure and you could tell she wasn't finicky about her vittles, but I wasn't about to point out to Flora that her mother could have put sawdust with gravy on the table, and the Queen would have bolted it down.

"Your mother has been here since the castle opened? Goodness! Have the other servants been here as long?"

Flora massaged her scalp, studying herself intently in the mirror. "Lots of them have been. And the newer ones are usually sons or daughters or cousins, taking over from someone in their family who is retiring from service."

"And the scrumptious Robbie Munro? He told me he had only been here a little while."

At the mention of Munro's name, Flora swooned dramatically, hand over her heart. "He is tasty, isn't he? Yes, he's new. Started work just a few days ago. His uncle is the under butler here, and he recommended Robbie. He was a footman at a house somewhere in the Borders. Kelso, I think he said. Or maybe it was Jedburgh. Anyway, we needed a footman here and Robbie's uncle said he'd do. One of the other footmen just upped stakes and left. Nobody knows where he went or why he was in such a hurry. You mark my words, though"—Flora laughed—"we'll find out in the spring, when one of the laundry girls shows up in the family way."

I joined in her laughter, but my mind was elsewhere, namely on how to communicate with French that he should enquire into the case of the disappearing footman and the background of handsome Robbie Munro.

"Do you like working here?" I asked.

"Oh, yes. It's the best job in the world, if you have to be in service. The Queen only comes up here once or twice a year, and then just for a few weeks, excepting this year, of course. While she's here, it's always a bit of a panic, all that rushing about and cleaning rooms and cooking for dozens of guests and all the servants. Still, it's worth it in the end. We have the ghillies' ball, you see, and that's ever so much fun."

"You mentioned the ball earlier. Tell me about it."

The ghillies' ball was a tradition instituted by the late Prince Albert, who liked to reward his faithful ghillies for their services in assisting the prince in slaughtering stags and netting salmon in the lakes. The prince landed on the idea of a Scottish country dance, rustic and simple, with plenty of victuals and enough liquor to slake the thirst of a Highland regiment, and thus the custom was born. Each year, when Prince Albert and the Queen visited Balmoral in September, a ball was held, with the royal couple leading a grand march into the ballroom, followed by their guests, the ghillies and all the other servants.

" 'Tis a wonderful affair," Flora gushed. "You wouldn't believe it, but the Queen steps as lively as a wee lass on the dance floor and stays up until all hours just to watch the fun."

I did find it hard to imagine Her Highness jigging to a Scottish reel (you'd have to step lively yourself to avoid coming in range of those flapping jowls), but I remained silent.

"Some of the lads will dance the sword dance, and the old folks will clap their hands and keep time to the music," Flora went on. "And this year, I plan to dance with that dashing chap with the black hair. There's always a 'Ladies' Choice,' and I intend to claim him."

I assumed she was referring to French. I'd have to warn him of the impending assault.

"I'll snaffle the handsome Robbie, then," I told her, and she chucked her shoe at me. "Sounds like the Queen does well by her good and faithful. Do the rest of the servants like working here?"

Flora shrugged. "I can't see why they wouldn't. We eat better than we would if we were crofters or shepherds or spun wool for a living. And when the Queen isn't here, it's very quiet. We do our work during the day and enjoy ourselves in the evening, playing cards and games. The only complaints I've heard are from some of the men. Her Majesty insists they wear kilts at all times, and most of the men hate to wear those things, especially in the cold weather. And then there are the Indians. No one likes having them about. The place smells of curry for weeks after they've gone, and we're always finding chicken heads in the courtyard."

She yawned widely. "I'm for bed. The day starts early for me tomorrow."

She shed her clothes and donned a nightdress, crawled under the covers and was snoring softly in minutes. I dozed restlessly until eleven o'clock, when I staggered downstairs to peel the marchioness out of her clothes and tuck her into bed, while she regaled me with stories of *tortue claire* and chine of pork, whatever the hell those were. Then I bade her goodnight, wandered wearily through the halls until I found Flora's room and collapsed on the bed, where I fell asleep like an innocent babe.

FOUR

I slept soundly until roused by a hammering at the door.

"Miss Black, are you there?"

I fumbled for the matches and managed to light a candle. "Who is it?"

Flora grumped and mumbled but didn't wake.

"It's Robbie Munro. The marchioness is asking for you."

"Damn and blast," I said. I put my feet on the floor and yelped at the cold. "I'll dress and be right there."

"Can you find her room, or should I wait and accompany you?"

Not even the prospect of roaming the halls with the dazzling Robbie Munro excited my interest. At this hour, *nothing* could excite my interest, except the warm bed I'd just left.

"I'll find it. Thank you, Robbie." I scrambled into my uniform (which looked a bit worse for the wear, since I'd dropped it in a heap on the floor) and began the long trek back to the marchio-ness's room. I found her sitting up in bed, with a log fire blazing and all the candles lit.

"Took ye long enough," she said by way of greeting. "Where've they put ye, out in the stables?"

"I'm sorry, Your Ladyship. The castle is so large, and I haven't learned my way around it yet. I shall endeavor to improve."

The marchioness thrust a book at me. "I canna sleep. I want ye to read to me."

Well, I suppose if you spend the day napping, a good night's sleep is hard to come by. I sighed resignedly, settled myself com-fortably in a chair near the fire (at least it was warm in here) and looked over the reading material the marchioness had selected. *Troilus and Criseyde*. I groaned. Possibly one of the most boring stories I'd ever read. I couldn't see why people made such a fuss about Troilus, raving about the purity of his love for Criseyde, his decency and goodness, his honour, and all those other qualities that supposedly make up the perfect gentleman. Personally, I found him cloying. There's nothing the least bit manly about cry-ing and mooching about, feeling sorry for yourself. And the fel-low is deuced stupid, in my view. If you're thick enough to get taken in by a woman, then it's your own fault when things go pear-shaped. And Criseyde? There's another sore point with me. She's supposed to represent the fickle nature of women, betray-ing Troilus by going off with that hairy Greek ape Diomedes, but what was she supposed to do, eh? Her scheming father Calchas had engineered her removal from Troy because he was sure the city would fall to the Greeks, and he wanted her out of harm's way. And what woman wouldn't throw in her lot with a virile chap like Diomedes, instead of that sheep Troilus? I know I would. (And as for Troilus throwing himself frenziedly into battle after learning of Criseyde's choice and getting himself skewered, there's only one thing to say about that: how typical of a man.) I suppose it's plain by now how much this particular fable annoys me, but I digress.

"From the beginning, my lady?"

The marchioness nodded and snuggled down in her blankets, snuffbox in hand, while I launched into the tale of star-crossed lovers and tried not to wretch. The marchioness nodded and snuffled, smiling gently whenever Troilus demonstrated his love for Criseyde by weeping like a schoolgirl and begging his friend Pandarus to stay with him through the long, lonely night (something fishy about that, I tell you). Her Ladyship frowned at Criseyde's perfidy while I silently cheered her on, and we read the whole damned story from start to finish. Thank God it's short, but even with that my voice was getting husky and my lids felt like iron bars near the end. The marchioness, damn her eyes, stayed awake for the entire performance. When I'd finished the book, it was nearly dawn. The cocks were crowing in the stables and the darkness was beginning to fade.

The marchioness gave me a gap-toothed grin as I closed the book. "There ye are. The perfect lesson in the power of women to deceive."

"And of men to be deceived," I added sourly.

She cackled. "Credulous idiots, most of 'em. On the other hand, many a maid has been taken in by the charms of men." She gave me a stern look through the rheumy eyes. "Ye would do well to remember that."

"That most men are credulous idiots?"

She laughed again and then yawned, her sparse teeth winking

in the candlelight. "When it comes to lyin', neither sex has the advantage over the other. Now off ye go. I always breakfast in bed, so I won't need ye again until it's time to dress for luncheon."

I was grateful for the opportunity to catch a few winks, but the marchioness's parting words had roused a nagging doubt in my mind. Usually, I'd agree quite readily with the assessment that women were skilled in the art of deception; I just hated having it pointed out to me while I masqueraded under false pretenses in the royal household. I cast my mind over the hours since I'd met the marchioness, but I'd be damned if I could remember any incident or word that might have revealed that I was not what I pretended to be. Oh well. Having not slept much over the last thirty-six hours, I was probably seeing dragons where none existed. A few hours sleep would see me right.

Which I was destined not to get, as shortly after I tumbled back onto my lumpy mattress (Flora still snorting like a grampus in the other bed), an eldritch screech poured through the window, shattering my slumber and jolting me upright, panting in panic. Good God. It sounded as though an entire platoon of felines was being run over by a mail coach. Slowly. And repeatedly.

Flora stirred, then stretched lazily. She glanced at the clock. "Och, time to rise." She didn't seem the least bit concerned with the unearthly wailing that filled the room.

"What on earth is that noise?"

She scratched her bum unconcernedly. "Why, it's only William Ross, the Queen's piper. He always pipes at dawn when Her Majesty's in residence. And he'll play again at sunset tonight."

The sound was fading, as the piper worked his way around the building.

"You mean we have to listen to that thing twice a day?"

"Every day the Queen's here," said Flora cheerfully. "Beautiful music, isn't it? The voice of the Highlands."

The voice of the Highlands sounded a great deal like a wagon wheel in need of grease, but one doesn't hope to have a rational discussion with a Scot about the Great Highland War Pipe. Sane people do not make musical instruments out of a sheep's bladder and a bundle of reeds. What prompts a bloke to pick up an internal organ from *ovis aries* and squeeze it in the first place? The mind boggles. "Great Highland War Pipe" indeed; I'm sure the Scots only charge in battle to get away from that horrible caterwauling. With luck, they'll be taken prisoner and never have to listen to the bloody thing again.

Flora was splashing water on her face. "That handsome toff I told you about? The one with the black hair? Turns out he's quite the devil."

Fleetingly, I wondered if French had paid a visit to Flora while I had been reading that vapid claptrap to the marchioness. Surely not. I shook my head vigorously. I was obviously befuddled from lack of sleep and being wakened by the dulcet tones of cats expiring.

"I had a cup of tea last night with Rosie. She's one of the other housemaids, and she tidies his room. Last night before dinner, she brought him some hot water and he made lewd suggestions to her and pinched her bottom." Flora laughed. "What a rogue! I may have to see if I can switch rooms with Rosie and clean up after that fellow. I'd give him a run for his money."

"And Rosie won't?"

"Not Rosie. She's a mouse. Scared her to death, he did." Flora drew her hair back into a tight bun at the nape of her neck and pinned on her cap. "But he doesn't scare me. After all, if you can work at Balmoral and stay a virgin while the Prince of Wales is visiting, your common, garden-variety swell is no challenge at all. Apparently, they've become fast friends."

"French and the Prince of Wales?"

"Rosie says they spent most of the night getting sozzled, gabbing about horses and flirting with the young ladies in the party. Princess Alexandra was in a right old state by the end of the evening. She practically dragged the prince off to bed by his ear."

I chewed on this for a bit, trying to summon up a mental image of French boozing and carousing with the lost souls, and found it hard going. Not the mannerly Mr. French, Public Schoolboy of the Year.

Flora put the finishing touches on her toilette. "I'm off. Breakfast on the table in fifteen minutes."

An hour later I had breakfasted well, drunk a half-dozen cups of tea and learned quite a lot about the events of the previous evening from the gaggle of maids and footmen who had been in attendance. Most of the conversation centered around the Prince of Wales, who was stiff as a plank in the presence of his mother and wife, but turned into Falstaff as soon as the old biddy and the ball and chain were out of the room. The prince had been joined in the festivities by French and a few of the male guests. Several bottles of champagne had been consumed, a large amount of the ready had changed hands at the card table, and the merits of Thoroughbreds and actresses had been discussed in clinical detail. One of the footman at the table had blushed at the memory of the conversation. I didn't hear the gory details as Miss Boss bustled in at that moment, and everyone at the table turned a guilty face to their plate and started gulping bacon and eggs as the housekeeper ran over the day's assignments.

I had hoped to spend some time cozying up to some of the other servants and pumping them for information, but Miss Boss had interfered with my plans, barking instructions to her staff and sending them off in a flutter to attend to their various duties. I was left to my own devices, and so I wandered off to the wing where the guest rooms were located. If I found a lad or lass shirking their duties, I could always enjoy an idle gossip, and if anyone questioned my own activities, I could retreat to the safety of the marchioness's room.

I sauntered along casually until I encountered a guest, and then I assumed an air of purposeful intent and quickened my pace until I was around a corner (there's always a corner to turn in Balmoral) and out of sight. Then I reverted to my slow peram- bulation. Once I found a wide-eyed girl mooning about the cor- ridor, eyeing herself in a hideous gilded mirror and arranging a curl on her cheek while the stack of linen on the table went unde- livered. I struck up the usual conversation between working stiffs, moaning about wages and hours and only having off Sunday eve- nings, and we commiserated awhile, but as she had all the intel- ligence of an aspidistra, I wrote her off as a possible assassin and ended our discussion as soon as decently possible. Yes, I know, every army needs its foot soldiers, but the girl wasn't even men- tally equipped to be cannon fodder. You can't feign stupidity of that caliber. Would have made a good whore, though.

I turned my back on another recruiting opportunity lost and worked my way through the maze of hallways, chatting up a for- bidding Scottish footman (hard going, that—no one does forbid- ding like a Scot), who had better things to do with his time than chat with the likes of me, and chasing down the girl emptying the chamber pots (on the whole, not the best move on my part), who professed to thoroughly enjoy her job at the castle. There's just no accounting for what some people are willing to do for money. I should know.

By midmorning I had given up my quest (temporarily) to find a talkative Balmoral servant, having decided that my best opportunity to chat up my fellow employees would be between the time I packed the marchioness off to dinner and when she retired. Truth to tell, I was feeling a bit fagged, having had so little sleep last night. I thought I might just have time to snatch a catnap before tarting up the old girl for luncheon and was making my way back to Flora's room when the door I was passing opened and a hand shot out, snatching my wrist.

Unlike most other members of the fair sex, I was not disconcerted. I've spent a goodly portion of my youth being grabbed unexpectedly by loathsome gents, and I've learned the simplest of maneuvers to escape. Instead of trying to pull away, one merely pushes forward, throwing the assailant off balance with this unexpected movement and, with luck, causing him to fall backward onto his arse. I would note that this tactic almost always works if one charges into the fellow with the intensity of a rugby forward with a wicked hangover, which I invariably do, planting my head in the fellow's stomach for good measure. Life is nasty and brutish, as Tommy Hobbes likes to say, but if India Black has anything to say about it, her life won't be short. Hence, I sometimes overreact.

As I did in this instance. I barreled into the bedroom at full speed, head lowered like a charging Hereford bull, only to find myself standing over French, who was sprawled on the floor and glaring up at me with those cold grey eyes.

"Oops," I said. I extended a hand, which he brushed away impatiently.

"Dash it all, India. Why can't you look before you leap?" He rose gingerly and brushed his coat.

"If you insist on getting my attention by accosting me, then you'll have to take the consequences. Next time, I suggest a simple 'Psst, India, in here.'"

"Next time, I'll send an engraved invitation." He hurried to the door, glanced up and down the hallway, and shut the door softly.

"Sit down, India. I don't expect us to be interrupted, but people have a way of wandering about here, blundering into rooms just when you think you've found some privacy."

"Are you referring to the servants or the guests?"

"Both. And the Queen. If she wants to sit in a room, she'll turf you out without a second thought."

"It is her house," I pointed out.

"Quite. Now, what have you learned?"

"Most of the servants have been at Balmoral since Methuselah was a boy. They seem content, for the most part, but I haven't really had a chance to dig below the surface. There are two things you may want to check, however. All of the arrangements for the Queen's visit are handled by the master of the household, who accompanies her from Windsor. But the master couldn't come this time; he's supposedly ill, and he's been replaced by James Vicker, his deputy. Vicker looks like a man who just had a game pie for luncheon that's been in the larder too long: white as sheet and sweating buckets. That could indicate a guilty conscience."

"Yes," French mused. "Or merely food poisoning."

I punched him in the bicep. "It might be worth verifying that the master really is down with something. And perhaps a review of Vicker's background would be useful: his length of service at Windsor, political views, that sort of thing."

"I agree. It's worth checking. Anything else?"

I told him about Robbie Munro and his recent hiring. "According to Flora, he's only been here a few days and came on his uncle's recommendation. That should be easy enough to confirm."

"I'll let Robshaw know immediately, and he can get a man on it right away."

"Your turn, French. The staff is agog at your behavior; apparently, you're giving the Prince of Wales a run for his money in the scoundrel stakes." Bit of an exaggeration, but how was French to know?

He grinned. "Good. Exactly the impression I hoped to make."

"You want to be seen as a dissolute Don Juan?"

"I do. People are much more inclined to let down their guard if they think they're talking to a dim-witted fool whose only interests are ponies, maids and cognac. No one would think that a brainless peer of the realm addicted to the racing sheets would have a political thought in his head."

"And you hope to lure someone into an indiscretion with that act?"

"I already have," he announced smugly.

"Not the bloke on the platform at King's Cross?"

"Oh, good Lord, no. That chap is as straight as they come. No, I've made a new friend here: Hector MacCodrum, seventh Baronet of Dochfour."

"Never heard of him."

"No reason you should have, until now. He's the favorite nephew of the Earl of Nairn, one the Queen's favorites among the

Scottish peers. The earl is sober, circumspect and completely loyal to the Crown. His nephew is not."

"What's he doing here? The baronet, I mean."

"Call him 'Red Hector.' Everyone else does. He's got ginger hair and a fiery temper."

"He doesn't sound like a pleasant fellow."

"He's not. Whinnies like a horse when he laughs, shouts abuse at the servants and is pickled most of the time. He's only here because the earl has made a bit of a project of him, trying to damp down Red Hector's impetuosity and teach him the art of diplomacy. The earl is trying to impress upon the young man the importance of the Queen's patronage, so he wangled an invitation to Balmoral to introduce Red Hector to the prime minister and Her Majesty's other advisors."

"Sounds as though the earl is taking a risk he may regret."

"Oh, I think he already does. Red Hector doesn't care a fig for the Crown or the Queen or anything to do with England, for that matter. And he made that quite clear at dinner last night and afterward over the port." French looked modest. "Encouraged by me, of course, who spent a fair amount of time egging him on."

"What did he say?"

"Just that England should shed its slavish allegiance to the royal family and send them packing. And the Scots could do very well without being tied to England's apron strings."

"Did the Queen hear those comments?"

"Thankfully, no. It's a very large table at dinner. But everyone within ten feet of Red Hector did. There was a scandalized silence, as you can imagine, while the diners tried to conjure up some response to this heretical point of view, and then the whole party broke into conversation at once, pointedly ignoring the baronet."

"Which he no doubt found satisfying."

"Indeed. Even drunk as an Irishman on Saturday night, he still had the indecency to look proud of his statement. Apparently, he's known for dropping conversational bombs such as that."

"He might be saying such things for effect. He sounds a bit of rascal."

"He is that. But I have to determine if he's just stirring up controversy for its own sake or if he means what he says."

"If he intends to assassinate the Queen, statements like that will guarantee he doesn't get anywhere near her. He should be fawning over Her Majesty, instead of slinging verbal arrows for everyone to hear and drawing attention to himself."

"I had thought of that myself, India. But it's possible he's merely running a bluff, counting on being so conspicuously anti-monarchical that if something happens to the Queen, he'll be dismissed out of hand as being too obvious a candidate. You know, the idea that only an idiot would so openly disparage Her Highness and then attempt to murder her. He could in fact be a red herring, sent by the Sons of Arbroath to draw attention away from the real assassin."

"What do you plan to do?"

"Red Hector and I are going to become fast friends. It means I'll have to drink like a fish and feign an interest in studs and bloodlines, but so be it."

"And here I thought I had the worst of it, wiping down the marchioness every time she takes a bit of snuff and staying awake all night reading the Holy Scriptures to the old trout. Lord, it must be hard work for you, French, quaffing champagne and discussing brood mares."

"Every man must do his duty." He smirked. "How are you getting on with the marchioness?"

"She's a pleasure to work for, if you don't mind sitting up most of the night and dodging a wall of spray every time she takes snuff, which is frequently. I was expecting someone a bit more elegant. The marchioness would be right at home with the fellows in the merchant marine."

French nodded. "I knew you two would have something in common."

I chose to ignore this ill-mannered comment. "I see you buckled under pressure from Vincent and brought the little blighter along with you. Has he had a bath, or have they had to remove the horses from the stables because they couldn't stand the odor?"

"He had a bath, of course. I made that a condition of his being allowed to come. He's actually going to be quite useful. Neither you nor I can penetrate the world of the outside servants—the grooms, the gardeners and so on. He can. He'll be snooping around the stables and the grounds to ferret out any disloyalties in the staff."

I had to agree that made a certain amount of sense, but I wasn't about to admit that to French. Besides, there was another matter I needed to take up with the man and our time was limited.

"How's the sire these days?"

"Sire?" French looked puzzled. Probably still had his mind on the nags.

"Your father."

"Ah." French had located a particular thistle on the wallpaper and was staring at it with single-minded concentration. "He's, ah, fine, of course. In blooming health."

"And the rest of the family?"

The thistle lost its attraction; French's eyes ricocheted around the room while he rummaged distractedly in his pockets. Luckily for him, salvation appeared.

The door to the room swung open, and before I knew what was

happening, French had seized me roughly in his arms and planted his lips on mine. Normally, that can be a pleasant experience with a man, but in bundling me tightly into his arms, French had squeezed all the breath from my body and then, having attached himself to my mouth like a giant squid, had cut off my only means of replacing the air in my lungs. I struggled valiantly to breathe, but French had a vise-like grip on my body and my lips.

I heard a throaty chuckle, and the Prince of Wales said, "Well, well. Sorry to interrupt, old boy. I didn't think anyone was in here, and I was hoping to have a little snooze before luncheon."

By this time the lack of oxygen to my brain was beginning to tell. I felt a warm drowsiness stealing over me. My knees were beginning to sag, and I found myself leaning into French for support. He wrapped his arms tighter around me. His lips seared mine. I felt myself begin to swoon, a not uncomfortable feeling, if I'm to be honest. Oxygen deprivation will have that effect, I'm told.

Just as I was about to collapse, French released me with a gentle shove. I stood gasping, wondering what to say, but French saved me from having to respond by taking my shoulders, turning me toward the door and saying: "Go on, my lovely. Go pet the old lady. We'll finish this some other time." And then the bastard slapped my ass and pushed me out the door.

I stood in the hallway, leaning against a sixteenth-century bureau, my chest heaving and my knees wobbling like a day-old blancmange. I was quivering with rage. How dare the bastard treat me like . . . like . . . like a bloody housemaid over whom he was exercising the ancient right of *droit du seigneur*.

It didn't help that I could hear French and the Prince of Wales neighing and snorting like two randy stallions.

"Fast work, brother," said Bertie. I'd have liked to have given him a good one right in his toolbox for that. "I spotted her in the hall yesterday. She's a handsome wench. I'd have had a go at her myself if I hadn't walked in on the two of you wrapped up together. But since you've got first dibs, I'll step aside. Can't promise I won't look that little wagtail up later, though. What a fine filly."

That's the aristocracy for you. Or, come to that, men in general. They just assume that every maid they meet would be thrilled to drop her knickers for them, regardless of how bald, fat or stupid they are. It's a hard truth, ladies, but the sooner you learn it, the quicker you can get on with learning how to buffalo the old farts and turn their arrogant confidence to your advantage.

"There ye are, Iris."

I winced at the raucous voice. The marchioness. Bloody hell. That was all I needed at the moment.

The old dame was tottering down the hall, peering nearsightedly into each room, like a laying hen just released from the coop and trying to work out where to find the corn.

"I need yer assistance, Iris. Now."

"Yes, my lady." My knees were still weak and my breathing ragged, but I followed her back to her room.

There, the marchioness collapsed into a chair and scowled up at me. "I heard male voices from that room. Were ye in there alone with two gentlemen?"

"Yes, ma'am. Mr. French and the Prince of Wales."

"Give me my snuffbox, Iris."

I handed her the box, along with a snowy square of linen. She waved the latter away. I shrugged. One can only try. So I beat a hasty retreat to the far side of the room until the ritual of dipping, sneezing and dripping was complete, then mopped up the aftermath.

The marchioness dabbed away a trickle of snuff. "Ye're new to my service, Iris, and also new to the Queen's residence. I feel I must warn ye. Ye should not, under any circumstances, permit yerself to be alone with any gentlemen here at the castle. They're likely to be friends with that bounder Bertie, and ye've surely heard what a scoundrel he is."

I didn't know whether I should admit to being au fait with the misdeeds of the Prince of Wales, as I was liable to get a lecture on gossiping with the other servants, so I merely nodded ambiguously and let the marchioness carry on.

She gave me a sharp glance from those rheumy eyes. "Ye keep to yerself, Iris. I don't want ye leavin' here with a bairn for a souvenir. Is that clear?"

"Yes, ma'am. Abundantly. And may I say that you need have no worries about that."

Truth to tell, I could probably have made the old lady's eyes bug out with the wealth of information I knew about this particular subject, but I didn't see the point of flustering her with knowledge that your average virginal maid should never acquire.

"You said that you needed me, Your Ladyship. Are you ready to dress for luncheon?"

"I'm havin' it on a tray in here. Then I'm havin' a nap. But ye should come back this afternoon. I'm havin' tea with Lady Dalfad, and I want ye to accompany me."

I nodded and took my leave, my spirits momentarily uplifted at the thought of seeing the marchioness partaking of snuff in Lady Dalfad's presence. Bound to be a show worth the price of admittance.

* * *

As I had anticipated, tea with Lady Dalfad was a chilly affair. The marchioness toddled in on my arm, and the countess gave her a stiff nod in greeting. I wondered why, if the countess so disapproved of the old girl, she had bothered to invite her to tea, but the Upper Ten does things differently than we do. I wouldn't give the time of day, let alone tea, to someone I disliked, but the aristocracy has to nod and smile and pretend they're deuced happy to see all sorts of simpletons, wastrels and dullards, just because they have money, a title, or an eligible son or daughter with one or the other.

Effie, the countess's maid, gave me an equally stiff nod. The gracious ladies seated themselves in chairs covered in that godawful Royal Stewart tartan, and the countess's maid and I were relegated to rigid wooden chairs along the wall, where we could keep an eye on our charges but they wouldn't have to spoil their tea by actually seeing us.

A footman waltzed in with a tray of sandwiches and cakes and a silver teapot. I was delighted to see that it was Robbie Munro. I could at least idle away some time in admiring his muscular calves (even the thick woolen socks couldn't hide those) and that handsome head of red gold curls. He looked as nervous as a schoolboy, treading carefully over the carpet (Royal Stewart, what else?) and placing the tray on the table before the countess with trembling hands. The china rattled and the teapot slid alarmingly to one side. Robbie recovered it quickly and replaced it on its lacy mat. Under the golden tumble of curls, his face was pink.

Lady Dalfad impaled him with a glance but said nothing.

The marchioness leaned forward, examining the food. "Smoked salmon. And those lovely fairy cakes. My favorites." She grunted in satisfaction, which made the countess wince.

Robbie served them, sloshing the tea and earning another

glare from Lady Dalfad, but he finally succeeded in getting tea in the cups and sandwiches on the plates without a major disaster. He went to stand in the corner, ready to spring into action.

Lady Dalfad took a sip of tea. "You may go, Munro. If we require anything, I'll send Effie to fetch you."

Robbie inclined his head and retreated quickly. He caught my eye as he went and grimaced. I gave him an encouraging smile.

"What a clumsy oaf that man is," said Lady Dalfad.

The marchioness crammed a bit of toast and salmon into her mouth. "Is he?" she mumbled. "I hadna noticed. Good lookin' chap, though." She laughed boisterously, and the countess's lips tightened.

"You would think he'd never been a footman before," she said. "The Queen usually hires only experienced servants."

"She's a stickler for protocol," said the marchioness, slurping tea.

"Her Majesty has high expectations of her servants, which is entirely appropriate," Lady Dalfad said primly.

"Well, the footman may not be up to snuff, but the cook is first-rate." The marchioness helped herself to more salmon.

"I daresay I shall have to have a word with Vicker about that young man. He ought not to wait on the Queen until he's gained some polish."

"Who's Vicker?"

"The deputy master of the household. Wilkins, the master, is ill and had to stay at Windsor. This is Vicker's first time to perform the master's duties, and I fear that things are not as they should be. If Wilkins were here, that young footman would not have served anyone until he'd proved his competence."

The countess went on prattling away about the difficulty of finding good servants, unlike her Effie, of course, who was a paragon of virtuous servitude, while Effie preened herself in the corner and darted little glances in my direction, to be sure I was listening. I wasn't, of course, having latched onto something Lady Dalfad had said about Munro: "You would think he'd never been a footman before." I distinctly remembered Flora telling me that Robbie had been a footman at a great house somewhere in the Borders. I daresay the countess had lots of experience with footmen, being one of the Queen's ladies of the bedchamber and consequently used to consorting with those chaps on a regular basis. If Lady Dalfad suspected Robbie had never acted as a footman before, then perhaps the handsome lad was here at Balmoral under false pretenses.

The marchioness had moved on to the cucumber sandwiches and was shoveling them into her mouth at a rate that guaranteed the countess wouldn't be having any. Lady Dalfad carried on at such length about the dearth of well-trained staff and the consequent hardships suffered by their employers that I soon lost interest and began looking about for distractions. Where were Robbie Munro's knees when you needed them? I had resorted to a minute examination of the pattern on my teacup when Lady Dalfad ignited my curiosity with a remark.

"Eh? What's that ye said?" asked the marchioness, who'd obviously been paying as little attention to the countess as I had been.

Mistaking the marchioness's inattention for deafness, Lady Dalfad raised her voice. "I said, I was quite surprised when Vicker applied for the position as deputy master. I've known him for years, and his mother before him. She was an Erskine, you'll recall."

The marchioness spooned jam onto a scone. "An Erskine, ye say?"

"Yes. You see the difficulty?"

"Aye," said the marchioness, through a mouthful of jam and scone. "The Clearanthes."

I didn't see the difficulty, but then I was not acquainted with the family Clearanth.

"Indeed," sniffed the countess. "The Erskines lost everything."

Thank God for the countess. The marchioness must have been referring to the Highland Clearances, when Scottish and English landlords had driven many of the Highland clans from their lands to create room for more sheep. The English Crown had stood idly by, not daring to interfere as most of the landlords were supporters of the monarchy. A good many families had been ruined in this way and carried a longstanding grudge against the English government as a result.

"Vicker's mother was infuriated at the loss of the family home and their farms. I can't imagine that she'd countenance a son of hers working for the Queen."

"She had a son?" asked the marchioness, squinting at the assortment of cakes on the tea tray.

"Vicker," Lady Dalfad said irritably. "Vicker's mother was an Erskine. That's why I think it odd that he applied to work for the Queen; no self-respecting member of the family would do so."

The marchioness's hand scrabbled through the folds of her skirt. "Where's my snuff, Idina?"

I fished the box from the bag at my feet and sprang up, but before I could reach the old lady's side, her eyes had alighted on the sugar bowl on the tray. Before I could stop her, she'd removed the lid and raised a heaping spoon to her nose.

"Oh, dear God," said the Countess in horror.

Now, I have never inhaled sugar in my life, and I can assure that I never will, after witnessing that scene. When the sugar crystals hit her sinus cavities, the marchioness blinked. Her head jerked back, and her eyes rolled upward until all I could see were the whites, yellow with age and threaded with thin red veins. She looked like a horse that had just had a pistol go off in its ear. Then her face twisted, and I knew the moment of reckoning was at hand. I seized the antimacassar from the back of the marchioness's chair and clapped it over her nose and mouth. I must admit the explosion was quieter than I had expected. Unlike the sneeze that followed the ingestion of the face powder, this one was almost subdued, sounding more like the crack of thunder than a blast of dynamite on a building site. Still, it was loud enough to render the countess mute with shock.

The marchioness sniffled and shook her head. "Lord, I must speak to that Mitchell. This batch of snuff is singularly unnatural."

"You inhaled sugar from the sugar bowl," the countess said icily.

"Nonsense. What a remarkable thing to say." The marchioness looked offended.

"Well, you did."

Had the countess asked my advice (no chance of that ever happening, of course), I'd have told her to drop the topic, but Lady Dalfad had worked herself up into a rare state of revulsion, and she spent the next quarter hour haranguing the marchioness for her egregious lack of manners, while the old lady grew increasingly sulky and silent. The party broke up shortly after, as you might expect, with the countess and her maid Effie flouncing out, and me petting and teasing the marchioness until I was rewarded with a smile as I dumped her into bed for a short rest before dinner. I closed the door with relief, wondering how many small containers of various materials might be found around a house the size of Balmoral and how I would ever manage to keep the marchioness from inadvertently dipping into the contents of, say, the Queen's tea caddy. One thing I knew for sure: I'd have to keep the old bag away from the gun room; there was no telling what might happen if she filled her sinuses with a hefty dose of gunpowder. She might even level the castle.

FIVE

I returned to my room to find an envelope bearing my name. I ripped it open and found a note from French, with instructions to feign illness and skip services at the kirk on the morrow, which was Sunday. For a moment I puzzled over this, wondering why the bloody man would ever imagine I'd spend the Sabbath sitting through a joyless service with a group of glum Scots, but then I recalled that Miss Boss had mentioned that all Balmoral servants were required to attend kirk. Accordingly, I woke up the next morning with a crippling headache and a bad case of diarrhea (imaginary, of course, but I've found that nothing works faster at clearing a room than a case of diarrhea). Flora heard the news, offered to bring me a cup of tea and looked grateful when I declined. After she'd gone, I rose and dressed, pulling on the hideous clothes I'd worn on the train, found a muffler and gloves in Flora's drawer, and slunk silently out the servants' entrance.

French had included directions in his letter to our rendezvous, and just beyond the dairy barn I found the path he'd instructed me to take. It wound steadily upward along a steepish incline, the landscape littered with boulders and a stand of spruce trees soaring overhead. There was snow on the ground and ice on the path, and I picked my way carefully. It was dead quiet out here in the woods, except for the occasional raucous cawing of a rook (which, the first time I heard it, caused me to look over my shoulder for the marchioness).

After thirty minutes of hard walking, I topped a rise and stood for a moment, catching my breath. I suppose the view was superb, if you cared for scenery: snow-covered crags that towered into the sky, a sweeping vista down the hill I'd climbed, with smoke rising from the castle chimneys and the pale granite of the building gleaming in the sun, acres of windswept moorland, the shimmer of tiny, jewel-like lakes in the distance. The air was fresh and cold, and smelled of pine and wood smoke. I shudder when I think about it. It's abnormal, living where you can't see a pub sign from your window.

I tightened my muffler against the wind and scuttled down the path. In the valley below stood a stone hut, thatched with heather. It looked cold and lonely and isolated, the latter state no doubt being the reason French had selected it as our meeting place. I looked in vain for a curl of smoke from the flue, but the place appeared deserted. I hoped French had at least brought along a bottle of whisky to keep us warm.

I circled around to the rear of the hut and whistled softly (not really my idea of proper etiquette when making a house call, but I had been directed to indulge in these antics per French's instructions). I was answered by a low trill, which meant French was in residence and no one else was about. Well, a knock on the door would have ascertained that just as easily. I sighed as I waded through the snow to the back door.

French ushered me into the kitchen of the hut, after scanning the countryside to ensure I had not been followed. Vincent was at a wobbly table in the corner, wolfing bread and cheese and drinking tea from a flask.

"'Allo, India," the scamp said.

"And hello to you, Vincent. Is there any more of that tea?"

He shoved the flask across the table. "'Elp yourself. French brought it along."

"And I'm glad he did." I found a tin mug on the windowsill (cold as ice, it was) and poured myself a cup. The tea was tepid at best, but I drank it anyway, grateful for even the slightest warmth.

French sliced more bread and cheese, and we tucked into our Sunday repast. He was looking a bit peaked, as if he'd spent the evening before quaffing copious amounts of liquor, breathing cigar smoke and laughing at asinine jokes. How I wish I had been there. He pulled himself together, though, like the dedicated agent he was, and chaired the meeting for us.

"We've each had a couple of days to form some impressions and take note of any peculiarities," he said. "I thought we should share our initial information and discuss our next moves. Why don't you go first, India?"

For Vincent's sake, I repeated what I had told French about Vicker and Munro. "There's a bit more to add," I said, and launched into my account of tea with Lady Dalfad and the marchioness.

"I'm sure that Flora said Robbie had served as a footman before, but Lady Dalfad wasn't convinced. And the information about Vicker being descended from a Highland family done out of their inheritance is suggestive. Have you heard anything from Robshaw yet about Robbie or Vicker?"

"Nothing," said French. "But then I only told him yesterday, after we met."

The mention of our "meeting" (if one could call the mugging I had suffered at French's hands such) reminded me that French and I had unfinished business. Unfortunately, with Vincent sitting there, it was not the time to discuss it. I gave French a scowl, though, just to let him know he was not getting off lightly.

French ignored the scowl. "And, of course, I've heard nothing more from Robshaw about Red Hector." He described the seventh Baronet of Dochfour to Vincent while the boy chewed ruminatively on a crust of bread.

"Blimey," he said when French had finished. "Them hassassin fellows are all over the place."

"Any out in the stables?" I asked.

"I got one suspect. Archie Skene."

"The fellow with the eyebrows?" asked French, and I remembered the old bloke with the caterpillars over his eyes who had stepped forward to help Vincent with French's horse on our arrival at Balmoral.

"Aye, that's 'im. 'E's a groom at the castle. 'E used to be the 'ead groom. 'E saddled the Queen's pony and led 'er around the castle grounds, makin' sure the ole bat didn't fall off, but then this Brown bloke comes along and pushes ole Archie out of the way. 'Pears the Queen likes this Brown bloke so much that she lets 'im do whatever 'e wants, includin' takin' over from Archie. Least that's the way Archie tells it."

I reached for a slab of cheddar. "And that made Archie mad enough to kill the Queen?"

"There's more to it, o' course. That Brown 'as a nasty temper, plus 'e's pickled 'alf the time, and 'im and Archie got into it real bad one day. I guess Archie 'cused Brown of shaggin' the Queen"—French's eyebrows climbed his forehead, but Vincent ploughed on, unfazed by the facts of life—"and Brown went off like a firecracker. 'E and Archie climbed into one another, and pretty soon there was blood all over the yard and the 'orses were thrashin' about and the stable boys were takin' bets and all the maids 'ad run out of the 'ouse to see wot all the blather was about."

Vincent stopped for breath.

"Goodness," I said. "I'm surprised Archie's still employed. I thought anyone who crossed Brown did so at his peril."

"That's wot everyone says about Brown. Them stable boys and grooms 'ead in the other direction when they see 'im comin'."

French broke in impatiently. "Finish your story, Vincent. What happened between Brown and Archie Skene?"

"Brown went straight to the Queen and told 'er that 'e and Archie had been into it, and she oughter fire Archie. So the Queen called Archie in and give 'im a tongue-lashin' 'e says 'e won't soon forget. Then Archie acted all sheepish and 'pologized about a 'undred times, and the Queen said 'e could stay, but 'e couldn't be 'ead groom no more."

"Brown must not have told her that Archie accused Brown of, er . . ."

"Shagging her," I said, finishing French's sentence for him. I am amazed at how even the doughtiest of men can't bear to refer to the act of sexual congress without stammering or blushing.

"If Brown had, I expect Archie would have been out on his ear," said French.

"Instead he's still here, nursing a grudge against Brown and presumably the Queen. Is it a grudge strong enough to provoke him to kill the Queen?"

"And is it merely personal animosity, or is there a connection to the Sons of Arbroath?" French mused.

"Would the Sons use Archie to assassinate the Queen?" I asked. "He needn't care a fig for Scottish independence, just be suggestible enough to be persuaded by someone like the Marischal."

French stroked his chin. "What do you think, Vincent? Is Archie's hatred of the Queen sufficient to drive him to kill her? Or would he be a willing tool for someone else, perhaps someone he looked up to?"

"Are ye askin' me if the man is stupid enough to do someone else's killin'? Naw, I wouldn't think so. 'E ain't no fool, not Archie. I don't think even Dizzy could talk Archie into doin' somethin' 'e don't want to. But 'e might do it on 'is own. After the Queen dressed 'im down, the stable boys say 'e ain't been the same. Spends all 'is time ravin' that 'Er Majesty ain't fit to run the country if she ain't got better sense than to 'ang around with that bastard Brown."

I had to admit to some general views along the same line.

"We have four suspects," said French. "Not bad work in such a short time. Now we must decide how to proceed."

"We've already got Robshaw on Vicker, Robbie Munro and your friend Red Hector," I said.

"He might not find anything. Remember, the Sons of Arbroath are reputed to be well organized and very cunning. They will go to great lengths to cover their tracks."

"So hit's down to us, his hit?" Vincent wiggled like a setter pup. "We got to do some more investigatin', ain't we?"

"We do," said French. "We've got to see if we can turn up anything else, but we must go about it cautiously."

"Search their quarters?" I asked.

"Yes, I think that's our next move. Vincent, you'll look through Archie's room for anything that strikes you as suspicious. I'll go through Red Hector's things."

"I'll search Robbie's room and Vicker's as well. All the servants are at kirk today. This will be my best opportunity to toss some rooms." I glanced at Vincent. "What about Archie?"

"Aye, 'e's off to wear out the knees of 'is trousers, just like all the rest. I'd lay odds I could be done in 'alf an 'our."

"I doubt Red Hector is contemplating his sins right now, though he might be committing a few. If he's not off for a canter, he may be sleeping off last night's excesses, but I'll try my best." French rose from the table. "Shall we meet back here between luncheon and teatime? After a heavy meal, I wouldn't be surprised if the whole household doesn't have a lie down."

That sounded like the perfect way to spend a Sunday afternoon. I hoped I had time to grab a hot meal and forty winks between my bouts of breaking and entering.

I hightailed it back to the castle along the path, with Vincent and French slipping away in opposite directions. This seemed like an inordinate amount of skullduggery for a situation that had yet to prove dangerous, but I supposed French was correct and we should be on our toes. The Sons of Arbroath and the Marischal could strike at any minute, and it wouldn't do for French, Vincent and me to be standing about with our mouths open and our thumbs up our arses. So I slipped and slid along the icy path, cursing the rocks and paying no mind to the scenery until the great pile of granite hove into view, and I stole in through the servants' entrance, keeping a wary eye out for any other serfs who'd shirked the Sunday services.

I conducted a quick reconnaissance of the kitchen, pantries and buttery, and was about to mount the stairs to the servants' quarters when I heard a clattering in the silver room, followed shortly by the sound of an expensive piece of the Queen's silver crashing onto the floor and an oath that would have burned even Vincent's ears. I stuck my head around the door to find Robbie Munro swearing a blue streak and trying to pick up the salver he'd just dropped, a task which was not made any easier by the fact that he was wearing a pair of white cotton gloves, smeared with silver polish. He'd just succeeded in getting a grip on the platter when I pushed open the door.

"Hello, Robbie," I said brightly.

The tray slipped out of his hands again and hit the floor for a second time.

"Damnation," said Robbie, spitting me with a glance. He fumbled for the salver, fingers sliding over the surface until he managed to pin it between his gloved hands. Gingerly, he lifted it to the table with all the proficiency of a newly ordained vicar conducting his first infant baptism. It slipped from his fingers just as he was about to set it down on the table, clanging loudly against the oak surface.

"Damnation," he repeated. His face was pink beneath his golden red curls, and a bead of moisture had appeared on his upper lip. "I thought you were sick and couldn't go to kirk. Why are you traipsing about, scaring the wits out of me?"

"I thought a breath of fresh air might help my headache. And why aren't you over at the church with the gospel grinders? I thought the Queen made everyone go to services."

"I volunteered to polish the silver for today's luncheon."

I didn't believe that for one minute. Granted, sitting in a wooden pew for a couple of hours while some dreary padre droned on about fornication, death and gluttony (on second thought, probably not the appropriate topic when Her Royal Rotundity attended services) was worth avoiding at all costs, but not, I thought, by volunteering to do an extra bit of housework around the castle. Especially when one did not seemed particularly skilled at the job. Robbie looked like he'd been wrestling crocodiles instead of polishing candlesticks: his curls were tumbled, there was that faint sheen of sweat on his face, and his collar was awry. I suppose I have a nasty, suspicious mind, but I wondered if Robbie had been doing what I had been planning to do, namely ransacking someone's personal belongings.

"Dull work," I said, nodding at the pile of hardware laid out on the table.

"Yes, and it has to be done within the hour." Robbie glanced at the clock on the wall and picked up the polishing cloth.

"Still, it must be exciting, working at Balmoral for the Queen."

"I suppose it's a step up from the marchioness," Robbie said grudgingly. "Some might think it an honour to work for Her Majesty, but it's not what I ever expected to be doing with my life." He looked distastefully at the silver. "Especially working up a sweat putting a shine on all this."

"You must prefer the outdoors."

"What?" Robbie looked up from his perusal of a pepper pot. "Oh, yes. Rather be outside any day than stuck indoors."

"Then why be a footman?" I asked. "Couldn't you get on here as a ghillie?"

"Well, there's my uncle, you see. He got me the place here, and I couldn't disappoint him. He needed another footman. One of the others had left."

"But if not for your uncle, you'd probably be building fishing traps or stalking stags?"

Robbie grinned. "That would be better than polishing fish forks."

"But weren't you a footman already, at Stirling, or was it Melrose?"

Robbie's smile faded. "Right. Well, we can't always do what we want, can we? Sometimes we have to accept our responsibilities."

I'd pricked him, no doubt. But exactly why, I couldn't work out. Because he didn't want to be a footman? Or because he wasn't one?

"I've got to finish this," said Robbie, turning away abruptly. "Everyone will be back from kirk soon and ready to dine."

"Then I'll leave you to it," I said, and did, but not before I caught him gazing thoughtfully at me as I made my exit.

With Robbie safely tucked up in the butler's pantry putting a gloss on the chafing dishes, I ran upstairs to shed my coat and gloves, then hotfooted it down the corridor to Robbie's room. There was no lock on Flora's door, and I thought it likely the same was true of Robbie's, Miss Boss being the type of housekeeper who believed privacy was a luxury reserved for the aristocracy. Robbie's door swung open at a touch, and I closed it hastily behind me. The room was as plain as Flora's, with a single brass bed that had seen much use, a dingy rag rug on the floor, a chest against the wall and a small table by the bed, which held a candlestick and a dime novel with a lurid cover (*Meehataska: The Scourge of the Mounties*). I suppose after a day of helping old duffers into their socks and pouring tea for the Lady Dalfads of the world, Robbie felt entitled to a bit of light relief. I flicked through the pages, looking for the sort of things assassins might hide in bad literature—notes of assignations, lists of co-conspirators and that sort of thing—but I was disappointed.

I moved to the chest and began rummaging methodically

through each drawer. I'd rifled through a sparse collection of vests, drawers (should have kept the gloves for that task), socks, collars and shirts when my hand touched paper. Probably news-paper, used to line the drawers, but I pulled it out anyway, very gently so that I wouldn't tear the thing, and found myself staring down at a political tract, cheaply printed in smeared ink on the flimsiest of paper. The cross of St. Andrew was emblazoned across the top, and under it, in bold letters, the headline proclaimed, "Arise, Sons of Arbroath, and Free Scotland from English Bond-age!" The writer had added a verse from Robert Burns (a nice touch, I thought, if a bit heavy on the exclamation marks):

> Lay the proud usurpers low!
> Tyrants fall in every foe!
> Liberty's in every blow!
> Let us do—or die!

There were a half-dozen articles with titles such as "Scotland Betrayed" and "The Audacity of English Governance," but the one that caught my attention was an article written by "Marcus Junius Brutus" (whoever he was when he was at home), which, if you know your Shakespeare, was not surprisingly a screed against the tyranny of Vicky, the present Monarch of the Realm, and a call to arms to exterminate Her Royal Highness for the good of the Scottish people. I dug under the clothes and unearthed a few more polemics, all of the same type, advocating that the Queen be dispatched with haste, along with any other English scum cur-rently exercising dominion over Scottish affairs. I pondered the idea that the handsome Robbie Munro might be an ardent Scot-tish nationalist who saw himself as Brutus and the Queen as Ju-lius Caesar. It would be a shame for such a handsome lad to end up on the gallows, and a waste of muscular calves, but I supposed it wasn't that much of a stretch to see the chap as a potential killer. What did I know about the man, anyway? I'd have to tell French about the propaganda I'd found, and I'd have to keep a close watch on Robbie, which would be nearly impossible given my responsibilities with the marchioness. I was considering this dilemma, making a final sweep of the drawers and rooting through Robbie's meager belongings, when my hand touched something that I recognized immediately: a revolver.

The Queen's party and the servants had returned to the castle from kirk by the time I'd finished examining the .450 Tranter center-fire revolver hidden under Munro's socks. He might be a sportsman, but no self-respecting woodsman would pot a rabbit with that weapon; there'd be nothing left but fluff. When I heard the carriage wheels in the drive, I hurriedly replaced the gun in the drawer just as I had found it and scampered back to Flora's room, where I donned my uniform, smoothing my hair and pinning on my cap just as Flora walked in.

"Feeling better?" she asked.

I gave her what I hoped was the wan smile of a semi-invalid. "A bit. But I expect the marchioness will need me before luncheon."

"You've plenty of time. It's a madhouse downstairs. The Queen makes everyone go to services, then we have to sweat like slaves to get luncheon ready for her. She's cross if she doesn't get fed by two o'clock."

That was welcome news, as it was only one o'clock now, and that meant all the servants would be engaged in preparing luncheon, with the toffs off to their rooms for a quick nap or a tot of sherry. Vicker would no doubt be occupied with all the details of serving the Queen a fortifying meal of a dozen courses, and I would have an opportunity to slip into his room and fish about for incriminating evidence.

I left Flora changing back into her working clothes and scurried down the stairs to the main floor, where Vicker's room was located. I peeked into the kitchen, to see Miss Boss and Cook working like stevedores, the former bullying the maids and the latter bustling around with her cap askew, her usually genial expression replaced by one of intense concentration. I passed on, before Miss Boss noticed my appearance and dispatched me to the marchioness.

Outside the butler's pantry the footmen were lined up, with McAra, the head butler, giving them the once-over while Vicker stood to one side, teeth clenched and his face pale, shifting nervously on his feet like a pugilist ready to step in the ring.

McAra consulted the paper in his hand. "And the buffet will include a game pie and a woodcock pie, as well as beef and tongue. For the fish course, the guests have their choice of turbot or sole."

Vicker was fidgeting restlessly, his watch in his hand. "For God's sake, McAra, can't you move this along? We've got to be ready to serve in less than an hour."

McAra turned toward Vicker, as slowly and stately as a transatlantic liner. "With all due respect, sir, I know what I'm about here. I've served the Queen these fourteen years, and we'll have the food on the table and serve it up just as we always have, to Her Majesty's satisfaction." He turned back to his charges. "Now then, *éclairs au chocolat* for dessert."

Vicker made a strangled noise in his throat and stalked off in the direction of the kitchen, where doubtless he would soon be irritating Miss Boss and Cook. The sweat on his bald head glittered in the light of the gas lamps. He was on edge, no doubt about it, but was it because he was here to assassinate the Queen, or had he just forgotten the place cards for luncheon?

I bobbed and ducked my way past McAra and the battalion of footmen, and once out of sight, I hared away to Vicker's room. It was risky, with Vicker still stalking the halls, but I calculated that he would stay in the center of activity and not retreat to his room until luncheon had ended and the Queen was safely tucked away for a snooze. I could only hope that in his agitation, Vicker hadn't wet himself, necessitating a quick trip to his room and a change of linen.

The deputy master of the household rated a far superior room to that allocated to the Marchioness of Tullibardine's maid. The double bed looked comfortable and the quilts warm. Vicker also had a writing desk and a drinks table with etched crystal glasses and a half-empty bottle of rather superior whisky, along with a set of bookshelves and a cozy armchair near the fire in the inevitable Royal Stewart tartan. But the room had an air of seediness about it, as though the occupant wasn't quite a respectable fellow. A dip pen and several sheets of writing paper were scattered on the desktop, and the stopper to the inkwell had not been replaced. A dirty collar hung over the back of the armchair, and one of the whisky glasses had been used, then set upon the polished surface of the bedside table. I picked up the glass and found it sticky to the touch; a thin ring of spilled whisky had eaten into the polish of the table. Perhaps Vicker was a drunk, which might go some way toward explaining the tremor in his hands, and his pale, perspiring face. I could not imagine, however, that the Queen (as persnickety as she was said to be) would tolerate a rum hound as deputy master.

I foraged through Vicker's belongings at a flying pace, keeping an ear cocked toward the door in the event the poor bugger felt

the need for another infusion of liquid courage to quiet the
nerves. The wardrobe held only duplicates of the same getup
Vicker wore every day: starched white collar and shirt, black neck-
tie, waistcoat and suit. He had a pair of polished black half boots,
a sturdy pair of hobnailed boots in brown leather, and a baggy
suit of dusty green tweed (presumably for his rare moments of
relaxation away from the confines of the castle). I perused the
bookshelves, pulling out the volumes and letting the pages flutter through my fingers. There were a few improving books of ser-
mons and essays on the moral condition of man (the pages had
yet to be cut on these; apparently, neither the room's previous occupants nor its current one were overly concerned with their im-
mortal souls) and the complete works of Sir Walter Scott. I chose
Rob Roy from the shelf and thumbed through it, but there were
no hidden messages written in secret code, no underlining of
words that marked the time and place of the Queen's assassination. If owning a set of the laird of Abbotsford's books indicated
disloyalty to Her Majesty, then half the literate population of
Britain would be considered traitors. I stifled a yawn and moved
to the desk.

The sheets of paper I'd noticed earlier were wrinkled and blot-
ted with ink, as though a schoolboy had been tasked with neatly
copying out his lessons but failed numerous times. A drawing under the writing paper caught my eye. I moved the sheets aside to
have a gander and found myself staring at an architect's drawing
of the castle interior, with the inhabitants of each room marked
in pencil. A useful thing for an assassin to have in his possession
but equally as useful to the deputy master of the household, who
doubtless had to know where to send the chamber pots and
which earl required a spittoon. I replaced the drawing and arranged the papers over it, taking a moment to hold them to the

light to see if they revealed anything incriminating. I could make out a faint impression on one of the sheets: "Dear Mother." I put it down and sighed. I suppose assassins can be dutiful sons, but somehow I couldn't imagine anyone as dull as Vicker having the gumption to thrust a pistol to the Queen's head and shout, *"Sic semper tyrannis,"* as he pulled the trigger.

One of the sheets had been crumpled into a ball and discarded in the wastebasket. I picked it up and smoothed it out on the desk. I might as well be thorough. With luck, I'd stumble across the killer's to-do list:

1. Make sure gun is loaded (or knife sharpened, as the case may be).
2. Buy railway ticket.
3. Sign last will and testament.
4. Pack sandwiches.

But I found nothing so explicit. Vicker had indeed been penning a letter to his mumsy, but there was no way for me to tell whether he'd actually finished the missive and posted it. Certainly, the contents of the sheet I held in my hand were evocative.

"Dear Mother," it read, "by the time you receive this letter I shall be gone, bound for South Africa."

I filed away the information to report to French, crushed the letter in my hand and dropped it back into the wastebasket. I made a final survey of the room, rummaged under the mattress, tapped all the stones on the fireplace for secret hiding places and searched the oak floorboards for the same. Satisfied that I had missed nothing, I poked my head out of Vicker's room and scanned the hall. Damn and blast! At the end of the corridor, the deputy master had waylaid a footman and was barking instructions at him like a drill sergeant. It wasn't the footman's plight that aroused my anxiety, but the fact that he and Vicker were positioned so that I'd have to squeeze past them to return to Flora's room, and I had no real reason to be loitering in this particular hallway. There was no choice but to bugger off in the opposite direction and take a circuitous route back to my sanctuary. To my right, just steps from Vicker's doorway, was a convenient corner to disappear around. Of course, if Vicker happened to look up and see my back vanishing down the passage, it might occur to him that I had to have emerged from one of the rooms that lined the hall, and it might have been his own room I had just exited.

If I lingered any longer, Vicker would finish his tirade against the footman and turn toward his quarters. It was time to go. I took a deep breath and edged out of the room, closing Vicker's door gently behind me. I was torn between the urge to bolt and the desire to appear completely innocent of tossing Vicker's room. I adopted a nice compromise, I think, moving purposefully but with speed, as though I had just gotten a summons that Vicky needed me to spoon up the pudding. I fairly flew along the hall, my feet skimming the floor, until I reached the corner and was home free. Then I took a moment to collect myself and consult the rather hazy plan of the castle I carried around in my head. From what I could recollect of the layout of the place, the quickest route back to Flora's room was a shortcut through the guest wing. I wouldn't look out of place mucking about there; I could always claim a summons from the marchioness if I was seen.

I was pattering along the main floor of the guest wing, wondering if I might bump into French (which reminded me that I still owed him a punch in the chops for taking liberties with my person) when the portly figure of the Prince of Wales stepped into my path. It was French's fault; if I hadn't been fulminating over the way he'd slapped my bum, I'd have been on the lookout for Bertie. It was common knowledge that you didn't want to be caught alone with the heir to the throne, as you were liable to be dragged into a broom closet and impregnated. I added this latest issue to the list of those that I meant to take up with French the next time I saw him.

"It's Miss Black, isn't it?" Bertie asked in a jovial voice. "Friend of Mr. French's, I believe."

I tried to blush and look virginal, which as you can imagine is infernally difficult for me. "I've made his acquaintance, sir, but we're hardly friends."

This turned out to be the wrong thing to say. Bertie raised his eyebrows and smoothed his whiskers with a thumb. "Ah, so I wouldn't be stepping on the old boy's toes if I offered my own friendship to you?"

Bugger, bugger, bugger. How to play this? Saucy and pert, a flirtatious promise of a later assignation (that would take place when Hades iced over)? No, that would likely just inflame the randy chap. Shy and demure, a maid uncorrupted by men? From what I'd heard of the prince, he liked nothing better than deflowering the innocent. So, I was bound to rouse the old boy's predatory instincts either way.

"I'd indeed be honoured if you bestowed your friendship upon me, Your Highness." I edged away from the plump lecher, trying to put some space between us. Where was Miss Boss when you needed her?

The prince erased the distance between us, moving with surprising quickness for a prize porker. He touched my cheek with one plump finger, stroking it lightly.

"I've a nice bottle of champers in my room. I was planning to have a glass before luncheon. Care to join me?"

I ducked my head. "Oh, sir, I couldn't. The marchioness is expecting me."

The prince was beginning to look impatient. Apparently, I was taking rather longer than a maid should in succumbing to his charms. "Damn the marchioness. Come on, girl. I've only a few minutes before I have to be downstairs."

He encircled my wrist with his hand, put his arm around my shoulders and began dragging me toward the nearest room. Now, I had no doubt that I could make him stop this behavior in an instant; all it required was a swift blow to the conkers and Bertie would be collapsed on the floor, gasping like a hooked trout. But what that might mean for my future, I could easily guess.

I was just about to capitulate gracefully, resigning myself to a brief contemplation of the state of England (Bertie had said he had only a few minutes) when a raucous cry split the air.

"Christ," said Bertie, bounding away from me like a scalded cat. His head swiveled as he searched for the source of that piercing scream. No doubt he expected to see his mater bearing down on him, flourishing a riding crop and ready to use it on her wandering boy.

"Isadora?" the voice croaked again. The marchioness came weaving down the hallway, her cane thumping in a ragged rhythm against the stone floor. "Where have ye been? I sent for ye an hour ago." She hacked up a clot of wet snuff and spit it on the floor.

I shot the prince a regretful glance, as if to say, "Sorry, Bert, maybe next time," knowing full well that he'd never get a second chance at me, not without employing a few rascals to carry me off against my will. Bertie retreated sullenly, with a thunderous look at my rescuer, but he had the grace to nod his head at her as he passed her.

The marchioness waited until he was out of sight, then rounded on me, spraying snuff. "What did I tell ye about that man? Ye're not tryin' to cozy up to that ne'er-do-well, are ye? Ye'll be sorry if ye do, just mark my words. Ye'll end up with regrets, not to mention a fat baby to feed."

"Oh, no, ma'am. I know my station in life. I wouldn't dare make overtures to a member of the royal family." Especially one who resembled a sperm whale (aptly named, that species, when compared to our Bertie). "His Highness stopped me in the hallway as I was on my way to your room." I didn't challenge the marchioness's allegation that she had sent for me; she might very well have done so while I was busy tossing my suspects' rooms. On the other hand, the old dear might have imagined she'd summoned me and gone lurching through the halls in search of her missing maid. Whichever the case might be, I was grateful for her intervention, saving me a quick (and, damn it all, free) session with England's next king.

I escorted her back to her room, spiffed her up for a lengthy stay at the feed table and left her in the custody of one of the footmen. Then I took myself down to the kitchen and put on my own feedbag. Cook had laid out a sumptuous repast, and I fortified myself with rare roast beef, Yorkshire pudding and apple crumble with a slathering of yellow custard. It was a far cry from Mrs. Drinkwater's boiled beef and cabbage, and I pondered the circumstances of life that entitled a podgy neurotic who communed with the dead to a chef of Cook's caliber, merely because she was the British monarch, while I had to make do with a cook whose best dishes might only be appreciated by the inhabitants of a besieged city. After the meal, I wanted nothing more than to collapse on my bed for a nap, but there was still the marchioness to see to (I'd heard no report of explosions in the dining room, so presumably, the marchioness had refrained from dipping into her snuffbox with the Queen present). I trundled back upstairs and met the marchioness at her door, removed her shoes and dress, then wrapped her in a dressing gown and stuffed her into bed. I added logs to the fire and drew the curtains, and I hadn't even left the room before she was snoring like an ancient bull mastiff.

Mercifully, Flora was nowhere to be seen when I returned to her room. Probably flirting with Robbie Munro, since the servants had Sunday afternoons off until teatime. I donned my outdoor clothes again (I debated adding Flora's muffler and gloves but decided against it; I didn't want her to find them missing) and crept out of the castle. I hoped Miss Boss had retired for a siesta; it would be deuced awkward to run into her and have to explain that while I was too ill to attend kirk that morning, I now felt up to a longish hike through the woods. However, I gained the outer door without incident and set off up the steep rise behind the castle.

Half an hour later, huffing like a steam train, I had reached the stone hut. Once again I followed French's instructions, whistling softly to let him know I had arrived. The back door opened and French appeared, waving me inside. He still hadn't lit a fire, but there was a bottle of whisky on the table and three crude tumblers of clay. Vincent was already nursing a drink, the tops of his ears and the tip of his nose a bright cherry colour from the cold.

"Did you have any difficulty in getting away from the castle?" asked French.

"No, all the servants were having a rest."

"Or a snog," said Vincent, sniggering.

"You've a nasty mind for a young sod," I said. "But you're probably right."

"Would I be imposing if I asked you two to focus on the matter at hand?" French asked, rather superciliously, I thought, given that Vincent and I were doing this for free, not to mention chapping our hands in the process while French hovered around warm fires and depleted the Queen's liquor supply.

"Righto, guv," Vincent said. He swallowed some whisky and topped off his glass. "I got into Archie's room with no trouble at all." Vincent being an accomplished cracksman, I suspected he was telling the truth. "There wasn't much there, only a shotgun under the bed that looks about a 'undred years old. A twenty-eight gauge, so I reckon Archie uses hit for rats and crows and the like. It ain't exactly the weapon I'd choose to kill 'Er 'Ighness, 'less you could get in real close, and then, 'er bein' as fat as she is, I reckon the shot just might hirritate 'er."

French hid a smile behind his tumbler of whisky. "Well done, Vincent. There was nothing to connect Archie to the Marischal or the Sons of Arbroath?"

"I didn't see nothin'," and I went through the place hinch by hinch."

"Well, I can't say I was any more successful at turning up incriminating evidence in Red Hector's room," said French. "Naturally, he's got weapons: one of those *sgian dubhs* the Scots love, and a brace of pistols in a fancy case. There's no reading material in the room, other than some pornographic pictures under his combinations and a dozen reports from breeders with a wealth of detail about bloodlines, dams and studs."

"Wot's a skin do?" asked Vincent.

"A ceremonial knife, with a short blade and pommel. The Scots wear it tucked into their socks."

Vincent mulled over this addition to his knowledge of the world's weapons.

"And how did you fare, India?" French asked.

"I think I've done rather well." I informed them of the letter in

Vicker's wastebasket. "He's clearly planning on leaving the country, and soon."

"'E could be 'avin' a 'oliday," said Vincent.

"A man of his class would more likely spend it in Brighton than South Africa." I sipped the whisky and found it very fine. So far, it was the only thing I'd enjoyed in Scotland.

"I shall get Robshaw on it right away," said French. "Did you find anything else of value?"

I told them about the house plan with the names of the guests lettered on it. "It's suggestive but not terribly suspicious. As deputy master of the household, I think it's something Vicker would likely use."

"'Less there was a big ole 'X' on 'Er Majesty's room, hit probably don't mean nothin'."

"As much as I hate to acknowledge your perspicacity, Vincent, I expect you're right."

"Wot's that mean?" Vincent bridled.

"She's flattering your intelligence, Vincent, although in a rather oblique way," French said. Vincent's brow wrinkled at the word "oblique," but as it had been issued by his hero, he did not demand an explanation.

French twirled his tumbler in his hands. "What about Munro?"

"Ah, there's an interesting lad." I informed the two of them about the reading material and the revolver I had found among Munro's possessions.

"Hit's 'im," Vincent pronounced firmly. "Got to be, with all that hincriminatin' evidence."

"He's almost too perfect as the villain," mused French. "Robshaw shall hear of this immediately, of course. In the meantime, India, you've got to keep a close eye on the man."

"And how am I supposed to do that? Remember, I'm the zookeeper for the marchioness, and it's not as though I could follow Robbie around anyway, even if I had free time on my hands."

French dismissed these rather serious obstacles with a vague wave. "Oh, you'll figure out something. You always do. I'm not concerned about what he's doing while on duty, but rather what he gets up to when he's off the clock."

"I don't think servants ever get off the clock. I shall have to inform the marchioness that I am unavailable after midnight and before breakfast." I tipped my cup at French. "When Munro is on duty, you'll have to see that he doesn't get close to the Queen. I mean, if you're not preoccupied with pinching the maids and getting sozzled with Bertie and Red Hector."

French gave me the glare that comment deserved.

"I s'pose you want me to follow Archie around and see that 'e don't get up to nothin' with that shotgun of 'is?"

"Yes, Vincent. If he slips off, try to follow him. But be careful. We don't know yet what we're up against. One or more of these fellows could be members of the Sons of Arbroath, and they could be in league together." French drained his whisky. "I'll get on to Robshaw as soon as I return to the castle. It certainly looks as though Munro is our most likely suspect, but we cannot afford to ignore the others. Let's keep our wits about us."

SIX

It was fully dark by the time I'd navigated my way along the path and down the hill to the castle. The kitchen was bustling with preparations for tea, and I slipped in during the hubbub and reached the safety of Flora's room. I shed my coat and slipped into uniform, then hopped it down to the kitchen again where I found Flora and Effie, Lady Dalfad's maid, sharing a table and a cup of tea. Effie wasn't my first choice as dining companion, and I had been hoping to speak to Flora alone, to see what additional insight she might provide into Munro's background, but that would have to wait for the moment. I poured myself a cup of tea and buttered some bread. Flora was regaling Effie with a tale about a hapless laundress who had burned a hole clean through the Earl of Roseberry's best dinner jacket with a hot iron, which made Flora giggle and Effie purse her lips sanctimoniously. Did the woman ever smile?

"How are you feeling, India?" Flora turned her attention to me.

"Much better, thank you. I had a good rest and now I'm fit as a fiddle." I selected a sandwich from the platter. "And how did you two spend your time off today?"

"I read the Bible," Effie announced. "It is my custom to do so on the Sabbath."

Lord, what a twit.

"What did you get up to, Flora? A walk with handsome Robbie? Or more than a walk?" I grinned conspiratorially at her.

"Och, wouldn't I have liked that?" Flora sighed theatrically. "Alas, the dear boy wasn't anywhere to be found today."

This was interesting news. "I saw him polishing silver before luncheon," I said.

"Did you now?" Flora looked at me sharply. "I thought you were resting this morning."

"Oh, I was. But it seemed a little close indoors, and I thought a breath of air would settle my stomach."

"He must have had something to do, as he wasn't in his room nor anywhere around the castle," said Flora. She snickered. "I should know; I went looking for him."

At this news, Effie looked shocked.

"He wasn't with you, was he?" Flora was smiling at me, but there was an edge to her voice.

I didn't want the girl to imagine that I had fixed my sights on Munro, and I hastened to assure her that my beau back in . . . (bugger, *where* had I supposedly worked before joining the marchioness?) well, my beau was the man for me, and I had forsaken all others.

"Robbie is a catch," I told Flora. "How lucky for you that his uncle lost a footman and Robbie was available to take on the job. Although Robbie told me he'd rather be out in the fresh air than serving soup to the swells. I wonder why he became a footman. Did he ever tell you?"

Flora shrugged. "He's not said a word to me about his job. I just assumed he'd been brought up to be in service, like most of us here at Balmoral. You know, his father was a valet and his mother a housemaid, that sort of thing."

"Do you know his uncle well?"

"Old Murdoch, the under butler? He's a fine gent. He was ever so fond of Prince Albert, and he's totally devoted to the Queen."

"Did you know he had such a luscious nephew?"

"If I had known, I would have been after him to hire Robbie before now," Flora simpered.

"I wonder how he occupied his Sunday afternoon," I mused, sipping tea. "Maybe he went for a walk, being the type that prefers the outdoors."

"Perhaps he found a secluded place where he could smoke," Effie contributed.

A look of suspicion had taken lodgings on Flora's face. Clearly, I had exhibited too avid an interest in the whereabouts of Robbie Munro. It was time to direct the conversation elsewhere.

"I understand Lady Dalfad is one of the Queen's ladies of the bedchamber."

Effie swelled noticeably with pride, as though she inhabited the role along with the countess. "Indeed she is."

"And what, pray tell, does a lady of the bedchamber do?"

Effie looked shocked at my ignorance. Well, I could have informed her that there were "ladies of the bedchamber," and then there were ladies of the bedchamber, and while I could give her quite an education on the role of the latter, I had no idea what the former got up to.

"The countess acts as a companion for the Queen, taking tea with her, or meals. If the Queen desires, she accompanies Her Majesty for outings: a ride in the carriage, perhaps, or a walk, or sometimes she will keep the Queen company while she's sketching or listening to music."

Sounded deuced dull to me, especially since Vicky looked like she'd be about as much fun to be around as a funeral director after Judgment Day.

"And how does one become a lady of the bedchamber?" I asked.

"One is invited by the Queen," said Effie. "It is a great honour." She paused a moment, then added, "Although Lady Dalfad does not always seem to think so."

Flora bit into a fairy cake. "Really? Why is that, I wonder?"

I could have given my own theory (see above) but remained silent.

Effie frowned, either because she was truly puzzled over her employer's lack of enthusiasm for her position with the Queen, or because Effie herself had spilled the beans and wished she hadn't. "I'm not sure," she said hesitantly. "Sometimes she finds it all a bit tiresome, having to do what the Queen wants to do, when the Queen wants to do it."

"That would wear on anyone. At least the Queen doesn't snort castor sugar and spray it all over her dining companions."

That got a laugh, as I knew it would. "By the way, what does the Earl of Dalfad do while his wife gallivants around with the Queen?"

Effie put down her teacup and gave me a look of severe disappointment, like a sixth-form schoolmaster who'd just been told that Epicurus was some Roman chappie with a propensity for hair shirts and self-flagellation. "There is no Earl of Dalfad."

"Is he dead? Is she actually the Dowager Countess?"

Flora looked a bit shocked as well. "Didn't you know, India? There is no Earl of Dalfad. The countess has never been married. She holds the title in her own right."

Their reaction made me uneasy, not to mention puzzled. Every Englishman knows that a countess is a countess because she married an Earl, and that titles pass only along the male line. This means that Dear Old Blighty is run by a small, very select group of braying, inbred nincompoops who inherited their estates and titles by virtue of being the first infant with a penis to pop out of the womb. In this scheme of things, women are just so many brood mares, chosen for their bloodlines or fortunes, and if they're lucky, they acquire in the marriage process a title and a husband who doesn't spend much time at home. I was dying to know how the countess became a countess, but as Flora and Effie had reacted as though any fool would know the answer, I didn't fancy asking more questions. I'd drawn enough attention to myself.

I had attended to my duties, smartening up the marchioness for tea and dinner, filling her snuffbox, sponging the wet snuff from her tea gown and then her evening gown, listening to her croak admiringly of the sweetbreads and meringues she'd shoveled into her gullet, and finally bundling her into bed with a hot water bottle at her feet. I'd collapsed into my own narrow cot, having had a rather long day. I'm a Londoner, born and bred, and probably don't walk four blocks without calling a hansom cab. An hour spent straggling over rocks and hills in the cold air had left me exhausted. I snuggled under the covers and was asleep before I'd pinched out the candle.

I slept soundly until roused by a hammering at the door.

"Miss Black?"

By now I recognized Robbie Munro's voice. I groaned.

"The Marchioness?" I asked. Unnecessarily.

"Yes. She requires your presence."

I struggled upright and into my clothes, wiping the sleep from my eyes and hoping that the old lady hadn't forgotten we'd already read *Troilus and Criseyde*. There was no way I could endure that again.

My employer was propped up in bed with a shawl around her shoulders and a glass of whisky in her hand, which she waved vaguely in my direction, leading me to believe that she'd indulged in a glass or two of the stuff already.

"There ye are, Iphigenia."

Iphigenia? I was beginning to feel like French. Correcting the old lady, however, was just so much wasted breath.

"What can I do for you, my lady?"

"I'm in the mood for a story tonight. Fetch the Bible, and ye can read me the tale of Samson and Delilah."

I breathed a sigh of relief. I had only to plough through three chapters of the Book of Judges. With luck, the old lady would be asleep before Samson got hold of the pillars and buried the Philistines in a heap of rubble. Besides, I quite like Samson, being a towering oak of a fellow and a womanizer who consorted with harlots and ripped lions apart with his bare hands. I'm not sure I buy the part where he slays a thousand men with the jawbone of an ass, or ties torches to the tails of three hundred foxes so they can scamper across the Philistines' fields and set them alight. I suppose a donkey's jaw could be an effective weapon initially, but it would be smashed to bits after crushing twenty craniums or so. And as for the foxes, well, hard to imagine how the first two hundred and ninety-nine occupied their time, waiting for the three hundredth to get prepped and ready ("I say, old chap, ready for a run? Makes a bit of a change from the hounds, what?") But it makes for a good story, and I'd rather read about a hairy brute with superhuman strength than that milquetoast Troilus any day. But I digress.

The marchioness sipped her drink, and I started in with chapter 13, the most boring bit where Manoah and his wife (never identified by name, but you'll find that quite common in the Good Book: the most inconsequential fellow has a moniker and his poor barren wife, who has to do the hard yards, remains anonymous) get a visit from an angel informing them they'll have a son, but for God's sake, whatever you do, don't cut his hair. Things pick up after that, what with the jawbone incident and the foxes and Samson getting married but being betrayed by his wife (another woman who shall remain anonymous because old Samuel the author was either a misogynist or an amnesiac).

I had just gotten to the part where Samson makes the fatal mistake of marrying that trollop Delilah, when the marchioness sat up straight and cackled into her whisky glass.

"Have ye noticed, Iphigenia, that the fair sex always brings a man to his knees?"

I could have elaborated on that theme, but I didn't think the marchioness was strong enough to hear the catalog of sexual positions available at Lotus House.

"Mmm," I murmured in agreement.

"There's Samson, as strong as an ox"—and about as smart as one, I might have added—"and he falls for some little bobtail who's willin' to deliver the secret of his strength to the Philistines."

"Well, the remuneration was tempting," I said. "Eleven hundred pieces of silver from each of the lords of the Philistines if

Delilah discovered Samson's secret. I mean, even I might find that too enticing to pass up."

The marchioness peered at me over the rim of her glass. "I'm not surprised that Samson is taken in by Delilah, for when it comes to women, most men have the brains of a stag durin' the rut, which is to say, none at all. Samson should have confirmed his choice with another lass. She'd likely have seen through Delilah's charms and saved Samson from endin' up as the afternoon matinee for the Philistines."

"You think women are better judges of character than men?" I asked.

"I am," she announced. "I hope ye are as well." She looked uncharacteristically sober for a moment, with the shawl tucked up under her chin and the tumbler of whisky trembling in her hand. "I don't think either of us would have been deceived by Delilah."

I turned a few pages while my mind worked furiously. Had the marchioness rumbled me? If not, why this pointed conversation about treacherous sluts lining their pockets with ill-gotten gains? It was enough to make me wonder if I had allowed my disguise to slip in some way. But even if I had, surely the old topsy was too dotty to have noticed that my service as a lady's maid left something to be desired? And how could she have made the leap from servant to whore? It beggared belief that a woman who couldn't tell snuff from face powder had the wit to uncover a bint in the castle.

I did not have to confront this issue, however, being saved from doing so by the sound of running footsteps thundering past the marchioness's door.

"Who can that be at this hour?" said the marchioness. "Don't they realize people are tryin' to sleep?"

I bit back a response that would have included acid agreement on the lack of consideration on the part of those who disturbed the slumbers of others.

"Don't just sit there like a dolt, Iphigenia. Get up and see what's goin' on out there."

I put down the Bible and cracked the door. Officious-looking servants were bustling along the hallway, and I saw the night-capped heads of half a dozen guests popping out of their rooms. Effie, Lady Dalfad's maid, came scurrying past, her lips pinched and her face colourless.

"Psst, Effie," I hissed. "What's happening?"

She hesitated, torn between ostentatiously going about her duties and being the first to spread the gossip. "It's the Queen. She's fallen ill. Lady Dalfad has been summoned. And Doctor Jenner, the Queen's physician." She scuttled off with an air of self-importance.

"Well?" the marchioness demanded.

"Her Majesty is ill. The doctor has been summoned."

The marchioness snorted. "That idiot Jenner? His idea of treatment is to bring out the leeches and then go off to smoke his pipe. Hope it's nothin' serious; God help the poor woman if it is. Nothin' we can do, of course. I was just about to nod off until all that uproar occurred."

I cursed under my breath.

"I don't believe we'd finished Samson yet. Start again, will ye? At the part where Delilah fastens Samson's hair with a pin. That always gives me a laugh."

So I read the old lady to sleep but not before we'd finished the story of Samson and Delilah, and plodded through several more uplifting stories from the Old Testament. The marchioness was a great one for fire and brimstone, and she kept me at it through the destruction of one city after another by sword and treachery until she finally fell asleep with her empty glass clutched in her hand and her mouth open. I pried the glass from her grasp and smoothed the covers, then slipped off to my own bed. The corridors were silent but for a few grim-faced coves wondering about and conversing in low whispers. As I turned into the servants' stairwell, I caught a glimpse of Dizzy and French conversing by candlelight. I considered trying to attract their attention, but a stern-visaged footman carrying a ewer and a towel was bearing down on me, and I decided to retreat to Flora's room. If French needed me, he knew where to find me.

I was awakened the next morning at dawn (which, I should point out, was only minutes after I had fallen into bed) by the strangled wail of the Great Highland War Pipe.

Flora sighed at the sound. "That's 'Hieland Cathedral.' Isn't it fine? It's one of my favorites."

"I thought it was a calf bawling for its mother," I said sourly.

"Oh, India, you are a card. You'd think you'd never heard a bagpipe before." Flora flung off the covers. "Did you hear? The Queen was sick last night. Her doctor had to come."

I yawned. "I was down the hall with the marchioness when it happened. Do you know what ails Her Highness?"

Flora shrugged. "Dyspepsia, I think. That sounds likely, given how Her Majesty can put away the food. She probably had too much pudding for dinner last night. It's happened before."

I rinsed my face and donned my uniform, shivering. Downstairs I helped myself to a cup of coffee and a plate of sausages and sat down at the table for a leisurely breakfast. The mood was subdued, the usual chatter muffled, and the flirtatious exchanges between maids and footmen that I had heard during previous meals were absent. A young footman, hair slicked back and his kilt and jacket immaculately brushed, sidled up to me. He surveyed the room quickly, reaching into the pocket of his jacket.

"Miss Black? I've a message for you." He glanced around quickly once more, then palmed the envelope into my hand.

I slid the envelope into the waistband of my skirt while I finished my breakfast. Then I found a quiet corner and tore open the message. As I expected, it was from French, requesting that I meet him at half past noon in the front parlor. The time did not present an obstacle, but the location did, as I had no idea how to find it on my own. I went off in search of Flora, composing as I went a plausible excuse for needing to visit the parlor.

How French and I were supposed to hold a private conversation in the parlor was anybody's guess, as another of the Queen's guests might drop in at any moment, or a maid might take it upon herself to run the feather duster over the furniture at any time. Still, I arrived at the room at precisely the appointed hour (having extracted directions from one of the footmen, saving me from what would no doubt have been a good deal of curiosity from Flora). French had arrived before me and was leaning casually against the mantelpiece, examining a bust of Prince Albert.

"Don't you get enough of him?" I asked.

"He is ubiquitous," agreed French, smiling.

"Bit spooky, if you ask me." I took care to stand a few feet from French, with my hands clasped, just in case anyone wandered in and assumed a tryst, which would earn French points with the other rogue males and mean the end of my employment by the marchioness.

French took a step in my direction and I backed away.

"What are you doing? Come closer so I don't have to raise my voice."

I explained why I kept my distance. "Besides, I'm not getting within a foot of you ever again unless you promise you won't snatch me like an undergraduate on his first visit to a brothel."

"India," French said reproachfully. "Do you think I intended to, to . . ."

"Have your way with me?" I asked.

French reddened. "That is not what I meant. I was merely trying to project a plausible image of an aristocrat taking advantage of a servant since the Prince of Wales had wandered into the room. I had no intention of taking it any further than that."

I had not expected French to ravish me when he had wrapped himself around me like a python in front of Bertie, but I must admit to feeling a hint of disappointment at the news. That hint of disappointment gave rise to a hint of unease; what the deuce was I doing feeling deflated that French hadn't intended to sweep me up and carry me off like a Viking raider? I was well aware of the effect I had on men, and just such a reaction to my proximity would not be at all unusual. Were my charms fading? Surely not. The Prince of Wales had certainly seemed enamored with me. French, on the other hand, had never done a single thing that might be interpreted as forward, save for that tango we'd performed for Bertie's benefit. Was that time's winged chariot I could hear rumbling in the background? If I looked in the mirror, would I find a wrinkle? Had I lost the power to bewitch men? Had I ever bewitched French? And, confound it, why was I asking myself these questions? It was totally unlike me to doubt my abilities and totally unlike me to seek confirmation of my beauty from French. The Archbishop of Canterbury would have adhered to the tenets of Buddhism by the time French even noticed I was a woman. With difficulty, I wrenched my thoughts away from these vexing questions and tried to focus on what French was saying.

"The Queen always has a cup of cocoa before nodding off. Last night, an hour after drinking the cocoa, she awoke, complaining of stomach pains. Doctor Jenner was called. When he arrived, Her Majesty was suffering from cramps and vomiting copiously."

"What was the doctor's diagnosis?"

"He thinks perhaps she overindulged at dinner. The food was quite rich, and apparently, this isn't the first time the Queen has eaten without restraint."

"You were at the table. Did she eat more than usual?"

"Hard to say," said French. "She's got an appetite like a blacksmith. In any case, she didn't complain until several hours after she'd eaten. Apparently, she felt fine until after she drank the cocoa."

"You think the cocoa was poisoned?"

"We can't discount the possibility."

"But Doctor Jenner doesn't think so."

French smiled. "I rather think Doctor Jenner is here to jolly along the Queen, handing out sugar pills and listening to her complain about the Prince of Wales."

"How do we determine if the cocoa was spiked with something?"

"I'd like you to find out who made the cocoa and who delivered it to the Queen. That should be an easy task. I imagine the servants are gossiping like—"

"Aristocratic ladies at tea," I concluded his sentence for him.

"Quite. In any case, please see what you can learn downstairs."

By some miracle, we'd been allowed to finish our conversation without interruption, but just as I was about to broach the subject of French spanking me like a seven-year-old who'd thrown her dolly in the pond, the door to the parlor opened and Miss Boss waltzed in.

"Forgive me, Mr. French. I thought I heard voices and wondered if any household services were required." She scowled in my direction, and I thought it best to disappear while she was being obsequious to French.

"None at all, Miss Boss," said French in a hearty voice. "The girl was just straightening the cushions for me."

Miss Boss did not appear convinced, but I gave a cursory pat to one of the pillows on the sofa as I darted out of the room. I knew she'd bow deferentially out of French's presence and be after me like a barn cat after a rat, so I shot down the corridor and fairly leapt for the servants' stairs, shoulders hunched in anticipation of the housekeeper's call. I made the stairs and nearly collided with Flora, who was carrying a broom.

"Lord, India! You nearly sent me flying."

"Sorry," I said over my shoulder, as I plunged downward. "Got to run."

"The marchioness isn't ill, is she?"

"Perfectly fine, as far as I know. Why?"

"I just thought the old pussy might be sick, with the way you're carrying on."

"She's in fine fettle, full of vinegar." I heard the door to the stairs swing open. I grinned impishly at Flora and put a finger to my lips. "Miss Boss," I mouthed. "I'm trying to avoid her."

Flora smiled back. "Run away, then. I'll create a diversion for you." She headed upstairs with her accoutrements. "Miss Boss, is that you? May I have a word?"

She neatly intercepted the housekeeper before she'd stepped into the stairwell and began peppering her with questions about work schedules and which rooms Flora should do first and would there be fresh flowers for the Queen's room and so on. I thanked my lucky stars that Flora had missed her calling on the stage and ended up as a housemaid at Balmoral. I hoped she could keep Miss Boss occupied for so long that the housekeeper would forget she'd been on her way to find one India Black and scold her for wasting time with one of the guests, who just happened to be a handsome wastrel who was pals with the Prince of Wales.

Most of the servants were off performing their duties, and the hallways downstairs were almost empty, save for a few laundresses carrying loads of dirty linens and the odd footman with a tray on his arm. I found Cook in the kitchen, having a cup of tea after the morning rush of preparing porridge and kippers for the swells. She looked downcast, her ruddy face unusually somber as she stirred milk into her tea. I helped myself to a cup from the urn and sat down across from her.

"Where is everyone?" I asked by way of breaking the gloomy silence, though I had no real interest in the location of my fellow serfs.

"Running about like headless chickens. The whole house is in an uproar, what with the Queen getting sick last night. I've had Doctor Jenner and Mr. Vicker underfoot, peering into saucepans and rummaging through the larder. That delayed breakfast, and now the guests are complaining."

As the aristocracy was prone to complaining at the best of times, I ignored that tidbit of information and focused on the one that interested me.

"What were the doctor and Mr. Vicker doing?"

Cook snorted. "They had some ridiculous notion that something was wrong with the Queen's dinner last night. Didn't I tell them that if there had been, then every other guest would have been sick, too? And what right have they to come in here and cast aspersions on my cooking?" Her face and neck had turned a mottled red. "As if I'd serve spoiled food to the Queen! What are those two thinking?"

I patted her hand soothingly. "There, there. It's nothing to get worked up about. They're just taking precautions. I'm sure they didn't mean to imply that you would ever do anything to endanger the Queen's health."

"Of course I wouldn't. She may be a queer old bird, but she's always been good to me."

"Well, then. There's nothing for you to worry about. As you said, everyone else ate the same meal, including Doctor Jenner and Mr. Vicker, and those two are still gadding about in perfect health. I expect the Queen just had one too many helpings of your excellent cuisine."

The flush had been receding from Cook's face, but now it grew pink again at the compliment.

"Oh, go on with you. I do my best, and that's always been good enough for Her Majesty."

"Do you make her cocoa at night?" I casually dropped the question into the conversation and hoped Cook wouldn't find it odd.

"Naturally. Everything the Queen puts in her mouth comes out of my kitchen, and I oversee everything that goes out of the kitchen."

I gave Cook a sly smile. "I don't suppose there's any chance of sampling some of that cocoa sometime? Flora says it's excellent." Now this was taking a risk, as Flora might bloody well be allergic to chocolate, but I needed to keep the conversation on cocoa until I'd found out what I needed to know.

"Any night, my dear. I usually make up a pan around eleven for the Queen. I wouldn't mind letting you have a cup."

"Perhaps I could save you the trouble and brew up some for myself. How do you make it?"

"Fresh milk from the Balmoral dairy, the finest cocoa powder from Fortnum and Mason, and lots of sugar. The Queen has a sweet tooth, you know. But don't you worry about making your own. You just let me know when you'd like to try some, and I'll have it ready for you."

"Do you just leave it on the stove?"

"I will for you. But for the Queen, I serve it up in a china pot and some nice china cups with the royal crest, and leave the tray on the buffet by the door for a footman to take up to her."

"Oh?"

"That's a job for the footman with the least seniority. He always delivers the cocoa. That's how it's been done since I came to work here."

She glanced at the clock. "Mercy, is that the time? I must fly." She drained the last of her tea and carried the cup to the draining board. "Sorry to leave you, India, but I've luncheon to prepare."

I smiled and waved her away. I didn't need anything further from her, as I already knew that the most recently hired footman was Robbie Munro.

I went in search of the handsome young man and found him polishing a pair of gentleman's boots in the gun room.

"Hello, Robbie."

He glanced up and gave me a shy smile, but his face looked drawn and his movements were agitated.

"Bit of excitement last night," I said.

"You mean the Queen?"

"Yes. I understand it's nothing serious, though. Apparently, the doctor thinks it was merely a stomachache."

Robbie nodded, his attention on the boots in his hands. I wasted a few seconds trying to develop a strategy for cracking this nut, something subtle and indirect that wouldn't arouse Robbie's suspicions, but that was a waste of time, as I'm constitutionally incapable of being either subtle or indirect. I'm better at jumping off cliffs before ascertaining there's anything waiting for me below. So in keeping with my impetuous and direct nature, I plunged in.

"Did you see the Queen when you took her cocoa to her?"

He glanced up, startled, smearing his cuff with a streak of black polish. "How did you know I took up Her Majesty's cocoa?"

"Cook told me," I said. "I was reading to the marchioness last night when all hell broke loose, and I was just curious about what happened. Did you see the Queen? Was she awfully pale? Did she vomit?" I supposed Robbie had met his share of gossipy maids before, as he relaxed a bit at my questions, taking me for just another of that simple-minded species.

"I didn't see her. I knocked on the door and Lady Dalfad answered. She often shares the Queen's cocoa with her."

I adopted a disappointed expression. "So you couldn't see if she was sick?"

"No. I didn't lay eyes on her." Robbie returned to the task of buffing boots, noticed the splotch of polish on his cuff and swore under his breath.

"So you were surprised to hear she'd become ill?"

"Yes, but then I've served at dinner before, and the amount of food that woman can eat would put an entire platoon to shame."

"I've heard she likes her provisions," I said. Then I twiddled my thumbs (figuratively) for a minute and wondered what other information I could pry out of Robbie. I had asked my questions and could think of no plausible reason to linger in Robbie's company, so I moved toward the door.

Robbie paused, brush in hand. "I was surprised to hear about the Queen, especially after the incident with Mr. Vicker."

I halted in my tracks. "The incident with Vicker?"

"Yes, he was also ill last night."

"I hadn't heard."

"The only reason I know is that I was on my way to Her Majesty's room when I passed Mr. Vicker in the hall. He was leaning against the wall and looked deuced odd, all white and shaking. I asked him if I could be of service, and he requested that I find Doctor Jenner and send him to Mr. Vicker's room."

"And you did that?"

"Yes, I set down the tray on a chest in the hall and went to the doctor's room. He wasn't best pleased at being roused at that hour for anyone but the Queen, but he went anyway."

"And did Vicker return to his room without any assistance?"

Robbie shrugged. "I assume so. He was gone when I returned to collect the tray. I was afraid the cocoa would be getting cold, so I hurried to the Queen's chambers and left it with the countess. She was a bit stiff about it; I suppose I was a few minutes late."

"Ah, well, not to worry. The countess is stiff about everything." I gave Robbie a comradely wink. "She's never satisfied with anyone's service. In fact, she's convinced you've never been a footman before."

The brush dropped from Robbie's hand. His face was hidden as he bent to retrieve it, but not before I'd glimpsed the look of alarm that spread over his features.

* * *

I was swinging down the hallway, feeling rather pleased with myself for completing the mission French had assigned to me and was in search of the patrician bastard himself so as to deliver the news, when the paunchy figure of the Prince of Wales hove into view. He was without his usual retinue of jolly, half-drunk sycophants, which spelled trouble for yours truly. I cast about for a hiding place and found my options were few. I debated the wisdom of diving into one of the rooms along the corridor, but there I'd be cornered like a vixen in her den. It was better, I reasoned, to stay in public view and hope that before Bertie could fling me over his shoulder and cart me off to the nearest bedroom, rescue would appear in the form of a guest or Miss Boss or even the marchioness.

"'Allo, 'allo," said the Prince, beaming. For a fat man, he could move surprisingly quickly. Only a second ago, he'd been ambling down the hall toward me, and now he was encircling my waist with a brawny arm, breathing a potent mix of stale whisky and cigar smoke in my face.

"Your Highness," I said, wiggling strenuously. "How very nice to see you."

He nuzzled my neck and breathed into my ear: "It appears we both have a few moments free from our official duties. Shall we take advantage and indulge in a bit of slap and tickle?"

I'll grant you, Bertie was bold, if not wise. He pinched my bum and I squealed, which produced a lusty chuckle from the heir to the throne.

I sucked in my breath and feigned panic (well, feigned is probably not the correct word, as I was in fact feeling some consternation at the moment), slapping away the prince's hands. He let out another throaty laugh and tightened his grip around my waist.

"Oh, good Lord," I hissed. "Is that the Queen?"

At least Bertie was predictable. He recoiled from me like a snake charmer dodging a cobra strike, his eyes bulging from his head.

"Where?" he asked, but I had already sidestepped him and was rocketing along the hallway, with very little idea of where I was headed, other than out of reach of the next King of England. I heard a stifled shout of rage behind me as Bertie realized he'd been hoodwinked, and the sound of footsteps on my trail. Confound it, where was everyone? The castle seemed deserted, except for me and the unhappy prince, who had not taken kindly to being duped by a lowly maid. I careered past a series of closed doors, hoping to find an open one, where I planned to waltz inside regardless of the status of the room's occupant and claim sanctuary. I could hear the prince's heavy tread and labored breathing. He was a determined chap, I'll grant you that, especially when his plans had been thwarted.

I had nearly reached the end of the corridor when I spied the handsome figure of French emerging from one of the rooms. I must admit to feeling the merest hint of relief when he stepped into view. He raised an eyebrow as I swooped in behind him and clutched his arm.

"Hide me," I commanded.

"Too late," he said. He cleared his throat. "Good afternoon, Your Highness. Pleasant day, what?"

The prince bumbled to a halt, wheezing. "Indeed it is, Mr. French. Though I suspect you had planned something even more pleasant for yourself," he said, his voice heavy with sarcasm.

French chuckled self-consciously. "'Fraid you've caught me out, sir." He reached around and snagged my arm, dragging me forward. "Miss Black has volunteered to help me adjust my mattress. Frightfully bad night last night, lumps everywhere."

Bertie nodded, looking daggers at me. "Well, we can't have one of our guests being uncomfortable. I shall certainly let Vicker know of your discomfort. He's just the chap to remedy the problem." The prince smiled humourlessly at French and gave me a last significant glance before he marched away, back rigid, smoothing his hair with his hand and straightening his tie.

French pushed me into his room and locked the door behind us.

"Curse it," I said, expelling a breath of relief. "That man is a menace. I can't seem to go anywhere without running into him. If I disappear, look in Bertie's room. He's likely to have me stuffed in his wardrobe." I smoothed my apron modestly. "Of course, if I weren't such a deuced good-looking woman, I wouldn't have such trouble."

French snorted. "Don't flatter yourself. The Prince of Wales is as about as discriminating as a stoat during mating season." As stoats are promiscuous little devils, copulating with any number of females and then darting off in search of greener pastures (or more females) and leaving their discarded partners to raise the resulting little stoats, I found the comparison apt.

French flopped into a chair and draped one leg elegantly over the arm. "Have you learned anything?"

"Never walk alone in the halls while the prince is in the castle," I said, helping myself to a seat without waiting for an invitation from French. "Have you any whisky? Or brandy? I could do with a tot after my narrow escape."

I expected to be directed to the bottle, but to my surprise,

French rose to his feet and poured us each a brandy and soda. I sipped mine gratefully and summarized what I had learned of the travels of the cocoa tray. When I finished, French lit a cheroot and watched the smoke eddy to the ceiling while he thought this over.

"How is the Queen?" I asked.

He stirred himself. "She is much better this morning. She seems to have ejected the contents of her stomach during the night and is now resting peacefully."

I winced at the image that had formed in my mind.

French carried on: "Doctor Jenner is inclined to believe it was merely a case of too much rich food; at worst, a mild case of food poisoning. It's difficult to disagree with that diagnosis, but I would not think food poisoning would be limited to one or two persons. Literally dozens of guests and staff ate the same thing last night. If it were food poisoning, one would expect many more people to have been sick."

"The only other person who exhibited any symptoms of illness was Vicker, and as he's one of our suspects, the validity of his infirmity is questionable."

French tapped the ash from his cigar. "Quite."

"Not food poisoning, then. Overindulgence by the Queen?"

"In view of the threats on her life, I do not think we can merely assume the Queen ate too many meringues for dessert. And the diversion of the footman Munro by Vicker is interesting."

"Have you seen Dizzy? What is his opinion?"

"He is concerned, of course. He expressed his disquiet to the Queen. She refuses to countenance his fears. She was not, in her opinion, intemperate in her choice of food last night. She is inclined to think that, if anything is amiss, it was with the chocolate. She remembers feeling quite ill immediately upon drinking it and then beginning to vomit. But she is disinclined to believe that anyone tampered with the cocoa. She believes the milk used to make it was spoiled."

"I think that's doubtful. The kitchen is spotless, and Cook is too experienced not to have noticed if the milk was off. There was ample opportunity for someone to doctor the cocoa. Not only did Munro leave the cocoa in the hall while he went off to fetch the doctor for Vicker, but Cook left the tray on the counter in the kitchen for Munro to collect. God only knows how many people knew the nightly routine and knew where they could find the cocoa. Vicker's diversion of Munro looks suspicious, but it's just as likely that someone took the opportunity to add the poison while the tray was in the kitchen. If the cocoa was poisoned at all," I added.

"Robshaw has taken away the remains of the cocoa to have it analyzed," said French. "But it will take weeks to get any results."

"By which time the Queen could be safely back in Windsor, or Dizzy might be attending a state funeral."

French frowned. "I find black humour inappropriate, India."

"I wasn't trying to be funny." I polished off the remains of my drink. "It seems that we need to confirm whether Vicker was indeed ill last night."

"I'll have a quiet word with Doctor Jenner. The more difficult problem is narrowing down the list of people who passed the tray in the hallway, or were in the kitchen after Cook made the cocoa and before Munro picked up the tray."

I groaned. "Surely you're joking. I'd have to question every servant, and how am I to do that without giving away the game? And you'll have the same issue with the guests. They may think you're an amiable fop, but how many of them will sit still while you grill them about their whereabouts at midnight last night?"

French nodded glumly. "A dead end, I'm afraid."

"When is Robshaw going to get us some information about our list of suspects? We might eliminate Vicker as our potential assassin if the superintendent would put on some speed."

"It does seem to be taking an inordinately long time to investigate a few chaps," French mused. He extracted his watch from his pocket. "Good Gad, I'm late for luncheon."

"Try to avoid sitting near the marchioness, if you can," I advised. "And if you must, carry a large handkerchief."

SEVEN

The rest of the day and evening passed uneventfully, save for the usual struggle to manhandle the marchioness into an evening gown and out of that into her nightclothes, all the while picking flakes of snuff from her person and listening to her chunter on about the quality of the vittles she'd ingested, but eventually, I had the old dearie swaddled in blankets with the fire banked for the night. I yawned my way back to Flora's room. I was spent from reading the Holy Scriptures to the marchioness during the wee hours, interrogating Cook and Robbie Munro, and narrowly escaping becoming the Prince of Wales's latest conquest. I needed a tranquil night, which, of course, I was not to have, for just as the long-case clock in the hall struck midnight, a footman I hadn't seen before knocked loudly on the door and woke me from my slumbers. I opened the door to him in my shift, which struck the poor man dumb.

"The marchioness?" I queried, and the bloke nodded silently, tearing his eyes away from my décolletage with difficulty and stumbling away down the hall, having delivered his message. I dressed, not without difficulty as my fingers were clumsy and stiff from the cold and lack of sleep, and blundered groggily through the corridors with a candle in my hand.

The marchioness was sitting up in bed, nursing a whisky and looking damnably pert for this hour of the night. Dispiritedly, I contemplated another session with that lively band of fun seekers, the Old Testament prophets.

"How are you, my lady? Can I bring you anything? A cup of tea? Some coffee?" A dose of morphine? I added silently.

The marchioness snuggled into her covers. "I'm well set up, as ye can see," she said, waving her whisky glass at me. "Help yerself to a dram."

She didn't have to ask twice. I found a glass and poured a generous tot. The whisky burned like fire, and for the first time in a long while, I felt warm.

"There are five reasons to drink, lass. Do you know 'em?"

I shook my head.

"Good wine, a friend, or bein' dry; or lest you should be bye and bye; or any other reason why." The marchioness hooted and lifted her glass. She was well into her cups. One of life's small ironies, I supposed, that she hadn't passed out and left me to a night of restful repose, but instead looked ready for a night of carousing.

"I canna sleep," she announced.

I conceded the point; it would be difficult to doze off at night, having spent a good part of the day slumbering.

"Would you like me to read to you?" I looked around wearily for the marchioness's Bible.

"I would. But not from the Good Book." My sigh of relief must have reached her ears, for she gave me a sharpish look. "I'm in the mood for somethin' else tonight. Trot downstairs to the library and find the Queen's copy of Miss Greenhow's book."

"Miss Greenhow's book?"

"Surely ye've heard of her?"

"I can't say that I have."

The marchioness honked in derision. "Come now. Everyone has heard of Rose O'Neal Greenhow. The society matron in Washington who spied for the Confederacy during the War Between the States?"

"Oh, *that* Greenhow. I had confused her with someone else."

The marchioness's rheumy eyes swam with suspicion. "No matter. Just fetch the book, and together we'll renew our acquaintance with the lady."

I rose from my chair. "Yes, ma'am. And the name of her book? It's on the tip of my tongue, but for some reason"—probably because I'd never heard of it—"I can't recollect it."

"*My Imprisonment and the First Year of Abolition Rule at Washington,*" the marchioness snapped.

"Of course," I murmured and slipped away. Catchy title. I hoped the contents were an improvement.

I took up my candle and wandered out into the hallway. I knew the library was the first room past the entrance hall, in the corner of the castle, which meant that even someone as congenitally indisposed to navigation as I was should be able to find my way there. I bypassed the servants' stairs and descended the grand staircase to the first floor. As luck would have it, the entrance to the library was directly across from the stairs, and the door was open. I slipped inside and let out a curse: the walls were lined with books, hundreds of them, it seemed. At this rate, the marchioness would have forgotten she'd sent me to the library and fallen asleep while I spent a hellish night examining titles by candle-light. The thought was appealing, and I was debating whether I could just stretch out on the tufted leather sofa and catch a few winks when I heard distant laughter, a muffled chorus of "Drink, puppy, drink," and the muted crack of billiard balls. Some of the toffs must still be up, having a nightcap and a game.

I peeked out into the hallway. Now I confess that I am not without faults (I'll thank you to keep your snide comments about my profession to yourself), and among them is an innate curios-ity that occasionally leads me to venture into areas best left unvis-ited (like the Russian Embassy, or a smuggler's boat bound for Calais, as I have previously recounted). So it was no surprise to me that I was seized with the temptation to suss out the billiard room and see what the boys were getting up to. I left my candle on a table in the library and followed the gleam of light down the corridor until I could see a corner of the billiard room, ablaze with light and awash with the blue smoke of cigars. Smoking be-ing strictly verboten at Balmoral, I half expected to see Vicky charging into the room in her nightie with a whip in one hand.

I spotted French leaning languidly on his cue stick, a snifter of cognac in one hand and a cheroot in his mouth. His hair was rumpled, and he'd assumed an expression of affable dissolution. A bloke with a shock of ginger hair had buttonholed French and was talking animatedly, emphasizing every other word by stab-bing his cigar perilously close to French's waistcoat. Stewed to the gills, the young fellow was, and swaying dangerously on his feet. This could only be Red Hector MacCodrum, seventh Bar-onet of Dochfour, the favorite nephew of the Earl of Nairn and rabid Scottish nationalist. From the looks of him, Red Hector had made a heroic effort to polish off the Courvoisier single-handedly. French must have wound him up on the political situation, because the baronet's face was contorted with the fanatical passion that only taxes or blood sports can arouse in the aristocracy.

In the dark hallway behind me, someone cleared his throat. I spun round, no doubt looking guilty as hell, even though I hadn't done a thing (this time). Vicker emerged from the gloom, looking overwrought and wrung out.

"Mr. Vicker," I said. "I see you've recovered from your illness. That's wonderful." I had thought to disarm him with a show of interest in his welfare, but he wasn't having any of it.

"What are you doing down here?" he asked. You could have iced lemonade with his voice.

"The marchioness sent me to look for a book in the library." I grinned sheepishly. "I heard voices and was just curious about what the gentlemen were doing."

Vicker gripped my elbow. For a pasty fellow he was devilishly strong. "What they are doing is no concern of yours. Is that understood?"

I tried to disengage my arm, without success. "Yes, Mr. Vicker. I'm sorry, sir. I'll just go look for that book now."

He stared into my eyes for a long minute, then nodded stiffly and released his hold on me. He watched as I retreated to the library, where I snatched up my candle and began to peruse the bookshelves. I heard footsteps, and Vicker appeared in the door.

"What book does the marchioness want?" he asked.

Confound it, what *was* the name of that book? Something about prison, but I was hanged if I could remember the rest of it.

"Er, it's by a woman who was a Confederate spy, and she wrote a book about going to prison," I babbled. "That's all I can remember. Oh, and her name is Greenhow."

Vicker nodded dubiously, no doubt nonplussed at my description of the book (which sounded like a feeble fabrication even to me) or perhaps at the marchioness's choice of reading material.

"I shall return here in a few minutes," he said. "See that you have found the book and rejoined the marchioness by then, or I shall have to have a word with Her Ladyship about the situation." He stalked off silently.

Spurred on by the thought of another encounter with Vicker, I made a rapid search of the books in the library. For a good twenty minutes I pored over the titles, trying to read the letters in the wavering light from my candle, but I could not find the volume the marchioness had requested. Truth to tell, the whole concept of the Queen having a copy of a Confederate spy's autobiography in her library had sounded far-fetched. I was beginning to think my employer was pulling my leg, and my inability to find the book only confirmed my belief.

I was in a foul temper and covered with dust by the time I'd finished searching. Bugger Rose Greenhow, I thought. The marchioness will have to be satisfied tonight with more stories from the Pentateuch. My candle had burned to a stub, and Vicker was due back any second. I shut the door to the library and climbed the grand staircase again. Halfway up, my candle guttered wildly and the flame died, leaving me in darkness. Damn and blast. I had trouble finding my way around this pile in the daylight; without a candle or lamp, I was all at sea. I crept to the wall, hugging it and feeling my way up the stairs, one halting step at a time. I reached the second floor and turned toward the marchioness's room. Ahead of me, a candle flame floated down the corridor, illuminating a head of red gold curls. Robbie Munro stole quietly down the hallway, shielding the candle with one hand and searching the wall to his left. As I watched, Robbie's head turned, and I shrank into the nearest doorway. Then the candle flame wavered, and Robbie disappeared.

By the time I had groped my way back to the marchioness's room, it was getting on to two o'clock in the morning. The old lady was still upright in bed, and she gave me a murderous glare as I entered the room.

"Where've ye been? Ye've been gone for hours. I could have walked to Tullibardine and got the book from my own library by now."

"I'm terribly sorry, my lady. I searched the library carefully and could not locate the volume of which you spoke. Then my candle went out, and I had some difficulty finding my way back here."

"Hmmph. A likely story, Ingrid. Ye haven't been consortin' with the prince again, have ye?"

"Oh, no, ma'am. I can assure you I have not."

The marchioness shifted irritably. "Bother. I was lookin' forward to hearin' Mrs. Greenhow's story again. I canna believe the Queen doesn't have a copy of the book here. Did ye search carefully?"

"I did, my lady. I looked at every title. Is the book so very popular that you expected the Queen to have the volume?"

"Mrs. Greenhow once had an audience with the Queen, and she presented her with several copies of the book. Ye know how authors are, always pushin' ye to read their claptrap. Anyway, I expected the Queen to dump one of the volumes here at Balmoral. It's quite an excitin' story, actually. Sit down and I'll tell ye about it."

I don't believe the marchioness heard the whimper that escaped me as I dutifully took a chair.

"Mrs. Greenhow was a prominent member of Washington society at the beginnin' of the War Between the States. All the politicians and generals, imbeciles to a man, trundled over to her salon, where she milked them of the details about federal forces and Northern war plans. Ye must remember that Washington was full of Southern sympathizers, and Mrs. Greenhow was one."

I stifled a yawn and thought I heard a cock crowing from the castle farm.

"The lady turned over everything she learned to contacts in the Confederate government. She was exposed, eventually, as a Southern spy and was sent to prison, along with her young daughter. Are ye listenin', Ingrid?"

I must have dozed off. "Yes, ma'am."

"She was released after several months and wrote a book about her imprisonment. It was published in England in 1864, and Mrs. Greenhow visited the country then. That's when she had her audience with the Queen."

Fascinating stuff. My eyes felt as though they had been branded into my skull.

"What happened to Mrs. Greenhow?" I asked. Damned if I cared, really, but if I talked, I could stay awake.

The marchioness cackled. "Got her comeuppance, she did. Drowned on her way back to the States from England, tryin' to run the Northern blockade."

"What a shame," I said. If I didn't get to bed soon, I was going to fall out of my chair.

"Not really," said the marchioness, settling back into her pillow. "She took a risk and paid the consequences. If ye're going to do something daft and dangerous like betray yer country, ye can't expect any quarter to be given." She yawned, her gums pink in the candlelight.

"Well, I'm ready for a kip. Draw the curtains, will ye, Ingrid? And don't slam the door when ye leave."

I did as instructed. Then I blundered down the stairs and out through the kitchen into the bracing air of a Scottish winter morning, heading for the stables.

By the time I tumbled into my bed, dawn was breaking. You would think I'd have fallen to sleep the minute my head touched the pillow, but I was nagged by the image of Robbie Munro in the corridor. He had seemed to vanish into thin air. What was he doing up at that hour? And where had he been going when I had seen him? It wasn't impossible that the handsome Robbie had made such an impression on one of the Queen's female guests that he had been invited to her room (and for that matter, I supposed, the Queen's visitors might include an aristocratic Mary Ann who had singled out Robbie for attention). Hard to credit, but who knows? The nights are long and cold in Scotland. A third possibility presented itself, and that was that Munro was up to his eyeballs in the plot against the Queen and had been meeting one or more of his co-conspirators. I suppose there might be an innocent explanation: one of the guests had required a hot water bottle or a sandwich or a bedtime story read aloud. I would have to eliminate that possibility as well. I resolved to inspect the hall in the light of day, to ferret out which of Her Majesty's lodgers had entertained the footman last night.

The marchioness's behavior also disturbed me (not the explosions and floods that followed her ingestion of the evil weed—God knows the old pussy needed some consolation at her age), but her decided interest in tales of female deception. Perhaps I was being paranoid, but I was beginning to think Her Ladyship had smoked me out. But how on earth had she done so? Granted, when it came to pressing skirts and brushing on powder, I could manage, but no doubt I was a bit rough around the edges when it came to acting the servant. I was more used to barking orders at my whores than anticipating when to produce a handkerchief. The marchioness, however, had the eyesight of a bat who'd never left the cave; she probably hadn't a clue whether her bodice was starched or not. Even if she had rumbled me, she didn't seem in any hurry to terminate my employment (not that a Bible-reading insomniac who could do hair could be found on short notice in the local village). Had someone let slip my real role at the castle? It could only have been Dizzy or French, or Sir Horace Wickersham, the poor devil who had forged my letter of recommendation, but to what purpose?

As you can see, I had a lot to ponder, so I tossed and turned while Flora snored, until I fell asleep just as the sun rose over the horizon. Predictably, the skirl of the Great Highland War Pipe followed shortly thereafter, jolting me awake with another tuneless ululation that passed for song here in the north. No doubt the Scots found it stirring, but the only thing I felt inclined to do was close the window.

"Lord," I moaned from beneath my covers.

Flora laughed and bounced out of bed. "Don't you ever wake up in a good mood, India?"

"Not since I started work for the marchioness. If I don't get some sleep soon, I'm going to collapse." I struggled upright and regarded the world through bleary eyes. A look in the mirror confirmed my fears: I was looking deuced haggard.

I washed and dressed and went downstairs for breakfast, where fried eggs and toast and a cup of strong tea revived my spirits somewhat. The rest of the servants tucked into their porridge with the appetites of Arctic explorers, but I declined to join them. I don't much care for warm, soggy oats in the morning, or at any time for that matter, and the thought of stuffing them into a sheep's stomach along with bits and bobs of internal organs and boiling the mess up for luncheon is a stomach-turner. After the meal I wearily climbed the stairs and stopped by the marchioness's room to see if I was needed, but my employer was asleep over her breakfast tray, with her stiff white braid dangling in the milk jug. I considered extracting it, but if the marchioness woke up while I was performing the operation, I might be stuck for hours. I closed the door quietly and crept away.

After only a few false starts, I found my way back to the main corridor that housed the guest rooms, where Robbie Munro had apparently dematerialized last night. I walked slowly along the hall, trying to visualize the scene in my mind and identify the room into which Robbie had vanished. I paced up and down, measuring my steps and estimating distances for a good while, keeping a wary eye out for the Prince of Wales and planning an escape route in the event he wandered down the hall. After several minutes of hanging about, I had narrowed my search to three rooms on the left side of corridor, one of which I knew to be occupied by French. The second and third were separated by a dusty, threadbare tapestry depicting a few bare-legged Scots routing an unidentified enemy. Well, I suppose a wall hanging showing the English victories at Bannockburn or Culloden would have been deemed tasteless by the locals.

I struck lucky at the first room; the door was cracked and a housemaid was stripping the bed, humming under her breath as she did so. I knocked softly and she started like a spurred colt, spinning round with a look of terror on her face. Her face sagged with relief when she saw me.

"Lord almighty, I thought you were the Prince of Wales."

We shared a laugh at that and introduced ourselves, though I promptly forgot the girl's name. There were dozens of servants at Balmoral; why waste valuable memory on one name?

"I know you. You're the marchioness's maid. I've seen you at tea in the kitchen. She's a funny old sort, isn't she?"

I bristled at this description of my employer, then gave myself a mental thump on the head. I rarely gave a tinker's damn about anyone but myself, and it was inconceivable that I had developed any affection for a snuff-spraying, slack-jawed crone who suffered from the curse of Hypnos. The lack of sleep I had endured was beginning to play tricks on mind.

"She's a character," I said neutrally. "Actually, I was just looking for her, and I thought I saw her come into this room."

The maid shook her head. "She's not in here and likely wouldn't be, unless she got awfully confused. This is the Earl of Kinnoncairn's room. They haven't spoken in twenty years."

"Right," I said, nodding sagely as if I knew of the long-running feud between the two. "Perhaps the marchioness is next-door," I said. "Do you know who occupies the room?"

"Oh, that's the prime minister's room. And his secretary is next door." The maid cocked her head and smiled dreamily. "That handsome Mr. French. Have you seen him?"

"The chap with the black hair and the vacant smile?"

My sarcasm didn't make a dent in the maid's ardor. She nodded happily. I thanked her for her time and made my exit. In the hallway, I hung about, thinking over the information I'd learned. Lord Kinnoncairn had a chestful of medals from various actions in Afghanistan, the Sudan and the Gold Coast, and was a distant cousin of the Queen and a member of the Cabinet. He might be the Marischal, but if he was, his disguise as war hero, royal relative and loyal member of the government was a good one. That left Dizzy's room and that of French as potential destinations for Robbie's midnight ramble. Surely the PM had been asleep in the wee hours of the morning. A chill ran through me; what if Robbie had visited the old man's room with the intention of eliminating one of the hated Englishmen on the premises? But if something had happened to Dizzy, the news would have permeated the castle by now. That left French's room as a possible destination for Robbie, which made some sense as I had seen French downstairs in the billiard room not half an hour before I'd seen Robbie skulking through the hall. Robbie could easily have known French was not in his room; the footman might even have been up late attending to the gentlemen at their games and drinks. I mulled over the possibilities. There might be a perfectly reasonable explanation for Robbie entering French's room. French might have sent Robbie to fetch something, or Robbie might have been instructed to prepare the room for French's retirement. Or Robbie might have tumbled to French's masquerade as Dizzy's secretary and learned of French's real purpose in visiting Balmoral.

I needed a word with French. I paused at his door, looked left and right, and seeing that I was alone in the hall, knocked gently. There was no answer. I turned the knob cautiously, but the door was locked. Probably breakfasting on deviled kidneys and nursing a hangover from last night. I'd have to run him to earth later.

Then a strange thing happened. I was facing French's door, with the tapestry of the battle scene hanging from an iron rod to the right of the door frame. Suddenly the tapestry billowed gently away from the wall and settled back into place. It spooked the hell out of me, being the tapestrial equivalent of the eyes in a painting following you around the room. I sucked in a breath and waited for my heart to stop fluttering. My nerves were clearly shot from long nights reading to the marchioness. There had to be an obvious explanation for the tapestry moving. I hadn't felt a breeze through the hallway, and I had been standing at French's door, so my passage along the corridor clearly hadn't created a draught of air that could stir the wall hanging. I inserted my hand behind the tapestry, pulled it gently away from the stone wall and peered behind it. I had no idea what I would say if I was discovered rummaging around behind the ornamentation, but I excel at the blarney and knew I'd think of something if the necessity arose.

Surely whatever force had made the tapestry balloon outward had come from behind the hanging. I probed the mortar between the stones, inching my way farther behind the tapestry as I did so. If anyone came down the hall now, I was buggered, as even the marchioness with her eyesight couldn't fail to decry the great lump moving about beneath the embroidery. My fingers traced the rough pattern of the stonework, exploring for cracks or openings of any kind. I had nearly exhausted my search of the area of wall that I could reach (and was ruminating on how to get a ladder behind the tapestry to complete the section I couldn't), when I heard the faintest susurration of air and felt a cool zephyr caress my fingertips. I probed the interstice between the stones where I had felt the breath of wind and discovered a slight irregularity in the mortar, a hairline crack running from the floor to just above my head. My fingers inched sideways and down, tracing the fracture in the mortar until I had outlined a door in the wall. Now, to locate the means of opening said door. This necessitated a great deal of pushing and pulling on damned near every stone in the vicinity, while trying to be as inconspicuous as possible, a feat nearly impossible to accomplish while rooting around behind a tapestry. But my luck held, and I finally stumbled onto the right stone, an irregularly shaped one at waist level that receded an inch into the wall when I prodded it. There was a satisfying click, and a section of the wall swung slowly open, revealing a dark passage.

"Open sesame," I murmured, before ducking inside. It was black as pitch in there and musky as a badger's den. I weighed the merits of looking for a means of closing the door (and perhaps thereby consigning myself to die a lingering death of starvation if I couldn't get out again) or leaving the door open to provide a ready escape. Predictably, I opted for the latter option. If the tapestry flapped about like a sail in a hurricane, that was just too bloody bad.

I waited for a moment as my eyes adjusted to the darkness. Those long Balmoral corridors were dim, and the tapestry had blocked out what little light might have come in from the hall. While I paused, I contemplated the uncharacteristic whimsicality of the secret passage. Dear departed Albert had been a bit of a stick, always blathering on about science, learning and progress, and certainly not a bloke given to flights of romance. Who'd have thought the old boy would have commissioned a hidden tunnel in his Scottish home? Perhaps he'd been inspired by the decidedly anti-Teutonic sentiment expressed in the English papers when he'd married Vicky; a concealed route to freedom might have seemed like a good idea in the event the natives took an intense dislike to German accents and attacked the castle with torches and pitchforks in hand. But I digress.

I had delayed my exploration long enough. I took a tentative step, my hand scraping the wall of the tunnel, and using it as a guide, I inched my way forward. I hoped there weren't rats. Or spiders. God, I hate spiders. The wall felt gritty under my fingers, and my feet scraped over the stone floor. I put one foot in front of the other, moving slowly and counting my footsteps as I went. Just as I reached thirty-three, the wall fell away from my hand and the passage took a sharp left turn. I tottered for a moment, having lost my balance when the wall disappeared, then my outstretched fingers found stone again and I regained my feet. I did a cautious survey of the area around me, to be sure that the tunnel had not branched into more than one direction, but it followed a single line. I moved forward counting steps.

At fifty-six, the wall again vanished from beneath my hand. This time, I turned right, took three steps forward and banged my forehead into the wall. I reeled backward, clutching my temple and moaning. Bloody hell. No doubt a qualified government agent would have come prepared for anything, with matches and a bull's-eye lantern tucked into her maid's cap, but I had plunged into the darkness without a second thought. There was no need, I thought, to mention my absence of forethought to French when I told him about the tunnel. I massaged my head and then pressed on. I felt my way around the wall, discovering as I did so that I had entered a small room, empty of furniture or adornment, whose purpose I could not discern. I did locate an opening opposite the one by which I had entered the room, and I groped my way through it and into the passage beyond. I had lost track of time by now and wondered if it might be getting on toward luncheon. My stomach rumbled at the thought of food.

At eighty-seven steps, the tunnel turned once more, but as I rounded the corner, my spirits lifted. Ahead of me I could see a faint luminescence. I must be nearing the end of the hidden passage. Fresh air (even bloody cold Scottish winter air) sounded wonderful. I picked up my pace a bit, not bothering to cover the ground as slowly and prudently as when I had been deprived of light. The radiance ahead of me in the tunnel grew steadily brighter as I moved forward, eagerly anticipating a release into the thin sunlight of a Balmoral morning. I blame myself for what happened next.

I was steaming along, not paying much heed to my surroundings, just anticipating the pleasure of emerging from this damp passageway, when it occurred to me that the illumination before me was more yellow than white, more akin to a lamp or candle than the natural light of day. I halted and stood warily, straining to see down the tunnel. I listened intently . . . and heard a muttered oath. The candle flame (for such it was: I could see it clearly now) oscillated, and a dark figure loomed.

I am not a fanciful person. I don't believe in ghosts or phantoms or any other kind of spirits, save those I can drink. But even I must admit that my knees quavered a tad as I surveyed the form in the tunnel. There was a shadowy, brooding intensity to it that made me instantly and distinctly wary. Thank God I'd been wise enough to leave the door open behind me. Discretion being the better part of valor, it would be best, I thought, to leave my exploration to another time, when the Stygian figure before me had returned to his lair, and I had a candle (and some sort of weapon) in my hand. Stealthily as a fox leaving the henhouse, I reversed direction and headed back the way I'd come. I tiptoed along at a glacial pace, fingertips grazing the wall, and trying to remember how many steps to the first turn. Was it fifty-six or eighty-seven? Was the first turn to the right or to the left? With that kind of memory, it was going to be deuced difficult for me to earn my official espionage credentials.

At least I'd had the presence of mind not to run right into the fellow holding the candle. My navigational skills in the darkness might leave something to be desired, but my instincts had kicked in when needed and disaster had been averted. I glanced over my shoulder, expecting to see the pale yellow light growing fainter. What I saw sent an icy current down my spine. The glow from the candle had not receded into the distance. Instead, it had grown brighter. Even in my present state of befuddlement (damn the marchioness and her insomnia), I recognized the significance of that fact: the sinister figure with the candle was following me.

I'm not easily frightened; I've had too many experiences fending off muggers and cutpurses and the occasional bloke whose tastes I didn't care to accommodate. True, I'd have felt better with the heavy weight of my Bulldog in my hand, but I would have to rely on my native skill and cunning in dispatching the gent now bearing down on me like the devil searching for stray souls to shanghai off to the abode of the damned. The thought of Hades spurred me to action. I wasn't entirely sure my ticket was punched for that destination, despite what the local curate might think, but why take the chance?

I wheeled round, intending to be as soft-footed as a monkey, but damned if I didn't catch my toe on the slightest protuberance in the stone floor. I pitched forward, crashing over with a noise akin to a yew tree being felled on a quiet summer day. There was a muffled shout from the passageway as the fellow with the candle realized he was not alone, then the sound of footsteps ringing on stone as he rushed toward me. I scrambled to my feet and fled, using my right hand on the wall as a guide and my left stretched out in front of me to cushion the blow if I missed a turn and crashed into the wall.

The candlelight danced on the walls as my pursuer gave chase, and my shadow jittered wildly, like a drunken sailor just out of the tavern. The cove behind was gaining on me; his footsteps thundered down the passage, and I could hear him snorting as he ran. Then the flame went out. It had proved impossible to run with a lighted candle, and my heart leapt at the unexpected reprieve. Except it wasn't much of a reprieve, if you thought about it, as all the fellow had to do was follow the tunnel and he'd eventually find me, unless I moved with dispatch, which I proceeded to do. I set off on tiptoe, determined not to make a sound that would reveal my position to the ruffian in the tunnel. It was damned hard going, moving so slowly and cautiously, not to mention that I was blowing like a cavalry mount that had survived the Charge of the Light Brigade. If the fellow with the candle stopped and listened, he'd have no trouble finding me in the dark. I resolutely put that thought from my mind and carried on.

It has always seemed most unfair to me that the Maker of Men sees fit to punish you just when you're doing your damnedest to avoid trouble. So it was in this instance. I was shuffling along rather well, putting some ground between the brigand and me, when my right hand fell into empty space and I yawed dramatically, floundering around and making an ungodly amount of noise as I tried to retain my balance. I had stumbled upon (literally) the small room I'd passed through earlier.

The cove was on me like a jaguar, throwing an arm round my neck and pressing his forearm into my windpipe while he dragged me to the ground. I twisted as I fell, but I still managed to plant one side of my face into the stone floor with a shocking jolt. This did not improve my state of mind, but it did have the salubrious effect of making me mad as hell. One does not trifle with India Black's appearance without repercussions. I'd been lying quietly, stunned by the blow to my face, which had caused my attacker to relax his hold round my throat by a fraction. More fool, he. I put up my hands and groped until I found his, then dipped my chin and sank my teeth into his hand with the energy and devotion of a she wolf protecting her young. There was an infernally loud roar, which, being loosed directly into my tympanic membrane, was deafening. Then the chap compounded the problem by boxing me on the ear with his unbitten hand. Constellations danced at the edge of my vision. I tried to stagger to my feet, but I was felled by another blow.

"Help!" I shouted, but it came out as a croak.

At the sound of my voice, my assailant stopped pummeling me about the head and paused. "India? Is that you?"

"French," I rasped.

"What are you doing here?"

"The same thing you are; following the secret passage to see where it goes."

"You should have told me you planned to do this."

"I stumbled across the tunnel," I said irritably. "I hadn't planned to go exploring today. How did *you* know about the passage?"

"I found the castle building plans in the library."

He was still lying on top of me.

"Get up, will you? I can't breathe."

"Oh, I beg your pardon."

He rolled off me and I sat up tentatively, nursing my jaw where it had hit the floor and fingering my ear where French had landed a blow.

"You've bunged me up, you bastard."

"You bit my hand. No, you bloody well mutilated it." He sounded hurt.

"Well, you attacked me first." I had him there; he had instigated the whole affair.

"I thought you were the Marischal."

"I thought *you* were the Marischal."

A match scraped on the stones and a flame danced between us. French pulled the stub of a candle from his pocket and lit it. He let a few drops of wax fall to the floor and set the candle upright in the wax. He gazed at me across the light and his brow wrinkled.

"Damnation. You look like you've been in the wars."

"I feel it." I touched the side of my face and winced. "Is my cheek scratched?"

He leaned forward and put his fingers under my chin, turning my face this way and that.

"A little," he said. "I'm so damnably sorry, India. You're going to have a hell of bruise, not to mention a bad scrape."

His hand lingered on my skin. His fingers were cool, and his breath caressed my cheek. I felt the startling urge to forgive the bastard.

His thumb moved along the line of my jaw. His mouth opened slightly. He had very white teeth. A good feature in a man, I thought. I admire a man with excellent choppers. And his lips. He had fine lips, did French. Not thin, like so many men seem to have, but proper lips. One might even call them feminine, they were so soft and inviting. I swallowed hard. I admit that I imagined (if only for the briefest of moments) what it would be like to kiss . . .

"Er, French," I mumbled.

"Eh?"

"Do you suppose we should . . ."

"What? Oh, yes, yes. I suppose we should."

His hand jerked away, and we both sprang to our feet (I can't say how French felt, but I got up feeling as the though the First XV had gang-tackled me), brushing off our clothes and looking everywhere except at each other. He stooped to pry the candle from its bed of wax, and when he faced me, he'd resumed his mask of indifferent politeness.

"Shall we see where the tunnel leads?" he asked courteously.

"By all means," I replied.

He led the way while I told him about my observations of Robbie's disappearance from the hallway last night and how I'd discovered the tunnel. He in turn had his own news to impart.

"I had a chat with Doctor Jenner this morning. It seems that Vicker also had some of the cocoa that Cook prepared. One of the footmen brought him a cup about half an hour before Munro took the Queen's cocoa up to her room."

"Did Munro deliver Vicker's chocolate?"

French shook his head. "No, not Munro. Another footman."

"I suppose the two could have been in league together," I said.

"It's possible. Of course, Vicker might have ingested a small dose of poison to divert attention away from himself." He stopped to examine a crack in the stones, holding the candle up to the wall. He probed the fissure with a finger until he was satisfied no secret passage existed behind the wall, then he resumed his progress.

"Do you recall if the house plans Vicker had in his room showed this tunnel?"

I cogitated for a moment, trying to recall. "I can't remember. I only glanced at the plans for a few seconds."

"Perhaps you should make some enquiries among the servants, to try and find out whether the existence of the passage is well-known." French glanced over his shoulder at me. "Have you noticed that the tunnel has been descending? I believe we're underground now."

We emerged from the tunnel by way of an ancient oak door, crossed with iron, which led into a stone grotto at the edge of the castle grounds. It was tiny, no more than six feet by six, with a stone bench and a marble statue of some classical type, looking out of place here in the Highlands in its thin drapery. In the summer, the grotto would have been cool, dark and ferny, but in winter it was as cold and desolate as the grave. The door into the tunnel had merged into the back wall of stone, covered with moss. You could find it if you knew it was there, but a casual glance into the grotto would reveal nothing.

"If the plans you found in the library included the passage, then I should think everyone would know about it."

"Not necessarily," said French. "The plans were locked away in a cabinet, not lying about for just anyone to peruse."

"What a terrible houseguest you are," I said. "Picking locks and going through the owner's private effects. How did you know the plans were there?"

"I flattered the Queen by admiring her late husband's architectural aptitude. He designed Balmoral, for the most part, though he did hire an architect from Edinburgh to handle the details. I merely asked the Queen if she had any plans of the castle, and she told me where they were kept."

"Devious devil. Surely she would have shown them to you if you had asked."

French smiled. "I'm sure she would have, but I like to practice my skills as a screwsman."

I bit my tongue at that; no point in embarrassing the cove.

EIGHT

I was having a bite of luncheon with some of the other lady's maids in the kitchen, spinning an elaborate tale of a tumble on the stairs and the consequent damage to my face, when Robbie Munro came rushing in, his curls askew and his cheeks flushed with excitement. He scanned the room until his eyes came to rest on me, and he bustled over with the all the urgency of a Viennese soldier come to deliver the news that the Saracens were at the gates.

"You're to come at once, Miss Black," he panted, skidding to a halt at the table.

"What's the matter?"

"It's the marchioness. She was dining with the Queen. There's been an incident."

"An incident?"

"Come along," said Robbie impatiently. "I've been sent to fetch you and we mustn't tarry. I'll tell you on the way."

I dabbed my mouth and straightened my cap and off we went, with Robbie galloping along in front of me, kilt swishing from side to side (offering a tantalizing glimpse of clearly defined hamstrings), and me struggling to stay up with him.

"What has happened?" I called to him.

He slowed to a trot. "The marchioness stuffed a wad of pepper up her nose. I saw her myself. You wouldn't believe what happened next."

"Yes," I said wearily. "I would."

"The Queen was not amused. You're to take the marchioness away." He grimaced. "You'll have to do a bit of cleaning up. Of the marchioness, I mean."

The dining room was unexpectedly quiet when we entered. There was the embarrassed silence among the occupants that one encounters at family dinners when Auntie Rose loses her false teeth in a wineglass or Uncle James breaks wind during grace. The marchioness sat sullenly at the table while a couple of footmen hovered over her, attempting without much success to mop up the table and sponge off the old lady's dress. Her nearest neighbors had the dazed look of survivors of an artillery bombardment. I caught sight of French at the end of the table, grinning like a schoolboy with Red Hector. Lady Dalfad was rigid with disapproval, lips pursed. As for the Queen, her little pudding face was quivering with fury. She crooked a finger at me.

Damn and blast. So much for slipping into the room and extracting the marchioness without drawing attention to ourselves. I crawled up the room like an obsequious spaniel and dropped an inexpert curtsey. The Queen fixed me with a pale and murderous eye. She noted the developing bruise and scratches on my cheek (evidence to her, no doubt, of the kind of disreputable maid the marchioness would employ), but she was so infuriated that she did not comment upon my appearance.

"Have you been told what occurred here today?" Her voice was trembling with suppressed rage.

"I have, Your Highness."

"We are not amused." She pointed a plump finger down the table. "You will escort the marchioness to her room and remove that, that . . . *filth* from her clothes and her person."

"Yes, Your Highness."

"In the future, you will accompany the marchioness to meals. You will stand behind her until she has finished eating. Your attention to her will be *unremitting*, and you will see that nothing like this *ever* occurs again." She waved her hand in dismissal.

"Yes, Your Highness."

I collected the marchioness, and we skedaddled out of the room, with the marchioness holding her head erect, clutching my arm and teetering defiantly. I had to hand it to her; the old trout had pluck.

"It wasn't my fault," she rasped when we'd escaped the view of the scandalized diners. "Some fool put pepper on the table in front of me."

"Anyone could make the same mistake," I said soothingly.

This blatant lie mollified the marchioness.

"Indeed," she said. She squinted at me. "What the devil has happened to ye?"

I gave her the same fallacious account I'd provided to the servants.

"Clumsy oaf," she said, clutching my arm as we tottered along.

In her room I stripped off her gown and tossed it in the basket for the laundress to clean. Then I moistened a flannel and applied myself to removing the dried grains of pepper that had adhered to the marchioness's face. This was as laborious as performing surgery, and my eyes were beginning to cross by the time I'd scrubbed her clean. The marchioness's head was drooping by then, and I left her snoring comfortably under an eiderdown and headed to the kitchen for some refreshment. A cup of tea would be nice. A belt of brandy would be better.

Alas, there was no brandy in the offing, so I settled down on a bench beside Flora with a cup of a tea and one of Cook's scones.

"I suppose you've heard the news," I said. "My employer has disgraced the house of Tullibardine."

"I hear the Queen threw a wobbly. I'd have given anything to see it." She poked me in the ribs. "And I hear you're going to attend the marchioness at meals. That should be a treat. I'd love to hear what the toffs talk about after a few glasses of wine. And I'd love to spend a couple of hours staring at that fine Mr. French over the table."

"I hadn't thought about it that way," I said. "It might be entertaining, as long as I don't forget my duties and let the marchioness stick any foreign objects up her nose."

"Oh, do. I'd love to hear what the Queen does if it happens again."

"Probably consign the marchioness to the Tower and lop off my head."

Flora clapped her hand on my arm, sloshing tea onto the floor. "I almost forgot to tell you! There was a robbery last night in Ballater."

"Oh?" This would not be news in London, but apparently Ballater did not see much criminal activity beyond the theft of the odd ewe.

"Someone broke the window out of the chemist's shop and

cleaned out the place. They say whoever did it made off with enough medicine to kit out a hospital."

"Fancy that," I said. "Do the authorities have any clues?"

"Not a single one. Of course, that's no surprise. Grant, the constable in Ballater, is dimmer than a dying candle. He'll never find the thief."

"Pity," I said. I finished my tea and wiped the crumbs from my apron. "Well, I've a few minutes before I have to wake the marchioness and beautify her for dinner. I think I'll step outside for a breath of air."

I popped out of the servants' entrance, prepared for a blast of searingly cold Highland air in my lungs, only to be met with the eye-watering aroma of curry. In a corner of the courtyard, a pair of shivering Hindoos huddled over a wood fire, stirring a vile yellow swill in a blackened pot. I pulled my apron up over my nose and hurried around the corner, where a stiff breeze from the Cairngorms brought the tears to my eyes and scoured the odor from my nostrils.

I found a bit of shelter behind one of the turrets that dear departed Albert had added to the exterior of the castle, and surveyed the grounds. Except for the visits to the stone hut in the woods, I'd scarcely been out of the castle since arriving, and I was getting heartily sick of swabbing down the old lady and reading the Bible until the wee hours. A bit of fun wouldn't go amiss, and I set to wondering about the ghillies' ball and whether the dour Scots race was capable of throwing a party that didn't involve a lot of morose, bearded coves comparing notes on sheep. However, Flora had indicated the ball would be festive, and she looked like a miss who enjoyed getting oiled and sharing a romp on the dance floor with a likely lad. She'd made clear her intention to dance with French at the ball; although, I've had the pleasure of waltzing with the bloke, and I could have told Flora not to bother as the man was about as attentive as a ten-week-old fox terrier. But at the time we'd shared our dance at the Russian Embassy, French had been playing serious-minded government agent. Now that he was masquerading as an aristocratic boob, he might be pleasant company.

I was gazing aimlessly around the grounds (which, at this time of year, were not at their best), wondering why on earth the Queen would choose to vacation in this frigid clime when the contents of the royal treasury were available to her, when a black blur caught my eye. I watched with interest as Robbie Munro slunk furtively from the castle. At this time of day, he should be polishing silver or laying cutlery in preparation for dinner. I perked up at the prospect of following him; this was real espionage work, unlike playing nursemaid to a dotty member of the Upper Ten. Munro walked rapidly, hugging the wall of the castle, head swiveling as he scanned the area. He was clearly nervous, checking over his shoulder every few seconds to ensure he wasn't being followed. I applied myself to the granite as well, ducking in behind turrets, pillars and bowed windows (thank God, Prince Albert had been inordinately fond of such decorations and piled them on with a heavy hand), keeping a close eye on the footman.

Robbie turned the corner and exited the courtyard, glancing behind him as he did so. I found refuge behind a buttress until my quarry was out of sight, then rushed forward, gathering up my skirts and skating over the slippery cobblestones. At the corner I paused and cautiously inched forward for a peek. Munro was in view, hands jammed in his pockets, nervously describing circles at the side of the stables, out of sight of the main entrance and the horse stalls. He pulled a watch from his pocket and looked at it anxiously, then resumed his nervous pacing. He kept a sharp lookout, peering back at my hiding place from time to time, making it difficult to stay out of sight. As he was clearly waiting for someone, I cooled my heels for a bit, tucked up behind the corner. After a few minutes, I took a gander and found that Munro's appointment had arrived: Archie Skene.

The two had their heads bent close together while Munro talked and Skene listened, nodding now and then and tugging thoughtfully at his beard. I conned the area between me and the men, but there was no way I could get any closer, unless I just sauntered out and joined them, which of course would have meant the end of the conversation I so wanted to hear. I waited impatiently as the two conversed. Munro did most of the talking, jawing away while Skene looked up at him from under those furry eyebrows of his. Skene shook his head a couple of times, once vehemently, at which Munro looked frustrated and spoke sharply to the older man. Skene drew himself up to his full height (which wasn't much, as he could just about look over the withers of a Shetland pony when he did so) and tapped Munro on the chest. The footman took a step back, then raised a placating hand to Skene. Well, if Munro was the Marischal and Skene the lackey, the Scots clearly had different ideas about the deference due to the leader of the cabal.

The cold had seeped into my bones and I started to shiver. It was also getting onto the hour when I should be sprucing up the marchioness and donning my best uniform to attend her at dinner. If Skene and Munro didn't finish their confounded conversation soon, I'd have to leg it back inside the castle. I hugged myself and jogged quietly in place, willing Munro to get on with it. After an eternity, he ceased jabbering, and Skene bowed his head, as though considering what the footman had said. Then the two shook hands, Skene headed to the stables and Munro strode purposefully in my direction.

Curse it. I'd been so absorbed in watching Munro and Skene that I hadn't given a thought as to what I would do when Munro returned to the castle. No use looking for a hiding place; those turrets and towers had served very well to slither behind while tailing the footman, but as he walked back to the servants' entrance, I'd stand out like a Pathan at a picnic. Nothing to do but brazen it out, so I assumed an expression of affability and sauntered around the corner to meet Munro.

He started guiltily when he saw me, halting abruptly and giving me a stony stare. By now he must be wondering why I kept appearing like a magician's apprentice.

I smiled amiably. "Why, Robbie, I didn't expect to see you out here. Don't you have duties to attend to?"

"Don't you?" He said it coldly. He was not best pleased to encounter me.

"I do. I was just having a stroll before the evening's work commences. You know I'm to accompany the marchioness to dinner. I needed to steel myself for the task."

He grinned and relaxed visibly. "I can't say that I blame you. I suppose I'll see you at dinner, then."

I nodded, and he marched away, leaving me to ruminate about the scene I'd just observed.

I suppose in my senescence, I'll be able to tell my grandchildren (if such creatures should ever exist) that their old grammy dined with Victoria Regina, Queen of the United Kingdom of Great Britain and Ireland and Empress of India. There'll be no need to mention that I did so decked out in a sober black skirt and shirtwaist, with a lacy white apron and a matching cap, standing several feet from the table. The little beggars won't believe me anyway. They'll hoot out loud at the news and say cruel things about my mental state, and I'll cuff them on the ear and send them running in tears to their mama. Ah, the joys of old age.

Dinner with the Queen was as stiff an affair as I've ever attended. The Queen sat at the head of the table, of course, where she could keep an eye on things and tamp down any fun in the offing that did not meet her approval. The chairs nearest her were occupied by officious-looking coves in black tie and gaudy ribbons and medals and such, and their pale, overfed wives stuffed into gowns of crimson and bottle green velvet. Dizzy had pride of place, next to the Queen, and he was putting on a brave face, though he looked pale and haggard, and he shook violently now and then as draughts of cold air circulated through the room. Even his dress was subdued this evening; he had donned his monkey suit like the rest of the men, and his only concession to his peculiar fashion proclivities was a pair of spotless white gloves and a half-dozen rings worn over them, their jewels winking in the firelight. He spent a good bit of time jollying the Queen along and making her giggle like a schoolgirl, but you could tell his heart wasn't in it. When one of the other chaps in the Queen's circle would jump in with a story about the campaign at Sobraon, Dizzy would lean back in his chair and let his eyes wander over the table while he sipped sparingly at a glass of champagne. On one of his surveys of the room, he caught my eye, and one of his own heavy lids drooped briefly in what might have been a wink.

Bertie, Prince of Wales, was situated at the other end of the table, which was both boon and burden. From this distance, he was free to fondle the knees of the ladies seated on either side of him and talk cards and horses with the men, but he had to keep a watchful eye on his mater, lest she catch him engaging in some hilarity. I rather enjoyed watching the royal lecher swill champers and gorge down course after course of fine French cooking while he pawed his female companions, all the while darting nervous glances the length of the table to see if his mother had noticed that he was enjoying himself. I felt a swelling of sympathy for the sybaritic swine, until I noticed he had noticed me and was leering over his wineglass in my direction. I dropped my eyes and strove for modesty.

Just down the table from Bertie, French and Red Hector had been seated opposite each other, and I had my first good look at the chap. He had the complexion of a dedicated sportsman and boozehound: chapped, freckled, pitted and pocked, and the colour of a well-used saddle. Flaming red hair receded from a domed forehead, which indicated a larger brain than French had indicated it actually held. The piggy eyes held not a glint of intelligence but plenty of malice, and his lips were the loose, red, wet lips of a libertine. All in all, he was the sort of coarse, crude character that French would have studiously avoided had he had the choice. I was glad to know that French's life at Balmoral was not without its complications.

Their dinner companions were considerably older than French and Red Hector (in one instance being so ancient and still I thought she might have left this vale of tears during the first course). I enjoyed a smirk at that; no doubt the crones who had been seated near the two men had been deliberately placed to stifle any untoward behavior. One of those crones happened to be the marchioness, and I breathed a prayer of thanks to the Bearded Cove in the Firmament that I was well placed to hear whatever indiscretions Red Hector might utter. He and French were engaged in a contest to see who could empty the Queen's cellar first, with Red Hector quaffing champagne as though it were water and French following suit. Red Hector looked as though he'd just rushed in from coursing hares, thrown off his outdoor garments and climbed into an ancient dinner jacket, doubtless handed down with the baronet's title. There appeared to be a blade of withered grass still tangled in his ginger hair. French was neater (no surprise there; he was as fastidious as a cat when it came to his appearance), although his hair had obviously not made acquaintance with a comb in some time. The two were cracking jokes and crowing with laughter, while their nearest companions looked askance and inched away from them. They were prattling on about the steeplechase circuit, each one trying to top the other with stories of the debaucheries they'd enjoyed at various races. The old pussies were growing purple and trembling with indignation, except for the marchioness, who was shoveling salmon mayonnaise into her mouth with all the finesse of a starving stevedore and grinning foolishly at the two young ruffians as she listened to their tales. That reminded me that my purpose tonight was to keep the marchioness from spraying the Queen's guests like an out-of-control fire hose, so I took note of the location of the salt cellars, pepper pots and sugar bowls. None appeared in reach of the marchioness, but I doubted that would stop Her Ladyship from embarrassing herself; she was remarkably adept at doing so. I poised like a ballerina, ready to leap if the marchioness's hand strayed toward any powdery substance.

Evidently, French had judged that Red Hector was ready to be plucked, for he leaned across the table in a confidential manner, cast a wary glance toward the Prince of Wales to see that he wasn't listening (of course he wasn't; he had his left hand up the petticoats of the nearest lass and was mooning like a love-struck calf into her eyes) and said: "I say, old chap, have you heard the latest about the Queen and that bounder Brown?"

Red Hector snorted. "Good Gad. An aging widow sporting about with a younger man is bad enough, but when she's the Queen and he's a commoner, it beggars belief. At least the bloke is a Scot. You know we Scots have a rough charm the ladies find irresistible." He smiled ferociously at the marchioness, who cawed with laughter.

"Apparently, Brown and the Queen have been seen sharing a glass of whisky before bed."

Red Hector's eyebrows waggled.

"And," French said, "Her Highness has commissioned a painting of Brown, to hang at Windsor. His Highness won't be pleased." French nodded significantly toward Bertie. It was no secret that the Prince of Wales hated John Brown and would have sent him packing with a foot up his kilt, but the Queen wouldn't allow it.

Red Hector shot a condescending glance at Bertie. "A Scottish mother wouldn't dare behave in such a way, and a Scottish son wouldn't allow it if she did. Those two have nerve, calling themselves royalty and ordering the rest of us about. It's bad enough they're not Scottish. Why, they're not even English. The Queen's half German, for Christ's sake. Her mother was princess of some insignificant German duchy, and then the Queen married that oaf Albert, who couldn't even speak English properly. What a tribulation for a great nation to bear."

French toyed with his champagne glass. "You mean England?"

"Of course I don't mean bloody England," roared Red Hector. Silence descended upon the dining table. The Queen looked up sharply.

Red Hector grinned at her and waved his glass. "A pleasant

wine, Your Highness," he said. The Queen glowered at him, but Dizzy leaned toward her with a witticism that brought a smile to her lips, and she settled down to flirt with her prime minister.

Red Hector wiped his face, which was shining with sweat and flushed from heat and drink. "I mean Scotland. We Scots have mortgaged our heritage, and for what? A chance to trade in the English colonies and be ruled by a cluster of German dolts who wear the plaid and pretend they're entitled to do so. My ancestors are turning over in their graves right now."

French shrugged. "There is nothing to be done. You Scots have tried to gain your independence and failed." He sipped his wine and added, by way of an afterthought, "Many times, in fact."

Red Hector swelled like a puff adder. I thought he'd pop his collar or have a stroke or pull out his *sgian dubh* and go for French's throat. The marchioness cackled appreciatively, and I contemplated whether it would be pistols at dawn or edged weapons on the lawn at noon.

"If I didn't like you so much, French, I might take offense at that. It's true, you cursed English have beaten down every uprising, but a few English toffs have watered the soil of Scotland with their blood in the process."

"Just stating the facts, old man," said French. "I don't have a dog in this fight. I really don't care if we have a German or a Scot or a bloody Hottentot on the throne, so long as it doesn't interfere with my fun. Besides, the present lot aren't going anywhere. Bertie's ready to assume the throne as soon as Mama corks it, and he's got a litter of half a dozen to choose from next, not to mention plenty of offspring from the other side of the sheets."

"Och, weel, you never know what the fates have in store for you."

"The clans may rise again, eh, Hector?"

Red Hector gave a sly smile and finished his wine. "Hard to say,

French. We Scots are unpredictable. The only loyalties we have are to kith, kin and the old ways."

"Hear, hear," mumbled the marchioness through a mouthful of veal, though I detected a note of disappointment that the two strapping young fellows weren't going to fling off their jackets and climb into one another.

After that, dinner passed without incident. I suppose French felt he'd baited Red Hector enough for one evening, and I suppose he was right. The Scot might hate the English monarch, but he wasn't foolish enough to openly advocate knocking her off while he enjoyed the delights of her table. The marchioness behaved herself admirably; only once did she grow restless and her fingers stray toward the salt cellar, but I leapt forward like a startled deer and shoved her wineglass into her outstretched hand. She seemed surprised to find it there, but she drank dutifully, and then the footmen carried in an enormous Bakewell tart and a variety of sherbets, and the marchioness forgot all about snuff.

I knew the test would come after dinner, when my employer would be hankering for the consolation of tobacco, especially given the joyless company she had to endure with the Queen and Lady Dalfad and more of their ilk, until the men finished their port and cigars and joined the ladies for a few hands of cards and some lively conversation. During the procession of the ladies from the dining room to the parlor, I spirited my old gal away to a dark corner, where I plied her with a healthy dose of Mr. Mitchell's best, held a thick napkin to her face while she expectorated most of what I had shoveled into her, and dabbed her clean. Then I shoved her back into the parade and followed dutifully.

After an evening among the swells, I could understand why their menfolk made a beeline to the likes of Lotus House at the first opportunity. I have never been as bored in my life as I was that night (save for the incident that ended the evening, which I shall recount in detail in half a mo). There were a few rum coves (French and Red Hector among them) who migrated to a distant corner and engaged in much merriment, assisted by the consumption of gallons of brandy, but the rest of the crowd was as flat as one of Mrs. Drinkwater's Yorkshire puddings. A doughy-faced girl played the piano, and a pale youth, slender as a whippet, sang sentimental songs in a reedy tenor that made the Queen wipe her eye. We were all made to suffer through "The Bonnie Banks of Loch Lomond" and "My Ain Folk" and a particularly dreadful version of "Dark Lochnagar," sung no doubt for the Queen's benefit to remind her of the brooding rocky crag that loomed over Balmoral from a distance. Then one of the minor Scottish aristocrats got nervously to his feet and cleared his throat and, after much blushing and mumbling, treated us to a recitation of a number of Rabbie Burns's poems. By the time he'd worked his way through "Man Was Made to Mourn" and "The Farewell," the Queen's face had screwed tight and her eyes were gushing, being reminded, I'm sure, of dear departed Albert. By then, I was considering running up to French's room to borrow his straight razor so as to slit my wrists and put an end to my misery.

But while the Queen was snuffling into her handkerchief and Lady Dalfad was patting her hand and whispering consoling words in her ear, I noticed Red Hector stagger away from the group in the corner and approach the Queen. French made a halfhearted attempt to catch the fellow's arm, but Red Hector jerked it away and lumbered on, his swinish eyes glittering with spite. He planted himself before the Queen, and she looked up in astonishment, her nonplussed expression quickly altering to one of fury. Apparently, Red Hector hadn't gotten the memorandum

that informed houseguests they were never to approach the
Queen without being asked to do so by Her Highness, but then,
as the man was clearly potted, he couldn't have read it any way.
Now, this, I thought, could be interesting.

One of the military chaps who'd sat near the Queen at dinner
stepped in with a snarl. "See here, old boy . . ."

Red Hector brushed him aside like a troublesome mosquito. A
terrible silence descended upon the room. The ladies huddled together, dismayed, with their lace mittens over their mouths. The
responsible male members of the party were holding sotto voce
conversations about the best way to subdue this drunken sot, and
the servants were exhibiting an unhealthy interest in the spectacle
taking shape. Dizzy's ebony ringlets bounced in agitation. French
looked on with a cold eye. I noticed he had followed Red Hector
and now stood nearly at his side, within easy striking distance of
the man. French's right hand had strayed into his pocket, where
no doubt it rested upon his Remington .41 rimfire derringer, beloved weapon of American gamblers in the saloons of the western
frontier, and a deadly weapon at such short range.

Red Hector swayed dangerously, then regained his balance.
"I'm pleased to see that Your Majesty is a great fan of our Rabbie.
He was a damned fine wordsmith. There's a song of his that I'm
verra fond of, and I think you'll like it, too."

He thrust back his head, fixed his eyes on the stag's head over
the mantle and opened his mouth. I can't say much for Red Hector's singing voice, but it hardly mattered. It was the song that he
sang that made the Queen's eyes pop out and shouts of protest
ring around the room. If you're the literate type, you'll recognize
it immediately as "Scots, Wha Hae," which is the bard's rendition
of Robert the Bruce's address to his army of Scotsmen, just before
they whipped King Edward's English forces at the Battle of

Bannockburn. If you haven't heard this verse before, I've set it out below, just so you'll get the flavor of the thing and understand the row it kicked up when Red Hector belted it out before the Queen.

> *Scots, wha hae wi' Wallace bled,*
> *Scots wham Bruce has often led;*
> *Welcome to yer gory bed,*
> *Or to Victorie!*

> *Now's the day and now's the hour;*
> *See the front o' battle lour:*
> *See approach Proud Edward's pow'r—*
> *Chains and slaverie!*

> *Wha will be a traitor-knave?*
> *Wha can fill a coward's grave?*
> *Wha sae base as be a slave?*
> *Let him turn and flee!*

> *Wha for Scotland's King and law,*
> *Freedom's sword will strongly draw;*
> *Free-man stand, or Free-man fa'?*
> *Let him follow me!*

> *By Oppression's woes and pains!*
> *By your sons in servile chains!*
> *We will drain our dearest veins,*
> *But they shall be free!*

> *Lay the proud usurpers low!*
> *Tyrants fall in every foe!*

Liberty's in every blow!
Let us do, or die!

Red Hector finished with a flourish, bowing deeply at the waist and nearly falling over as he did so. There was a moment of stunned silence, then a hellish babble broke out with all the military duffers wheezing asthmatically, the ladies chattering shrilly, and the politicos harrumphing into their beards.

"How dare you?" hissed Lady Dalfad.

"You impertinent little whelp," growled some earl or other.

There were cries of "cad" and "bounder" and "bloody Scottish louse," which fazed Red Hector not one bit. He grinned widely at his audience, his eyeballs drifted toward each other, then they crossed entirely, and he toppled over slowly onto the tartan carpet.

It was close on to midnight before the uproar had died down, with the marchioness cackling like a crazed hen (which earned her an almighty scowl from Lady Dalfad), and the ladies being bustled out of the room while the gents stayed behind to speak in outraged tones about what to do with such an irresponsible rogue. I expect a few were calling for his head, and I anticipated hearing the sound of gallows being erected in the courtyard at first light, but in the event I was disappointed.

I finally wrestled the marchioness into bed and drifted off to my own, musing about Red Hector's performance. If he was the Marischal, he'd passed up a first-class opportunity to scrag the Queen. I didn't number many political assassins among my acquaintances (well, none, if I tell the truth, and I always do, unless necessity dictates otherwise), but I didn't think there would be many who'd opt to sing a tune to their victims instead of knifing them in the gut. Puzzling. I resolved to raise the issue with French, when next we met. I fell into bed with my clothes on, not even bothering to remove my shoes, and my foresight was rewarded when the marchioness summoned me less than an hour after I'd left her. She was wound as tight as a spring from the evening's events, and she gassed on for ever so long about Red Hector and his boldness. She sounded half-admiring, but I suppose it was the Scot in her, as our northern brothers love nothing so much as a daring charge against hopeless odds.

"What do you suppose the Queen will do?" I asked.

"Send the boy packin', I should say. And tell the Earl of Nairn that his favorite nephew is a bloomin' idiot."

"I don't suppose Red Hector can expect another royal invitation any time soon."

The marchioness chuckled. "Och, he'll not be asked again. Still," she added wistfully, "'twas a fine ballad he sang, drunk as he was. It's one of my favorites, but our English cousins are always so touchy when Bannockburn is mentioned."

We talked Scottish history for a while, or rather the marchioness did, for I was falling asleep in my chair, but I woke just long enough to interject some question or comment before falling back into a muddled haze. The old trout had an encyclopedic knowledge of every battle fought between the English and the Scots (and if you know your history, you know there's a fair number of them), so I got an earful of Bruce's spider and the Young Pretender, and "Butcher" Cumberland and the perfidy of Clan Campbell at Glencoe. All very interesting, if you've a head for things of that sort, but I had to struggle to stay up with the narrative. I suppose the lesson I derived from the marchioness's maunderings was that Scots have long swords and short memories.

Toward daylight, Ross the piper marched in stately and solitary procession around the castle, his pipe bleating like a lost sheep, stopping the marchioness in midspate.

"Good heavens, it's nearly time for breakfast. Why on earth have ye kept me up this late, Ina? I should have been asleep hours ago."

I shrugged helplessly.

"And I've been invited by the Queen to visit the stables with her this mornin'. There's a new litter of collie pups I want to see. I breed 'em, you know."

I assumed she meant that she bred canine bitches to studs, but who knows what goes on north of the border?

"When are you to be ready, my lady?"

"Eleven. Or was it noon? Cursed if I know."

"I'll find out and be here in time to get you dressed and ready. Shall I have breakfast sent up?"

The marchioness nodded vigorously. "Yes, do. And tell them to put extra marmalade on the tray. Bit stingy with it yesterday. There wasn't enough to cover a shillin'."

Toward noon I corralled the marchioness, and we joined the small party invited by the Queen to see her new pups and the Highland ponies in the stable. This interested me about as much as joining cricket practice, but Miss Boss had caught me in the kitchen and informed me that the Queen was still shaken from Red Hector's outburst of the night before, and it would be best if the marchioness were kept under surveillance to ensure she did nothing to upset Her Highness. So there I was, diligently following the requisite three steps behind the marchioness across the frozen cobbles and wondering what the old turnip might find to inhale in the stables.

French was a member of the party. He leered at me, touching the brim of his hat. One or two of the old ladies in the group spied his greeting and tut-tutted under their breath. They gave

him the cold shoulder for the rest of the tour, but he just sauntered along, twirling his walking stick in his hand and looking
unconcerned.

The Queen led the parade with John Brown, her hand resting
delicately on his arm, while the Prince of Wales stamped along
behind with a scowl on his face. You'd have thought Brown was
the King of England himself as he strutted along with his whiskers blowing in the wind and Her Majesty leaning against him,
looking adoringly into his face. I could understand how Bertie
must feel, watching his mother, ruler of almost a half-million
souls around the globe, behaving like a giddy schoolgirl in the
throes of first love. So much for dear departed Albert, I thought.

It was a beautiful day. The sun on my shoulders was warm,
and though there was a sharp wind off the mountains, we were
protected from it in the walled courtyard. We visited the pups
first, and as dogs go, they were adorable. The ladies billed and
cooed over the tiny wriggling bundles of black and white, and
stroked them delicately while the marchioness pinched one
by the nape of the neck and hauled it up for a critical perusal.
I didn't know you could look at a dog for that long, but the
marchioness examined every detail of the mutt, muttering appreciatively at the length of a toe or the thickness of a whisker,
while the bitch (I mean the pup's mother, of course) whined
and fretted and capered about nervously underfoot. When my
employer had finished inspecting the little fellow, she dropped
him briskly back into the pen, to be nuzzled anxiously by his
mum and pushed about by his littermates. He went searching
for the milk dispenser, apparently none the worse for his experience.

"Deuced fine litter, Yer Highness," said the marchioness to the
Queen.

The Queen's sour countenance split into a genuine smile. "Do you think so? They're out of Megan by my old fellow Sharp."

"If Sharp's the father, then I shall certainly take one. There's never been a finer dog than Sharp. Sharp is his name, and sharp he is," the marchioness announced.

The Queen beamed. "There will never be another like him," she cried.

While Her Highness and the marchioness chatted about the merits of various collies they had known, and the kennel master and his assistants stood around silent and respectful, I wandered off a bit and surveyed our party. The ladies were still making eyes over the pups, and the gentlemen had formed little knots and were chuntering on about politics, the state of the Empire and the next winner at Exham. French had removed himself from the crowd and was enjoying a cheroot. John Brown was chewing on one of the lads about the straw bedding in the kennels, and watching Brown from a distance, his mouth puckered with hatred, was Archie Skene. Brown must have felt the man's gaze upon him because he straightened abruptly and turned to face Skene. Brown didn't acknowledge Skene, just gave him a look of such arrogant superiority that I immediately decided to back Skene, whether he was a member of the Sons of Arbroath or not. I sucked in my breath, waiting for fisticuffs to break out, while the rivals stared at each other across the yard. Skene looked ready to burst with rage, fists clenching and unclenching, face contorted, and his eyebrows twisting like trapped weasels. Brown was a cool customer, haughty as a young lancer, smirking as he watched Skene wrestle with the urge to lay him out in front of the Queen. After a staredown that lasted for an eternity, Skene turned and stalked away, while Brown's smile broadened until his attention was claimed by the Queen, who wanted confirmation of the intelligence of the dear departed Sharp.

French discarded his cheroot, grinding it beneath his heel, and crooked his finger at one of the doors into the stables. Vincent scuttled out and held a brief conversation with his lord and master. French patted him on the shoulder, and Vincent stole off in the direction Skene had taken.

Our party moved into the stables for a visit to the equine residents. No stylish Thoroughbreds here; these were Highland ponies, built to trek the mountain trails and pick their way over the moors. I could see why the Queen was so fond of them, for they bore a decided resemblance to one another, both being stout, broad and rather dowdy in appearance. The ponies had bright, kind eyes, but their colours were muted and dull, ranging from cream to mouse to grey. They put their heads over the stall doors and neighed softly, expecting a handout, which of course they got in spades, as both the ladies and the gentlemen of our group vied to hand out carrots and apples and lumps of sugar. The Queen pointed out her favorite and described the many wonderful rides she and Mr. Brown had shared through the nearby mountains, while Brown simpered and played up to the old bag, and the two teased each other like married folk. I figured Skene must be frothing at the mouth somewhere, listening to this drivel.

I had seen the exterior of the stables when I had followed Robbie Munro to his rendezvous with Skene. The interior was neat as a pin, with stalls and loose boxes for the horses arranged along one of the exterior walls and on either side of a dividing wall down the center. The fourth wall was reserved for tack; bridles, saddles and harnesses of various types hung on pegs on the boards or were laid out on sawhorses and tables. Overhead, a long loft ran the length of the stables, where, the helpful Brown informed us, bedding and fodder for the animals was stored. I was pleasantly relieved that the floors were clean, though I supposed

I shouldn't have been; I doubt the Queen would have tolerated even a speck of manure on the floor. There were openings in the ceiling above each stall or box, so that hay could be forked into the mangers below, and two large openings through which hay and sacks of grain could be hauled into the storage room above. There was a block and tackle at each of the large apertures, so the stable boys wouldn't strain themselves. All in all, it was a neat operation, and about what you'd expect to see when the owner of the stables is a monarch and has the cash to throw around on such things.

The Queen and her guests had finished petting the ponies and we were all moseying toward the door, when there was a metallic screech overhead, followed by an ear-splitting creak as wood splintered. All eyes turned to the block and tackle overhead, which had tilted precariously to one side, where it teetered and held for a moment, then succumbed to the pull of gravity and tumbled through the opening. There was a bloody great commotion, as you can imagine, with the ladies shrieking and the gentleman dashing about, throwing themselves on the nearest feminine flesh and shoving the females out of the way of the plunging machinery. I made a grab for the marchioness and caught one wispy arm, yanking her from harm's way and tossing her aside as though she'd been a rag doll. Then French bore down on me like a demented wrestler, wrapping me in his arms in a flying tackle that knocked the wind from me. We crashed into the side of a loose box, which collapsed under our weight, and tumbled into the hay.

"India, are you alright?"

My mouth was full of hay and my ribs had been crushed by French's overzealous defense of my person. It was impossible to speak.

French seized my arms and shook me vigorously. "India, speak to me!"

I tried to draw breath, without success. My uncharacteristic silence spurred French to action. His brow furrowed with concern, he thumped me sharply between the shoulder blades. This had the effect of removing the hay from my mouth but left my lungs bereft of air. Consequently, I remained speechless. French squeezed me to his chest, his grey eyes boring into mine with an intensity I found both irritating and strangely touching.

There was an infernal hubbub going on, with some of the weaker sex wailing like banshees and several of the elderly gentlemen mumbling hysterically (especially the politicos, who were used to nothing more upsetting than weak tea in the afternoon), but I could hear one of the retired military types barking orders and chivvying the groomsmen and servants. As yet, no one seemed to notice that one of the nobility seemed preoccupied with a certain lady's maid, but it was only a matter of time before one of the aristocratic harpies noticed French ministering tenderly to me, and then we'd both be in the soup.

I drew a strangled breath. "The Queen?"

At the sound of my voice, some of the intensity drained from French's gaze. He reluctantly dragged his eyes from mine and gazed around. "She appears to be unscathed. It looks as though Brown pulled her aside."

Wheezing like a Welsh pit pony, I struggled to sit upright.

"Here," said French anxiously, "let me help you."

I shook my head. "The marchioness?"

French issued a soft bark of laughter. "She's wandering around the sight of the accident, telling the young ladies to pull themselves together."

"I need to tend to her."

French raised an eyebrow. "She looks more capable of tending to you at the moment." He touched my ribs gingerly. "Does that hurt?"

"Ouch! Stop that, you damned heathen."

"I believe you've cracked a rib." French probed carefully.

I winced, inhaling sharply. "Stop poking me. I'll be fine. And you need to get over there in the general melee and stop hovering over one of the servants."

"You need medical attention."

"I wouldn't have, except some well-meaning oaf poleaxed me when I wasn't expecting it."

French scowled. "That's the thanks I get for saving your life?"

I waved a hand, indicating our near surroundings. "I was twenty bloody feet from that block and tackle. There's no way it could have hit me."

French grunted. "Ungrateful wench. Rescue yourself next time." He pushed himself to his feet.

I don't know what possessed me. It must have been the effect of being flung about like a rat in a terrier's jaws and being deprived of oxygen for such a long time that the part of my brain that rendered me incapable of being nice to French had been damaged, but I reached up and caught his sleeve.

"French," I muttered, looking at his boots, "thank you."

He took my hand and pulled me to my feet. There was a ghost of a smile on his face.

"My pleasure, India." He trotted off in the direction of the Queen.

I tracked down the marchioness, who was haranguing one of the lesser nobility, Lady Somebody or Other, who was weeping copiously and trembling like a frightened doe.

"Come on, lass. Buck up. Show some of that English courage."

The girl continued to sob. The marchioness sighed in exasper-ation and gnawed her lip with one of her yellowed stumps.

"Are you well, m'lady?" I asked.

Her rheumy eyes gleamed dully. "Bit of a hullabaloo there. I thought the old girl had pegged it for sure, but that bloody man seems to have pushed her out of the way just in time."

"It doesn't look as though anyone has been hurt," I said.

"Not a scratch on any of us," said the marchioness. She looked contemptuously at the sniveling girl. "Although ye'd think some-one had been smashed to bits, by the way this young booby is carryin' on."

The marchioness rounded on me. "Where have ye been?" Her eyes narrowed. "Ye haven't been with the prince, have ye?"

"Of course not," I said, my dalliance with French in the loose box making me feel a bit guilty and, consequently, snappish. I mean, I know Bertie is a bounder of the first rank, but would he really use the opportunity afforded by his mother's near-fatal ac-cident to drag a maid off into the nearest stall for a bit of the rumpo? Doubtless the fellow had other things on his mind at the time, such as just how close he'd come to laying hands on the crown and getting out from under Her Highness's thumb. The prince did look a bit disappointed, I thought, stroking his beard regretfully while John Brown petted his mama and the guests milled about.

The marchioness slipped her arm through mine. "I need a cup of tea, Irene. Take me back to the house. I wonder if this will delay luncheon?" she mused as we wound our way through the splin-tered timbers and around the block and tackle, now smashed to bits on the stable floor. We had nearly reached the door when the young lady the marchioness had been chiding issued a scream that would have made the witches of *Macbeth* envious. I whirled round in time to see Vincent stagger out of one of the stalls, his face pinched and white, his hand to the back of his head. French ran to meet him, and the little fellow made it as far as French's arms before he collapsed. French cupped Vincent's head tenderly, frowned, then examined his palm. Even from where I stood, I could see that it was covered with blood.

NINE

" 'Course," Vincent said through a mouthful of cake, " 'twasn't about to tell anyone wot really 'appened to me. I figured it 'twas better just to say I'd fallen out o' the loft and let 'em think I was a hidiot, than say I'd been bashed on the 'ead and halert the hassassins."

"Except that presumably the assassins are already on the alert, given that someone felt compelled to put a dent in your skull." I helped myself to some of the cake before it all disappeared down Vincent's gullet.

French, Vincent and I had repaired to the stone cottage before tea, the frightening accident in the stables having sent the Queen and her guests off to their rooms with cold compresses for a collective lie-down. The Queen had managed to choke down enough luncheon for a family of four before submitting to her attendants' demands that she retire to her room and rest. I know, for I was there, seeing that the marchioness didn't inhale anything she shouldn't. My employer did me proud, however, forging with abandon through the courses but otherwise behaving herself. After luncheon, I put her down for a nap and escaped to the hut.

"Tell us again how it happened," said French.

"I was followin' Archie, just like you told me," Vincent obliged. "'E went 'round the corner of the stables and I 'urried after 'im, peekin' round to see where 'e'd got to. I saw 'im climbin' up a ladder to the loft. 'E went inside and I clumb up after 'im." He found a stray raisin on the table and put it daintily into his mouth. "When I got up there, Archie 'ad disappeared. I snuck round the place for a while but couldn't see nobody. Then I 'eard voices and right then, I 'eard a noise over by the block and tackle. I crept over there, quiet as a mouse, but there was no one about. I was lookin' down at the Queen through that there openin', and the next thing I know, I'm wakin' up in one of the stalls, my 'ead poundin' like I'd been drinkin' that swill Ned Palmer at the Helephant and Castle calls gin."

Vincent's wound had been cleaned and bandaged by Doctor Jenner, and he'd changed out of his bloody coat into a clean one. He looked rather cheerful, considering he'd been tomahawked and thrown into a stall down one of the shafts used to toss fodder to the horses.

French was turning a bun in his hands, staring absently at the wall. "It could be coincidence."

"First the poisoned cocoa, and now the accident with the block and tackle?" I snorted. "I think it unlikely under the circumstances."

"*If* the chocolate was poisoned," interjected Vincent. "Wot's ole Robshaw got to say about that?"

"Nothing yet. The tests at the laboratory aren't complete."

"Wish that bloomin' cove would get a move on," Vincent grumbled. "Wot's 'e waitin' on, anyway?"

French shrugged, shredding the bun into tiny pieces, which he dropped onto the table. "Suppose the incidents did not occur by happenstance. Does that strike anyone as odd?"

I hate it when French plays the bloody schoolmaster, as though we were all back at Eton, studying the classics. I thought for a bit. There was something unusual about the episodes involving the Queen.

"Neither seems to have been a serious attempt to kill her," I said. "If you planned to poison someone, wouldn't you make sure there was enough of the stuff in the drink to do the job? And as for the block and tackle, well, it made enough noise to wake the dead when it fell over. Even someone as immobile as the Queen would have plenty of time to get out of the way. If the nationalists do have someone in the castle, why haven't they done as they've threatened and carked Her Highness by now?"

"Yeah," agreed Vincent. "'Ow come the hassassin ain't shot 'er or stabbed 'er? 'Ow come 'e's pussyfootin' about?"

"Good question, Vincent. The nationalists made it clear they intended to kill the Queen," said French. "We've assumed that meant a very public act, one in which the assassin himself might die, as a means of making a political statement."

"Instead, the attacks on Her Highness have been the kind in which the killer remains anonymous. Obviously, he wants to remain alive and undetected." I ate some cake and ruminated over a few things. "If these really were attempts on her life, the perpetrators are bloody clumsy, or the deeds weren't meant to be taken seriously."

"The nationalists' idea of macabre fun? Frighten Her Highness to death instead of killing her outright? If that's the idea, it hasn't been successful." French gathered his crumbs from the table and wadded them in his handkerchief for disposal. "The Queen refuses to countenance the 'absurd notion,' as she describes it, that anyone is trying to assassinate her here at Balmoral. She has complete trust in her servants and guests. Dizzy is about to pull out his hair. He's begged Her Highness to return to London, but she says to do so would contravene dear Albert's wish, and she refuses to go."

"So we have two incidents, which might be accidents or warning shots across the bow or actual attempts on the Queen's life. Which do you think it is, French?"

"The block an' tackle fallin' 'tweren't no haccident," said Vincent, "not with me gettin' clobbered on the noggin like that."

I had to admit he had a point. "So we eliminate the idea that the Queen has had a run of bad luck lately. Is the Marischal trying to put the wind up Her Highness's sails?" I adopted my best Scottish brogue: "Here we are, Your Majesty. We can come for you anytime we want, so we're having a bit of fun, watching you and your advisors squirm about like insects in a jar."

"Except," said French, "as I have already pointed out, she's not squirming."

"Dizzy is. And I'll bet Robshaw's not sleeping well at night. Have you spoken to him?"

"I see him every day, and I spoke to him after the affair in the stables this morning. He believes they were genuine attempts on the Queen's life. But it's his job to protect her, and hence you would expect the man to treat these occurrences as authentic."

"We were told the Marischal was intelligent and forceful, and the Sons of Arbroath were a dangerous organization," I said. "Is Robshaw's intelligence wrong? Are we dealing with a group of bumbling clowns?"

"You may be correct, India," said French, which shocked me so much I choked on a bite of cake.

Vincent shot to his feet, overturning his chair, and gave me a thump on the back. "Ya want to watch them raisins. You can swaller one down the wrong 'ole and kill yourself."

I thanked him for his concern. Between French's exuberant rescue in the stable and Vincent's boisterous heroics just now, I was not going to be fighting fit in the morning. My ribs ached, and my spine felt as though Thor had been playing the scales on it.

Assured that I would live, French resumed his professorial air. "I believe you were right when you said the killer wants to commit the deed and escape, er, scot-free, as the saying goes. There would be tremendous publicity value in killing the Queen and evading capture. Just think of the effect on government officials and politicians. They'd be terrified that they might be the next victims. The Sons of Arbroath could create a climate of fear that sweeps the land, and engender contempt for the government for failing to catch the Queen's killer."

Vincent nodded sagely, as if he discussed the effect of political assassinations on public opinion on a regular basis. "That ole Marischal would be pleased as punch if 'e could stir up people like that. 'E'd be a legend."

"Thereby attracting more supporters to his cause," I said briskly. "Now that we've figured out these were real attempts on the Queen's life and that the Marischal is behind them, let's deal with the most important issue: who is he?"

"Robshaw has not turned up any evidence that Vicker, Red Hector, Skene or Munro have any affiliations with the Sons of Arbroath," said French. "He finally heard from London this morning."

"You're joking," I cried. "I found nationalist tracts in Munro's room. Why would he keep them if he didn't have an interest in them? Robshaw's agents must be incompetent."

"Or perhaps they've found nothing because there's nothing to find. Someone might have given the tracts to Munro, and he's thrown them in the drawer and forgotten about them."

I sniffed. Munro didn't strike me as being too lazy to ball up a political leaflet and toss it in the trash. He must have kept it for a reason.

"I recognize that stubborn look, India. I'm not saying that Munro isn't a member of the Sons of Arbroath, only that Robshaw hasn't turned up any evidence that he is. There may be an innocent explanation for the pamphlets in the drawer."

"What about the revolver in Robbie's room? I still think we should keep an eye on him."

"I agree."

"And"—I looked at French—"if you were paying attention at the concert last evening, you'll remember that one of the verses of Burns's song that Red Hector sang is printed on the leaflet I found in Munro's drawer. You know the verse: 'Lay the proud usurpers low,' " I began.

"Yes, I recognize the verse, and it had not escaped my notice that both Munro and Red Hector are acquainted with it. But then, I would expect most of the population of Scotland to be, as fond as the Scots are of Robert Burns."

"That's true," I admitted. "Even the marchioness likes that ditty."

"Well, then," said Vincent (he'd consumed the last of the cake and was getting bored), "which one of them fellers is it?"

"The Marischal is reputed to be eloquent and charismatic," I said, recalling our briefing from Dizzy. "I should think that would eliminate Vicker and Skene. From what I've seen of them, I don't think either of them could inspire a thirsty horse to drink water. Vicker has the lineage and connections of a Scottish patriot, at least on his mother's side of the family, but he hardly has an air of command about him. Half the time he looks as though he'd faint if you said 'boo' to him. What do you think of Skene as our villain, Vincent?"

"'E's a nice feller, if you can keep 'im off the subject o' John Brown, but I don't think 'e's a natcherall leader, if you know wot I mean."

"Red Hector?" I asked French.

He shrugged. "He can gas on for hours about the evils of English rule and the plight of the Scots, but he's usually in his cups when he does so. He had a perfect opportunity to pull a pistol out of his belt or the *sgian dubh* from his stocking and go for the Queen last night, but he sang instead." His brow wrinkled. "I suppose I can see a group of inebriated Scotsmen following Red Hector to the nearest pub, but not to gaol, and certainly not to the gallows."

"'E's a blow'ard," Vincent piped up. "'Is stable boy says that all 'e does is drink and talk, drink and talk, and when 'e gets tired of that, 'e takes out 'is whip and lays into the 'elp."

"That leaves Robbie Munro," I said. "Who looks like a leader, with that square jaw and handsome physique."

Both Vincent and French swiveled to look at me.

"What? I'm only saying that Munro cuts a fine figure. He has a soldierly look about him. I daresay he'd look a treat in a military uniform."

I could see that French was not even attempting to visualize this image.

"And on that basis, you think he is the Marischal?" Did I imagine that French's voice was the teeniest bit chilly?

"Don't be ridiculous. I was just pointing out that of the four men we suspect, Munro most looks the part. But I do not think we can discount any of them, except perhaps Skene. As a groom, he would have had a more difficult time than a guest or house servant in gaining access to the castle to poison the Queen's cocoa."

"The same theory applies to Vicker or Robbie Munro with respect to the stables; they'd have looked like fish out of water out there. Someone would surely have noticed the deputy master of the household or a footman fiddling about with the block and tackle." French's voice was still flinty.

"They could all be in league together. I have seen Skene with Munro." I related my tale of the meeting between the two men outside the stables. There was a lengthy silence as we all contemplated this possibility.

Vincent brushed the crumbs from his jacket and burped loudly.

"Pardon me," he said, "but hit seems to me that we ain't any closer to findin' this 'ere hassassin than we were when we rolled in 'ere. Wot're we gonna do next?"

"We continue as before. Keep watch on the suspects, and alert each other if something unusual occurs," French said with authority, but even he seemed a bit downcast at our inability to lay hands on the Marischal. All it would take was one more "accident," and the whole lot of us might be going back to London in disgrace, not to mention that we'd be accompanying the Queen in her coffin. It was a glum prospect indeed.

Our meeting broke up then. As we were putting on our coats, I pulled Vincent to one side. "Haven't you got something for me?"

He grinned. "Aye. 'Ow much will you give me for hit?"

Cheeky sod. "I expect you carried off enough stuff to flog in

London that you'll be living like a king when we get back there. Now, give it to me."

"You ain't payin'?"

"It would serve you right if Superintendent Robshaw got an anonymous tip to search the stables," I hissed.

"Oy," said Vincent, feigning terror, "I'll 'and it over, India. Promise me you won't rat me out." He extracted a bundle from his pocket, and I slipped it into mine.

French caught the motion from the corner of his eye and opened his mouth to speak but thought better of it.

That evening I brought the marchioness a cup of warm milk. The old dear grumbled a bit as she preferred her usual dram of whisky, but as I'd laced the cup with brandy, she greedily sucked it down and smacked her lips once she'd tasted it, pointing at the Bible and asking me to find a passage or two I thought might be appropriate for the evening. I selected something from the New Testament (the Apostles are so much more uplifting that those wild-eyed prophets from the Old). I'd read only a few verses when I looked up to see my employer's eyes closing and her head bobbing on the pillow. I shut the Good Book, pulled the bedclothes up to the marchioness's chin and blew out the candle. I smiled in anticipation as I shut the door to her room. I hadn't had a decent night's sleep in ages, but I would tonight. In addition to the brandy, I had added several drops of laudanum to the marchioness's milk, courtesy of Vincent, who'd lifted the drug for me from the chemist's shop in the village.

It certainly hadn't been my idea for the lad to clean out the place; all I'd wanted was the laudanum. Vincent, however, was a disciple of the temple that believed that the trouble with resisting temptation is that it might never come your way again. He also had an eye for the main chance and a nose for profit that would have done a Rothschild proud. I'd no doubt that stashed under Vincent's cot in the stables was a sack stuffed with enough morphine, laudanum and chloral hydrate to render the entire population of Edinburgh unconscious. Vincent could have any price he asked in London. I can't say that I blame the boy for taking the lot and selling it, as there didn't appear to be any benefactors lining up to help the little bugger off the streets.

I, therefore, went off to dreamland with a clear conscience. Between sleuthing during the day, babysitting the marchioness at every meal, and renewing my acquaintance with Holy Writ into the wee hours of the morning, I was fair knackered. I fell into bed like a toppled oak, prepared to sleep the sleep of the righteous (and I'll thank you not to point out that my claim to such status is dubious).

The sound of someone hammering on the door woke me. I shot upright, head spinning. My first thought was that I had perhaps overestimated the amount of laudanum necessary to render an ancient crone unconscious and had inadvertently killed the marchioness. That would look bad on the old curriculum vitae, not to mention being a criminal offense. Then the voice at the door penetrated the fog in my brain.

"Miss Black, Mr. French has summoned you."

Even through the thick wood I could hear the disapproval in the words. I stumbled to the door and opened it to find a footman named Grant (or MacBeath or Macdonald—who remembers or indeed cares?), one of the elder statesmen among the crowd of servants employed at Balmoral. He was an evangelical Kirk o' Scotland man—I could tell by the sour frown on his face and the disgust with which he informed me that a male guest of the Queen had requested my presence in his room. I could have informed him that French leaned toward the lesser offenses of blackmail, conceit and the odd white lie in the service of duty but had little interest in the sins of the flesh (at least to my knowledge, which, admittedly, was minimal in this area, French being as loathe to talk about his background as I was). I yawned in the footman's face and informed him that I could find my own way to French's room, which scandalized the fellow even more. He went away with his handlebar quivering, grumbling about Jezebel, Sodom and Gomorrah, and the morals of the aristocracy.

Flora was as still as a mouse under her covers, and I took care not to wake her. I found my traveling clothes and slipped them on in the dark, then took my coat and scarf from the wardrobe, and carrying my boots in my hand, slipped out the door. I felt my way to the servants' stairs and lit the candle, shielding the flame with my hand. I sat on the top step to lace up my boots and then hurried through the silent corridors. The coat and scarf were a precautionary measure; the last time I'd shared an escapade with French, we'd spent a fair bit of time freezing off our fingers in a blizzard.

A thin wedge of light spilled out from under the door of French's room. I knocked softly and he opened the door immediately, drawing me safely inside and conning the hall to see if anyone was about. He was dressed for the outdoors, in topcoat and muffler. I congratulated myself on my intelligence in foreseeing just this possibility.

"Vincent was here," he whispered, pulling on his gloves. "Archie Skene and one of the other grooms slipped out of the stables an hour ago. Vincent followed them long enough to be sure he could stay on their trail, then raced back here to tell me. We're to join him in the stables."

"What's happening?"

"A meeting of sorts, in the woods. Vincent will tell us more.

Now hurry." He shoved his hat firmly on his head. "We must get there as soon as possible."

Vincent was hopping silently in place, blowing on his hands, when we found him at the rear of the stables.

"There you are, guv," he said. "I scouted out the territory whilst you and India were puttin' on your duds. Archie and the other fellow met up with some blokes out there in them trees. They got a fire goin', and there's people comin' from all over to join 'em. I saw four or five slip out o' the castle, too."

"Maybe they're off to have a drink together, away from the house," I said, thinking of my warm bed and not relishing at all the prospect of a stroll through the snow.

"They may be 'avin' some whisky, but hit ain't a social affair," said Vincent. "You'll see when we get there. We'll 'ave to be quiet as cats to get up close enough to 'ear wot's goin' on. Follow me." He slipped away into the dark, and French and I fell in behind him.

The night was moonless, with a cold wind blowing off the icy peaks of the Cairngorms, scouring the snow on the ground and rustling the boughs of the spruce trees overhead with a devilish whine. It was not, in my opinion, a fit night for a party, unless it was being held indoors in front of a raging fire. I gathered my coat about me and pulled my scarf tighter. Vincent had struck out on a straight line due north from the stables, away from the trail the others had taken. We walked briskly for several minutes, covering rocky ground patched here and there with a light skiff of snow. We reached the tree line behind the castle, where the ground began to ascend, and the walking became more difficult. We inched up a rocky slope, brushing aside snow-laden branches and scrambling over and around granite outcroppings, some as large as a house. The cold air made it difficult to breathe, my ribs hurt like the devil, and I was winded in no time. We struggled on

like that for a bit, with Vincent pausing now and then to correct
our course, and me sobbing for breath at the rear of the column.
You'd think an urchin from the streets of London would be lost
within sight of the castle, but Vincent had the instincts of a Paw-
nee scout and the night vision of an owl (how else do you think a
boy his age managed to survive in the Big Smoke?), and we
trekked on unerringly, until ahead of us a tiny light gleamed in
the darkness, and Vincent crouched low and crept forward slowly
for a distance of twenty feet or so (it felt like a mile, waddling
forward in the that thigh-burning posture), then halted abruptly,
dropping to his haunches behind a waist-high cairn of rock,
which afforded us an excellent vantage point of the scene below.
French and I knelt, and peered over the edge of the cairn.

"There they are," Vincent whispered.

We had topped the crest of a ridge and were looking down into
a shallow clearing, littered with huge boulders. Someone had lit a
bonfire fit for Vulcan, with sparks leaping high into the air and
giving off a great light that illuminated the two dozen figures
gathered around the flames. The crowd contained mostly men,
but there were six or eight women among them, easily marked by
their skirts and bonnets. In the weird, flickering light the faces of
the watchers were white and waxen, but for the few whose faces
were shadowed, their eyes ringed with black. I shook my head,
wondering if I'd accidently imbibed some of the laudanum I'd
intended for the marchioness and was having a nightmare, having spent too much time chasing assassins and too little sleeping.
But the mystery solved itself when I looked closer; the figures
round the fire wore masks of varying shapes and sizes. I scrutinized them closely, and after a few minutes I was able to nudge
French and Vincent and point out Skene, whose bushy eyebrows
rested on top of a black mask like a dead mink draped over a cur-

tain. I scanned the crowd, looking for the figures of Red Hector or Vicker or Robbie Munro, but I could not be sure if any of them were among the group.

There was no discussion among the congregation at the fire. They stood silently, facing the flaring light, seemingly oblivious to the biting wind. Vincent put his hand on my arm and nodded his head toward the encircling woods. A dark figure glided out of the trees and joined the merry band around the fire, then another came and yet another. It was eerie, sheltering there among the rocks with the wind gusting around us and those faceless forms gathered in the circle below us. Clearly, all that Bible reading had inflamed my imagination: the crowd below me looked like they were putting on a tableau of the ninth circle of hell, where traitors to their liege lords stood frozen in ice, as close to Old Harry as a sinner could get. Poetic and picturesque, you might say, if you hadn't been freezing to death in the theatre seats and wondering what the devil was going to happen, as I was. I pushed the unpleasant images of Lucifer and his cronies from my mind by reminding myself that it was just old Archie Skene and his pals down there, no doubt enjoying a bit of playacting, but otherwise harmless. If their idea of entertainment was to wade through the snow on a bitter night and stand in a circle staring holes through each other, well, it's not my place to judge. I've known stranger ideas of a good time.

Vincent clamped his fingers around my wrist, and French sat up straight. The crowd round the fire had stirred, turning expectantly toward a mighty spruce that towered overhead. Two human forms had appeared at the edge of the woods. There was a murmur from the masked audience, a throaty hum of affirmation and adoration that rose above the noise of the wind. The figures stepped forward out of the shadow of the tree. They might just as well have stepped out of a painting by Ronald Robert Mclan. Both wore tartan trousers (wisely, I thought, given what the wind might do to a kilt on a night like this), dark masks that covered their faces, flowing capes and soft Scotch bonnets.

One figure, the slighter of the two, sat down upon a boulder at the edge of the clearing, while the second, a brawny chap with the shoulders of Hercules, strode forward into the light. He flung his cape over one of those giant shoulders, revealing a brace of pistols in his belt. He raised a hand for silence, though he needn't have bothered as a hush had descended over the onlookers at his approach.

"Friends," said the tartan-clad behemoth, in a brogue so thick you could have stood a sword in it. "We have gathered tonight to affirm our bonds of loyalty and trust. The time draws near when the head of the Sassenach serpent will be severed from its body, and the rightful heir of King Duncan will reign once more in Scotland."

This drew an appreciative chorus from the crowd.

"Wot the devil is a Sassenach?" whispered Vincent.

"From the Gaelic word 'sasunnach,' meaning 'Saxon.' It's used now as a slur against the English."

Trust French to take time to deliver a lesson in linguistics while treason was being plotted in the clearing below.

"Through many long years and through many generations, we have endured the English boot upon our neck. We have suffered and sacrificed for the English crown, sending our finest sons and brothers to die on dusty battlefields in far-off lands, to protect the rights of English merchants to rape and pillage these foreign territories. And why must we do this? Because there is no future for the sons of Scotland in their own land."

The congregation was beginning to get worked up. At the speaker's words, an angry buzz ran through the crowd.

"There are no prospects here for young men, and so they are reduced to taking the Queen's shilling and boarding ships for Bombay and Mombasa, for Singapore and Cape Town. Our young women chap their hands doing laundry for the English overlords, and our old women pine for the youth who lie buried in the soil of India and Africa. Those who remain behind till the hard ground, dig the coal from the earth or fish the cold waters to earn a pittance. Our children starve and our women wither, while the English grow fat and rich from our toil."

I found that a bit rough, as I was personally acquainted with quite a few Englishmen and Englishwomen who might have thought a Scottish peasant with a patch of corn and an outdoor privy had a damned good life. I stole a glance at Vincent to see how he was taking the news that the Scots had been supporting his lavish lifestyle, but he didn't seem overly concerned.

The figure below us raised a hand again, but this time 'twas clenched in a fist.

"It is time that we reclaimed our birthright, as an independent nation of free men and women. It is time to cleave the Union between England and Scotland, and if blood must be spilled to affect such a separation, then so be it!"

There was a huzzah from the crowd. If this was the Marischal, I could understand the English government's trepidation about the man; he had the silver tongue of a gifted orator. There were raised fists among the crowd now and a few cries of "Kill the bloody English" and "Off with the Queen's head."

"The Sons of Arbroath have pledged to rid Scotland of the plague of English pests. We wait only for the proper time to strike, when the royal imposter is beguiled into complacency and our act of fealty to our nation will shock the world. Victoria, for I cannot call her Queen, will not leave Scotland alive!"

This evoked a roar from the gathering, and I squirmed uncomfortably. If we were discovered now, the mob below probably wouldn't hesitate to tear us limb from limb, once they heard our English accents. Of course, they would likely go first for French, who was everything a posh English gentleman should be. That might leave time for me to rocket away through the woods while the Scots were occupied with striking their first blow for freedom against the hated English aristocracy. I was sussing out escape routes when French nudged me.

The seated figure had risen and now stood immobile with the cloak billowing about in the wind and the firelight playing across the masked features. It was a romantic scene, I'll tell you, with the sparks from the fire flying up into the treetops and the smoke rising like incense, and the silent figure standing there as silent and inscrutable as an Oriental god.

The titan who'd been doing all the yammering stretched out a hand to the quiet figure. "Before you stands the instrument of Victoria's destruction—the Marischal, whose life's work shall be accomplished when Victoria lies dead."

There was a great shout that shook the boughs of the tree and made my knees turn to jelly.

"You know the Marischal and the Sons of Arbroath are now hunted like stags through the fields and forests of Scotland. You know that we must hide our identities, and gather in secret in hidden glens and the caverns of the earth. But soon, very soon, my friends, the Marischal shall remove the mask and step forward as the rightful heir of King Duncan, restoring a Scot to the throne of Scotland and running the English cowards from our kingdom. The Marischal has come to Balmoral to see that our destiny is fulfilled."

The crowd couldn't get enough of this, and there was a deuce of a perturbation amongst the masked supporters, with enough howling and whooping to make you think you'd stumbled onto some pagan ceremony and the human sacrifice was just minutes away. I hoped that wasn't true, as I didn't stand a chance of out-running French or Vincent if the mob decided that just any old victim would do. I was preparing my speech about being an in-nocent bystander, roped into this little jaunt by the unscrupu-lous English nob at my side, when the Herculean fellow spoke again.

He'd pulled a bottle from under his cloak and was holding it aloft. "Let us drink to victory and to a free Scotland."

Like all good Scots, every bugger there had brought a cup or a tumbler, it seemed, and now they whipped them out and waited patiently while the big fellow went round the circle, pouring a jot into each vessel and saying a few words to each person, and now and then clapping some bloke on the shoulder in a gesture of manly concord. Lastly, he turned to the Marischal, who had pro-duced a quaich, the shallow Scottish drinking cup, and poured a liberal measure for the boss. Then the Herculean cove filled his own quaich and raised it high in a toast.

"To the Sons of Arbroath," he cried.

A ragged echo rose up, and then everyone of that assembly quaffed their thirst.

Again, he raised his quaich to the stars. "To the Marischal."

There was a general hue and cry over this, and the Marischal nodded humbly at this recognition of his superior personage.

For the last time, the giant lifted his quaich and shouted, "To a free Scotland!"

The folk in the firelight went off like a sell-out crowd at the local football derby.

Then they all crowded together with their arms wound round

each other, including the big man and the Marischal, and they raised their voices in a ringing chant. "As long as but a hundred of us remain alive, never will we on any conditions be brought under English rule. It is in truth not for glory nor for riches nor honours that we are fighting, but for freedom—for that alone which no honest man gives up but with life itself."

It was stirring stuff, no doubt, and I felt like rising to my feet with a great cheer and hurrying down to the clearing to join these brave men and women in ridding the Scottish ship of English rats, but French put a restraining hand on my arm and gave me a look that made me sink back to my knees. I could tell he'd found it rousing as well, though, for his eyes were bright, and I thought I detected in the firelight a faint flush on his cheeks. Later, he told me that those words came from the Declaration of Arbroath, written over five hundred years before, when the Scots had had a bellyful of the English Edward I crushing their attempts at rebellion. As I have learned, the Scots have long memories.

The toasts seemed to mark the end of the formal portion of the meeting, for bottles of whisky were dragged from pockets and haversacks, and the crowd settled down for some serious tippling. The next item on the agenda appeared to be getting blind drunk, which would provide us the perfect opportunity to steal away and return to the safety of the castle. French leaned over to Vincent and whispered in his ear, gesturing at the Marischal, and I was sure the lad had just received instructions to tail the slim figure. Sure enough, Vincent half rose, balancing on his toes, ready to follow the scent when the Marischal and the bruiser took their leave. French touched my hand and jerked his head, indicating that we should retire in the direction from whence we'd come—a very good plan, I thought, as the only thing worse than a mob of fanatics intent on spilling English blood was a mob of drunken fanatics intent on spilling English blood.

The two tartan-clad figures had taken their farewells and were moving toward the tree line, French and I were backing slowly away from our hiding place, and Vincent had taken one covert step to follow our quarry, when the most awful thing happened. Usually, you can depend on Vincent to be as silent and stealthy as a Thuggee, but tonight his (and, consequently, our) luck turned. His step dislodged a stone, which bounced down the hill toward the fire, and as it bounced, it collected pebbles and gravel and other stones until there was a veritable torrent of rubble headed toward the nationalists. Worse luck, they were all still sober, and it didn't take long for one of them to spy the avalanche of rock descending toward them and raise a shout that reverberated around the clearing. The Marischal took one look and scampered into the woods like a startled rabbit, while his companion drew his pistols from his belt and ran toward the commotion, signaling to the others to follow him. The crowd let out a lusty roar, and a dozen *sgian dubhs* winked in the firelight.

"Confound it," said French. "Run, India."

I had no need of such instructions; I had already bolted and was running at full speed, spurred on by the image of being carved up like a roasted ox by the screaming horde behind me. A few steps into my flight, it occurred to me that I had no idea where I was in relation to the castle, having spent the trek here following blindly behind French and Vincent. Next time, I would pay more attention. I ran on, stumbling over rocks and colliding now and then with a tree. The nasty things made a habit of looming up out of the darkness at the last minute. I had taken a few thumps and scratched my face on a spruce bow when I pulled up for a moment to catch my breath and get my bearings. I turned, half-expecting French to be at my heels, but he was nowhere to be seen. Where had the bugger got to? Without him, I was as likely to end up in Glasgow as at Balmoral.

Away to my right, I heard someone hurtling down the slope, crashing through the trees and bellowing like an angry bull. French, I thought, but what the devil was he doing? Then I heard the yelps behind him, and cries of "Over here," and "There he goes!" I felt a surge of affection for the bloke then, for it was clear that French was deliberately drawing our pursuers after him, giving me the chance to slip away undetected. It was damned sporting of the man and completely in character. I resolved to be a bit nicer to the cove and thank him properly, if I ever found my way back to the castle and he escaped from the howling mob behind him. I thought it more likely that the former would occur than the latter; I might be lucky enough to stumble upon Balmoral by morning, but French had a habit of taking pratfalls in the snow and being ambushed by villains, as I've recounted in my previous tale of adventure. I wasn't worried about Vincent, as he could hide behind a snowflake and would no doubt be snoring in his bed while I was still trudging through the woods in search of the castle.

It was a bloody long night. After the hue and cry had died away (though it still continued in the distance, as the nationalist band pressed on in pursuit of French), I spent a good many hours walking around with my hands held out in front of my face, bumping into tree branches and great boulders, turning my ankles a half-dozen times on the uneven ground, and generally careering about like a ship without a sail. The first rays of the sun had just touched the summits of the Cairngorms when I caught the scent of wood smoke in the air and spied the chimneys of the castle. I must have walked over half of Scotland by then. I was exhausted, hungry, bruised and battered when I staggered into the stable yard and tapped at the window of Vincent's room. The sash flew up instantly and Vincent looked out. He looked a bit worse for the wear as well, with a brutal cut from a tree limb across his cheek and bits of leaves and sticks decorating his hair.

"Blimey, where you been, India? We thought you was lost."

"We?"

"French and me."

"So he made it back safely?"

"Aye, 'e made it to 'is room a couple of hours ago. 'E said if you didn't come back by daylight, we'd 'ave to go lookin' for you."

I found their masculine concern irritating. If they hadn't left me alone out there in the woods in the first place, I'd have been in bed hours ago. And I'll thank you not to point out the logical inconsistency of thanking French for drawing off my pursuers and then blaming him for deserting me. In my defense, I need only point out that I am a woman and thus entitled to entertain as many logical inconsistencies as I please.

"Well, I have returned safely, so you two can rest easy now. Did you follow the Marischal? Did you see who it was?"

Vincent shook his head mournfully. "I tried, but them nationalist buggers was all over the place, 'untin' me down like a bloody jackal. I 'ad a 'ard time shakin' 'em. They was on my 'eels all night, and I didn't take an easy breath till I made the stables and shut the door and crawled under me cot."

"Could you tell how many people returned to the castle?"

"A 'alf dozen, at least. Maybe more. 'Twas 'ard to count 'eads whilst them fiends was bayin' for me blood. Not to menshun hit was dark as the inside of a helephant out there. You better get on into the 'ouse. French said we'd meet again soon." Vincent slid down the sash and disappeared from view.

I hobbled across the courtyard and into the castle. Dawn had yet to break, but already there were a few servants about, lighting fires and lamps, and getting ready for another day of activity. I climbed the stairs wearily and cracked the door to Flora's room as quietly as I could. There was a hump in her bed, and I heard her breathing gently. I pushed the door to, wincing as it closed with a sharp click, then sat on my bed to take off my boots. My head was swimming with fatigue, and my fingers fumbled the laces.

"And how was your night of sin, my girl?" Flora asked, with a laugh in her voice.

"I thought you were asleep."

"Rather difficult to sleep through old Grant knocking on the door in the wee hours and you dressing up for a ramble with Mr. French."

I yawned widely, my jaw creaking. "My night was exhausting," I said honestly.

"Weel, now." Flora giggled. "You'll have to tell me all about it. I'm a simple country lass, I am, and there are lots of things I'd like to know."

I threw a pillow at her and collapsed on the bed.

TEN

As the sun kissed the castle grounds, William Ross, piper to the Queen, destroyed the morning with an enthusiastic rendition of the "Bonnie Lass o' Fyvie" (or so I was informed by Flora—all compositions tend to sound alike to me when played on the Great Highland War Pipe). I groaned and rolled over, shading my eyes from the light streaming through the tiny window. One of these days I was going to lie in wait for Ross, rip his *sgian dubh* from his stocking and plant the blade in that cursed instrument of his. I bathed and dressed and contemplated the irony of having drugged the marchioness in expectation of a solid eight hours of sleep, only to spend the night playing Duck, Duck, Goose with a group of Scots dressed for a masquerade party.

Robbie Munro found me after breakfast, having a second cup of coffee and feeling like a pony that had been stabled without a rubdown. I inspected the footman closely for any signs that he had spent the evening hunting Englishmen through the rocks and snow, but he seemed chipper enough, clear-eyed and smiling pleasantly.

"The marchioness has asked for you," he said.

"What? At this hour? She's never awake by now."

He shrugged and returned to his duties, and I went to do mine with a foul temper.

The marchioness was sitting up in bed, bright as a new button. She gave me a gap-toothed smile. "Splendid mornin', ain't it, Imogen?"

I nodded dully.

"I'm thinkin' of dressin' and breakfastin' downstairs this mornin'. I never feel like gettin' out of bed this early, but today I feel grand."

Oh, dear. I had expected the marchioness to enjoy a peaceful evening's repose, but I hadn't considered the idea that the old dear would wake up so full of pep.

"Breakfast won't be ready for an hour, ma'am. Should I bring you a cup of tea?"

"An hour," said the marchioness in disbelief. "I'm famished."

"I've got just the thing to take the edge off your appetite," I said, collecting her snuffbox from the dressing table and pouring her a stiffish peg of whisky.

The old lady cackled. "Capital idea, Imogen."

I held the snuffbox while the marchioness ladled a large portion into her nose, snorting like a spent artillery mule at the water trough, and I wiped her dry after an attack of sneezing that would have killed a countess.

"Take a pew," said the marchioness when her sinuses had cleared. "I've a hankerin' to hear about harlots."

I gulped (I hoped not visibly). If the old gal had rumbled me, why not come out with it and stop these not particularly subtle messages?

"Second book of Joshua, if ye please." The marchioness settled herself comfortably among the pillows.

There was a fine tremor to my hands as I turned the pages of the Bible and commenced the story of Rahab the harlot. You may already be acquainted with it, but as I find that the vast majority of readers tend to doze through the lessons at Sunday services and are loathe to crack open the Good Book themselves unless absolutely forced to do so, I'll fill you in on the story and save you the trouble of looking it up. As I've said, Rahab was a member of the world's oldest profession (and you'd think that would earn it a bit of respect, wouldn't you, as it indicates the native intelligence and cunning of women who learned how to turn a profit before the male sex had climbed down from the trees). That wily Israelite Joshua was planning to attack the city of Jericho (where Rahab had her place of business), and he sent a couple of coves in to suss out the lay of the land. These two blokes, like most soldiers who finagle their way out from under their commander's thumb, went looking for a good time and wound up spending the night at Rahab's establishment. Now, Joshua says that when the soldiers of Jericho came in search of his two spies, Rahab hid them under a bundle of flax, and being deuced grateful for the help, the men agreed to spare Rahab and her family when Joshua's troops attacked the city. I reckon they had such a good time (and being conscious of the waste of a talented whore, of course), they didn't want Rahab to end up skewered on the tip of an Israeli spear. I leave it to you to find your own moral of the story.

Anyway, the sign the spies agreed to with Rahab was the hanging of a red cord outside her house, which some scholars seem to think was the origin of red lights outside brothels. It's no matter to me where the idea came from, for I run a discreet establishment and would no more think of painting my lantern red than I would of having a sign printed up and hung on the door. There's never the slightest need to advertise your location, in my experience, as word of mouth is the best recommendation, and what respectable gentleman wants to be seen slipping into a bawdy house by his fellow MPs through a crimson fog?

Apart from my concern that the marchioness was toying with me by dropping hints that she knew my background (and I still couldn't see how she'd managed to learn the truth, without some assistance from French or Dizzy, and why would either of them have disclosed my identity to the old cat?), I rather enjoyed the story of Rahab. For once, the bint in the story didn't end up as a pillar of salt or consumed by fire, but instead bet on the winning horse and reaped the reward. I like an uplifting tale like that. But I digress.

The marchioness's breakfast arrived, and I helped her sit upright long enough to fork in a wagonload of deviled kidneys and toast, and by the time she'd finished and I'd given her a sponge bath (resolving to mention to French in the future that while I might be willing to shoot a Cossack guard or two, I was disinclined to bathe flabby members of the aristocracy), it was time to drape my charge in a clean costume for luncheon.

"I'm dinin' with Lady Dalfad and the Queen," the marchioness announced glumly, doubtless remembering her shaming and banishment from the dining table two days prior.

"Not to worry, my lady. I shall be in attendance and ensure that nothing untoward happens."

The marchioness sniffed, but I thought I detected the merest trace of gratitude on her face.

The ladies' luncheon, being a small social function on the Balmoral calendar, was served in the library, where the Queen and dear departed Albert had preferred to dine. I'd been in the room before, on my ill-fated excursion to locate Mrs. Greenhow's book, but it took the daylight to reveal how utterly gloomy the room was: dark as pitch with rows of bookcases around each wall, surmounted by yet more hideous thistle-patterned wallpaper, and the ubiquitous Royal Stewart tartan carpet. There was a handsome sofa of button-tufted Moroccan leather and a set of matching chairs, and in the center was a table for six. The marchioness joined the Queen, Lady Dalfad, and three other sterling examples of inbred, blue-blooded nitwits.

It was a jolly affair, with all those fine Christian ladies freezing out the marchioness for offending the Queen, but the marchioness affected not to give a damn (and probably didn't, as the comestibles on hand were sensational), while Her Majesty sat stiffly at the head of the table with one of her Hindoo servants standing at attention behind her. He was a comely fellow, the colour of a shelled walnut, with a set of sweeping, dignified mustaches and a powder blue silk kurta and matching turban that many ladies would have killed for. The marchioness sniffed when she saw him, but she didn't let the presence of an infidel interfere with her appetite. The only one who matched her in putting away the provisions was the Queen. She didn't waste breath on polite conversation; she let her ladies-in-waiting do all the chatting while she devoted her fullest attention to each course. She worked her way steadily through soup, salmon, veal cutlets, York ham and a roast or two. There were three kinds of puddings, and she sampled each, and when she'd decided which one she liked best, she had a second helping just to make sure her decision had been wise. I'll tell you, it was like seeing the crew of a man-o'-war going through the grub that day, and I felt faintly sick watching those pudgy jaws grinding away relentlessly. Hard to credit that this plump matron greedily licking the icing from a cream cake was the monarch of our sceptred isle and the Great White Queen to her heathen subjects.

I kept a keen eye on the marchioness, and she did me proud, not once snuffling about among the pickle dishes and sugar bowls for something to inhale. Finally, after the Queen had emptied the custard bowl, she pushed back her chair and signaled to the waiting footmen to clear the table. The pagan in the turban brought her a finger bowl, and she delicately washed her hands, and the group relaxed, now that Her Highness had eaten her fill.

One of the ladies at the table (a baroness or a duchess, I can't recall exactly, but as she plays no further part in this story, there's no use getting exercised about the details) beamed at the Queen.

"I am so looking forward to the ghillies' ball tonight, Your Highness. It will be such a treat."

I had been so busy sleuthing and tossing rooms and evading masked Scots in the woods that I had forgotten that tonight was the big night. Everyone chimed in at the woman's comment, to make sure the Queen knew how much each one was looking forward to the dance and, that's right, more food.

"Wouldn't Prince Albert have loved to have been here for the ball," one of the old cats said wistfully.

The Queen's face contorted, and she dabbed at the corner of her eye with her serviette. "Poor, dear Albert. How he loved these dances for the servants. He adored watching the ghillies dance with the domestics. And dear Albert looked so handsome in his kilt the last time we led the grand march into the ballroom."

Lady Dalfad sipped her coffee. "Indeed. The dances are most enjoyable. Your Highness should be commended for carrying on the tradition after the prince's passing. It must be difficult for you, ma'am, but I know the servants are most grateful. My Effie looks forward to it every year."

Effie squirmed but nodded.

"And what a rare delight," Lady Dalfad carried on. "We'll have *two* dances this year. The customary occasion last September and now a ball in December."

"It is how Albert would have wished it," said the Queen lugubriously. "We always have a dance when we are at Balmoral, and as he expressly wished me to spend the Christmas holiday here, I see no reason why we should depart from tradition."

"Very wise," said Lady Dalfad. "Especially under the present circumstances."

The Queen cast a sharp eye down the table. "What do you mean by that statement?"

There was an infinitesimal movement of the countess's shoulders. "I was referring to the incidents that have occurred. Continuing to observe the customary habits will reassure the servants and guests that nothing is amiss."

"Nothing *is* amiss." The Queen's tone was freezing.

A lesser woman than the countess might have quailed, but Lady Dalfad smiled sweetly. "But Your Highness, you must know of the talk that surrounds your illness and the occurrence in the stable."

"Bah!" spat the Queen. "Those were accidents, nothing more. I don't understand why everyone is so excitable. Mr. Disraeli has even suggested that I return to Windsor."

"Everyone is concerned with your safety, ma'am," Lady Dalfad said gently. "We are all aware that the Sons of Arbroath have vowed to kill you. Why, even the servants have heard of the threat to your life. Isn't that right, Effie?"

The Queen turned a basilisk glare upon Effie, who flinched but nodded affirmatively.

"*I* do not allow my servants to sit idle and spend their time gossiping," sniffed the Queen.

The marchioness was hanging on every word, her fingers inching unconsciously toward the sugar bowl. Well, whatever happened, it was bound to make Her Highness angry, so I resolved to bear the burden and sprang to my feet, seizing the marchioness's hand just as her twitching fingers had found the handle of the sugar bowl, and reaching for her water glass at the same time.

"Your medication, my lady," I said smoothly, and prayed the old trout would cotton on. The marchioness snarled at first, but I waggled an eyebrow at the sugar bowl and she took the hint, muttering, "Thank you, Ima," and pretending to swallow the imaginary capsule with a copious draught of water to wash it down. I returned to my seat and tried to ignore the daggers being flung at me by the Queen and Lady Dalfad.

"Those dreadful nationalists," one of the other ladies of the bedchamber said. "Whatever is wrong with them? Why, it's not as though the Queen had anything to do with the Act of Union."

"Besides," another of the grannies added, "the Queen *adores* Scotland."

"And my Scottish subjects," the Queen added unctuously.

"Some of your Scottish subjects apparently do not return the sentiment," said Lady Dalfad. "Are you quite sure, Your Highness, that you should appear at the ball tonight?"

The Queen swelled with indignation, looking like a displeased dumpling. "Lady Dalfad, you forget yourself."

The countess inclined her head under the weight of her monarch's wrath. "Forgive me for speaking so bluntly, Your Highness. But believe me when I say that I do so only because I have your

best interests at heart. The country and the Empire would floun-
der without your steady guidance."

The Queen settled back, mollified by the abject flattery. Lord, I
thought, what a job, smoothing the old kite's rustled feathers every time she gets her back up, which, with Vicky, was a frequent
occurrence.

"I thank you for your concern, Lady Dalfad. But I assure you
that the incidents you mentioned were mere accidents, and even
if they were not, I am well protected here, among my faithful servants and my invited guests."

I shuddered a bit at that, as I never like to tempt fate, but the
Queen just looked defiantly around the table.

"I shall go to the ball," she said firmly. "I shall lead the grand
march, and I shall dance a reel or two with Mr. Brown, and I shall
watch my servants enjoy an evening of amusement."

That seemed to settle matters, and it was a good thing, as the
marchioness was getting restless, her gnarled hand jumping like
a tarantula on the table. I didn't know how long she could hold
out; if I didn't get some snuff in her soon, there was bound to be
some sort of dustup at the dining table. Luckily, the party broke
up on the Queen's pronouncement of her intentions. I hustled
the marchioness into the nearest cubbyhole and satisfied her nic-
otine addiction, wondering as I did so if the Queen's last words
would be "Et tu, Brute?"

The marchioness retired for a nap, which sounded like a grand
idea to me, but I figured that I'd been sent to protect the Queen,
and as the stubborn fool was planning to put herself on display
to all and sundry at the ghillies' ball, it would be best to conduct
a recce of the ballroom and check on the preparations for the

event. So I wandered down to the main floor, sidestepping carpenters and tradesmen, and ambled to the ballroom for a looksee. The place was bustling with footmen and maids, setting up tables and chairs and fussing with hothouse flowers and tartan bunting (would there be any other kind?). The room was a long one, with a raised dais in the middle of the floor against one wall, where an elaborate carved chair served as the Queen's throne during the festivities. At the end of the room a minstrel's gallery jutted out from the wall, just below the great oak beams of the roof.

I noticed Robbie Munro assiduously laying silver, and I ambled over for a chat.

"It looks like it will be a grand night," I said. "I hear the Queen goes all out for these shindigs."

Robbie aligned a fork and knife. "No expense spared. We'll eat like kings tonight and dance until we fall down."

"I've heard a rumour that there will be whisky and ale."

Robbie leaned toward me conspiratorially. "*And* brandy. A whole cask, just for the servants."

I glanced idly at the balcony. "Where do you find a band around here?"

"Local lads, all of them. But I'm told they're quite good. We'll have nothing to complain about." He surveyed his work with satisfaction and dusted his hands. "There's that job finished. Now I'd better find Mr. Vicker and see what else I'm to do."

Vicker looked ill. I wondered if he was feeling the aftereffects of the cocoa or just the pressure of putting on a ball on a couple of weeks' notice. His mustache bristled with effort, and his collar was stained with sweat. He had a sheaf of papers in his hand and was flipping through them furiously. A queue of builders, joiners, maids and footmen had lined up before him, stamping their feet impatiently. One fellow pulled out his watch and consulted it, sighing theatrically. Vicker was doing his best, but every question left him goggle-eyed and openmouthed.

"Poor fellow," said Robbie. "He insists on checking everything personally. There are too many decisions for one man to make. He should have handed some of it over to Miss Boss."

I heard bleating and scuffling from the hallway. The band had arrived, a pack of ruffians by the look of them, with long beards and country attire. I doubted that we would be waltzing to the latest tune from Vienna tonight.

Robbie saw my face and grinned. "They don't look impressive, but I'm told the fiddler is first-rate, and the rest of the boys aren't far behind. There'll be country dancing tonight."

"The Queen said she intended to dance a reel with John Brown."

"I've heard they'll share a dance," said Robbie neutrally. "If you'll excuse me, I'll offer to show the musicians the stairs to the balcony. Vicker's got more than enough on his hands at the moment."

Robbie marched off, his kilt swaying mesmerizingly. What a damned looker he was. I hoped he wouldn't turn out to be the Marischal; it would be a dreadful waste of a handsome man. Robbie put a hand on Vicker's arm to draw his attention, and Vicker shied violently. Good Lord, the man was on edge.

Vicker cocked an ear to listen to Robbie, then shook his head vehemently. He'd obviously nixed Robbie's proposal to guide the musicians to the gallery where they'd be playing. Instead, Vicker hailed the fiddler, a twinkly man who must have been a hundred if he was a day, and instructed him to fall in behind and be dashed quick about it. The old codger looked affronted at the brusque command but waved down his fellow musicians and trailed after

Vicker, who led them out of the ballroom. A few seconds later, they appeared in the gallery.

There was obviously an entrance to the gallery in the hall, and I considered that it might be useful to know its location. I exited the ballroom and strolled slowly along the hall, until I saw Vicker emerge from a paneled wall. He brushed past me, reeking of perspiration, his face as wan as a typhoid survivor's. I glanced around to be sure no one was watching, then searched the oak panels swiftly until I found a metal latch, half-hidden behind a hideous portrait of Prince Albert lording it over a dead stag in a mountain meadow.

After locating the entrance to the gallery, I retraced my steps to the ballroom, noting all the entrances and exits from the room, the possible hiding places for the nationalists (could Archie Skene fit behind that potted palm?), and otherwise thinking about where I was likely to conceal myself if I were going to take a shot at the Queen or leap on her with dagger drawn. There were two points of access into the room: a set of double doors off the main hall, through which the grand march would enter the ballroom, and a smaller door at the opposite end of the room, for the use of the servants. One end of the room was jammed with tables and chairs, and the dance floor occupied the other. Counting guests and servants, there might be a hundred people in the room tonight, with the Queen seated smack in the middle where the revelers could see their monarch and bow obsequiously when the occasion demanded. It would be bloody difficult to keep an eye on everyone but not impossible if Vincent, French and I went about our business in a professional manner. And even if the assassin was one of the crowd, it would be confoundedly difficult to get close to the Queen, whack her like old Caesar and then scamper off without being brought down by a dozen hirsute Scots in kilts. My conclusion, at the end of twenty minutes of poking around, was that any assassin worth his salt wouldn't dare try to pot the Queen tonight, at least if he wanted to escape alive.

French had entered the room and was making a great show of admiring the decorations and arrangements. He ambled past Flora, twirling his stick and brushing against her. She emitted a little shriek and simpered at him, and the ass simpered back. Must have pinched her bum as he wandered by, I shouldn't wonder. He caught my eye and jerked his head and in a moment we were secluded in a corner, while I fiddled with the flowers on the nearest table (spilling most of them onto the tablecloth—floral arrangements are not my forte).

"How do you assess the situation?" he asked.

"I wouldn't give Flora any encouragement, or you'll spend the evening trying to fend her off."

"That's not what I meant."

Of course it wasn't. I filled him in on my survey of the hallway and the ballroom, and my conclusion: an attack might come, but if it did, the perpetrator would be bent on suicide.

French gnawed his lip. "We can't discount that idea. It would make the perfect political statement, demonstrating the sacrifice of true Scottish patriots. The press would have a field day."

"What of Robshaw? Will he have anyone on duty in the ballroom?"

"He's got trouble enough securing all the entrances to and exits from the castle, as well as patrolling the grounds. We'll be on our own tonight. I'll stay close to Red Hector, and you can monopolize the dashing Robbie Munro."

"Which leaves Vicker and Skene on the prowl, not to mention dozens of other servants and a score of guests unaccounted for."

"You and I will share the burden of tracking Vicker tonight, and I'll put Vincent onto Skene. As for the others, we'll have to watch the crowd constantly and be alert for anything out of the ordinary. It's not ideal, but we must play the odds and focus on our suspects."

I had forgotten that Vincent would be attending his first royal soiree. "Do you think he can stay away from the buffet tables long enough to watch Skene?"

French smiled humourlessly. "I shall issue strict instructions."

I could have informed French that to Vincent strict instructions were as water over the proverbial duck's back, but there are some things a man must learn for himself. And to be fair to the young scallywag, when he took on a task, he generally saw it through, unless, of course, tempted by cake or gewgaws he might flog or any sort of liquor at all. Well, I'd have enough to worry about tonight, between making sure that the marchioness didn't inhale the dry mustard set out for the sirloin of beef, keeping tabs on the delectable Munro and scanning the crowd for signs of incipient violence, so I went off for a bit of a kip, leaving French to skulk around the ballroom and poke his walking stick into the aspidistras in search of hidden weapons.

The marchioness elected to have her dinner in her room, so that she would be fresh and lively for the dance, a decision that I applauded as it meant I didn't have to spend a couple of hours standing behind her at the dining table. I went to spruce her up as the hour for the dance approached and found her puttering about her room and practicing a few steps. As wobbly as she was when she perambulated, you would expect this exercise to be disastrous, but the marchioness proved surprisingly light on her feet and managed a brief caper before she crashed into the bedpost and keeled over onto the mattress, where she lay laughing and spitting (she must have just inhaled a prodigious amount of snuff, to judge by the quantity of the stuff that was streaming out her nose). I got her upright and mopped her clean with a wet flannel.

"Are you looking forward to the ball tonight, my lady?"

"Indeed, I am. It's been as gloomy as a mortuary around here. A dance is just what we need."

"Do you think the Queen is in any danger? Lady Dalfad seemed to think so."

The marchioness honked loudly, which necessitated another swipe with the flannel. "Time was when the aristocracy had more backbone."

I didn't know if this was a jab at the countess or the Queen, but I doubted the marchioness was inviting my assessment, my being a member of the lower classes, you see. So I held my tongue, and my employer maundered on about cowardly types who went about tampering with cocoa and shoving machinery onto unsuspecting persons, and the equally timorous souls who now saw traitors lurking among the bushes and behind the curtains.

After she'd finished this tirade, it was time for another; this one directed at me. The marchioness lifted her cloudy eyes to my face. "It's time we had a talk about tonight, Irene."

"Ma'am?" I dragged the comb through a tangle of hair and she winced.

"Ow. Take some care, ye bloody fool."

"Yes, ma'am." It would be easier to snip off the snarl with a pair of scissors, but that would leave the marchioness with a noticeable bald spot. I withdrew the comb and tried a flank attack.

"There will be heavy drinkin' tonight, which sometimes leads to perverse behavior."

Finally, I thought, a bit of fun.

"Not," the marchioness hastened to add, "that I have ever personally witnessed such activities. No, I have only heard of 'em, from unimpeachable sources."

"Perverse behavior, my lady?" I was innocence itself.

The marchioness sniffed, detecting sarcasm. "Don't mock me, India."

India?

"I know ye lasses think ye know all there is to know of the ways of men, but believe me, I could tell ye stories that would raise your hair."

Doubtful, that. More likely I could provide an education to the marchioness she wouldn't forget, but it would be a waste, wouldn't it, as the days in which she might have made use of my lessons were long past.

"Choose yer dance partners well. The youngsters from the castle are good boys. They know they'd be flogged within an inch of their lives if they step out of line. As much as it pains me to admit it, the real cads are to be found among the guests. Reports have reached me that ye've been seen on several occasions with that Mr. French. And I myself have stumbled upon ye with the Prince of Wales."

"I am completely blameless," I said, and I didn't have to feign my indignation. If the marchioness wanted to school someone, why didn't she march off to Bertie's room and shame him? But it was ever thus: men are free to impose their will on women, while women are denounced as sluts and bobtails for submitting to it. Give me the old-fashioned exchange of goods and services any day; there's no disgrace in conducting a business transaction among consenting men and women.

The marchioness waved away my protests. "Regardless, I am

instructin' ye to refrain from flirtin' with that French fellow, or ye'll end up just like . . ." She shut her trap abruptly and glared at me in the mirror. "Anyway, just do as I say, and remember that I'll be watchin' ye."

"Yes, ma'am," I said obediently, but it would be bloody hard to slip around the ballroom and follow suspects if the marchioness kept her eye on me.

When the marchioness had finished chastising me before I had sinned, I spiffed her up until she bore a passing resemblance to the title she carried and then escorted her down the hall, where we joined a stream of excited guests and eager attendants. She doddered along on my arm, her eyes alight and her few visible teeth displayed in a deranged grin of pure delight. We descended the stairs into the main hall, where all was chaos. Everyone and his second cousin had arrived to join the grand march into the ballroom, and there was a bit of shoving and braying about seniority and there were ill-humoured remarks, all from the toffs, of course. I am proud to say the servants conducted themselves with a bit more dignity.

As one of the Queen's oldest relatives, the marchioness had a place of honour near the front of the pack. Vicker, face blanched white and lathered like a Boer's ox, was carrying around another of his infernal lists. When I presented the marchioness, he thumbed through the pages, then barked at me to conduct Her Ladyship to the fourth place in line. Mr. French would join her there and escort her into the ballroom. I nearly made myself sick with silent laughter as I positioned my employer in line, thinking of the fastidious French offering a snowy cuff upon which the marchioness would place her snuff-stained glove. I hoped he had an adequate supply of handkerchiefs, as he'd likely need them ere the night was over.

I realized that I had not found my own place in line, so I reluctantly consulted Vicker again and endured the subsequent snarling and spitting. I was walking in with one of the ghillies, a shy youngster named Jock MacBeath, with jug ears and red down on his cheeks, who blushed when I introduced myself. But I'm a dab hand with raw youth, and within ten minutes I had the pup twisting around my legs in delight. Thank God, I'd be spying tonight, or I never would be able to shake my new admirer.

It was quite a sight, that assemblage of hairy, kilted men and bright-eyed ladies in their best dresses. The male servants wore the Royal Stewart tartan, topped with black wool Argyll jackets with gauntlet sleeves and epaulettes on the shoulders, or the more elaborate Prince Charlie, a cutaway jacket of fine wool with short tails and braided epaulettes. Each wore a bristling sporran of fox or rabbit fur (the Scottish version of a wallet, though I suspect most of the chaps had a flask tucked in there tonight) dangling over his goolies (a dashed odd place to carry your cash, but then the Scots are an odd lot). I'll tell you true, those men were so dashing and romantic, I almost wished I'd been born in the Highlands, so I could gaze on their hirsute magnificence to my heart's content. All the male guests wore white ties, though some had put a sprig of thistle through their buttonholes. The female guests were decked out in ball gowns of pink satin, gold moiré silk and cerise tulle. There was gold blond lace, red velvet bows and trains of light blue silk and white satin in abundance. Even the female servants were decked out festively, in muslin gowns in pastel shades, which contrasted sharply with their reddened hands and large knuckles.

Flora was a fantasy in a creamy satin dress with a swatch of the Royal Stewart tartan for a shawl, her strawberry curls twisted into an elaborate affair. Her pale cheeks were flushed with excitement, and her eyes sparkled. She had provided me a simple silk gown of robin's egg blue, with a low neckline that set off my décolletage to full advantage (which I must admit, is a considerable advantage indeed) and accentuated the cobalt of my eyes. I'd put up my hair and rouged my cheeks, and the male staff went down before me like wheat before a threshing machine. I looked ravishing, if I do say so myself. But I digress.

Silence fell over the assembly, and the Queen, looking as pink, plump and complacent as a well-fed pig, descended the stairs. She was dressed in black, of course, but she'd made some concessions to the occasion by donning a striking little hat of ermine and an ermine collar and cuffs, with a miniature rosette of the royal tartan pinned to her breast by a yellow cairngorm. Bertie had been loitering about, flirting with anything in skirts and trying to avoid the irate gaze of his dearly beloved, Princess Alexandra. When the Queen appeared in view, Bertie stiffened at the sight, broke off his conversation with the youthful baroness he'd been ogling and scrambled to the front of the line. I expected him to escort his mother into the ballroom, but he slunk up to his wife and took her arm, while she looked with loathing at the baroness and the baroness pretended not to notice.

'Twas John Brown who materialized at the Queen's side, tucking her arm under his and gazing about with an arrogant grin. Bertie snarled. Disraeli, third in line and spanned with Lady Dalfad, looked bored. He'd wriggled his way into the Queen's good graces, and he didn't fret about sharing them with Brown. In fact, the crafty old Hebrew had encouraged the Queen's affection for Brown, earning Dizzy the Queen's devotion. Bertie, pondering whether the monarchy would survive the lurid tales in the newspapers of "Mrs. Brown" (and thus be worth inheriting), could hardly contain himself when Brown was in the room.

From inside the ballroom I heard the scrape of fiddle strings and the wheeze of an accordion. There was a buzz amongst the crowd, with a few of the youngsters standing on tiptoe for a glimpse of the band and gabbling excitedly. Then Brown, acting as drillmaster, raised his hand and signaled for silence, and an expectant hush settled upon the revelers. The band issued a desultory note or two to finish tuning their instruments, and then they launched into "Hielan' Laddie," which young Jock MacBeath was pleased to inform me was the regimental quick march of the Forty-Second (Royal Highlanders) Regiment of Foot, popularly known as the "Black Watch." It's a damned fine song, inspiring enough to induce young soldiers from the glens to forget their fear and charge the French line at the Battle of Quartre Bras, and John Brown and the Queen marched into the ballroom to its stirring refrain with their heads held high. We followed after them, making a circuit of the room with everyone grinning foolishly (except Dizzy, who looked as though he'd rather be having a tooth extracted). Red Hector, already well in his cups, was bouncing along, probably hoping for a chance to slaughter some English infantryman before the night was over. The marchioness looked as giddy as a schoolgirl at her first dance, and even French's lips were quirked in a tight smile. I'm not ashamed to admit I was beaming; the prospect of an evening of dancing and drinking and . . . oh, curse it, I'd forgotten I had to be vigilant tonight. Well, it always pays to make the best of things, as my mother used to tell me when we'd been chucked out onto the street because we couldn't make the rent (again), and I resolved to enjoy myself (a bit of dancing and a nip of whisky now and then) while keeping a close eye on Munro and Vicker.

When the whole troupe had squeezed into the room, we formed off into groups of eight (Jock MacBeath still dancing attendance on me), and the band swung into the "Reel of the Fifty-First Division." I hardly knew what I was doing, but MacBeath proved as lively and quick as a hare and had me weaving and bobbing right along with the others in no time at all. Scottish country dancing is simple, really, once you pick up the basic steps, as you tend to repeat them several times before moving on to another set of steps, which are then repeated, and so on. Sounds dull, but in fact it was great fun, even if I was dancing with a spotted youth with ears the size of water pitchers.

I caught sight of French, with a grim expression on his face, dutifully flinging the marchioness around the room. Dizzy had opted out of the athletics and was nursing a whisky at one of the tables with Lady Dalfad, a prim expression of disapproval on her face as she watched Effie dance with one of the under butlers. The Queen . . . Lord, there was a surprise. She and Brown were scampering about like a pair of frisky fox cubs. For a plump woman, Her Highness proved remarkably spry. It was said that she couldn't stand anyone touching her, and so I was amazed to see Brown grasping both her hands and draping his arm around her shoulders during the dance. Perhaps there was some truth to the rumours of conjugal visits between the two.

Between twirls, I checked the room for assassins. Flora had proved prescient; she had Robbie Munro in a chokehold as they cantered among the other couples. Vicker was studying the buffet table, ticking items from the list he carried and frowning. Now and then, he reached down to straighten a bowl or line up a fork with its fellows. I hoped he wasn't sweating into the horseradish.

Those two were my responsibility, but I figured it wouldn't hurt to check on the other fellows. Archie Skene had a pewter tankard in his hand and was disporting himself with the boys from the stables. They were dressed formally, in jackets, ties and kilts, but they still looked as if you could pull hay from their hair. Vincent had attached himself to Archie, and as I watched, he took the old man's jug and filled it for him from a barrel of ale standing nearby. Ho, ho, Vincent, I thought. What a clever way to keep tabs on the fellow: get him falling down drunk and you won't have to move ten feet from the liquor the whole evening long. Red Hector's ginger hair was tousled and his face flushed with brandy. He was gamboling with one of the housemaids, who was pleased as punch to be dancing with one of Scotland's eligible bachelors. I could have warned her things wouldn't end well, but it wasn't my business to interfere, so I turned my attention back to Jock MacBeath.

Dancing was hard work, so after the reel ended the band gave the crowd a chance to slake its thirst and sample the comestibles on the buffet. French sauntered up with a glass of whisky in his hand.

"You and the marchioness make a fine couple."

He scowled. "It's not the dancing I mind; it's the sneezing. It's like swimming upstream through a Nile cataract. Care to dance?"

I'd danced once before with French, a waltz at the Russian Embassy several weeks ago, and he proved as attentive a partner now as he had then, which is to say, he paid no mind to me at all, except for the minimum of effort required to rein me in and set in on the right path when I was inclined to miss a step. He was busy looking over my shoulder for Red Hector and Munro and the others. We executed a mechanical turn and I bumped into Flora, who was dancing in the next group to ours. She did not look happy.

"Here," she hissed at me. "I'm supposed to dance with French."

"You've Robbie Munro attached to your arm. Don't be selfish."

We swung away from each other, and the next time she glided past she gave me a meaningful glance.

"Don't spoil my chances, India. I loaned you that dress, remember?"

"Don't worry yourself, Flora. You can have him next, as long as you hand over Robbie."

What better way to keep an eye on the lad than holding his hand and laughing up into his eyes? His red gold curls and handsome knees were merely icing on the cake.

We did switch out on the next dance ("The Rakes of Auld Reekie," if I recall correctly), with Flora and I changing partners so deftly the two men looked surprised to find themselves in another woman's arms. I had thought French a distracted partner, but Robbie was worse. We whirled and jigged and stepped our way through dance after dance, but the footman never once looked at me. His eyes were constantly active, and he was as twitchy as a stag on the first day of the hunting season. Naturally, this made me suspicious, as he did seem to be the leading contender for the role of Marischal, but curiously, his attention seemed to be everywhere but upon the Queen, who had retired to the chair on the dais and was now fanning herself energetically, while Brown looked on with a lofty air.

After a blistering rendition of the "The White Cockade," the band finally cried off, pleading for drink, and Robbie bowed shortly and hurried away through the crowd. I followed him just long enough to see him safely ensconced at a table with some of the other servants, sinking a glass of the Scottish national drink. I refreshed myself with some of the same and was pleased to combine business with pleasure as Vicker had taken up residence behind the table containing the liquor (to ensure that none of the servants made an ass of himself, I suppose), and I could watch the man while I sipped my whisky.

The dance floor had cleared, and now four of the ghillies marched into the center from the four corners of the room. They were strapping coves, with broad shoulders and sturdy legs beneath their kilts, and each carried a sword. Silence descended upon the merrymakers. The men faced one another, holding their weapons before them with the blades extended upward. Slowly, they raised the swords to the roof beams, once, twice and yet a third time. Then they knelt as one and laid the swords on the floor so that the points touched.

Jock MacBeath had reclaimed me (by bringing me another drink, and who was I to turn him away, even if you would have to stay out of range of his ears in a high wind).

"The ghillie callum," he whispered.

"Eh?"

"The Scottish sword dance. Have you ever seen it?"

I had not, but if all the performers were as grand-looking as those at Balmoral, I'd been missing something.

The band tuned their instruments, and at a nod from one of the ghillies on the floor, the piper commenced a slow, skirling tune. The kilted chaps simultaneously rose to their toes, then floated into the air and began to dance. I've seen some astonishing performances in my life, including Ellen Terry the night she forgot her lines in *She Stoops to Conquer*, Fred Archer riding Spinaway to victory at Epsom Oaks and the war dances of the Zulus (more about that in a later volume), but I was knocked flat by those ghillies and their footwork. They capered about like young fawns, their feet barely touching their floor, kilts swaying and the muscles in their calves flexing, the sword blades twinkling in the candlelight, and the entire audience hardly daring to breathe as the dancers executed the intricate and ancient steps. Arms raised to the sky, skipping lightly among the blades and points, setting one foot down and now the other, they seemed to levitate above the swords. All the while the pipes droned, filling the ballroom with that eerie sound, at once resonant and electrifying.

When the chaps had finished, collecting their swords and bowing to the Queen, the place erupted. The audience clapped and shouted and whistled. Even I admit to an unladylike whoop, in response primarily to those extraordinary calves. Jock Mac-Beath was cheering like a mad man, his ears aflame. He gave me a wild grin, bursting with pride, and for the first time, I thought I might see some merit to being a Scottish patriot. We've plenty of tradition in England, but the Scottish brand will make your skin crawl, what with the blades and the pipes and the fine, strong men. Belatedly, I realized I had become caught up in the exhibition, and I spent a few anxious minutes tracking down my suspects. Vicker hadn't moved from his place behind the buffet tables; he was scowling at a stable boy who'd taken a rather too generous serving of boiled potatoes. To my relief, Munro had wandered over to the group that included Archie Skene and was now engrossed in a conversation with him. Vincent had edged close to the two men. He was gobbling a meat pie and pretending not to listen to Munro and Skene.

I thought I'd seen the zenith of entertainment, but I was proved wrong. As soon as the band members had refreshed themselves with hot punch and biscuits, they let fly with a savage tune that I thought would have the crowd on the dance floor in seconds. To my surprise, however, the only couple who stepped onto the floor was Her Majesty and John Brown.

"'Tis a *hullachan*," said Jock, who was clearly serving as my native guide to these strange rites.

It looked less like a dance than a skirmish. The Queen and Brown were hurling each other about with abandon. Her Highness's jowls were shaking like jelly, and she'd lost the tartan rosette she'd been wearing. Normally, she mooched about the castle like a sick dog, but here she was, leaping and cavorting like a spring lamb. Brown looked as blown as if he'd just completed the jog from Marathon to Athens, but he was giving it his best, prancing like a man half his age. The music ended (and a good thing it was, as I expected to see both the Queen and Brown keel over any moment), and the two bowed to each other and the crowd, the Queen a bit sheepishly, as if she'd done something unseemly, and Brown with all the natural arrogance of a barnyard rooster. There was a good deal of shouting and applause, and the Queen retired to her chair on the dais, flushed and perspiring.

The band (rascals, they were, as they wouldn't give us a moment's rest) began to play, and Jock MacBeath swung me out onto the dance floor again. That part of the evening is a blur, for we danced and danced and then danced some more, while my head swiveled constantly to keep Vicker and Munro in view. We danced to "The Dundee Whaler" and "The Westminster Reel," and then we slowed for a stately strathspey, to the tune of "The Wishing Well." I wore my soles off to "The Dashing White Sergeant," "The Bees of Maggieknockater," "Lamb Skinnet," and "The Wee Cooper of Fife." Don't ask me the story behind the names; I barely had time to hear Jock's shouted title to each song, and then we were away, galloping giddily around the boards while the bystanders stomped and cheered.

ELEVEN

It must have been close on to one o'clock in the morning when the shot rang out. I had expected the Queen to have retired by then, but she was still on the dais, smiling at the shenanigans on the dance floor and leaning over to whisper into Brown's ear from time to time. It was one of those comments to Brown that saved her. She had inclined her head for a tender exchange when the bullet splintered the chair exactly where her head had rested not a second before. The music ended abruptly in a cacophony of screeches and groans, and the revelers stopped dead in their tracks. The sound of the shot echoed off the roof beams. Then some ninny screamed (there's always one woman in every crowd who demonstrates the truth of the phrase "the weaker sex"), everyone began babbling, and suddenly, Lady Dalfad was on her feet, pointing at the minstrel's gallery and shouting, "Up there, on the balcony!"

I shoved Jock MacBeath and spun wildly, looking, concurrently, for French, Vincent, Skene, Munro and Red Hector. Skene was staring, gape-mouthed, at the balcony, his hand frozen in the act of raising his glass to his lips. Vincent had attached himself to the old duffer like a limpet. He caught my gaze and raised his chin, letting me know he had the situation well in hand. Vicker had left his post behind the buffet table and disappeared. I spent an anxious few minutes, my heart in my mouth, trying to spot the pale and harried deputy master of the household, but he was nowhere to be seen. Neither was Red Hector. Nor was Munro. Damn and blast.

French, tie askew and his black hair waving, shouldered his way through the crowd to me. He had to put his lips against my ear to make himself heard over the tumult.

"Lady Dalfad says a man appeared behind the musicians and fired a revolver at the Queen."

"Was she hit?"

"No, thank God. She had leaned over to gossip with Brown and the assassin missed." He was conning the room while he spoke.

"Munro?" he asked.

"Gone."

"Vicker?"

"Vanished."

He scowled. "Damn your eyes, India. You were supposed to keep them under surveillance."

That stung. "Where the hell is Red Hector?"

"Damned if I know."

Apparently, French seemed to think my lack of diligence was a fault, but his own indifference was nothing to worry about.

"I need to find Vincent."

"He's with Skene."

French gripped my arm. "Good. At least one of us is doing our job. Come with me."

We darted through the partygoers like a couple of London fingersmiths, dodging bearded coves and fainting maids, pushing aside anyone in our path. Robshaw had blockaded the double doors into the ballroom and was roaring instructions to his men to escort the Queen and her guests to safety. A hefty chap in a hideous tweed suit hustled Dizzy out of sight; the PM looked displeased at being manhandled away from the action. Two more burly lads in billycocks and overcoats had the Queen between them and were dragging her along the floor, ignoring her protests.

French seized Robshaw's arm. "We must get through," he bellowed, and Robshaw waved us by.

We pelted down the hall toward the door that led to the balcony. It was open when we reached it, and French dashed up the stairs for a look, returning almost as soon as he'd gone. He shook his head, but, of course, neither of us expected to find anything there. Only a colossal idiot would have hung about to observe the reaction to his attempt on the Queen's life.

"Which way?" I asked.

French glanced to his right. "That hall leads out to the garden. Robshaw's men would have intercepted anyone passing that way."

We turned left and thundered off between the rows of stag heads and paintings of dear departed Albert. I was the first to see the revolver on the floor.

"French," I cried, and pointed at the weapon.

But he had spotted a bigger prize. Ahead of us, Robbie Munro was sprinting down the passageway.

Without slowing his pace, French swooped down and scooped up the revolver, shoving it into his pocket.

Now it's God's truth that if only women had upper-body strength, they'd rule the world. As it is, they have to be content with letting men posture like peacocks and pretend to be in charge. However, I will admit that when it comes to things like chasing down assassins, chaps do have the advantage. French put on a burst of speed that left me panting in his wake. Hearing the footsteps of his pursuer, Munro peeked over his shoulder. I heard his exclamation when he saw French on his heels. The footman turned the corner, followed by French in hot pursuit.

I was constrained to follow at a more leisurely pace, having perhaps imbibed a wee bit more tarantula juice than was advisable for a woman of my size. There was a tremendous crash in the corridor ahead of me, and I rounded the corner to see Munro and French pummeling each other like two prizefighters, neither of whom had made the acquaintance of the Marquess of Queensberry. Munro's fingers were probing for French's eyes, and French had a knee lodged in Munro's groin. They rolled over, grunting like two Russian boars, and Munro took his hands from French's face long enough to wedge them under French's knee and remove that threat to his manhood. French put his palm under Munro's nose and shoved upward. The footman shrieked in pain and grasped a handful of French's hair, tugging vigorously. French yowled and shoved a thumb into Munro's windpipe. Munro gagged and let go of French's lustrous locks.

By now both men were winded and gasping for breath. Blood trickled from Munro's nose, and there was a knot on French's temple that threatened to turn nasty. The two circled warily, each looking for an opening. I sighed. This could go on forever. I'll swear two whores could have accomplished more in less time.

I picked up a Chinese vase from the nearest dresser and advanced on the men. Munro's eyes flickered in my direction as I marched up to them. That was just distraction enough for French to slip in and launch a savage blow to Munro's kidney. The footman collapsed, moaning piteously.

I hefted the vase over his head, ready to deliver the coup de grâce.

Munro glared up at me. "I'm from the Yard, you bloody idiots," he spat. "I'm Robshaw's man."

I thought French was going to hit him again. "You work for Robshaw?" he demanded. "Why didn't he tell us you were one of his?"

Munro shrugged, grimacing.

I tugged at French's sleeve. "You can take as long as you like when you kill Robshaw, but at the moment, we've other things to do."

French nodded reluctantly. He addressed Munro. "Did you see who fired the shot?"

"Just some bloke running down the corridor in front of me," Munro said through clenched teeth. He pointed down the hall. "He's there somewhere. I lost sight of him, of course, when you saw fit to drag me down."

Vincent careered around the corner and drew up short at the sight of us. "Wot's all this?" he demanded. "'Ave you got the bugger, then?"

I explained (briefly, as I was still hoping we could move on to the task of chasing the real assassin).

"Wot the bloody 'ell are you playin' at, mate?" Vincent sputtered, inches from Munro's face.

"We'll settle scores later," I said to Vincent. "Now, we've got to find the man who fired the shot."

"What about Skene?" French asked.

"Drinkin' like a damned fish when the shot was fired. I was right there with 'im. I didn't leave 'is side all night."

"Right," said French grimly. "We need to find our other suspects. Vincent, see if you can locate Vicker. I'll find Robshaw"—he looked murderous when he uttered the superintendent's name—"and tell him to search the grounds, and then I'm off to track down Red Hector."

"I'll check the secret tunnel," I said, to French's back.

French turned on his heel, with a look of alarm. "Don't do that, India. Robshaw's men will seal off the exit, and if our quarry is there, he'll have to return to the house. We'll get him then."

"Oh, very well," I said grumpily, looking vexed that French had quashed my plan. Naturally, I had every intention of proceeding to the tunnel as soon as he was out of sight. He hesitated, no doubt perplexed by my capitulation. He's a suspicious bastard, is French, although in this case he was perfectly justified.

"Go on," I said, giving him a brisk shove. "We've got to find this fellow."

He waggled a finger at me. "Behave yourself, India."

I dutifully followed him back to the entry hall, where I waited until he had snagged Robshaw by the sleeve (with a bit more force than was strictly necessary to get the man's attention) and was engrossed in a conversation with the superintendent, then I sidled away and slipped up the stairs to the main corridor, where I raced off in the direction of French's room and the door to the secret passage. I was moving at such pace that I nearly crashed into the couple tottering down the corridor toward me: a ponderous under butler escorting the marchioness to her room. The marchioness's hazy eyes focused, looking directly at me.

Bugger.

She waved her cane at me. "Here, girl! Where have ye been?"

"No time to talk, my lady," I panted, and attempted to squeeze past.

The marchioness deftly inserted her cane between my legs, and I crashed to the floor, my face skidding across the Turkey carpet. I rolled against the wall and glared up at her, rubbing my bruised shin.

The marchioness looked at me accusingly. "Ye disappoint me, Idina."

It was hardly the time to listen to complaints about immoral behavior or indolence. "I took ye for a clever lass, but I see ye've missed the point."

"The point?"

"Ye want to know who the Marischal is, don't ye? Ain't that why ye're here?"

"What do you know about the Marischal?" I jumped to my feet, rejuvenated by this unexpected news.

"More than ye, my girl. F'r instance, I'll bet ye're runnin' in circles right now, lookin' for the man who tried to shoot the Queen."

"I am. And I've no time to waste talking to you about it."

The marchioness cackled. "Suit yerself. But ye'd do well to remember the stories we've been readin' this past few days."

I am not a patient person, and the marchioness was trying what little quantity of that characteristic I possessed.

"Whatever you're trying to say, just say it. I can't wait around all night while you flap your gums."

The marchioness turned regally and put her hand on the under butler's arm. "Ye give it a think, while ye're harin' about the castle, lookin' for the man ye're after."

She lurched off down the hall. I shook my head and trotted off toward the tunnel, fuming and sputtering like a Catherine wheel. I had a wily Scottish nationalist to find, and the dotty old bird wanted me to cogitate about the Scriptures. And Rose O'Neal Greenhow. And how, by all that was holy, had the marchioness known about the Marischal? Despite my inclination to hurry, I found my pace slowing as my mind raced. What had she been trying to tell me? I'd been certain she had learned my true identity and wanted me to know she knew, hence those stories about whores and deceitful women. As far as I knew (though there were no doubt some amateurs in the building), I was the sole professional at Balmoral. I certainly didn't consider myself the only liar in the pack; I was a dilettante in deceit, compared to all the bloody politicians on hand.

By now, of course, alert readers will have deduced the theme that the marchioness had been harping on since she'd instructed me to read to her for the first time. I can only plead a lack of mental clarity, brought about by an almost complete absence of sleep since arriving at the Queen's Highland home. But it came to me now, and I stopped dead in my tracks and slapped my forehead with my palm. Treachery and treason. All the ladies I'd been droning on about to the marchioness had betrayed someone or something: a lover, a city, a country. What the marchioness had been trying to tell me was that the Marischal was a woman. I thought I had detected some sarcasm when the marchioness had referred to the "man ye're after."

I actually smiled when I realized I was hunting one of my own sex. There isn't a woman alive who frightens India Black. I've held my own on the streets of London, when another bint and I have gone toe-to-toe over a customer, clawing at each other like two cats. I've vanquished a half-dozen other madams intent on stealing my customers or my sluts. And I've sparred for my life with that damned Russian agent, Oksana. When it comes to fighting another damsel, I'm hot pickles and ginger. I didn't care what kind of political fanatic the Marischal might be; she couldn't hold a candle to a whore when the chips were down. I bustled off cheerily, already anticipating the surprise on French's face when I delivered one Scottish nationalist and failed assassin to his feet, trussed like a Christmas goose.

Two of Robshaw's men were in the hall, opening bedroom doors and darting in and out, searching for the Marischal. It would take hours to search every room in the castle, and by the time the job was done, our assassin could have doubled back and found a refuge in some part of the building already searched by Robshaw's men. This, however, was not my concern. I waited until the boys from the Yard had disappeared into one of the guest rooms and then flashed past the open door and around the corner. I might be on a wild-goose chase myself, but I was determined to search the secret passage. Call it woman's intuition (or, in retrospect, sheer bad luck).

The bare-legged Scots on the tapestry were swaying gently when I arrived. I slipped my hand behind the wall hanging and felt a gentle breeze, as cold as the Thames in January. I groped for the stone that triggered the locking mechanism. The door swung inward, and I craned my neck around the opening. A soft yellow glow filled the tunnel. I tamped down the excitement rising in my breast; the bearer of the light could easily be one of Robshaw's men, for surely the superintendent knew of the tunnel. Still, with luck, I might lay hands on the Marischal.

I was halfway through the door before it occurred to me that I needed my own light, so as not to be left stranded in the dark again. More important, I needed a weapon. I snatched a candle from one of the half-dozen candelabras scattered on chests up and down the hall, and rummaged through a half dozen of those before I found a box of matches. The weapon proved easier to find. I had only to take a few steps to find myself in front of one of the numerous martial displays that dotted the castle walls. I scanned the board swiftly. The great two-handed claymore caught my eye, if for no other reason than it looked intimidating as hell. Unfortunately, wielding it effectively would require the strength of Hercules, which I did not possess. I took down a *sgian dubh*, weighing it in my hand. I could certainly handle this, but I'd have to move in close to the Marischal to use it, and I didn't fancy that notion. I tossed the little weapon to the floor, wishing fervently as I did so that I had been allowed to bring my Webley Bulldog along. It looked as though the assassin had discarded her revolver in the hall, but that didn't mean she didn't have another. If the Marischal had a revolver, I would be wandering the Elysian fields before dawn, and it would be just my luck to bump into dear departed Albert there and have to natter with the poor soul about Vicky and Bertie and all the rest. Well, there was no use standing here all night, dithering about which edged weapon would best protect me from a bullet. I snatched a Scottish broadsword from the wall, waggled it experimentally and took some solace from the comforting sound of the double-edged blade swishing through the air. Then I plunged into the tunnel.

The glimmer of light could still be seen, though it had receded some distance into the passage. I didn't bother to light my own candle, not wanting to give myself away to my prey, so I edged forward cautiously, scarcely breathing. It was tedious work, following that murky gleam down the stone-walled corridor, and it seemed to take forever. I occupied my mind by imagining the various scenarios that might occur and calculating how best to ambush the woman in the limited confines of the tunnel. It was deuced cold in the passage at this time of night, and my teeth began to chatter like castanets. I clamped my jaws together and hurried stealthily onward. The sooner I ran the Marischal to ground, the sooner I could have a stiff drink and crawl into a warm bed. Perhaps if I captured the Marischal, I'd receive an appropriate reward: six pieces of coal instead of three.

The conclusion of the chase came sooner than I had expected. The pale golden gleam of the light ceased moving, flickering over the walls of the small room I'd found in my earlier exploration of the tunnel. I sucked in a breath and glided forward. I moved as silently as a Red Indian, albeit one wearing a silk ball gown, the rustling of which sounded like a typhoon approaching. Too late, I remembered my earlier vow (made while hunting those damned Russian agents) to acquire a pair of trousers for use in chasing spies, hand-to-hand combat and similar pursuits. But luckily for me, the figure I now saw was too preoccupied to hear the whispery fluttering of my skirts.

A slender form stood before me, dressed in tartan trews and a short, dark jacket, a Balmoral cap perched on its head. A black woolen cloak lay discarded on the floor. The figure bent over, rapidly untying the laces of a pair of stout boots. I was tempted to retreat, find the marchioness and bash her over the head with the butt of my broadsword. I'd been expecting to find a woman; now I'd have to take my chances with a member of the male sex, who looked lithe and fit as a champion hurdler. The sensible thing would be to silently retrace my steps and summon help, but I find it infernally difficult to do the sensible thing when my blood is up, as it was now. I could hear French's posh voice in my ear, telling me not to be rash, but I shut it out. I had two things going for me: the element of surprise and an aversion to fighting fair.

"The Marischal, I presume?" To my relief, my voice was steady.

The figure spun to face me, mouth agape. A mouth shaped like a rosebud.

Good Lord, that couldn't be . . .

A hand reached up and swept off the cap, releasing a mass of strawberry blond curls that tumbled to the shoulders of the figure I confronted.

"Flora!" The sword in my hand wavered.

Flora saw my indecision and sprang for the cloak, the folds of which had concealed a small sword. It was a vicious thing, almost three feet in length, with a razor-sharp point that Flora now brandished under my nose.

I raised the broadsword in defense. From a purely objective view, this should be an interesting match: I carried a weapon with a cutting edge on each side of the blade, giving me the ability to do damage with any contact to the body, while Flora's small sword was to be used not to hack or slash, but to bury its point into the opponent. We seemed equally matched, as far as height and weight, and we were both young and in our prime. From the subjective point of view, however, I was damned concerned.

"You seem surprised to see me here, India." Flora had dropped the amiable housemaid act and now looked as cordial as a trapped wolverine from the wilds of Michigan. "But I am not surprised to see you. It was clear you were up to something from the moment you arrived, pestering the servants with your questions, watching Robbie Munro and Vicker like a hawk."

That made my dander rise, but I fought it down with some effort. French would have been proud.

"And thank God you and your accomplices are a pack of dunderheads," I said. "Your attempts on the Queen were amateurish."

She bridled at that, which is just what I had planned. I wanted her raving mad when she came after me with that brochette in her hand.

"Your ignorance was breathtaking. You knew nothing about Scotland and its noble families. You had no idea that Lady Dalfad held the title in her own right, as Scottish peerages are allowed to pass through the female line."

I mentally applauded the liberality of the Scots in permitting aristocratic ladies to enjoy the same privileges as their menfolk, but the subject did not warrant much consideration at the moment, especially with the point of Flora's sword inches from my face.

"Indeed, I knew you weren't a lady's maid the moment I set eyes on you."

"Having never been a servant," I said, "I did find it hard to behave like one, unlike you, who seemed damned good at tugging your forelock."

Her eyes flamed, and a bitter smile formed on her lips. "Och, we've tugged them for too long, to a pack of rascals who care not a whit for our proud nation. But that will change soon enough."

"The Queen is still alive, Flora."

"She won't survive long. I'm not the only one prepared to sacrifice my life to rid the land of the Sassenach plague." She took a step toward me.

"Do your best, Flora."

Her face twisted with rage. "I am not Flora," she spat. "I am Fionnghuala MacGhillechoinnich"—I admit, I learned this later, as when she flung the words at me, they might have been Lithuanian for all I knew—"of the Clan MacGhillechoinnich, hounded by the British, our lands and kine confiscated in the Clearances, our sons reduced to dying for a monarch we loathe, our daughters forced into servitude, our name erased from history and anglicized to Mackenzie for the convenience of the bloody English."

Nothing I might have said could have provoked her more than her own fiery speech. She lunged at me, howling like a Fuzzy-Wuzzy intent on breaking the British square, the cruel point of her small sword aimed at my breast. I pivoted to avoid the rush and got my blade up to counter her thrust. I felt the shock along my arm and into my shoulder as the blades met, and I stumbled backward. Flora (and I'll continue to call her that, as the name she prefers takes such a deuced long time to write out on the page) pursued the advantage, advancing on me while I tried to regain my balance, the tip of her sword weaving like a black mamba about to strike. Then she flexed her wrist and the point of the blade flicked across my cheek. Shocked, I clapped my hand to my face and felt the warm gush of blood between my fingers.

But this was no time to worry about finding a mirror. Flora's successful strike had infused her with energy. She charged toward me, and I thrust my blade between us, shoving hers upward as she bore in on me. Once more, I staggered backward at the ferocity of her attack. Previous thoughts of delivering the Marischal to French were chucked out the window. The way things were going, I'd be lucky to survive this bout.

Flora swept forward and came in under my arm, dropping her shoulder and stabbing upward. I leapt away, hammering my blade down on hers and parrying what might have been a fatal thrust. I would have congratulated myself for escaping almost certain death, but I now had a real problem: my back was against the wall. Literally. Flora had pushed me backward until I had run out of room. I felt the damp, cold stone through my dress. Flora tilted her head, a mocking smile playing around her lips. Then her eyes hardened and every sinew of her body tensed. I knew she would be coming in for the kill.

I could almost hear French's voice in my ear, telling me that now was the perfect time for a counterattack. I thought so too, but not because I'd had the odd lesson in fencing strategy. No, it was pure, unadulterated fear at the prospect of being spitted on Flora's small sword that caused me to consider launching my own assault.

Flora was bobbing and ducking, looking for an opening, when I sprang off the wall, sword slashing upward. I found her blade and lifted it cleanly, but Flora was too fast for me to press home the advantage. She danced away from me before I could touch her, but I could see my attack had flummoxed her. She didn't look half so cocky as when she'd had me pinned against the wall, and I was bloody glad to have dented her confidence. I feinted toward her, and she swung gracefully out of reach of my blade, then glided forward with her own extended. I stepped to one side and blocked her advance. Steel rang on steel and the blades quivered. Flora sprang away and I followed, slashing at her retreating figure. Her hands moved deftly, countering my every move.

By now I was winded, and I could see that Flora had lost a good deal of her spark as well. We conducted a slow waltz in that tiny stone room, orbiting each other like two dying planets. Now and then, one of us would skip forward, trying to lure the other into a fruitless charge, but neither of us wanted to take the bait. The room echoed with our labored breathing, our slow, measured footsteps, punctuated now and then by the thump of an unsuccessful foray and the grating and scraping of blade against blade. We'd been at it like that for a while, and I was wondering whether Flora would be amenable to calling it a draw, shaking hands and having a wee dram together in the spirit of good sportsmanship, when her head snapped up and her eyes were drawn to something beyond my shoulder.

"Marischal," she breathed, a look of adoration on her face, which dissolved into puzzlement and then melted into a mask of disbelief. "No!" she cried, and I started to turn, to see what had horrified her so, when the world exploded.

The concussion from the shot sent me reeling. The damned gun must have gone off right in my ear; I believe I lost my hearing momentarily, for the room was quiet as a tomb, and the flash of the gunpowder had half-blinded me. I collapsed to my hands and knees and finally keeled over, like a ship that had been holed below the waterline. I rolled over onto my back, moaning loudly.

Then my hearing returned, though I wish it hadn't, for the sounds I heard now, albeit coming to me faintly, were sounds I never wish to hear again. I don't suppose many of you have heard the sounds of a woman dying of a sucking chest wound, and I hope you never will. I turned my head to see Flora stretched out beside me, the bodice of her blouse and jacket soaked with blood. There was blood everywhere, it seemed. My silk gown was spattered with the stuff, and for one crazy moment I dreaded the look on Flora's face when I told her I'd ruined her second-best dress. Flora, however, was past caring. Her eyes were still open and she was still breathing, but it was a dreadful hissing noise I shall never forget as long as I live. She was staring with an unfocused gaze at the ceiling, as though she could see beyond the veil and didn't much care for the view. Blood gushed from between those rose-bud lips.

"Oh, my Christ," I whispered, forgetting for a moment that I was not a practicing member of the C of E.

Over the ghastly sound of Flora Mackenzie's last breath, I heard a footfall and the soft rustle of cloth. You'd think I'd have been glad to hear this tangible evidence of my rescuer, but some instinct stirred in me. No Good Samaritan would be so furtive. Turning my head painfully, I searched for my sword and saw it lying in a pool of blood, inches from my hand. I stretched out my fingers, and a slippered foot descended onto my wrist. I looked up into the face of Lady Dalfad. I was also looking down the barrel of a revolver.

"You!" I exclaimed, which was a bit lame, but it was all I could manage after being concussed by that explosion in my ear.

Those sea green eyes were as calculating and merciless as a panther's. She kept her gaze locked on me as she lifted her foot from my wrist and used it to nudge my sword out of reach of my extended arm.

"That's better," she said. "I wouldn't want to raise your hopes by leaving that sword nearby."

"You're a cool one, considering you just shot one of your lieutenants in cold blood." I was rather surprised that my voice sounded almost normal but for a slight tremor and the tiniest hint of shrillness.

The countess spared Flora a glance and made a moue of distaste.

"I did hate killing the girl; she's a damned sight more intelligent than half the peers in Scotland. But unfortunately, I had to sacrifice her. She's one of the few people who could identify me as the Marischal. And, she's rather upset my plans. I was expecting the Queen to die at Scottish hands, on Scottish soil. Now, I shall have to wait for another time."

I'm no Socrates, but even I grasped the logical implications of that statement: if the countess was to have another crack at Her Highness, India Black would have to be removed from the picture.

"You can't escape, you know. Superintendent Robshaw's men are everywhere."

The countess smiled mirthlessly. "I don't intend to escape, Miss Black."

"But, what . . ."

"I intend to kill you. Then I shall run from here in hysterics and raise the alarm. No doubt the prime minister and Mr. French will be thrilled to hear of your gallant effort to prevent the Marischal's escape. Unfortunately, you died trying. I happened upon the scene not long after the Marischal had shot you, and I grasped at once that here was the villainess who had attempted to assassinate my Queen. I was too late to save you, but I did fling myself upon Flora, and by sheer luck, I managed to turn the revolver upon her and kill her." She looked down at her ball gown. "Pity, I've always liked this dress, and now I shall have to ruin it by smearing it with Flora's blood."

"Your story is weak," I sneered, but I was glad the light was dim; with luck, the countess might not notice my lips flapping like a ship's pennant in a stiff breeze. "How did you know about the passage, and why did you decide to venture into it alone? Why did you assume Flora was the Marischal? I can think of any number of questions you'll be asked, and you won't have any answers to them."

Lady Dalfad's nostrils flared. "You stupid girl. Do you think anyone will presume to challenge my statement? I am a lady of the bedchamber, the Queen's trusted confidant. No one would dare imply that I was involved in the plot against the Queen, least of all that fat, silly, selfish wretch who dares call herself a monarch."

"I agree the Queen leaves a bit to be desired in some areas, but then none of us are perfect. Is it really necessary to scribble the old girl?" I didn't expect a rational answer; it was clear the count-ess had stepped over the thin line dividing "dedicated patriot" to "one sheep short of a flock." I just hoped to keep her talking until help arrived, for surely someone in the castle had heard the gun-shot and should even now be rushing to the sound.

Lady Dalfad's face contorted into a mask of disgust. "The Queen isn't fit to rule Scotland. She dresses her servants in tar-tans like they were dolls. She cannot venture into the countryside without an army of servants to carry her tea and her sandwiches. She covers the walls with thistles and tartans and she thinks that makes her a true Scot. She has no appreciation of what it means to be born in this country, to live and die here. And have you no-ticed that fake Scottish brogue she affects? Just yesterday, she was saying that the Baroness of Kirkcudbright is 'woon prood wum-man.' I could have screamed with disgust. For her Scotland is a fairy realm, and the Scots are picturesque rascals who cater to her every whim. Just look at me, a member of one of the great families of Scotland, reduced to stirring her cocoa and sitting in on sé-ances while charlatans play upon her gullibility. Thank God for her stupidity, though. It was dead easy planting the idea that Al-bert wanted her here at the castle."

She shook herself then and leveled the revolver at my heart. "But I've wasted enough time talking to you. Good-bye, India Black."

"Lady Dalfad!" The voice belonged to French. "Pray put down that revolver, my lady. If you surrender, it will go much easier for you at the trial."

The countess spun and fired in the direction of French's voice. For the second time that night, the chamber rocked with the concussion of the explosion. I heard shouts from the passage, in-cluding an agonized cry that chilled me, but there was no time to lose. I rolled to my side and swept my leg in the direction of Lady Dalfad. My shin connected with her ankles, and I felt her stumble. The revolver in her hand waved wildly, then with an effort she steadied herself and aimed the weapon at me. There was despair in her eyes, the hollow anguish of someone who knows that the battle is lost. But there was hatred, too, and there was murder. I closed my eyes. This was the point where I presumed I should have a quick word with the Chairman of the Cosmos, but as he and I weren't on familiar terms, I thought it might be a bit presumptuous on my part to bother him with my present situation.

As it turned out, I was spared the indignity of having to cram my confession of sins into the seconds I had remaining (God knows, I wouldn't have been able to account for many in that amount of time), for there was an almighty bellowing from the other side of the room. I opened my eyes in time to see Vincent launch himself at Lady Dalfad, cutting her down at the knees and seizing the hand that held the revolver. The countess screeched and clawed Vincent's face like a wildcat, but the little pagan hung on grimly and did not let go of the weapon.

Munro arrived, with a look of grim determination on his face, and fell on the heaving pile that was Vincent and Lady Dalfad. More men of Robshaw's appeared, until we were having a veritable lodge meeting with all the Masons in attendance. The superintendent himself followed shortly. He was clutching his arm, and the sleeve of his tweed coat was dark and wet. It's the least the bugger deserved, in my opinion, for leading us astray and making our job that much more difficult. In a moment, Munro had wrestled the revolver from the countess's hand and Vincent was counting the furrows in his face left by her fingernails. I looked round for French, and then I felt his arms encircling me. His hands roamed my body, searching, I presume, for wounds.

I shoved him aside. "Bloody hell, French. I've had less intrusive exams by my doctor."

"Are you alright? Did she hurt you?"

I remembered Lady Dalfad's eyes, the cold green of the North Sea, and shuddered. "She was about to shoot me."

French pressed my face into his chest, his hands in my hair, murmuring soothingly in my ear. "It's all over," he said. "She can't do anything to you now."

I sat for a moment, inhaling the pleasant smell of sweat (he had been tussling with Munro, as you recall), tobacco and whisky. His fingers moved slowly through my hair. Was I swooning? My reverie was fated to end.

"She'd 'ave plugged you, India, if I 'adn't shown up." Vincent squatted on his heels next to us. "Look wot she done to my face."

"If anyone asks, you can tell them they're dueling scars," I said, disentangling myself from French. It had been pleasant there, in the cocoon of his arms, but Robshaw's men, having subdued and carted off the countess, were now looking at French and me with entirely too much interest.

TWELVE

It was a far jollier carriage ride from Balmoral to Ballater, where we caught the train for Perth, than the trip from Ballater to the castle so many days ago. We weren't traveling with Lady Dalfad, naturally, as her transport back to England had been arranged specially for her by Superintendent Robshaw. Effie, shocked to the bone by her employer's treason (or so she said—I never did trust that girl), had been reduced to sobs and was last seen being comforted by one of the under butlers, who, I was reliably informed, had been carrying a torch for her lo, these many years (poor fellow). The marchioness and I shared a carriage with Red Hector, who turned out to be a charming chap, being only half-drunk at this time of day. He and the marchioness gassed on about foaling stalls and stud fees and proper conformation, and when they were finished with the equine world, they moved on to canines, and I had to listen to a lengthy panel discussion of distemper and worms that left me breathless with boredom.

It wasn't until the marchioness and I were settled in our carriage for the journey back to Perth, and Red Hector had seen us off with a cheery wave and an invitation to the marchioness to visit his breeding kennels in the summer, that I had a chance to bounce the old girl about Lady Dalfad.

"Alright, my lady, time to come clean. How did you know about the Marischal?" I demanded.

"We've got newspapers in Scotland. O' course I knew the Marischal and the Sons of Arbroath were collectin' English heads and blatherin' on about killin' the Queen. And ye'd have to be a prize ninny not to know there was a ruckus brewin' at the castle. When the Queen said she'd be comin' to Balmoral for Christmas, I saw the hands of those Scottish traitors in it. Her Majesty's a great creature of habit, she is, and if she comes to the Highlands in the winter, ye know somethin's afoot."

There were several largish leaps of logic in that statement; I was not convinced. "Are you sure someone didn't tell you the Marischal would be at the castle?" I could think of some likely culprits, namely Dizzy, French or even Robshaw, though I found it difficult to imagine the superintendent exposing a spotless tweed suit to Her Ladyship's presence long enough to brief her on the nationalist plot.

The old trout gave me a crafty look and wagged her finger. "I canna tell you that, lass."

Was it possible my employer was also an agent of the government? Hard to credit, I know, but if the prime minister could employ a tart, he surely wouldn't balk at a decrepit aristocrat dripping snuff. If the marchioness was in the Queen's employ, I'd extract the information from French and make sure it was a painful exercise. Or was the marchioness herself a disaffected member of the Sons of Arbroath, who'd grown tired of Lady Dalfad at the helm? Well, even if she were, I didn't like to think of the old crone in a cold cell, trickling snuff over her straw mattress.

"Why didn't you just tell me that the countess was the Marischal?" I asked as I draped a blanket over her knees and put her snuffbox close to hand.

"I didna know she was."

"Come, now. She must have given you some reason to be suspicious."

"All I knew was that someone close to the Queen had turned traitor, and after thinkin' on it for a spell, I thought she was the most likely candidate, knowin' her family history as I did. I tried to give ye a hint, startin' ye out with those stories of Delilah and Criseyde, but ye didn't catch on. I figured I was goin' to have to throw ye a lifeline, and so I turned to Rahab and Mrs. Greenhow, but ye still kept flounderin' around like a drownin' sailor."

She fumbled for the snuffbox, and I handed it to her impatiently, priming myself with a large lawn handkerchief. I waited until she inhaled and expectorated, and wiped the trickle of tobacco from her nostrils.

"Anyway, I gave ye enough bloody clues, a blind pig could have found that acorn," she snuffled.

"What clues? We read a heap of maddening drivel about treacherous women. I thought you'd tumbled to my identity, and you were trying to tell me you knew I wasn't a lady's maid at all."

"I knew the day you dropped yer first curtsey to me that ye were no more a maid than I was a hippopotamus."

"What? How?" I spluttered. The old bag's criticism was a bit harsh, considering I've played every role from virginal shepherdess to Nell Gwynne without a word of complaint from my customers.

"Ye tried, I'll give ye that, but ye're about as docile as a collie bitch in heat. Besides, when Horace showed me yer resume, I knew there was a worm in the apple somewhere. Nobody with references like yers would be chompin' at the bit to work for the likes of me. I've got a reputation to keep up as the worst employer in Scotland." She nudged me with her cane. "And I'll thank ye not to spoil it fer me by tellin' everyone how I took pity on ye and solved yer little mystery for ye."

"And how did you know I was here to solve a mystery?" I snapped. My suspicion of French was growing rapidly. He had been the one who'd arranged this little masquerade, after all.

The marchioness pursed her lips and gave me a prim little smile. "Since ye weren't at the castle to do my hair, I reckoned ye had another job to do. I've never seen such a one as you for snoopin' and askin' questions and skulkin' around the halls."

"How would you know what I was doing? You were asleep most of the time."

She batted an eyelid at me. "Maybe I was and maybe I wasn't. Ye ain't the only woman who could ha' had a career on the stage."

My money was still on French having had a word in the marchioness's ear; I simply couldn't have been so transparent, especially to an ancient narcoleptic who had trouble distinguishing face powder from snuff. I felt the slight sinking sensation (quite rare, that) of my ego deflating.

"It's not my fault ye couldna find your arse with both hands." The marchioness heaved a great sigh and twisted the dagger she'd plunged into my self-respect. "I suppose I should have told ye what I was aimin' at, but I thought ye were bright enough to figure it out on yer own. Well, I suppose I'm to blame, really, for overestimatin' ye."

"I'm sorry to have disappointed you." I said it sarcastically, but of course that was wasted on the marchioness. She looked at me as though I was the village simpleton and to be pitied.

"Och, it's simple, really. The countess may be a tiger, but she's descended from an utter jackass: James Dalfad, fourth Earl of Haldane. Despite being an heir of old King Duncan, Dalfad was a ne'er-do-well of the first order. Next to him, Bertie looks like a Presbyterian missionary. The earl was just a young chap when he inherited the title, and within a year or two, he'd run through all the money his pa left him and had mortgaged the estate to pay for his bad habits. Luckily, 1707 rolled around, and the English government was lookin' for tame Scottish peers to sign the Act of Union. Dalfad took the thirty pieces of silver the English were offerin',' but instead of payin' his debts like a sensible lad, he gambled and drank it away, just as he'd done the family fortune. He was desperate for money, but he found he had no friends in Scotland. Half the country despised him for signin' the act, and the other half, who'd drunk his whisky, disappeared when they found out the money was gone. Dalfad went up to London, but the King wasn't partin' with any more gold. Weel, who can blame him? Dalfad would ha' spent it and been back beggin' for more within a year. But the King needed a few Scottish peers in his pocket, so ever since then, the monarch offers some middlin' post to the earl's descendents, which provides a little money and a smidgen of prestige, provided they can stand all the bowin' and scrapin' that goes along with it. It's a tragic fate for a noble family."

I'd been following this with difficulty, still trying to wrap my mind around the central thesis of the marchioness's history lesson. "Do you mean to tell me that Lady Dalfad became the Marischal and decided to kill the Queen because she was ashamed of something her great-great-grandfather had done?"

"Naturally," said the marchioness, astonished at my ignorance. "There's many like her who canna live down the shame of havin' a traitor for an ancestor. And it must have been humiliatin' for Lady Dalfad to have to follow the Queen around like a pet spaniel. I'd be mad enough to choke if I had to converse with the old biddy and watch her paint and listen to her whinge about Albert all day long."

"I see your point," I said. The latter would have been reason enough to scribble Her Highness, in my book. I had a more difficult time imagining that the actions of some long-dead ancestor of mine would engender enough shame to drive me to murder. Of course, family ties were rather loose in my case, and I'd long since ceased to feel any remorse for my own actions, let alone those of my forefathers, whoever they might have been. Try as I might, I simply couldn't fathom how the countess could get so worked up about events that took place almost two centuries ago and then take out her anger on that dull dumpling Vicky. I expressed as much to the marchioness, who hooted loudly.

"Ye're not from here. Unless ye are, ye'll never understand. We Scots thrive on thievery, religion and bloodshed, and our feuds are older than time itself. We've an ancient quarrel with England, and it will likely never end, unless the English get tired of our broodin' and mutterin' and cut us loose someday. Until then, there be plenty of caber tossers who'd be glad to raise the cross of St. Andrew and welcome back the heirs of Bonnie Prince Charlie. Ye know what they say: 'All ye need are twelve Highlanders and a bagpipe, and ye've got a rebellion on yer hands.'"

"If you suspected that I was there to winkle out the Marischal, why didn't you say something to me, or pass the word to the prime minister or Superintendent Robshaw?"

"And what would I ha' told 'em? The same thing as I'm tellin' ye, and I can see from the look on yer face that ye're havin' a hard time graspin' the essential point. What do you reckon that Robshaw would ha' thought of my intuition pointin' the finger at Lady Dalfad? Those chaps from Scotland Yard deal in facts, and I didna have any to give 'em. Yer Superintendent Robshaw would ha' rolled his eyes and sent me back to my room with a hot water bottle and somethin' to calm my nerves. Ye know how men are about acceptin' help from a woman. They'd rather have a leg cut off with a dull saw than take advice from the fairer sex. And the older you get, the harder it is to get a fellow to pay you any mind at all."

I had to leave it at that, as I was no closer to understanding Lady Dalfad's motivations after the marchioness's explanation than I had been before (though I concurred heartily in her assessment of the male sex). I suppose I find it hard to get worked up about such notions as patriotism and national identity and whether my monarch was weaned on porridge or roast beef. My concern had always been with more immediate and pressing matters, like whether I'd have a crust to eat that day.

The marchioness put her head back and fell asleep then, snoring like a bulldog until we shuddered to a halt at the station in Perth. She woke with a jerk and reached for her snuffbox. For the last time, I held the container for her while she shoveled a healthy measure into her nose, and for the last time, I stood well to one side to avoid being drenched by the deluge. Sir Horace Wickersham's ruddy face and halo of white hair appeared around the door. He cleared his throat bashfully.

"Horace," the marchioness cried. "We've had a deuced fine time at Balmoral."

"I read about it in the papers," said Sir Horace, twisting his hat in his hands.

"The papers!" the marchioness said scornfully. "What do they know about it? I'll give ye the inside story on the journey home."

"Wonderful," said Sir Horace, without much enthusiasm.

The marchioness flung the traveling rug from her lap. "Let's get on with it. I've seen garden statues move faster. Get my baggage, Horace. Ina, collect my things. Hurry, Horace, our train leaves in twenty minutes."

The beleaguered Sir Horace and I hopped to it. He summoned porters for the luggage, and I gathered up the snuffbox and the marchioness's Bible, and rolled up the rug and strapped it to her trunk. We straggled out of the carriage together, with the marchioness wobbling along on Sir Horace's arm while I brought up the rear. The train to Tullibardine was waiting on the other side of the platform, and I helped guide the marchioness into her carriage while Sir Horace deferentially asked the porters to look lively and have a care, please, which requests were rather rudely ignored by the hulking gentlemen who were busy tossing the bags into the baggage car.

The marchioness plopped down on the seat, and I placed the rug over her knees and her snuffbox in her lap, along with a supply of handkerchiefs, though I doubt the old pussy would have use for them.

"Well, Irma, this is good-bye," she said cheerfully. "I can't say ye're the best lady's maid I've ever had, but ye were certainly the most interestin'."

"And I can't say that you're the best employer I've ever had, but you were certainly the most interesting."

She liked that, hee-hawing silently, with the yellow stumps of her teeth winking at me from her gaping mouth.

"I was brought up never to touch the servants, unless ye were goin' to thrash 'em, but here"—she thrust out a hand in a dirty glove—"let's shake hands, as two prime examples of the female species."

I took her hand willingly, despite the knowledge that I'd need to find some soap and water before I resumed my journey.

She let go of my hand and looked around irritably. "Where did Horace get to? I've got dogs that mind better."

Sir Horace returned, red-faced and puffing from the effort of shepherding the stowing of the marchioness's luggage. A great cloud of steam enveloped the platform, and the conductor stalked the boards, hustling the remaining passengers into their carriages and checking that the doors were securely fastened behind them.

The marchioness whacked my shin with her cane. "Don't loiter about, Irene. We'll be leavin' any moment, and if ye miss your train, ye'll be stuck in Perth for days. If there's a more godforsaken place, I don't know it."

I massaged my shin. "Good-bye, my lady."

"And farewell to ye. Remember to keep yer eyes open and yer wits about ye. Read yer Bible, and don't fall for any handsome toffs with wild black hair." She winked.

"No worries there," I said. "Except for that injunction about the Bible. I've read enough of the Scriptures to hold me for the next few years."

I said good-bye to Sir Horace, who mumbled and blushed and swept off his hat. Then I stood on the platform while the engines revved and steam pulsed out from the locomotive. Slowly, the wheels began to turn. I took a few steps, still gazing at the old lady's window. I felt a pricking in my eye and had to knuckle it away. Damned cinders were a nuisance in these stations.

Sir Horace wrestled with the window to the marchioness's carriage. She put her head through the opening as the train began to roll.

"I forgot to tell ye that while ye can't fix hair for tuppence, yer a damned brave girl," she cawed.

I smiled and lifted my hand in acknowledgement.

"Ye are yer mother's daughter, India. Ye remind me of her. She was a brave girl, too."

My hand fell to my side and my smile faded to incredulity. My mother? What the hell did the marchioness know of my mother?

The train was gathering speed. The marchioness was waving dementedly from the carriage. I flung myself down the platform after her.

"Wait!" I shouted. "What about my mother?"

But the marchioness had disappeared in a billow of smoke, and the rumble of the train began to recede into the distance. I stood on the platform and watched it vanish from sight.

I was in a right state when I entered the railway carriage that would bear me back to London, but fortunately, the other occupants were engaged in a rancorous argument and paid no attention to me. Robshaw, immaculately dressed, with his arm in a sling, occupied a chair on one side of the private car. Robbie Munro, his nose swollen to alarming proportions, sat next to him. Both men were glowering across the room at French, who was scowling back. Vincent, God bless his soul, was providing moral support to his hero, staring blackly at the men from the Yard. Dizzy, like any sensible politician, had chosen a chair between the two camps and was busy scrutinizing his fingernails.

"I can only assume," French said coldly to Robshaw, "that you did not trust the prime minister and his agents to protect the Queen inside the castle."

Dizzy looked pained at having been dragged into the dispute.

"Hold on, old cock." Robshaw smoothed his whiskers. "It merely seemed prudent to have someone else in the house. And if you were unaware of his identity, you and your, er, associates would not slip up and divulge it." His glance ricocheted from Vincent to me, and a smirk tightened the corners of his mouth.

Officious clot.

A muscle twitched in French's cheek. "My associates and I spent a great deal of time trying to eliminate Munro from the field of suspects; time, I'm sure you'd agree, which could have been spent more wisely trying to find the real culprits."

Munro ran a hand through his curls. Since I'd discovered the handsome devil had been a red herring, planted by the Yard, I'd ceased to find him attractive. "I may have distracted you, French, but I did succeed in infiltrating the Sons of Arbroath."

"My dear boy," drawled French, "you'd made the acquaintance of poor Archie Skene, whose only motive in joining the nationalists was a grudge against John Brown. You attended one meeting of the group. You hadn't exactly penetrated the inner circle, nor did you learn enough from your contacts with the group to prevent the attacks on the Queen."

"At least I didn't trip over my own shoelaces and have to run away like a frightened rabbit," Munro said hotly. "And what about Miss Black? She was sharing a room with Flora Mackenzie, for God's sake. You'd have thought Miss Black might have noticed *something* was amiss."

"Now, now," murmured Dizzy. "Perhaps we should simply agree that things might have been handled better by all parties involved, rather than attempt to cast blame on one another."

"That's easy for you to say, Prime Minister," said Robshaw. "But you're not the one catching it in the papers."

Dizzy waved a hand airily. "Oh, the press. You are much too sensitive, Superintendent. My advice to you in dealing with journalists is to develop a skin like a rhinoceros. But I shall see that several of our journalist friends receive a communiqué from the prime minister's office praising your efforts in capturing Lady Dalfad and dismembering the Sons of Arbroath. The uproar will die down eventually."

French uttered a guttural noise of disgust.

"Bah!" Vincent exclaimed.

I remained silent, being in no mood to argue over who would get credit for removing the threat to the Queen. If anyone received the accolades, it should be John Brown, in my opinion. If the old girl hadn't been leaning over for a chin wag with the chap, she'd be dead now.

Bells clanged and the locomotive emitted an earsplitting whistle.

"Ah." Dizzy sighed. "We shall soon return to civilization. Superintendent, perhaps you would oblige me by describing the aftermath of the attempt on the Queen's life. I find that I have been so preoccupied in calming Her Highness and attending to affairs of state, that I have little knowledge of what has transpired. For instance, what of Vicker?"

"I can tell you that," said Vincent, before Robshaw could open his mouth. "I 'unted the cove down right after Flora tried to shoot the old . . . er, 'Er 'Ighness. 'E was tryin' to 'ush the maids, who 'ad gone 'ysterical on 'im, and they were flutterin' about like a bunch of chickens about to 'ave their necks wrung. 'E was soaked with sweat and white as a sheet, and babblin' about the Queen gettin' killed on 'is watch and, oh, the shame of it. I 'ustled out and found one of the men from the Yard"—a murderous look here at Robshaw—"and told 'im to collect Vicker and bring 'im in for questionin'. Which, I might add, 'e proceeded to do."

"Vicker may have acted suspiciously," said Robshaw, "but he wasn't involved with the Sons of Arbroath."

"The man was as nervy as a middle-aged spinster," I said.

"Yes, he was, and it turns out that he had good reason to be," said Robshaw. "It seems Vicker had developed an affection for one of the Queen's dressers at Windsor. One thing led to another, as it often does in these situations, and the young woman found herself with child. To Vicker's credit, he did right by the girl. They were married a few weeks ago at a small parish in London, where neither was known."

Vincent's forehead wrinkled. "Wot's the problem, then?"

"I expect the Queen would not have been pleased," said French.

"And Vicker knew it. He'd be out on his ear, and his wife with him, as soon as the Queen found out. As you know, Vicker wasn't supposed to accompany the Queen to Balmoral, but the master of the household fell ill and Vicker had to fill in for him. Vicker had been intending to tender his resignation while Her Highness was away in Scotland. Instead, he was forced to join the Queen's household for the holiday. He was doubly anxious, as he was now responsible for running things at Balmoral, and because he dreaded the return to London, when he'd have to give his notice."

"Poor devil," muttered Dizzy. "What will he do now?"

"He's off to South Africa," I said, explaining to Dizzy about the letter I'd found in Vicker's wastebasket.

"With his new bride," added Robshaw.

"Wot about Archie?" Vincent had found a hamper of sandwiches and was helping himself, opening them one by one and discarding the watercress and cucumber varieties.

"He's been arrested."

"Go easy on 'im, won't you, guv? 'E's a decent bloke. I reckon I'da done worse than join a bunch of blokes in skirts if John Brown 'ad 'umiliated me like 'e done Archie."

"I think you can rest easy on that score, Vincent," said Robshaw. "Skene was never more than a bit player in this drama. As you said, he was drawn into the Sons of Arbroath because he was angry that the Queen had demoted him on Brown's recommendation. He denies any involvement in the incident with the block and tackle in the stable, and I'm inclined to believe him. Skene resented the Queen but didn't really want to see her killed. I think he simply fell in with a bad lot and got in over his head. Just because he drank whisky with the conspirators doesn't make him one."

Vincent nodded emphatically. "Archie'd drink with anyone, long as the liquor was free."

"We've arrested Flora's mother, the cook. Unlike Archie, she freely admits to being a member of the nationalists. What's more, she's confessed to poisoning the cocoa, at Flora's direction. Flora, of course, had received the order from Lady Dalfad."

"I'm still baffled as to why the countess didn't have the Queen killed by the cocoa," I said.

"She intended to kill her, but evidently, Cook bungled the amount of poison she added to the chocolate. That accounts for the amateurish attempt with the block and tackle. That," Robshaw added, "was put together rather hurriedly by two lads who'd recently joined the Sons of Arbroath and were anxious to prove their commitment to the cause. We've picked them up in Leith, and we're questioning them now. One of them has already confessed to cracking Vincent's noggin. As for Cook, she'll most certainly be tried for attempted murder, and she won't make a good witness on her own behalf: she says she'd kill the Queen if she had the chance again."

French had been brooding, rubbing the knot on his forehead. "Why didn't you tell us about Skene's connection to the nationalists, when we asked you for information?"

Robshaw and Munro exchanged glances.

Munro spoke. "We were cultivating him as a source of information and as a means of introduction to the nationalists. We didn't want you to interfere."

French's face was a study in rage. "Interfere," he repeated, softly.

Dizzy leaned over and put a restraining hand on French's arm. "Whatever our personal feelings about the way affairs were handled, the important thing is that the Queen is safe."

French subsided, but I reckoned that Superintendent Robshaw would be receiving a visitor in the near future that he wouldn't enjoy seeing.

Vincent had cherry-picked the sandwiches and had progressed to the cakes. He shoved one into his mouth. "Wot about the countess?" he said through a mouthful of crumbs.

Dizzy brightened. It was his turn to talk. "Under the Treason Act, she will be tried by the House of Lords. I have no doubt that she will be found guilty."

"And wot then. This?" Vincent jerked an imaginary rope around his neck, crossed his eyes and stuck out his tongue.

"Theoretically, hanging could be the punishment. But I think it more likely that because she is a woman, and a member of the aristocracy, her sentence will be reduced to life imprisonment. Punishment enough, I suppose."

"The way I see it, you orter string 'er up. She tried to knock off the Queen, after all. Wot's the world comin' to, if criminals don't get punished for their crimes?" Vincent was outraged, as only those guilty of lesser crimes can be when a rogue of the first order gets off lightly.

"What's the punishment for theft in Scotland? Say, theft of medicine?" I asked. There were puzzled glances all around, except for Vincent, who rolled an eye at me, and French, who bore an expression of slowly dawning comprehension.

"There is the question of what should be done with the marchioness," said Robshaw.

"The marchioness?" I asked. "Why must something be done with the marchioness?"

Robshaw shifted irritably in his seat. "Miss Black, I'm still unclear about the role you played in this affair. Indeed, I am curious as to why you and the lad there"—he nodded at Vincent—"were involved in this matter at all. What exactly are your responsibilities, and to whom do you report?"

"To me," Dizzy interjected swiftly, presumably because he'd seen the homicidal glint in my eye. "And I must confess to being as confused as Miss Black with respect to your statement about the marchioness."

"Obviously, she knew Lady Dalfad was the Marischal but did not see fit to inform us," said Munro.

"Now, wait just a bloody minute," I said. "The marchioness didn't know about the countess; she only assumed she was the leader of the nationalists because of what the marchioness knew of Lady Dalfad's family."

"How do you know that?" Robshaw asked.

"Because she told me."

"Naturally, that will suffice as evidence," Robshaw sneered.

I sniffed. "She said you wouldn't have believed her if she had come to you with her suspicions, and your reaction proves she was right."

Robshaw rolled his eyes, just as the marchioness had predicted he would. He cocked his head at the prime minster. "I repeat my question, Lord Beaconsfield. Should we charge the marchioness?"

"No." The negative had come simultaneously from Dizzy, French and me (not that my opinion counted for much, but if the marchioness went to gaol, I wouldn't have a chance to winkle out whatever information the old bag might possess about my mother).

"Why not?" asked the superintendent.

"I won't allow it," said Dizzy, but he said it gently, for he could see that Robshaw was steamed.

Robshaw looked thunderous and Munro no less furious, but Dizzy put up a placating hand to forestall their protests. "I'm afraid that is all I'm prepared to say on the matter. You must leave the marchioness alone." My suspicion that the marchioness was one of Dizzy's soared into full flight.

I dug French in the ribs. "I expect a full report on the marchioness's activities from you and Dizzy when we get back to London," I whispered.

He massaged his side, the picture of injured innocence. Crafty bastard. I'd get the truth out of him, one way or the other.

A few days later, French arrived at the door of Lotus House, carrying a large box with a pretentious bow of bloodred silk. Mrs. Drinkwater admitted him, cooing with admiration at the parcel, and at his instruction, bore it off to the kitchen. I could have informed French that bribery would not improve Mrs. Drinkwater's culinary skills, but if he wanted to waste his money on hothouse flowers at this time of year, it was his decision.

French's usual expression of aloof arrogance had been replaced by a genial smile, which made me instantly wary. He settled himself in a chair by the fire and propped his boots on the fender.

"Make yourself comfortable, French. May I offer you a whisky? Brandy and soda? A tankard of ale?" French's blithe familiarity at Lotus House was beginning to irk me.

"Whisky, please. Make it a double."

I delivered it with ill grace. I was going to have to start charging French for the cost of his liquor, just like any other customer.

"How fared Lotus House in your absence?" he asked after he'd savoured the first taste of his drink.

"As I expected, Clara Swansdown is refusing to have anything more to do with men. Says she prefers women now, after Rowena introduced her to the Sapphic pleasures."

"What will you do?"

"Oh, she'll come round, once she realizes there's no money to be made in that trade. I'll feed her for a week, and if she doesn't toe the mark, I'll send her on to Rowena with a note. Rowena can pay to keep her, if she wants."

"You're a harsh woman, India."

"I'm in business, French. Would a racing stable keep a lame nag? Would the railway keep a blind conductor?"

There was a scuffle in the hallway, and Mrs. Drinkwater arrived, gripping Vincent by the collar. How that young pup could discern French's presence at Lotus House was a mystery to me; the boy must do nothing but loiter about the neighborhood all day on the off chance his hero would appear on the scene.

"I tried to keep this dirty cur out, but he darted past me and made straight for your study," said the cook, breathing heavily.

"You're losing your edge, Vincent. I can't believe Mrs. Drinkwater was able to catch you."

Vincent shot me a venomous glance and wrestled his collar free from the cook's grasp.

"She tripped me with 'er rollin' pin," he said sulkily.

"It's alright," I said to the cook. "Let him in. We're having a drink, Vincent. Care to join us?"

"Too right." Vincent lunged for the drinks cabinet, but I leapt to my feet and intercepted him. That boy had a hollow leg. I poured out a moderate measure, which Vincent looked at dubiously but accepted. He plunked down in one of my best chairs before I could stop him. I closed my eyes. I'd have to have the fumigator around.

French raised his glass. "To success in Scotland."

We drank (well, who needs an excuse, really?), but I was shaking my head before I'd finished.

"How can you call that a success? There were three attempts on the Queen's life, and the last one would have succeeded if Her Highness hadn't felt the sudden urge to whisper sweet nothings into John Brown's ear."

Vincent had polished off his drink and slithered over to the whisky bottle without me noticing. "The old bird's been shot at before. She must be gettin' used to hit by now."

French smothered a smile. "And we caught the brigands this time, India. The perpetrators are in gaol, and the Sons of Arbroath are scattered to the four winds."

"This special-agent business seems to turn out rather inconclusively," I said. "I was expecting something more definitive."

And a bit more heroic on my part, if I must tell the truth. I'd managed to survive my bout with Flora, but it hadn't been me who dispatched her, or Lady Dalfad for that matter. I admit to feeling some disappointment at not being the heroine. It's all well and good to blather on about the Queen and the monarchy and saving the country, but a little personal glory wouldn't go amiss.

I was brooding on the topic when French rose from his chair. "I've brought you something, India. An early Christmas present."

"I hope it's a bottle of whisky. You and Vincent seem to have emptied this one."

French bellowed for Mrs. Drinkwater, and the old cat came simpering in, bearing the parcel French had deposited with her.

He presented it to me with a flourish, laying it across my lap. Vincent came to look over my shoulder. I still shudder when I think about the smell that accompanied him.

The box certainly did not contain hothouse flowers. It was heavier than I'd expected, and the weight inside shifted as I positioned the box to open it. I removed the bow, tossed it to the floor and lifted the lid cautiously.

"'Urry up," said Vincent.

The lid followed the ribbon to the floor, and I sifted through the tissue paper in the box. The gaslight flared and twinkled upon a metallic object. I lifted it carefully from the box and looked at it with some dismay. A rapier, of the finest English steel, with a tooled leather case of maroon leather scrolled in gold leaf.

"Blimey," breathed Vincent. "That's a beaut'." I could see he was already calculating its worth at the nearest pawnshop.

"From Wilkinson," said French, beaming. "The finest swordsmith in the country."

"You shouldn't have," I said.

Really.

No wonder the bastard was still a bachelor.

Or was he? I remembered French's awkward attempt to deflect the prime minister's inquiry into his holiday arrangements. Then there was the matter of the marchioness. Was she on the prime minister's payroll? Was she in league with Dizzy and French? What did she know about my mother, and did French know what she knew? I had several points to clarify with the poncy bastard, and if I didn't get some satisfactory answers, I might find some use for my new Christmas present after all.

"I say, French—"